D1360435

PRAISE FOR ANDREW VACHSS

———

"Many writers try to cover the same ground as Vachss. A handful are as good. None are better." —*People*

"Vachss's stories . . . burn with righteous rage and transfer a degree of that rage to the reader."
—*The Washington Post Book World*

"Writing in a style so sleekly engineered that it purrs when you pop the hood, Vachss gives us such a smooth ride that it's easy to forget someone is driving this thing." —*The New York Times Book Review*

"Vachss is red-hot and as serious as a punctured lung."
—*Playboy*

ANDREW VACHSS

MORTAL LOCK

Andrew Vachss is a lawyer who represents children and youths exclusively. His many books include the Burke series and two previous collections of short stories. His books have been translated into twenty languages, and his work has appeared in *Parade*, *Antaeus*, *Esquire*, *Playboy*, and the *The New York Times*, among other publications. He divides his time between his native New York City and the Pacific Northwest.

The dedicated website for Vachss and his work is
www.vachss.com

BOOKS BY ANDREW VACHSS

— THE BURKE SERIES —

Flood

Strega

Blue Belle

Hard Candy

Blossom

Sacrifice

Down in the Zero

Footsteps of the Hawk

False Allegations

Safe House

Choice of Evil

Dead and Gone

Pain Management

Only Child

Down Here

Mask Market

Terminal

Another Life

— OTHER NOVELS —

Shella

The Getaway Man

Two Trains Running

Haiku

The Weight

That's How I Roll

Blackjack

A Bomb Built in Hell

Aftershock

— SHORT STORY COLLECTIONS —

Born Bad

Everybody Pays

Mortal Lock

MORTAL LOCK

INNISFIL PUBLIC LIBRARY
P.O. BOX 7049
INNISFIL, ON L9S 1A8

MORTAL LOCK

STORIES

ANDREW VACHSS

Vintage Crime/Black Lizard

Vintage Books • A Division of Random House, Inc. • New York

A VINTAGE CRIME/BLACK LIZARD ORIGINAL, MAY 2013

Copyright © 1999, 2001, 2002, 2003, 2007, 2008, 2009, 2010,
2011, 2012, 2013 by Andrew Vachss

All rights reserved. Published in the United States by Vintage Books,
a division of Random House, Inc., New York, and in Canada by
Random House of Canada Limited, Toronto.

This is a work of fiction. Names, characters, places, and incidents
either are the products of the author's imagination or are used
fictitiously, and any resemblance to actual persons, living or dead,
events, or locales is entirely coincidental.

Some of the stories in this collection originally appeared in
Another Chance to Get It Right; *Dark Horse Presents*; *Ellery Queen's
Mystery Magazine*; *Esquire*; *Hard Looks* (Dark Horse); *L.A. Noire*
(Mulholland); mullhollandbooks.com; *Playboy*; *The Strand*;
vachss.com; *Veil's Visit* (Subterranean); *Year of the Lizard*.

The Cataloging-in-Publication Data is on file
at the Library of Congress.

Vintage ISBN: 978-0-307-95083-3

www.weeklylizard.com

Printed in the United States of America
10 9 8 7 6 5 4 3 2 1

for Sonny . . .

You left too quick for us to say goodbye, brother. Hell, you left too quick, *period*. But you also left a stunning legacy. I'm still listening and learning. And always will be. Next time we meet, we'll *both* be able to smoke. And maybe even roll down 104, in that Police Auction Special.

CONTENTS

———

MORTAL LOCK

GHOSTWRITER

1

I was born a gifted child. By the time I started school, everyone was telling me I could be anything I wanted, do anything I wanted to do. At home, too—I had very supportive, encouraging parents. But there was only one thing I ever wanted to be: a writer. Just a writer.

That's the wrong word, "just." It trivializes something sacred. Writing is my connection to the universe. My only connection. If some magical surgery could scalpel it out of my soul, there would be nothing left. Without my writing, that's what I'd be: Nothing.

I knew this years before teachers started telling my parents about my "talent." I felt it inside me, growing. It suffused every cell in my body, surging with such power that I couldn't have suppressed it even if I had wanted to.

That force crushed everything in its path. By the time I was in grade school, it was so potent that it took over my world. It wasn't just that writing was the only thing I cared about; writing *owned* me. Every sense was always tuned to that same signal. If I wrote something great, that's how I'd feel. And if I wrote something lousy, that's how I'd feel, too.

I don't know the exact time it happened, but, after a while, writing was the only thing that could make me feel anything at all.

The topic didn't matter. Even if it was supposed to be writing *about* writing—like when you do a book report—it was always about *my* writing. It didn't make any difference if I liked the book or I hated it, the only thing that counted was *how* I said whatever I thought—that was the power-source.

I knew the grade didn't matter. Of course I'd get an A, but so would other kids. There was no grade that could measure my writing. I was the only judge.

But I was never smug, never satisfied. I'd spend hours deciding on just the right phrase, always trying to get it . . . perfect. I didn't care about being the best writer in class. What did that mean? I always knew there was more than that. Much more. Some place where I rightfully belonged. Don't mistake me for some petty narcissist—I was always my harshest critic, even when I was my *only* critic.

2

It wasn't until tenth grade that I saw my name in print. I could actually feel my synapses flame with this confirmation of my destiny.

The editor told me it was very unusual for a sophomore to get a bylined story. Even though I knew I could have written the whole school paper by myself, every single word, I told her how grateful I was to have gotten the chance.

I wasn't even lying. Not then.

The staff of the school paper always picked the editor. Every member got to vote, but it wasn't like the other elections at school. It wasn't the most popular kid who won—it was the one who was willing to do the most work. Some of the kids just wanted to do their own thing: take photos, or write poems, or do a gossip column, silly garbage like that. But putting the whole thing together, that wasn't a job most people wanted.

They always said the editor should be someone who had *earned* the job. Worked their way up from the bottom, paid their dues. So, naturally, they always picked a senior for the position.

High school has all kinds of rules—the kind they put on posters, and the kind you learn by watching how things work. It doesn't take long before you realize that the rules don't apply to everyone. Certain kids get to do certain things; other kids don't. Nobody had to spell that out. It was just the way things were—and so blatantly obvious that even the dullest kids picked it up quickly.

I saw this as an operational system, a weird blend of objectivity and favoritism. Like with the jocks: the best players got to be first string, no matter what year they were in. So the stars actually *earned* their positions. But once they got to *be* stars, they got their own set of rules as well.

I thought writing would work the same way. So whatever the editor told me to cover, I jumped on it. I was never late with an assignment. And I always nailed it, too: If they wanted three hundred words; they got three hundred words. Who, What, Where, When, and Why, just like the faculty advisor said had to be in every story.

The faculty advisor was Mr. David. The school hired him because he had a master's from the Columbia School of Journalism, and he had a lot of pieces published, in magazines with big names. He won some prizes for writing, too.

Mr. David had been what they called an "investigative journalist" before he retired. I guess they had to pay him a lot of money to get him to teach at a high school. But that wouldn't be a problem. In the town I lived in, the parents always demanded the best teachers. They paid a lot of taxes to keep their public school as good as any private one. Better, even. That was very important if you wanted to get into the best colleges.

I remember hearing my father tell my mother that was why we moved there from the city. It made the commute worthwhile, he said.

Besides the school paper and the journalism class, Mr. David taught creative writing. He even worked with the Debate Club.

Maybe he was one of those men you read about—the ones who can't stand being retired. He was busy all the time. I don't think he needed the money, so I guess that teaching was what he really wanted to do.

I thought a lot about Mr. David because I was trying to come up with a solution for my problem, and I thought he might have the experience to help me.

My problem was the editor of the paper. She was a fat, pasty-faced toad, with frizzy hair and thick ankles. Outside of the paper, she was so marginalized that you wouldn't believe she could squeeze her disgusting presence into that tiny bit of space. But when it came to the paper, everybody always gave in to her, because she did just about all the work.

That made her really valuable. If someone turned in a pile of slop, Amanda would fix it up for them—even if she had to rewrite every word. That meant a lot, especially to the crowd who needed every extracurricular activity they could grab. They were obsessed with getting into the best colleges, and they knew grades and SATs just weren't enough. Their competition always had more than that to offer, so they needed more, too.

They were always saying Amanda was a real lifesaver. Saying it *to* her—I don't what they said about her at the cafeteria tables where she knew she'd never be allowed to sit. Or even if they ever mentioned her at all.

But to me, Amanda was no savior, she was a roadblock. She changed *everything* I turned in. I would get it back, all marked up. The first time, I told her I wasn't going to rewrite it. She hadn't made what I wrote better, she'd just changed it to be what *she* wanted it to be—she was in control, and she wasn't letting anyone else join that one-member club.

She didn't like me saying that, I could tell. But she didn't lose her temper or anything. She just said everyone on the paper had to be edited, and if I didn't "go through the process," my article would have to be spiked.

I knew what that meant—Mr. David taught what he called "newspaper vocabulary" to all of us. He was the first person I ever heard use words like "byline" or "jump" and expressions like "above the fold" or "column inches."

I couldn't *stand* the thought of anything I wrote being spiked—it would be like the spike going into my own body. So I made all the changes. Every single one. Because we were so close to deadline by then, I had to make them with Amanda looking over my shoulder, watching the screen.

I wanted to spike her eyes.

3

Nothing was going to change until Amanda graduated. A whole school year away. I couldn't live with her having so much power over me for that much time. I couldn't let her keep changing everything I wrote. It was like she was slicing pieces off me. If I didn't find a way to stop her, there would be nothing left. Not of my writing, so . . . not of me, either. By then, there was no dividing line.

I knew I could never say anything like that out loud.

Nobody would ever understand. And if I tried to explain it, they'd probably want me to see some "counselor." That's when I started to plan.

I waited a few weeks, then I took one of my articles home with me, all marked up with Amanda's "editing." By then, she didn't watch me make the changes in front of her anymore—she knew I'd do whatever she said, even if she didn't know why. So when I told her I'd bring the article back to her the next morning, all fixed, she believed me.

I waited around for the stupid Debate Club to be over. Then I asked Mr. David if I could talk to him for a minute. I asked if I could meet him somewhere off campus. To talk about something in private. Anywhere he wanted, but . . . well, it was kind of an emergency.

He didn't even look surprised when I said that.

He drove me to a coffeehouse. Not a Starbucks, a real coffeehouse. It was all older people there, and the music they played was old. I guess it was, anyway—I'd never heard anything like it before.

The waitress knew Mr. David; she didn't even ask him what he wanted, only me. I asked her if I could have some green tea. She waited for a few seconds, like she expected me to say something more, then she walked away.

That's when I showed Mr. David my article. It was about a boy in our school who had gotten a perfect score on his math SATs. That kid was in a wheelchair. What I wrote about was how everyone knows kids in wheelchairs sometimes develop really powerful arms—one part of their body doesn't work, so they compensate by building up another part that does. But the barbed point of *my* piece was how important sports are in high school, and how this boy knew he could never be part of that. He hadn't just wanted to fit in; he wanted to excel. Arm-wrestling wasn't a school sport, so he found another way.

My piece was supposed to be all about his perfect score. But I wrote it about how that kid didn't like the place people wanted to put him in, so he made one for himself. And then he rolled his wheelchair right into it.

Mr. David read it right there, sipping his coffee. Not too fast, not too slow . . . the way a real editor reads, not the way a teacher grades.

When he was finished, he looked over at me, but he didn't say anything.

"I know I must be doing something wrong, Mr. David," I said. "Every time I turn anything in, it comes back looking like this."

Then I handed him Amanda's edits. "The thing is, I can't figure out *what* I'm doing wrong. I mean, I always make the changes she tells me to, but they never make sense to me. This isn't an ego-thing; I just want to improve. I need to be the best writer I can possibly be. But how can I learn to be a better writer if I just keep changing what I write without ever knowing why I'm doing it."

"Doesn't Amanda explain her edits to you?"

"I . . . guess she does. I mean, the first few times I asked her, she said some things. But she only used adjectives, and those are . . . well, flabby. If someone says they want to change what I wrote because it needs more punch and they don't tell me what 'punch' is, I can't get better. And I *have* to get better."

Mr. David gave me a look I didn't understand. I waited a long time, but he didn't say anything. So I did.

"I'm not criticizing Amanda," I told him. "She must know a hundred times more about writing than I do. I'm just . . . embarrassed, I guess. I mean, how come I don't get it? I *try.* I read her edits over a dozen times, but I still can't see how they make whatever I wrote better. So I know I must be missing something.

"I need to find the key, Mr. David. Because if I can't unlock the door, I can't get inside the only place I want to be. The only place I truly belong."

"Surely that's not the school newspaper, Seth?"

"No, sir. I want to be a writer. I want the best writer I have in me to come out. I know how important it is to learn from others. But if I can't even do *that,* how can I ever hope to . . . ?"

Mr. David sipped his coffee again. Took off his glasses and rubbed his temples. Then he said something to me I never forgot:

"You'll get better at it, Seth."

"But how can I get better if—?"

"Better at manipulating people," Mr. David cut into what I was saying. "You just keep practicing." He sounded sad when he said that.

He drove me home without saying another word.

4

Amanda never edited another of my pieces. She just ran them exactly as I turned them in, word for word.

Mr. David never spoke to me again, except in class, and then only when he had to.

I was sorry about that. I had learned so much from him. One of the books on the "optional" list he handed out is where I first read about how some editors have a need to mark their territory. The book called it "pecker tracks," but I knew that was probably a real old expression, from before women were in positions of power. Like editors were.

5

The literary magazine in college had an editor, too. But she didn't believe art *should* be edited—she would say things like "Kerouac and Corso showed us all the way." I thought what they wrote was some kind of drugged drivel. But everything in her magazine— and it *was* her magazine, the same way the high school paper had been Amanda's—was "art." And one doesn't judge art. At first, I thought she was being sarcastic. But she was worse than stupid; she was a believer.

By then, everyone knew what a gift I had. But they saw only the part I wanted them to see. I had to hide the other one.

I wasn't just a writer; I was a researcher. I could scan gobs of material really quickly, and weave it into whatever I was writing. So getting an A on a short story or an essay, that was nothing.

But for something like a term paper—one where they counted the footnotes without actually reading them—I needed my second gift . . . the one nobody knew about.

6

After I graduated, I had to make a decision. Not about being a writer—I *was* a writer—but how to find the quickest way to force others to acknowledge it.

I was accepted by every MFA program I applied to. But I applied only to make my parents happy; I wasn't going to spend any more years of my life getting some credential that wasn't good for anything except *teaching* writing. A few of my college professors had that MFA degree. I always took their courses, but none of them taught anything I could use . . . like how to get published by the best houses.

All they did was pose and posture. One of them, he was so "ironic" that he was always able to get a couple of the girls taking his class to think he was brilliant. He never saw the irony in that.

Another one, all he did was scream at students. He'd make us read our work out loud, in front of the class, and then he'd do a "critique." After that, the class would all give "feedback." Like the professor was the king shark, so he got the first rip, but he'd leave plenty for the others to feed on.

Once, after I finished reading, he said my story was vapid. "Writing isn't just mastery of words," he said. "Even the most perfect prose will die on the vine if it isn't nourished by narrative force."

I could feel the class nodding approval, waiting to jump in. But I was ready. I'd been waiting for it. Training for it like a prizefighter.

"Who says so?" I said to the professor. "You?"

"Well, I *am* the one who gives out the grades."

The class laughed. A herd of sheep, bleating on command.

"Sure," I said. "But this is the *only* place you get to make those kinds of decisions."

The class went quiet, not knowing what to do . . . waiting for their next cue.

"Is that supposed to be clever?" the professor said. "Or just some deep profundity you read in a comic book?"

Some people in the class started to laugh, but they were nervous laughs, like they weren't sure they were doing the right thing. When the rest didn't join in, they stopped.

"It's just the truth," I said to the professor. "In this little class, you get to decide what's 'good' writing and what's 'bad' writing. But out in the world, you don't get to make those decisions, other people do. And they already made their decision about your writing, didn't they? Otherwise, you'd have a whole bunch of your own books published by now, wouldn't you?"

"You apparently have some serious problems, young man," the professor said, his face all blotchy from trying to sound blasé while he was raging inside. "Maybe the school counselor could be helpful."

Nobody laughed at all.

After class, one of the girls came up to me. "That was the most amazing thing I ever saw," she said. "I would have been terrified to stand up to him like that."

"The only way you can be hurt is if you care," I told her.

She didn't understand what I meant until the next semester. Once she saw for herself what I meant, she dropped out of school. I don't know what happened to her after that.

7

I didn't want to teach. And I was sick of all the generic advice. I knew that desire *isn't* all it takes, and "try, try again" is wasted when "again" is a synonym for "infinitely."

What I found out is that everyone wants to be a writer. *Everyone.* Right this second, more people are writing books than reading them. They don't understand that only a micro-percentage of them actually have that special gift.

Not that I blame people for being confused about that, especially people my age. Anyone can get "published" now. Some of them put their writing in their blogs, beyond-all-doubt convinced they have thousands and thousands of "fans." Some of them use one of those "print on demand" outfits. Amazon will "publish" your book, guaranteed. All you have to do is agree to make it a "Kindle original." Now any twit can e-mail all his Facebook friends with a URL that proves he's a "writer."

They've all read actual books that seriously suck, so they know the bar is low enough for them to jump over, too.

They don't look at writing as an art. It's not playing the violin, or sculpting, or opera singing. They think being able to do those kinds of things is *truly* special—a God-given "gift" that might take a whole lifetime to perfect. Everyone's heard of child prodigies in the "arts." Three-year-olds who play the piano, kindergarten kids who paint . . . they're on TV all the time. But writing, who *can't* do that?

I read a survey once: almost ninety percent of the respondents rated themselves "very good" drivers. If the question had been: "Do you have writing talent?" the percentage would probably be the same. And just as accurate.

That's because writing has no standards of value. It isn't measured by how many pounds you can lift. Or who is first across the finish line in a race. Those are objective criteria, uniformly applied. Writing is nothing like that. What's "good" is what people say is good. Only a privileged few people get to say that; the rest are entitled only to listen to their wisdom.

The *literati* rule. And the sheep obey. Even if the opinions they are told to treasure *call* them sheep.

And it is beyond dispute that any book can instantly turn from rancid to wonderful the instant someone makes a movie out of it. That's the closest thing to a yardstick people ever have about writing. And if the movie turns out to be a hit, everyone runs out to buy the paperback of the book they wouldn't touch in hardcover.

But, first, it has to be published.

It took me quite a lot of rejections to learn this.

8

After I graduated, I knew I couldn't continue living at home. My parents would have let me, but that house could never provide the atmosphere I needed. Too much noise, too many distractions. And too many things other people would expect me to do. Family stuff.

I needed my own place. Which meant I needed money. I thought about getting some college-graduate job, maybe even teaching high school English. But I remembered Mr. David. I didn't know if he was a real writer—I thought maybe he was, although I couldn't explain why I thought so—and I realized that a high school teacher never has any time for his own work.

I thought of being a cab driver, but that was too scary. In this city, cab drivers get killed all the time. And they have to work very long hours to make any money. I researched all that because I was trying to find a job where I wouldn't have people telling me what to do all the time.

Finally, I ended up working at this big office supply store. All I had to do was keep the shelves stocked, answer customer questions sometimes, and not get fired for breaking the rules. Simpleton rules, like no smoking inside the building, not leaving your personal cell phone on, never taking stuff home . . . stupid, petty things like that.

All I really wanted to do was write. All the time. All day, every day. And this job let me get pretty close; I could put in four hours every night during the weekdays, and the weekends were all mine. Even when they changed the employee schedule—and they were always doing that—it didn't matter to me. When they put me on weekends, I still had Monday and Tuesday off. Days never mattered to me, only hours.

The only place I could afford wasn't nice in any way at all, and I didn't waste time trying to keep it clean. I knew some of the great writers had worked under much worse conditions. One day, I'd be telling the story of how I'd sacrificed so much for my art.

Telling the story to some interviewer, after I was famous.

9

It took me almost nine months to finish my first novel. I didn't know what to do next, so I went back to researching.

I joined a writers group. I thought it would be a good place to learn how to get my novel seen by the right people, but all they wanted to do was read their own stuff out loud, and then get "feedback" from the others.

Just like in college, only now, everybody was supposed to be "supportive." Like it was some sickening form of group therapy.

It always felt more like a secret society than a group of professionals. They all threw around insider terms like "hard-soft deals" and "The List."

The screenplay morons were the worst, dropping names like they were throwing coins into a wishing well.

They all had the vocabulary down pat, but it wasn't *their* vocabulary. In their mouths, those same words all turned into hollow dreams.

So I gave up on writing groups. I started going to open-mike readings. But the crowds there were always more interested in how the writer looked than anything he wrote. Some of them even brought their own cheering sections. The big favorites were always the ex-cons and the ex-hookers.

It was hard, but I did it. And all for nothing. Even the people who seemed to really love my work, all they had for me was *more* advice. Most of it was some variation of "What you need is an agent."

As if I hadn't known that! I'd tried researching agents, but it was like trying to negotiate a booby-trapped path through a forest of lies. Some of them wanted a "reading fee," some said they were "coaches," some were nothing but fronts for a vanity press outfit. It seemed as if the only *real* agents already had more clients than they needed.

That made sense to me. If you make your living off a percentage of what a writer sells, why would you want to represent a writer who's never sold a thing?

I felt stupid for not understanding what I should have known all along. Like when I was competition-checking in one of those giant Barnes & Nobles. I watched a middle-aged woman walk in the door. She didn't even look at the books, just asked the clerk at the front desk, "Where's the Bestseller List?" The clerk didn't even look up, just pointed her to a special shelf they had standing all by itself. She marched right over there, like there was nothing else worth reading in that whole giant store.

So I did more research. It seemed as if the major houses were always publishing first novelists, so they had to have discovered them somehow. *That* had to be the door I was looking for.

I could see how *some* books got published. If you were a famous person, you could always sell your life story, especially if you had sex with other famous people. But it didn't matter if you were a movie star or a serial killer, publishers loved "true" stories . . . even the ones that turned out to have been made up.

I thought of making up a story myself, but people are much more suspicious than they used to be, with so many frauds getting exposed all the time. Besides, even if I got away with it, all I'd have was money. Nobody would know me as a writer.

I *knew* the path to my destiny was its own test. I knew if I ever stepped off that path, I could never reach what was at its end.

So I looked even deeper. And I found one of the answers. All of those first novelists had a common denominator. Contacts. Connections. Somebody who could open doors for them.

I didn't have anyone like that. And I never would.

Even so, I never strayed from my path.

10

I met women in the places I went to for readings, but all they wanted was to hook up, as if the place were a singles bar instead of a showcase. I could use them for what they had to offer, and sometimes I did . . . just in case they knew somebody. But none of them ever did.

When I finally met the person who changed everything, it was in a place I'd never imagined. At work.

Her name was Julia. "Like Julia Roberts," she said, "except for my face and my figure." I knew that kind of talk. It's supposed to be self-deprecating humor, but it's really a test. And I knew all the answers.

Julia had been working there longer than I had—"Right out of high school," she told me, later—but I never actually noticed her until the day she caught me in the stockroom. I was supposed to be out on the floor, but I had an image in my head, and I had to get it into my notebook before it disappeared.

"I didn't know you were a writer," is the first thing she ever said to me.

From the moment she said I was a writer, I knew she was the one. But I had learned a lot by then, just like Mr. David had said I would.

"I never said I was—"

"Oh, you don't have to worry, Seth. I never could figure out why a guy like you would be working in a place like this, and now I know, that's all. I'd never say anything to the people who work *here*."

"I'm just—"

"Taking notes, I know. That's what writers do, isn't it? They all keep notebooks. I heard Stephen King say that once. On TV."

12

After she asked me a couple of dozen times, I brought one of my short stories to work and gave it to her.

The very next day, she told me I was the most amazing writer she ever read. She had stayed up all night, reading that story over and over again. "And every time I read it, I found something new," she said. Her eyes were pure and true as she recited my validation.

Listening to her, I felt the same way I had when I'd first seen my name in print. This was meant to happen. Destiny, finding its way. Rewarding me for never straying from the only path there was.

13

Julia had been saving for years. "What have I got to spend money on, anyway?" When I first saw her apartment, I was surprised at how big it was.

"I lived here with Mom ever since she moved back home after

the divorce. I was only four then, so I don't remember much about it. Mom moved back in with *her* mother. My grandmother. It was just the three of us. Then Nana passed, and it was just us two. I was twenty-three when Mom died. One day, she told me she had cancer. She only lived a couple of months after that.

"Mom didn't have any money to leave me, but, in a way, I guess she did. This place is rent-controlled, and now it's mine. I could never afford such a nice place otherwise."

I made some sounds. If people are getting emotional, it's better not to use words. If you stick with sounds, they'll turn those sounds into whatever they need to hear.

14

Julia had to talk me into it, but, finally, I moved in with her. Even half the rent on that place was much less than I had been paying for the little dump I had before. And Julia moved everything around, so I had plenty of space. Even a separate room of my own, just for working. She called it my "studio."

15

A couple of months later, I told Julia I had to leave.

"But why, Seth? Don't you have everything you want here?"

"It's a beautiful apartment, Julia. And you're a beautiful girl. But you know how I feel about my writing. I *have* to do it. But it's just too . . . hard this way. We come home from work, and I just disappear into my studio. It's like we live together, but we never see each other, you see what I mean?"

"That's okay, Seth. I know you have to—"

"It's not okay with *me*, Julia. I want to be able to . . . be with you, but by the time I get home from work, I know I've only got a few hours until I'm too tired to write any more. By then, you're already asleep. I live here like some ghost. And that hurts me. Because I know it's hurting you."

16

Julia got a second job, part-time. I stayed home and wrote. That way, I always had some time to spend with her. Every time I told her maybe I should go back to work so I could help pay some of the bills, she practically ordered me not to.

17

The writing I did in that place was my best work. When I told Julia I couldn't have done it without her, she started crying.

18

I kept going to writing conferences—the ones you have to pay for, like it was tuition. But I never came back with anything I could use.

I remember one of the speakers, though. After he made a little speech, this writer whose book was being made into a movie took questions from the audience. When someone asked the same question I would have, I couldn't breathe, waiting for the answer.

But it wasn't The Answer—it was just a mask, dropping. "The most important thing to remember is to *keep* writing. It may take a while, but cream always rises to the top."

As he said that, he looked like the cat who had just swallowed that cream.

Like he was smirking right at me.

19

One time, Julia and I were in a bookstore together. I opened a book that the *Times* reviewer called a "tour de force." I read a few pages. A red mist came over my eyes. I threw the book across the room. Nobody even noticed.

"I can write better than that in my sleep," I told Julia.

"I know you can, honey. None of them—"

"No, you don't understand," I told her. "It's not *about* being a better writer. It's not that kind of fight. I have to find another way."

20

But it was the other way that found me.

I was in one of those miserable little clubs, sitting at a table, waiting for the open-mike to start. Julia was working that night, so I was there by myself.

"Mind if I join you?" a man said.

He was older than me, wearing a fine suit and a silk tie. Nothing flashy; this wasn't a man who needed props to put on an act. My heart almost stopped; I knew he *had* to be an agent.

But it turned out he wasn't an agent, he was a writer. Well, not really, not yet. But he had plans.

"You ever write any crime fiction?" he asked me.

"I don't do genre stuff," I told him.

"But you *could,* if you wanted to."

I just shrugged, but I was impressed. Maybe he wasn't an agent, but he had the insight to understand what I was capable of. It was as if he knew the real reason I even came to those readings.

He leaned closer. "There's an endless market for crime fiction that the reader thinks of as 'realistic,'" he said. Not a lecture, an explanation. He didn't talk down to me like some pompous professor; he showed me respect. "That means the writer has to have some credentials, so the readers can tell themselves they're being let in on the inside stuff."

"That wouldn't be—"

"Enough? Of course not. Probably half the cops in L.A. have written screenplays. Medical examiners, forensic techs, psychologists . . . most of them have file cabinets full of crap they think are great novels. Any part of the criminal justice system you can name, even those idiot 'profilers,' they *all* think they can do it. DAs, Legal Aid lawyers, judges. . . . I'll bet *most* of them have some kind of half-ass 'book' they're working on right this minute."

As I lit another cigarette, I noticed his eyes were as flat and silvery as mirrors—I could see myself in them.

"That's what makes crap like *Law and Order* such a smash," he went on. "People know every episode is 'ripped from today's headlines.' Ripped *off* would be more like it, but you can't argue with success."

"My work is—"

"Original," he cut me off. "I know. I've listened to it. And read it, too. Not all of it, of course—only the short stories you've had published in those little magazines. But that was more than enough. This is the ninth reading of yours I've been to. What does that tell you?"

"That you go to a lot of readings."

He smiled away my wariness. "Scouting expeditions," he said.

"But you said you're not an agent, you're a—"

"I didn't say I *was* a writer. I said I wanted to be one. A rich, famous one. And I know how to make that happen. I've studied the process for a very long time, and I've decoded the formula. Want to hear me out?"

I just nodded.

"The first step is to understand that you *don't* have talent," he said. "The next step is to find someone who does."

21

That was almost ten years ago. Today, H. Emory Trelaine is a fixture on the bestseller lists. His Darrow series has been translated into a dozen languages, and the critics love the fact that he's "been there." They blather on about how Trelaine's real-life experience "informs" his novels.

And Trelaine *has* been there. Any reviewer could trace the origin of his protagonist, Clarence Darrow Nighthawk. A career prosecutor who proudly described himself as a "mixed-breed," he was the son of a brilliant biologist and a "special needs" teacher. When he was a freshman in high school, his mother had been killed by a drunk driver. The driver survived the crash.

While he was still in college, his father had been murdered. He was killed in prison, where he was doing a life sentence for mailing an envelope full of contact-poison to that drunk driver.

As a prosecutor, Trelaine had devoted his life to fighting crime. And the books were his "catharsis," since Darrow often worked outside the same law that was always tying his hands in court.

22

I wrote every word of every one of those books. First, I read nothing but crime novels for ninety days straight, day and night. I made notes. Took a little from some, a lot from others. When I had the formula down—and Trelaine had been right; it *is* a formula—I turned my gift loose and let it soar.

I wrote the first Darrow novel in less than two months. When I showed it to Trelaine, he promised to get back to me.

A week passed without a word. I got more and more anxious every day. "He'll call, honey," Julia kept telling me. "I know he will."

She was saying something like that one day when I'd finally had enough of her puerile nonsense.

"Could you just shut—"

But then the phone interrupted me.

23

Trelaine had no trouble getting himself an agent. "One phone call," he told me. We were sitting in a booth in a diner out in Queens at three in the morning—it would be the last time anyone could possibly see us together in public.

He said his agent had gotten a major house to take on his first book, especially when he was able to promise them this one was just the start of a series. A series with legs.

"Serious money," he said. "And plenty more to come."

Trelaine wanted to pay me a flat fee, like I was some hired hand. I told him it had to be a percentage.

I don't know what he heard in my voice when I said that. Whatever it was, he knew I meant it. And that it wasn't about money.

When I got back home, I told Julia it was just another false alarm.

She said the kind of stuff she always said.

I kissed her forehead, blessed her for having so much faith in me. And then we went to bed.

24

Three books later, Trelaine was rich and famous.

I was just rich.

25

The day after my first check cleared, I packed my stuff and moved out. When Julia asked me why, I told her that it wasn't right, her giving up her life for a man so obsessed with his writing that he couldn't give her any of the things she deserved.

It's easy to lie if you put enough truth into it.

It was time to face reality, I told her. I was never going to be a published author. But I was going to die trying.

Even that part had some truth in it.

"I'll never stop believing in you, Seth. Never."

That was the last thing she ever said to me.

26

The first four books in the series made The List, but Trelaine and I never met again, even in private. He never even called, except to tell me when his agent had signed another contract.

I was alone. But not alone with my writing, the way I'd always thought it was meant to be. Julia wasn't in the way, anymore, but that damn Darrow series was. Thanks to all the pressure from the publisher, I could work on my own stuff only part-time.

Just like I'd been doing when I'd first met Julia.

27

I never got invited to one of those launch parties the publishing houses throw for a book that they know is going to be hot. I never did any book signings. Nobody ever asked to interview me.

But I did get to talk to the editor of the Darrow series on a pretty regular basis, especially when he sent over his "notes" on a manuscript I'd just submitted.

Even with that kind of access, it took me a while. Mr. David had been right—some things came naturally to me, but other things I needed a lot of practice to get good at. Good *enough,* that is. By the time I'd made the deal with Trelaine, I knew how to get what I needed. I knew that patience is a weapon. And timing really *is* everything.

During one of our meetings, the editor let it slip that the publishing house had known the truth ever since the second Darrow book. I sat on that knowledge like a man with a powerful handgun in his pocket, but only one bullet for it.

When I *felt* it, when I knew it was *my* time, I just walked into the publishing house and asked for the editor. I didn't have an appointment, and I had to show ID at the security desk before they would even call upstairs. It took a couple of minutes, but then they gave me a badge and told me to go on up.

I didn't waste the editor's time. I told him he knew better than anyone what I was capable of as a writer. Just imagine what I could produce if I was liberated from the genre ghetto.

I showed him the manuscript of my own novel, the one I had been working on for years. He promised to get back to me.

28

A week passed. A hundred times, I reached for the phone. But I always stopped myself. I'd already fired the one bullet I had—acting all anxious could send it off-course.

Two more weeks. Then the editor called me and asked me to come in. He told me my novel was brilliant. Almost magical. "But there's no market for a novel of that complexity. Not now, anyway. The only way to make something like this a commercial success is by *major* promotion, Seth. And publishing today is all about consolidation, not risk-taking. Especially with the economy the way it is now."

29

Trelaine's next book had Darrow going after a ring of rapists who made movies of what they did, previewed them over YouTube, then sold them through a "back channel" over the Internet. It was his biggest seller ever.

A few weeks later, Trelaine's body was discovered in the front seat of his Mercedes. The back of his head was nothing but pulp.

The papers went insane with speculation. What had made him a target for assassination? Was it his courtroom fighting for justice? Or was it his novels, the ones that had carried his crusade even farther?

Trelaine's entire backlist was reissued, with new thematic jacketing of the paperbacks. On the back of every one was a collage of newspaper headlines about his murder.

They flew off the shelves.

30

I let six months pass. Then I called the editor, and told him I had something he *had* to see. I could hear the boredom in his voice until I said, "And I can't tell you about it on the phone."

Inside his office, I told him I had another three Darrow novels on my hard drive. All completed.

He wasn't bored anymore.

31

The head of the publishing house called a press conference to announce that Trelaine couldn't be silenced. "Whoever had him killed thought they could stop him from writing the truth, but they didn't know who they were dealing with," he told a rapt audience. "There are at least two more *completed* manuscripts already in our hands. That's all I have to say at this time."

The press corps had heard a version of that story before. Stieg Larsson died before *any* of his books had been published, and now he's the bestselling writer in the world. They did everything but shout "Amen!"

CNN ran the story every hour for a whole day and night.

The bloggers kept it alive for weeks more.

Preorders came in so quickly they almost crashed the company's server. It was probably even worse at Amazon.

32

On a special crossover episode between *Law & Order* and *CSI*, a crusading novelist was found dead in the front seat of his car.

At first, his wife was the prime suspect. Especially when they found she'd been having an affair, and that there was a big life insurance policy, too. But the murder turned out to be the work of a professional. The truth came out when they matched the assassin's "signature" to other crimes in the FBI database.

In exchange for the DA's office "taking the needle off the table," the assassin gave up the people who hired him—a cartel of kiddie-porn producers.

33

When the next Darrow finally came out, they couldn't print them fast enough.

HBO bought the series. *Variety* quoted a studio bigwig as saying "Darrow is too big for any one movie."

34

Trelaine's editor is my editor now.

My own novel was released, under my own name. The house

paid a respectable advance, and made a commitment to major pro-motion: full-page ad in the *Times,* thirty-city tour, a launch party at the publisher's mansion. Plus the stuff the public doesn't know about: window displays, end-caps, front-of-the-store dumps . . . you have to *pay* for all that. Throw in the top-tier Amazon "pack-age," a ton of favor-trade blurbs, and you can bet the farm on the outcome. It's simple math: pay*off* equals pay*out.*

I'm a lock for The List.

I wonder if Julia will see me on TV.

for David Hechler

SURE THING

When I got down to my last sixty-one bucks, I knew it was time to go.

My room rent was paid for that night, and they wouldn't lock me out until ten the next morning.

I couldn't die with money in my pocket.

So I put fifty on the nose of a trotting mare I always liked. Fancy Candy was a gross longshot, even against the pack of non-winners they had her in with at Yonkers.

That left enough for a better supper than I've had in . . . ah, who remembers? I blew the change on a tip for the waitress. For luck.

I never buy the newspapers—they tell you who's running, but not much else. You need the race program for real information, and the price keeps going up. The last four times I lost, I was betting on memory . . . on horses I remembered from better days.

I guess their better days were over, too.

I went down to OTB in the morning, holding my last ticket.

Fancy Candy paid $33.70 to win. My ticket was worth eight hundred and change.

—

That was seven months ago. At one point, I was up sixteen grand. Now I'm back where I belong.

—

This time it's forty bucks. I put it all down. Every last cent.

I can't die with money in my pocket, but I don't mind going out on an empty stomach.

for Frank Caruso

BLOODLINES

1

"What do I care what kind of horses they are? I'm not here to join some 4-H club."

The old man was looking out over the rail at a bunch of horses pulling little carts around the track. He never turned around, but I could hear him good enough. "A smart kid like you, I figure you probably know the difference between stupidity and ignorance, right?"

"I'm not sure," I answered him. Not challenging, asking. "Show him respect," is what they'd told me. I always do the job the way the people paying me want it done. That's my reputation, and I worked a long time to earn it. The better your reputation, the better you earn.

"You can do something about being ignorant," the old man said. "Not everybody gets the chance to do that. But if you do, and you pass it up, *then* you're stupid."

"Okay," I said to him, going along. "Could you tell me what's so special about those horses over there?"

"Those are harness horses," the old man said, talking like he was in church. "Harness horses, you understand? Not thoroughbreds, like they have over to Aqueduct or Belmont. Not thoroughbreds, *standardbreds*. What that means, they're all bred to race a standard distance. One mile."

"And the jockeys sit in those little carts—?"

"Not jockeys," he said, waving his hand like he was brushing some dirt off his sleeve. "Drivers. That's where this whole thing started from: horses doing *work*. Some guy's driving down a country lane, hauling a load, okay? Another wagon rolls up next to him. One guy looks at the other, and, *bang!* you got yourselves a race."

He talked the way a man does when he's just told you something important, wants to make sure you get it. Me, I got it, all right. You can see the same thing at stoplights every night, only with cars. But I just nodded, so he'd keep talking.

"And they do it the same way today," he said. "You see that big convertible over there on the back stretch? That's the pace car. It starts moving, nice and slow. Then a gate comes out of each side, like a butterfly opening its wings. It keeps moving, so all the horses can get lined up behind that gate. When the car crosses the starting line, the gate folds back up. That's the signal for the horses to go. The car keeps going until it gets away, then it pulls off to the side.

"A rolling start, see? Not like those *thoroughbreds*," he said, almost sneering the word. "Those, they start them out of little cages, like they was fucking greyhounds, chasing a fake rabbit."

"So the trotters, they're like Old School, huh?"

The old man gave me a sharp look, trying to see if I was jerking his chain. After a minute, he gave up. I may not know anything about horses, but I learned how to keep my face flat a long time ago.

"Those horses out there; you wanted, you could trace every one of them all the way back to the original stud. Hambletonian was his name, and every trotter you see today carries his bloodline. He was racing way before the Civil War, that 'Old School' enough for you?"

"Damn!"

"And when they're done racing, those trotters you see out there, what do you think happens to them?"

"They get killed?"

"Killed? You mean, like with those greyhounds? Nah. Some of them, the big winners, they use for breeding. The rest of them, well, they keep right on working. Those fancy carriages you see in Central Park? You know, the ones for tourists? Who you think pulls them? Those Amish people, down in Pennsylvania, where you think they get the horses, pull their buggies? They got some programs where they even get adopted. That's probably the best deal of all."

"The regular racehorses, they don't—?"

"'Regular' racehorses?" he said, like he was mad about something. "You mean, like the ones you see on TV, get movies made about them?"

I just nodded; I didn't say anything. That's always the best move when it looks like someone's going to lose it. I learned that one when I was just a little kid, even before I started getting locked up.

"You never been near a track in your life, but you heard of Secretariat, am I right?"

"Yeah. I mean, everybody's—"

"Sure. But I say, Nevele Pride or Une de Mai, I might as well be talking about fucking Martians, huh?"

"I guess so. I mean—"

"Thoroughbreds, that's all anyone knows. Let me tell you something, kid: Those nags, they're nothing but toys for rich men. That's why those spindly-legged things are always breaking down. They ain't from rugged stock, *working* stock, the way trotters are."

"But they're faster, aren't they? I mean—"

"A track star could outrun a prizefighter, too. But what happens when the runner gases out, got no breath left? Your trotters, they're the true tough guys in the business. Go out forty, forty-five times a year and *work* for their money. Race in the rain, race in the snow. Race in a damn hurricane, you let them. They pull whatever you put behind them, too. You don't have to be no midget to do it—some of those drivers are as big as you are. And you don't have to be from Saudi-fucking-Arabia to own one, neither."

"I don't want to own one. I just want to win some money on them."

"Uh-huh," the old man said. Meaning, whatever was really going on, it wasn't his business. "All right, here's how it works. Winning money on the trotters is part handicapping, part investment, and part luck. If the race is clean—and, a lot of them, they're not no more, not with exotics on every race—the edge goes to the man who really loves the horses. You got to have a feel for them. That takes—"

"What's 'exotics'?" I interrupted. I know it's not polite, but he was losing me, and I wanted to slow him down so I didn't miss anything.

"Combo betting. Like a trifecta, that's one example. To hit one of those, you have to pick the horses who come in first, second, and third, in that order. Long odds, big payoffs."

"What's wrong with that?" It sounded okay to me. That's the way life is—the bigger the risk, the bigger the payoff.

"What's wrong with it is that big money always brings out the guys who like shortcuts. Those kind of people, the ones I'm talking about now—all they have to do is pay two, three drivers to pull their horses—hold them back, make sure they don't finish in the money, okay? Then they bet the other horses in every possible combination. Long as they make sure the pulled horses are short-priced, they're guaranteed a big score, every time."

The old man lit a cigarette, hunching his shoulders and cupping his hands, even though there was no wind.

"They used to call a race like that the Big Triple. Usually had only one a night, on the last race; keep the crowd from leaving," he said. "Now, they got one on damn near *every* race. Superfectas, you got to pick the first *four* horses in the exact order of finish. High-Fives . . . well, you get the idea."

"Yeah," I said. And I did. There was a casino at the track—not a real one, just slots, mostly—and it was packed to the gills with gamblers. Not horse-players, gamblers.

"Look at it like this," the old man said. "The owner of the winning horse gets *half* the purse; the horse that comes second, his owner gets half of what's left, and so on . . . all the way down to fifth. So if you own a horse, he can get you a check even if he never wins a race. They do it that way because it's better for the game. It costs just as much to feed a horse that never wins a race as it does to feed a world champ, so the idea is to spread the purse money around, help the owners out, keep more of them in the game.

"Now the driver's take is ten percent of whatever his horse earns in the race. Let's say the purse is ten grand. That means five g's for the winner's owner, and five hundred for the driver, okay? So what you do, you tell the driver of the best horse, here's a couple of grand for your*self,* you do the right thing. No big deal. All you got to do is make sure your horse, it's not gonna be his night, see?"

"If that's the way it is, how come *you* bet on them?"

I thought that was a good shot I'd just landed, but the old man didn't even blink. "You stay away from those kinds of races. That's something you have to learn. Some guys, they strictly play the stakes races," he said. "A stakes race means the owners have to buy their way into them, keep putting up more and more money as the season goes along. The *stake,* see? You ante up, that lets you sit in. But you have to keep calling to stay in the pot.

"Some of those races, the purse gets so big, you could *never* get to the driver. It's not just that the driver's in for a fat check if he gets his horse home—any driver gets seen tanking in a big race, he's on the permanent shit list. You train one of the top horses, you *know* what he's supposed to do out there, and you watch *close.* So even if the driver doesn't get nailed by the track, the trainer, he'll know."

"A big race, like the Kentucky Derby?"

"Yeah," he sighed. "Like the Kentucky-fucking-Derby. Only for a trotter, that would be the Hambletonian. Named for the original, see?"

"I never—"

"I know." He spit over the rail. "You never heard of it." He took a breath, like he was taking control of himself. "Listen," he said, "you think the trotters don't run for big money, too? That Hambletonian I just told you about? Last year, the purse was two million, okay? That sound like chump change to you? They got all kinds of races for six figures, and a few go over that. There's plenty of money in this game, you got the right horse."

He sounded like a guy apologizing for something, but I didn't say that. I didn't say anything at all.

"You couldn't pay a driver enough to pull in one of those big races," he said. "And finding three of them crazy enough to try, forget it."

"So why wouldn't they cheat in the other direction?" I asked him. "Isn't there a way to make them go faster?"

"You mean like when they stick a garden hose down their throats and pump them full of baking soda? Sure. That's what they call a 'milkshake'—it stops their muscles from locking up so they still got plenty of zip down the stretch. But you mostly see that used on thoroughbreds, not trotters."

"How come? They're all horses, right?"

"No! That's what I've been telling you. Okay, look, they call all standardbreds 'trotters,' but it's not like they all trot. Some of them are pacers. Trotting and pacing, those are different gaits. But you got to hold that gait. If you start running, you're out."

He held up his hand to stop my next question, then he showed me what he was talking about, using the first two fingers of each hand: "Trotters move their outside front leg and inside rear leg at the same time; pacers move both outside legs, then both inside legs, like sidewinders, see?

"The big thing to remember is what I told you, they got to stay on whichever gait they pick. If they break stride, start galloping, the way the ponies do, you got to take them off to the side, settle them down, get them back to trotting or pacing before they can get back into it.

"That happens, ninety-nine times out of a hundred, their race is done right there. That's why you never want to hit a trotter with a speedball. He's likely to get all excited, start running. That's when you can tear up your tickets."

"But there's other ways, right?"

"With all the drugs they let them take now, who knows?" the old man said. He tapped a fresh cigarette out of his pack, looked at it for a second. Then he said, "Listen, you don't have to come around here with this fairy story, okay? I got asked to do a favor, and I'll do it. You want to pick up enough so you sound like you know what you're doing, let people think you're a handicapper, I can teach you enough. But you want to really look the part, you got to put in more than a few days, understand?"

"Sure."

"I can't be here every night. It's a long drive from where I live. But I can come maybe two, three times a week, until you're ready, fair enough?"

"You're the one doing the favor."

"That's right. Now, I got some books at home. About harness racing. When I come down Monday night, I'll bring some for you to look at. You willing to do that?"

"Yeah," I said, surprised. People don't ask me to read books. "Thanks."

"In the meantime, just hang out, watch the races. *Only* watch, for now. You start betting before you're ready, you could get lucky, think you actually know what you're doing. Worse, you could get hooked on the action. Then you'll never learn nothing."

"Okay," I told him.

It was early the next morning by the time I got back to my room. Motels are better than hotels—you can park right outside your room, and the desk clerk doesn't need to see you come and go.

I used one of the prepaid cells I always carry to make the kind of calls you make in my line of work. They never ask you for a credit card number, just an address.

The hooker they sent over was like they all are.

2

"Never fall in love," the old man told me a week later. "That's certain death for a handicapper. It's okay to have a couple, few horses that are like your guys, sure. You follow them, root for them, all that. But when it comes to betting on them, you got to make sure they're placed right, first."

"How do you do that?"

"Class is one way; you can see if the horse is going up against tougher company than usual. Or if he's in soft. But, mostly, you got to watch the conditions. See this race here," he said, pointing to the form. "It's a ten K condition layout, only for non-winners of eight thousand, last six outs, okay?"

"And even the winner, he only gets half the purse."

"You listen good," he said, like he hadn't expected it. "That's right. And remember, the horse comes in second, he takes half of what's left. All the way down to fifth."

"So, six races not to win eight thousand dollars, they couldn't be winning too often."

"Or," the old man said, smiling a little, "they were kicking ass, but the purses were real, real small. Sometimes, an owner don't expect much from his horse, so he keeps him at the small tracks."

"Small tracks, small purses?"

"Yeah," he said, handing me the program. "You got it down. So show me, which one of these is in cheap?"

"I think . . . this one," I said, putting my finger on a horse who won five out of the eight races they showed on the form, but the purses were all under two thousand.

"Maybe. Maybe so. Next thing is to look up the track," he said, taking the program from me and turning some pages. "That's Bangor, way the hell up in Maine. Speed rating for that track is two oh four, according to this little program you bought. What's it for here?"

I looked where he was pointing. "It says, 'Yonkers, one fifty-nine.'"

"Good! Now this here one we're looking at, he's been going in two oh two and change when he wins up there. And that's a real slow track. What's that speed translate to down here?"

"One fifty-nine?" I guessed.

"Closer to the deuce, I think, but you're in the right spot. So, could he win here, if he runs his number?"

I scanned the form, looking at each of the other horses. It was chilly out, with the wind blowing enough to move the flags. Maine, I'd never been up there, but I figured this kind of weather wouldn't be any big deal to a horse that made his living in worse.

I went over the race real careful. Taking my time, the way the old man had told me to. The horse would be fifth from the inside when the race started. It wasn't just the number on his blanket; the old man told me that every slot has to wear a color to match it, so you could tell them apart even on the back stretch. The horse had a black blanket.

"Early speed doesn't mean as much as it used to here," I remembered the old man saying. And, anyway, this horse never was first by the quarter mile even when he started from way inside, so I didn't count that much.

"Yeah," I finally said. "I think he could."

"Me, too," the old man said. "Even though those speed ratings are a pile of crap today, they give you some idea. Now I've been to that track in Maine, and, let me tell you, it's one rotten joint."

"The track itself?"

"Yeah. The track itself. See, the best tracks are firm, but they ain't like concrete. A horse moving to a track like this, he's going to feel like he's floating."

3

One of the things I had been reading about was the movable hub rail they have at Yonkers. The old man hated it. "Just another sign," he'd said to me, when I asked him about it. "This whole track has gone lousy. One time, it was one of the top spots in the whole country . . . maybe the whole world. Had the best horses, biggest purses, huge crowds. Now look at it.

"First, they had to go and fuck with the starting line. Used to be, there was a long distance between the start line and that first turn, okay? Now, naturally, that means a real short home stretch, right? So, tell me, what kind of horse does that favor?"

"One with early speed?"

"You've been hitting those books," he said. "I'll have to bring some more down for you next time. More advanced stuff. Now listen: Before they had that movable rail on the inside, you could see the strategy and tactics play out right in front of you. Get to the front, dictate the fractions. That means, shoot that first quarter, then back off on the second. You want to keep the pace slow, because you know they're all going to be coming at you down the stretch.

"Now, you go the whole way on the front end, there's no cover, so it may be a tougher trip. But it's a shorter distance home, too. If you're still in front looking at the wire, you can't block the others off—that's a sure DQ—but you can ease your horse out a little to the right, give the other guys a few extra feet to cover, see?"

"Yeah," I said. And I did.

"But you can't do it that way no more," the old man said, like been out to cheat him, personal. "Now it's all gimmicks.

This track, they even run some of the races at a mile and a sixteen. What's that supposed to be, a joke? These horses aren't bred for that distance. You can't handicap them, 'cause you got no background to look at. Might as well make them run uphill."

"Not standard."

"Yeah," he said, looking at me close. "That's right. They say this track's coming back. Big purses again. That's true enough. But that's all down to the fucking 'casino' they got inside. That's where the real money is."

4

A month went by with him talking to me like that. "You been making paper bets for a while now," he said one night. "You ready to pick one for real?"

"I think so."

"You already got one, don't you?"

"I . . . guess," I said. Wondering how he knew.

"Show me."

He studied the form I held out. Asked me a bunch of questions. Kept nodding. Finally he said, "Your guy's no overnighter; he's been on the grounds for five weeks now. Been going in the same class every week, just one step down from the top. Hasn't won here yet, but he's been holding his own. And there's a driver change, too. You see that?"

"Yeah. John Campbell. He's good?"

"Good? The man's an artist. Some of these drivers, they're nothing but thugs. Campbell, he knows you can't whip a horse into winning, you have to guide him home, act like you expect him to get there first. With pacers, he's pretty good," the old man said, "but you put him behind a trotter, there's no driver out here that can touch him."

5

My horse was a chesty bay named Little Eric, a Noble Gesture trotter out of an Arsenal mare. He was sluggish out of the six-hole, but he fired up and went first-over just past the quarter, which had gone in a soft thirty-flat. Just as he caught up to the lead horse, Simple Justice, that one picked up speed, and kept Little Eric parked out. The half went in fifty-eight and four.

Little Eric finally got clear by going slingshot on the clubhouse turn, but he'd come a long way without cover and the heavy chalk, Bruno's Boy, had popped down into the inside lane, as the movable hub rail lived up to its name.

Bruno's Boy was really rolling, but my horse kept chugging on, dead game. Little Eric held off Bruno's Boy by a neck. The tote board said he paid $18.20 to win. On the program, he'd been what the old man told me was a classic overlay. That meant he wasn't the favorite, and he didn't deserve to be, but he was a lot better than the 13-1 morning line made him out to be.

"Nice," is all the old man said. I didn't know if he said that because I'd picked the horse, or because I didn't jump up and down and scream as they came down the stretch, the way some people do. "Lames," the old man called them. "Like chumps who yell at the dice in a casino. The horses hear all that shouting about as much as the dice do. Makes as much difference to them, too."

I made my way to the window, waited my turn on line, the program open in front of me, heavily marked up in red. Under the brim of my hat, my eyes swept the area. But I didn't see what I was looking for.

6

" the old man said, when I handed over the beer I brought 'm.

He took a sip. Looked over at me. "You never get one for your-self," he said.

I just shrugged.

"You don't smoke, neither. Against your religion?"

"I don't do that, either," I said.

He closed his eyes like he was thinking something over, but he didn't say anything for a while.

I went back to looking at the program.

The old man tapped me on the forearm. "See that?" he said, pointing at the giant tote board in the infield. "Forget that Morning Line crap—you can watch the real action right here. Remember, the track don't set the odds, the bettors do. That's all 'pari-mutuel' means: you're betting against all the other players. The track takes its piece off the top. Same as the house does in a poker game. That's the only sure way to make money, any kind of gambling. Live off the takeout."

"What about when you bet with a bookie?"

"Don't bet with bookies," he said, like we were done talking.

I studied the tote board. Watched the numbers jump around.

"Any chump can be a gambler," he said. "All it takes is money. Or credit, if you're fucked up enough. You, you're learning to be a handicapper."

"Handicappers don't bet with bookies? Where do they go, then, OTB?"

"OTB? That's Sucker Paradise. You bet with those thieves, there's another takeout, on top of the track's. A horse that pays ten dollars at the track, he'd be a nine-eighty horse at OTB, see? You let politicians run anything, the first thing they do is drain it dry. OTB, that's the only bookie operation in history to lose money. A pro wouldn't go near that joint. Let's say you hit a big enough number—like a Pick 4, which is a righteous play for a handicap-per, 'cause you're stringing winners, not betting on horses to come in third or crap like that. At OTB, IRS takes its cut right at the window. They rob you at both ends."

I didn't say anything. That's the way things are, everywhere.

"Used to be, you got a wino to cash a big ticket for you," he said. "Ten-percenters, we called them, 'cause that's the piece they got out of it. All they had to do was show a Social Security card. It got reported to the IRS, sure, but they didn't take out the money off the top. You walked off with ninety percent, all cash."

I studied the tote board for a few minutes. "How come the show pool has so much money in it?" I asked him.

"There's a bridge-jumper in the house," he said.

"What's that?"

The old man lit himself a smoke. "This is how it works. The more the bettors like any particular horse, the less it's going to pay, understand? By law, the track has to pay at least $2.10 on each race, no matter what the odds. Now, you see the seven horse up there?"

"Yeah."

"Look at those odds: one to nine. Only time you see something like that, the horse is a monster. The next race, you see it's a Sire Stakes elimination, okay? There's maybe fifty horses eligible for the final, so they break them into groups, then the winners get to race each other. See, on the program? There's six of these races tonight. You with me so far?"

"Uh-huh."

"What's happening here is that the seven horse, Stephen's Susie, she got put in with a bunch of stiffs. Those others don't belong on the same track as her. Look at her lines: she's already won a couple of hundred grand, see there? Next best filly to her has banked thirty-something and she had to run twice as many races to get even that much. Stephen's Susie, she's already gone in fifty-three. For a two-year-old trotting filly! Only one other horse in the field ever got below two flat, and that was at Woodbine, where they all fly. The next race, it's going to be a slaughter."

"So, if everybody bets on her, it's not going to pay anything?"

"Not if you're a ten dollar bettor, it won't. But look at that board. Look at it close. When the odds get like that, you get the same $2.10 whether your horse comes in first, second, or third. So you play the monster to show, you've got the closest thing to a mortal lock you'll ever see on a racetrack. Figure it that way, it's a five percent return on your money in under two minutes. But that only works if you throw serious coin. You plunk down two, three hundred K, and, so long as the monster gets at least third, you get your stake back, plus ten, fifteen thousand profit."

"But what if the horse, I don't know, breaks stride, like you said? Even a great horse wouldn't win, then."

"That's why they call them bridge-jumpers, kid."

7

Back in my motel room, I studied the photographs they'd given me before I left.

"This is him," the man who'd hired me said. "He knows he's marked, but the fucking rat's a degenerate gambler—he *has* to play. And he's gotta watch the action, see it with his own eyes. He's not crazy enough to walk into a real casino, so we figure it's got to be the track. This one, it's got those slots, too. Sooner or later, he's going to show.

"So what you need is a reason to be there every night. And we've got that covered for you, too. You're going to be a real hard-core gambler, the kind of guy who practically lives on the premises, never misses a day. After a while, you're part of the scenery; nobody pays attention."

I didn't say anything. That's what people like him expect.

"We might even get lucky with a heads-up," he told me. "The only racehorses this little weasel knows anything about are the kind you rent by the hour. This Arnie guy, he's all about flash. Never goes anywhere without full front. He picks the wrong whore to bring with him one night, we'll get a call. That happens, you'll get one, too. But don't count on it, all right? Just study those photos; make sure you'll know him if you see him."

I knew what they'd expect me to do with the photos after I was done studying. The man gave me half the money in front, like always. Said it was mine to keep even if I didn't do the job. I knew that meant they had other people working the same job, but I didn't ask any questions. That's not my place—I'm a contract man, not a family member.

So I put in a couple of months, seeing the old man two-three nights a week, just like he'd said. Some days, too—he told me the real pros never miss the baby races—two-year-olds racing for stakes their connections put up when they were born—or the Qualifiers—where horses coming in from another track have to prove they can go the course in under a certain time.

You can't bet on any of those races, but it's the best place to get advance info. "Like scouting a farm team, see who's going to be a star in a couple of years," the old man said.

He kept a notebook, and he made a separate section for each new horse he liked. Every time that horse would go after that, the old man would be there, making his notes.

He showed me how to make a notebook of my own, but he never showed me what was in his—that wasn't part of the deal.

"Every handicapper's got his own system," he said. "And it all comes down to weight."

"I thought weight didn't matter with trotters. You said it's only the thoroughbreds who have to—"

"Not the weight they pull," he said. "The weight you put."

"Huh?"

"Look, kid, you see this program?"

"Sure."

"Got all kinds of information, if you take the time to learn how to read it. Most of the suckers who come here, they don't even bother to do that, and that's good, because they're the ones we're betting against, remember? But even if you learn to read the program perfect, even if you check the breeding books, read everything you can get your hands on, you're still working with the same information anyone can get: Like how many times the horse has been out, how much money he's won, his fastest time, what class he's been in . . . right?"

"I . . . guess. Sure. But, all that information, how do you know what piece is more important than another?"

"That's the trick!" the old man, said, like he was proud of me for figuring it out. "That's the weight I was talking about. Some handicappers, they're speed whores. Others, they go for horses that race better in the mud. Or take a drop in class."

"What about the breeding? You said there were books on it, so that's real important, right?"

"To some people, yeah. To them, bloodlines are everything. Me, I never went much by that. You got horses, you look up who their mother and father was, you'd think they'd be rockets. But they turn out to be duds, never even make it to a racetrack. Other ones, you never heard of any horse in their whole family tree, just a bunch of mutts. And they turn out to be world-beaters."

"What do you look for, then?"

"Heart," the old man said.

"Where's that on the program?"

"It's not supposed to be on the program."

"So how—?"

"That's mine," the old man said. "I was asked to teach you the game, and I'm doing that. And one of the things you learn is, a real handicapper, he puts together a system that works, he don't share it with anyone, ever. You ever watch those commercials on the TV in the middle of the night? The ones where this guy, he's made a zillion dollars in real estate, now he's going to show you how to do the same thing for a couple of hundred bucks?"

"Yeah," I said.

"You believe them?"

"Come on."

"Let's get something to eat," the old man said.

8

"You don't think you know enough yet?" the old man asked me.

I'd been going to the track with him for more than three months straight. I'd moved around a few times, just in case anyone was paying attention. It's easy for me to move, only takes an hour or so. I don't own a lot of stuff.

"No," is all I said.

"You got all the lingo down, now. You know how to read the program, how to bet, that's more than ninety percent of the lame *stugotz* that hang around any track."

"But there's more, right?"

"Sure. There's always more. Me, I'm still learning, picking stuff up."

"Okay, then."

He gave me a look, but he didn't say anything. That night, we sat in his favorite place in the grandstand. "You know why this is the perfect spot?" he told me the first time we sat there. "You can see the action in the turns, on the backstretch, and coming home, too. That's 'cause this is a half-mile track, get it?"

"No. What difference could that make? I mean, they all run the same distance, right?"

"Half-mile track means two circuits to get the whole mile in, okay? Two circuits, four turns."

"They're not all like this one?"

"Hell, no. Most of them are mile tracks, now. Like the fucking Meadowlands. Used to be a lot of five-eighths courses, too—that'd be three turns, real long stretch. Like Sportsman's Park just outside Chicago, that was a real beauty."

"So, one mile, that's only two turns?"

"Yeah," he said, like he was sucking on a lemon. "Gives you faster times, sure, but you can't actually see most of the race, unless you're one of those guys don't mind wearing fucking opera glasses.

"By me, binoculars narrow it down too much. You can only watch a few horses at the same time, depending on how tight the flow is. You miss a lot that way. Most people like the two-turn tracks, because the horses run closer to form there. That means the favorites win more often.

"I'm not talking about horse people; I mean the guys who bring their girlfriends to the track, watch them bet their birthday numbers, think it's cute."

I thought about the guy I was watching for. Then I said, "That's good for guys like us, right?"

He gave me one of his looks, but he didn't say anything.

10

"How long have you been doing this?" I asked him one day. We were at a diner, a short distance from the track, having breakfast, waiting for the gates to open so we could watch some new shippers qualify.

"All my life," he said. "My old man used to take me, when I was just a kid. That's why they ran the trotters at night, so working guys could go. But I didn't do it like this, come anytime I want, I mean, until I retired."

"You had a regular job?"

"What, you think everyone's like you?" he said. "Con Edison, just like my old man. Thirty-five years I put in."

"That's a long time."

"Didn't seem long to me," he said. "I figured, I had things to look forward to. My old man, he died on the job, when I was still in high school. I remember him always saying he was going to retire someday, spend all his time playing golf.

"My old man loved golf, but he only got to play once in a blue moon. He was going to move to Florida—they got a golf course down every block, there. But he never got to go. Me, I could have had what I wanted right here in Yonkers."

"So what got messed up?"

"Everything got messed up. My wife, Pam, she had plans, too. Just like my old man. She never got to see any of them come true, either. Fucking cancer."

He looked down at his hands. Big hands, I noticed. I always look at a man's hands—the eyes show you the right-now—it's always the hands that show you the history.

After about a minute, he said, "My kids, I got a boy and a girl. He's a lawyer, she's a schoolteacher. Only she don't teach. Anyway, the boy, he lives in Los Angeles, and my daughter, she's all the way down in South Jersey. After Pam passed, I started coming here all the time. But then it turned lousy, like I said.

"So now, I got me a place upstate. There's a sweet little track twenty minutes from my house. It's not major league, but it's got some nice horses going. And not just the old campaigners that aren't fast enough for the big purses anymore; the prospects, too. You can pick out the ones that are going places. It's kind of fun, watch them after that. Not in person, I mean in the papers. See how they made out."

"You miss your kids?"

"About as much as they miss me," he said. "I always worked second shift. Put in a lot of overtime, too. Always adding to that goddamned pension, that was me."

11

One day, the old man said he'd showed me what he knew—a *piece* of what he knew, he made sure to tell me. That's how I knew it was time for him to split.

"You don't have to do this . . . what you do, Henry." That was the first time he ever said my name. "I know you must get paid good, but there's not even a pension at the end, right?"

I nodded. The old man knew more than I thought he did. There's only one way a guy who does my kind of work gets to retire.

12

After the old man went away, I did the same stuff he did. I was there every night. I kept my notebook, and I watched. They never called me off, and I got paid expenses every week, so I figured they hadn't found that Arnie guy yet.

One Tuesday night, there wasn't a single pacer I liked in the first race, but I was crazy about a trotter going in the second—a tough little gelding named Sheba's Pride, eleven years old and he still knew the way home. That was something the old man taught me, how some of the older horses had the track figured out better than the drivers did.

Sheba's Pride was in with 5K claimers, grinders who weren't ever going to get claimed, just there to pick up a pick of the purse. My horse had a life mark of fifty-one and one, but he took that when he was a four-year-old. Three of the other horses had gone faster, and much more recently. But not one of them had taken their mark on a half-mile track, like my horse had.

It was a nasty day, cold with heavy clouds; the infield flags showed a hard wind, too. None of that was going to bother my horse. I had watched him qualify when he shipped in from

Freehold—another four-turn track. His driver had him pocket-sitting all the way; he could have cruised home second, qualified easy. But he pulled outside, challenged, and put together a last quarter in twenty-eight and three, open lengths between him and the horse that had been on top.

"They have to want it," the old man had told me. I knew that was what he meant by "heart," even though he never said the word.

I had wheeled Sheba's Pride, so I had the Double covered if he could pull off his half. I didn't care who won the first, but I watched anyway. The seven horse tried to cut across, but he moved too sharp. The interference break took out the front-runners . . . lucky none of the horses went down.

Some rat with no business winning anything managed to stagger home ahead of what was left. Paid a ridiculous forty-seven bucks for the win.

When I checked the board, it was like the stakes just shot up. I knew if Sheba's Pride came through for me, I was looking at a real bundle.

The marshal called the trotters, and they rolled in behind the moving gate. When the pace car pulled away, three of them fought for the lead, but Sheba's Pride showed nothing going into the first turn. He was shuffled back, sixth on the rail, and he stayed there all the way through the first two quarters, even though the second went in a stone-slow thirty and four.

Just past the half, Sheba's Pride pulled off the rail, but he wasn't the only one with that idea. Usually, that's good—you want to flush cover to run behind if you can. But he was parked deep, with two horses ahead of him on the outside instead of just one.

I glanced at the timer, the three-quarters had gone in 1:27.4, so I knew the lead horse wouldn't be able to hold on, but he was trying like hell anyway.

The first horse coming up on the outside slingshotted the club-house turn and made his move. The horse behind him had his nose in the other driver's helmet. Just as those two pulled past the leader, Sheba's Pride swung out three-wide and made his own lane.

Down the stretch, it looked like the two horses who'd been running outside were really flying. Sheba's Pride was just grinding away on the outside, closing on the leader, but not fast enough. But he kept grinding, right to the wire. The photo had his nose in front. The Double paid $709.50, and I had it five times.

I didn't go cash my tickets right away. I wanted to watch the replay on the monitors. And make some marks in my notebook.

I wished the old man had been there, but I didn't know why.

13

Late one afternoon, I got a call. They told me the job was over. They didn't say why, and I didn't ask. Instead of going to the track that night, I checked out of the motel and drove to a new one, all the way over by JFK.

The next morning, I packed my duffel bag: my clothes, my tools, and my notebook. I would have ditched everything except the notebook, but I didn't know how this would come out. That's why the virgin semi-auto I'd bought for the job I never did went into the slot built behind the glove box. Then I threw the duffel in the trunk of my car and started driving.

I'm going to try my luck at this sweet little track upstate I heard about. If I can be good at anything besides the one thing I already knew I was good at, maybe I could be good, period. A good man, I mean.

I don't know. I guess I'll find out, soon enough.

for Stephen Chambers

PASSAGE TO PARADISE

Beyond the border is everything they pray for. Pray *for*, not pray *to*. The border is no plaster shrine; it is a gateway to Paradise. The only one.

My life is to take them there.

They pray to God, but they cannot see God. They pray for the border, but that, too, they cannot see. God is only a belief. And the border; it is only a line on a map.

That line is not God's work. There is no river to swim, no mountains to climb. The terrain is exactly the same on either side. The borderline is not made by God; it is the mark of the Conqueror, a dry moat surrounding his palace.

Those who pray, those who dream, those who risk all they have against what they could be . . . they are no threat to the Conqueror. They do not want the palace; they dream only of tending its grounds.

On the Conqueror's side of the border, pay for such work is meager by their standards. It is not irony that the people of the Conqueror call it "slave wages." But on the other side, such wages can transform a life. Many lives. For eternity.

A man can live for years in a hovel if he knows each day brings his family closer to glory. A man can live with many others, packed in as if in prison, treated with contempt, driven like a mule. He can look at a tattered picture of his wife and children and feel his chest swell with pride. Why? Because he is their hero. Their provider and protector. His children will have clean water to drink. His children will never be beggars. His wife will not sell her body to feed them. Someday, there might even be a house. And school.

And his grandchildren will prosper, because their parents will have carried on his name, each generation climbing higher than the one before, because each will have begun higher.

All because of their foundation. The foundation he is building with his body-crushing labor.

His wife will be the envy of the others in the village. Her husband is not one of those fat, drunken cowards who tell big stories but never do big things. They make babies, but what is that? A dog can make puppies.

Someday, his name will mean something.

And if he dies in the attempt, he will be forever honored as a man.

Those who guard the border know none of this.

There is no gate. The patrols are as random as the packs of bandits that live in the lawless land between hell and Paradise. But not as merciful.

I am no coyote. Those who hire me are not crammed into an airless truck, to be abandoned at the first sign of danger. I am no deliverer of cargo; I am a warrior.

The dreamers pay me to fight. And to guarantee that they are never, ever taken alive. Everyone knows what happens to those who are taken by the bandits. The tapes—the ones the bosses make inside their castles—they are sold even here. But anyone with the kind of money it would take to buy such tapes would not need to cross the border. For them, for the *narco-reys*, Paradise is on this side of the border.

I take anyone who has the money. I make a run only every two or three months, and I must be paid in advance. That money does not come with me—I, too, have my own obligations.

It sometimes takes years for me to be paid. Years before I take a person across. I keep records, and I never cheat. This is the opposite of the way some do it, I have heard. Some take them across, and wait to be paid with the money they send back. This I cannot do. Part of my pay demands that I must make sure they are not taken alive. How could they pay me then?

This business came to me from my father. My father's father before. Our family; this is what we do.

The truck I use, that is always new. But the business, that has been here since before there were such things.

I drive by night, without lights. The sounds of the truck carry through the open air, but not so far. The sound of my weapons carries a greater distance, but gunshots in the desert carry no significance.

I have electronic equipment, too. And explosives. My truck is camouflaged, but it flies a flag. Our family's flag, at the very top of one of the antennas.

Most of the bandits know that flag. They are not fighters; they are carrion-eaters. They know there will always be other trucks, carrying much easier prey. They do not interfere . . . at least, not anymore.

I take the border-crossers to the gateway, but I never follow them across. On each drive back, I pray they find their Paradise.

Sometimes, I cry because I had to send them to Paradise myself.

But I have my work. My oldest son is almost twelve. Soon, he will start riding with me.

My name will live through him, as my father's does through me. That is my Paradise.

for Michael A. Black

VEIL'S VISIT

By Joe R. Lansdale and Andrew Vachss

1

Leonard eyed Veil for a long hard moment, said, "If you're a lawyer, then I can shit a perfectly round turd through a hoop at twenty paces. Blindfolded."

"I am a lawyer," Veil said. "But I'll let your accomplishments speak for themselves."

Veil was average height, dark hair touched with gray, one good eye. The other one roamed a little. He had a beard that could have been used as a Brillo pad, and he was dressed in an expensive suit and shiny shoes, a fancy wristwatch and ring. He was the only guy I'd ever seen with the kind of presence Leonard has. Scary.

"You still don't look like any kind of lawyer to me," Leonard said.

"He means that as a compliment," I said to Veil. "Leonard doesn't think real highly of your brethren at the bar."

"Oh, you're a bigot?" Veil asked pleasantly, looking directly at Leonard with his one good eye. A very icy eye indeed—I remembered it well.

"The fuck you talking about? Lawyers are all right. They got their purpose. You never know when you might want one of them to weigh down a rock at the bottom of a lake." Leonard's tone had shifted from mildly inquisitive to that of a man who might like to perform a live dissection.

"You think all lawyers are alike, right? But if I said all blacks are alike, you'd think you know something about me, right?"

"I knew you were coming to that," Leonard said.

"Well," I said. "I think this is really going well. What about you boys?"

Veil and Leonard may not have bonded as well as I had hoped, but they certainly had some things in common. In a way, they were both assholes. I, of course, exist on a higher plane.

"You wearing an Armani suit, must have set you back a thousand dollars—" Leonard said.

"You know a joint where I can get suits like this for a lousy one grand, I'll stop there on my way back and pick up a couple dozen," Veil said.

"Yeah, fine," Leonard said. "Gold Rolex, diamond ring. . . . How much all that set you back?"

"It was a gift," Veil said.

"Sure," Leonard said. "You know what you look like?"

"What's that?"

"You look like Central Casting for a mob movie."

"And you look like a candidate for a chain gang. Which is kind of why I'm here."

"You gonna defend me? How you gonna do that? I may not know exactly what you are, but I can bet the farm on this—you ain't no Texas lawyer. Hell, you ain't no Texan, period."

"No problem. I can just go *pro hac vice.*"

"I hope that isn't some kind of sexual act," Leonard said. "Especially if it involves me and you."

"It just means I get admitted to the bar for one case. For the specific litigation. I'll need local counsel to handle the pleadings, of course. . . ."

"Do I look like a goddamned pleader to you? And you best not say yes."

" 'Pleadings' just means the papers," Veil said, his voice a model of patience. "Motions, applications . . . stuff like that. You wanted to cop a plea to this, Hap wouldn't need me. I don't do that kind of thing. And by the way, I'm doing this for Hap, not you."

"What is it makes you so special to Hap?" Leonard asked, studying Veil's face carefully. "What is it that you *do* do?"

"Fight," Veil said.

"Yeah," I said. "He can do that."

"Yeah, so can you and me, but that and a rubber will get us a jack off without mess." Leonard sighed. He said to Veil, "You know what my problem is?"

"Besides attitude, sure. Says so right on the indictment. You burned down a crack house. For at least the . . . what was it, fourth time? That's first-degree arson, malicious destruction of property, attempted murder—"

"I didn't—"

"What? Know anyone was home when you firebombed the dump? Doesn't matter—the charge is still valid."

"Yeah, well they can valid *this*," Leonard said, making a gesture appropriate to his speech.

"You're looking at a flat dime down in Huntsville," Veil told him. "That a good enough summary of your 'problem'?"

"No, it ain't close," Leonard said. "Here's my problem. You come in here wearing a few thousand bucks of fancy stuff, tell me you're a fighter, but your face looks like you lost a lot more fights than you won. You don't know jack about Texas law, but you're gonna work a local jury. And that's still not my big problem. You know what my big problem is?"

"I figure you're going to tell me sometime before visiting hours are over," Veil said.

"My problem is this. Why the hell should I trust you?"

"I trust him," I said.

"I know, brother. And I trust you. What I don't trust, on the other hand, is your judgment. The two ain't necessarily the same thing."

"Try this, then," Veil told him. "Homicide. A murder. And nobody's said a word about it. For almost twenty years."

"You telling me you and Hap—?"

"I'm telling you there was a homicide. No statute of limitations on that, right? It's still unsolved. And nobody's talking."

"I don't know. Me and Hap been tight a long time. He'd tell me something like that. I mean, he dropped the rock on someone, I'd know." Leonard turned to me. "Wouldn't I?"

I didn't say anything. Veil was doing the talking.

Veil leaned in close, dropping his voice. "It wasn't Hap who did it. But Hap knows all about it. And if you keep your mouth shut long enough, you will too. Then you can decide who to trust. Deal?"

Leonard gave Veil a long, deep look. "Deal," he finally said, leaning back, waiting to hear the story.

Veil turned and looked at me, and I knew that was my cue to tell it.

2

"It was back in my semi-hippie days," I said to Leonard. "Remember when I was all about peace and love?"

"The only 'piece' I ever knew you to be about was a piece of ass," Leonard said kindly. "I always thought you had that long hair so's it could help you get into fights."

"Just tell him the fucking story," Veil said. "Okay? I've got work to do, and I can't do it without Leonard. You two keep screwing around and the guard's going to roll on back here and—"

"It was in this house on the coast," I said. "In Oregon. I was living with some folks."

"Some of those folks being women, of course."

"Yeah. I was experimenting with different ways of life. I told you about it. Anyway, I hadn't been there long. This house, it wasn't like it was a commune or nothing, but people just . . . came and went, understand? So, one day, this guy comes strolling up.

Nice-looking guy. Photographer, he said he was. All loaded down with equipment in his van. He was a traveling man, just working his way around the country. Taking pictures for this book he was doing. He fit in pretty good. You know, he looked the part. Long hair, but a little neater than the rest of us. Suave manner. Took pictures a lot. Nobody really cared. He did his share of the work, kicked in a few bucks for grub. No big deal. I was a little suspicious at first. We always got photographers wanting to 'document' us, you know? Mostly wanted pictures of the girls. Especially Sunflower—she had this thing about clothes being 'inhibiting' and all. In other words, she was quick to shuck drawers and throw the hair triangle around. But this guy was real peaceful, real calm. I remember one of the guys there said this one had a calm presence. Like the eye of a hurricane."

"This is motherfucking fascinating and all," Leonard said, "but considering my particular situation, I wonder if you couldn't, you know, get to the point?"

Seeing as how Leonard never read that part of the Good Book that talked about patience being a virtue, I sped it up a bit. "I was out in the backyard one night," I said. "Meditating."

"Masturbating, you mean," Leonard said.

"I was just getting to that stage with the martial arts and I didn't want any of the damn marijuana smoke getting in my eyes. I guess I was more conservative about that sort of thing than I realized. It made me nervous just being around it. So I needed some privacy. I wasn't doing the classic meditation thing. Just being alone with my thoughts, trying to find my center."

"Which you never have," Leonard said.

"I'm sitting there, thinking about whatever it was I was thinking about—"

"Pussy," Leonard said.

"And I open my eyes and there he is. Veil."

"Now *that'd* be some scary shit," Leonard said.

"Looked about the same he does now."

"Yeah? Was he wearing that Armani suit?"

"Matter a fact, he wasn't," I said. "He looked like everyone else did around there then. Only difference was the pistol."

"I can see how that got your attention," Leonard said.

"It was dark. And I'm no modern firearms expert. But it wasn't the stuff I grew up with, hunting rifles, shotguns, and revolvers. This was a seriously big-ass gun, I can tell you that. I couldn't tell if he was pointing it at me or not. Finally I decided he was just kind of . . . holding it. I asked him, politely, I might add, if there was anything I could do for him, short of volunteering to be shot, and he said, yeah, matter of fact, there was. What he wanted was some information about this photographer guy.

"Now hippie types weren't all that different from cons back then, at least when it came to giving out information to the cops. Cops had a way of thinking you had long hair you had to be something from Mars out to destroy Mom, apple pie, and the American way."

"Does that mean Texas too?" Leonard asked.

"I believe it did, yes."

"Well, I can see their point. And the apple pie part."

"I could tell this guy was no cop. And he wasn't asking me for evidence-type stuff anyway. Just when the guy had showed up, stuff like that."

Leonard yawned. Sometimes he can be a very crude individual. Veil looked like he always does. Calm.

"Anyway, I started to say I didn't know the guy, then . . . I don't know. There was something about his manner that made me trust him."

"Thank you," Veil said. I wasn't sure if he was being sarcastic or not.

I nodded. "I told him the truth. It wasn't any big deal. Like I said, he wasn't asking anything weird, but I was a little worried. I mean, you know, the gun and all. Then I got stupid and—"

"Oh, *that's* when it happened?" Leonard asked. "That's like the moment it set in?"

I maintained patience—which is what Leonard is always complaining he has to do with me—and went on like he hadn't said a word: "—asked him how come he wanted to know all about this guy, and maybe I ought not to be saying anything, and how he ought to take his pistol and go on. I didn't want any trouble, and no one at the place did either.

"So Veil asks the big question. Where is the guy right now? I told him he was out somewhere. Or maybe gone, for all I knew. That's the way things were then. People came and went like cats and you didn't tend to get uptight about it. It was the times."

"Groovy," Leonard said.

"We talk for a while, but, truth was, I didn't know anything about the guy, so I really got nothing to say of importance. But, you know, I'm thinking it isn't every day you see a guy looks like Veil walking around with a gun almost the size of my dick."

"Jesus," Leonard said. "Can't ever get away from your dick."

"No, it tends to stay with me."

"How about staying with the story," Veil said, still calm but with an edge to his voice now.

"So I ask Veil, it's okay with him, I'm going back in the house and get some sleep, and like maybe could he put the gun up 'cause it's making me nervous. I know I mentioned that gun several times. I'm trying to kind of glide out of there because I figure a guy with a gun has more on his mind than just small talk. I thought he might even be a druggie, though he didn't look like one. Veil here, he says no problem. But I see he's not going anywhere so I don't move. Somehow, the idea of getting my back to that gun doesn't appeal to me, and we're kind of close, and I'm thinking he gets a little closer I got a small chance of taking the gun away from him. Anyway, we both stick. Studying each other, I think. Neither of us going anywhere."

"Neither the fuck am I," Leonard said. "Matter of fact, I think moss is starting to grow on the north side of my ass."

"All right, partner," I told him, "here's the finale. I decide to not go in the house, just sit out there with Veil. We talk a bit about this and that, anything but guns, and we're quiet a bit. Gets to be real late, I don't know, maybe four in the morning, and we both hear a motor. Something pulling into the driveway. Then we hear a car door close. Another minute or so, the front door to the house closes too. Veil, without a word to me, gets up and walks around to the drive. I follow him. Even then I think I'm some kind of mediator. That whatever's going on, maybe I can fix it. I was hell for fixing people's problems then."

"You're still hell for that," Leonard said.

"Sure enough, there's the guy's van. I'm starting to finally snap that Veil hasn't just showed up for an assassination. He's investigating, and, well, I don't know how, but I'm just sort of falling in with him. In spite of his sweet personality, there's something about me and him that clicked."

"I adore a love story," Leonard said.

"So anyway, I wasn't exactly shocked when Veil put the pistol away, stuck a little flashlight in his teeth, worked the locks on the guy's van like he had a key. We both climbed in, being real quiet. In the back, under a pile of equipment, we found the . . . pictures."

"Guy was a blackmailer?" Leonard asked, a little interested now.

"They were pictures of kids," I told him. Quiet, so's he'd know what kind of pictures I meant.

Leonard's face changed. I knew then he was thinking about what kind of pictures they were and not liking having to think about it.

"I'd never seen anything like that before, and didn't know that sort of thing existed. Oh, I guess, in theory, but not in reality. And the times then, lot of folks were thinking free love and sex was okay for anyone, grown-ups, kids. People who didn't really know anything about life and what this sort of thing was all about, but one look at those pictures and I was educated, and it was an education I didn't want. I've never got over it.

"So he," I said, nodding my head over at Veil, "asks me, where does the guy with the van sleep? Where inside the house, I mean. I tried to explain to him what a crash pad was. I couldn't be sure where he was, or even who he might be with, you understand? Anyway, Veil just looks at me, says it would be a real mess if they found this guy in the house. A mess for us, you know? So he asks me, how about if I go inside, tell the guy it looks like someone tried to break into his van?

"I won't kid you. I hesitated. Not because I felt any sympathy for that sonofabitch, but because it's not my nature to walk someone off a plank. I was trying to sort of think my way out of it when Veil here told me to take a look at the pictures again. A good look."

"The guy's toast," Leonard said. "Fucker like that, he's toast. I know you, Hap. He's toast."

I nodded at Leonard. "Yeah," I said. "I went inside. Brought the guy out with me. He opens the door to the van, climbs in the front seat. And there's Veil, in the passenger seat. Veil and that pistol. I went back in the house, watched from the window. I heard the van start up, saw it pull out. I never saw the photographer again. And to tell you the truth, I've never lost a minute's sleep over it. I don't know what that says about me, but I haven't felt a moment of regret."

"It says you have good character," Veil said.

"What I want to know," Leonard said, looking at Veil, "is what did you do with the body?"

Veil didn't say anything.

Leonard tried again. "You was a hit man? Is that what Hap here's trying to tell me?"

"It was a long time ago," Veil told him. "It doesn't matter, does it? What matters is: You want to talk to me now?"

3

The judge looked like nothing so much as a turkey buzzard: tiny head on a long, wrinkled neck and cold little eyes. Everybody stood up when he entered the courtroom. Lester Rommerly—the local lawyer I went and hired like Veil said to—he told the judge that Veil would be representing Leonard. The judge looked down at Veil.

"Where are you admitted to practice, sir?"

"In New York State, your honor. And in the Federal District Courts of New York, New Jersey, Rhode Island, Pennsylvania, Illinois, Michigan, California, and Massachusetts."

"Get around a bit, do you?"

"On occasion," Veil replied.

"Well, sir, you can represent this defendant here. Nothing against the law about that, as you apparently know. I can't help wondering, I must say, how you managed to find yourself way down here."

Veil didn't say anything. And it was obvious after a minute that he wasn't going to. He and the judge just kind of watched each other.

Then the trial started.

The first few witnesses were all government. The fire department guy testified about "the presence of an accelerant" being the tip-off that this was arson, not some accidental fire. Veil got up slowly, started to walk over to the witness box, then stopped. His voice was low, but it carried right through the courtroom.

"Officer, you have any experience with alcoholics?"

"Objection!" the DA shouted.

"Sustained," the judge said, not even looking at Veil.

"Officer," Veil went on like nothing had happened, "you have any experience with dope fiends?"

"Objection!" the DA was on his feet, red-faced.

"Counsel, you are to desist from this line of questioning," the judge said. "The witness is a fireman, not a psychologist."

"Oh, excuse me, Your Honor," Veil said sweetly. "I mis-phrased my inquiry. Let me try again: Officer," he said, turning his attention back to the witness, "by 'accelerant,' you mean something like gasoline or kerosene, isn't that correct?"

"Yes," the witness said, cautious in spite of Veil's mild tone.

"Hmmm," Veil said. "Be pretty stupid to keep a can of gasoline right in the house, wouldn't it?"

"Your Honor . . . ," the DA pleaded.

"Well, I believe he can answer that one," the judge said.

"Yeah, it would," the fire marshal said. "But some folks do keep kerosene inside. You know, for heating and all."

"Thank you, Officer," Veil said, like the witness had just given him this great gift. "And it'd be even stupider to smoke cigarettes in the same house where you kept gasoline . . . or kerosene for that matter, wouldn't it?"

"Well, sure. I mean, if—"

"Objection!" the DA yelled. "There is no evidence to show that anyone was smoking cigarettes in the house!"

"Ah, my apologies," Veil said, bowing slightly. "Please consider the question withdrawn. Officer: Be pretty stupid to smoke crack in a house with gasoline or kerosene in it, right?"

"Your Honor!" the DA cut in. "This is nothing but trickery. This man is trying to tell the jury there was gasoline in the house. And this officer has clearly testified that—"

"—that there was either gasoline or kerosene in the house at the time the fire started," Veil interrupted.

"Not in a damn can," the DA said again.

"Your Honor," Veil said, his voice the soul of reasonableness, "the witness testified that he found a charred can of gasoline in the house. Now it was his expert opinion that someone had poured gasoline all over the floor and the walls and then dropped a match. I am merely inquiring if there couldn't be some other way the fire had started."

The judge, obviously irritated, said, "Then why don't you just ask him that?"

"Well, Judge, I kind of was doing that. I mean, if one of the crackheads living there had maybe fallen asleep after he got high, you know, nodded out the way they do . . . and the crack pipe fell to the ground, and there was a can of kerosene lying around and—"

"That is enough!" the judge cut in. "You are well aware, sir, that when the fire trucks arrived, the house was empty."

"But the trucks weren't there when the fire *started*, Judge. Maybe the dope fiend felt the flames and ran for his life. I don't know. I wasn't there. And I thought the jury—"

"The jury will disregard your entire line of questioning, sir. And unless you have *another* line of questioning for this witness, he is excused."

Veil bowed.

4

At the lunch break, I asked him, "What the hell are you doing? Leonard already told the police it was him who burned down the crack house."

"Sure. You just said the magic words: *crack house.* I want to make sure the jury hears that enough times, that's all."

"You think they're gonna let him off just because—?"

"We're just getting started," Veil told me.

5

"Now, Officer, prior to placing the defendant under arrest, did you issue the appropriate Miranda warnings?" the DA asked the sheriff's deputy.

"Yes, sir, I did."

"And did the defendant agree to speak with you?"

"Well . . . he didn't exactly 'agree.' I mean, this ain't old Leonard's first rodeo. We knowed it was him, living right across the road and all. So when we went over there to arrest him, he was just sitting on the porch."

"But he did tell you that he was responsible for the arson, isn't that correct, Officer?"

"Oh yeah. Leonard said he burned it down. Said he'd do it again if those—well, I don't want to use the language he used here—he'd just burn it down again."

"No further questions," the DA said, turning away in triumph.

"Did the defendant resist arrest?" Veil asked on cross-examination.

"Not at all," the deputy said. "Matter of fact, you could see he was waiting on us."

"But if he wanted to resist arrest, he could have, couldn't he?"

"I don't get your meaning," the deputy said.

"The man means I could kick your ass without breaking a sweat," Leonard volunteered from the defendant's table.

The judge pounded his gavel a few times. Leonard shrugged, like he'd just been trying to be helpful.

"Deputy, were you familiar with the location of the fire? You had been there before? In your professional capacity, I mean," Veil asked him.

"Sure enough," the deputy answered.

"Fair to say the place was a crack house?" Veil asked.

"No question about that. We probably made a couple of dozen arrests there during the past year alone."

"You made any since the house burned down?"

"You mean . . . at that same address? Of course not."

"Thank you, Officer," Veil said.

6

"Doctor, you were on duty on the night of the thirteenth, is that correct?"

"That is correct," the doctor said, eyeing Veil like a man waiting for the doctor to grease up and begin his proctology exam.

"And your specialty is emergency medicine, is that also correct?"

"It is."

"And when you say 'on duty,' you mean you're in the ER, right?"

"Yes, sir."

"In fact, you're in charge of the ER, aren't you?"

"I am the physician in charge, if that is what you're asking me, sir. I have nothing to do with administration, so . . ."

"I understand," Veil said in a voice sweet as a preacher explaining scripture. "Now, Doctor, have you ever treated patients with burns?"

"Of course," the doctor snapped at him.

"And those range, don't they? I mean, from first-degree to third-degree burns. Which are the worst?"

"Third-degree."

"Hmmm . . . I wonder if that's where they got the term, 'Give him the third degree' . . . ?"

"Your Honor . . . ," the DA protested again.

"Mr. Veil, where are you going with this?" the judge asked.

"To the heart of the truth, Your Honor. And if you'll permit me . . ."

The judge waved a disgusted hand in Veil's direction. Veil kind of waved back. The big diamond glinted on his hand, catching the sun's rays through the high courthouse windows. "Doctor, you treat anybody with third-degree burns the night of the thirteenth?"

"I did not."

"Second-degree burns?"

"No."

"Even *first*-degree burns?"

"You know quite well I did not, sir. This isn't the first time you have asked me these questions."

"Sure, I know the answers. But you're telling the jury, Doctor, not me. Now you've seen the photographs of the house that was burnt to the ground. Could anyone have been inside that house and *not* been burned?"

"I don't see how," the doctor snapped. "But that doesn't mean—"

"We'll let the jury decide what it means," Veil cut him off. "Am I right, Judge?"

The judge knew when he was being jerked off, but, having told Veil those exact same words a couple of dozen times during the trial already, he was smart enough to keep his lipless mouth shut.

"All right, Doctor. Now we're coming to the heart of your testimony. See, the reason we have expert testimony is that experts, well, they know stuff the average person doesn't. And they get to explain it to us so we can understand things that happen."

"Your Honor, he's making a speech!" the DA complained, for maybe the two hundredth time.

But Veil rolled on like he hadn't heard a word. "Doctor, can you explain what causes the plague?"

One of the elderly ladies on the jury gasped when Veil said "the plague," but the doctor went right on: "Well, actually, it is caused by fleas, which are the primary carriers."

"Fleas? And here all along I thought it was carried by rats," Veil replied, turning to the jury as if embracing them all in his viewpoint.

"Yes, fleas," the doctor said. "They are, in fact, fleas especially common to rodents, but wild rodents—prairie dogs, chipmunks, and the like."

"Not squirrels?"

"Only ground squirrels," the doctor answered.

"So, in other words, you mean varmints, right, Doctor?"

"I do."

"The kind of varmints folks go shooting just for sport?"

"Well, some do. But mostly it's farmers who kill them. And that's not for sport—that's to protect their stored-up harvests," the doctor said, self-righteously, looking to the jury for support.

"Uh, isn't it a fact, Doctor, that if you kill enough varmints, the fleas just jump over to rats."

"Well, that's true. . . ."

"That's what happened a long time ago, wasn't it, Doctor? The Black Death in Europe, that was bubonic plague, right? Caused by rats with these fleas you talked about? And it killed, what? Twenty-five million people?"

"Yes. That's true. But today, we have certain antibiotics that can—"

"Sure. But plague is still a danger, isn't it? I mean, if it got loose, it could still kill a whole bunch of innocent folks before they knew what hit them, right?"

"Yes, that is true."

"Doctor, just a couple more questions and we'll be done. Before there was these special antibiotics, how did folks deal with rat infestation? You know, to protect themselves against plague? What would they do if there was a bunch of these rats in a house?"

"They'd burn it down," the doctor answered. "Fire is the only—"

"Objection! Relevancy!" the DA shouted.

"Approach the bench!" the judge roared.

Veil didn't move. "Judge, is he saying that crack *isn't* a plague?

Because it's my understanding—and I know others share that understanding—that the Lord is testing us with this new plague. It's killing our children, Your Honor. And it's sweeping across the—"

"That is enough!" the judge shrieked at Veil. "One more word from you, sir, and you will be joining your client in jail tonight."

"You want me to defend Leonard using sign language?" Veil asked.

A number of folks laughed. Some of them on the jury.

The judge cracked his gavel a few times and, when he was done, they took Veil out in handcuffs.

7

When I went to visit that night, I was able to talk to both of them. Someone had brought a chessboard and pieces in and they were playing. "You're crazy," I told Veil.

"Like a fuckin' fox," Leonard said. "My man here is right on the money. I mean, he gets it. Check."

"You moved a piece off the board," Veil said.

"Did not."

"Yeah, you did."

"Damn," Leonard said, pulling the piece out from between his legs and returning it to the board. "For a man with one eye you see a lot. But you *still* in check."

I shook my head. "Sure. Veil gets it. And you, you're gonna get life by the time he's done," I said.

"Everything'll be fine," Veil said, studying the chessboard. "We can always go to Plan B."

"And what's Plan B?" I asked him.

He and Leonard exchanged looks.

8

"The defense of *what?!*" the judge yelled at Veil the next morning.

"The defense of manifest necessity, Your Honor. It's right here, in Texas law. In fact, the case of *Texas v. Whitehouse* is directly on point. A man was charged with stealing water from his neighbor by constructing a siphon system. And he did it, all right. But that was during a drought, and if he hadn't done it, his cattle would've starved. So he had to pay for the water he took, and that was fair, but he didn't have to go to prison."

"And it is your position that your client had to burn down the crack—I mean, the occupied dwelling across the street from his house to prevent the spread of disease?"

"Exactly, Your Honor. Like the bubonic plague."

"Well, you're not going to argue that nonsense in my court. Go ahead and take your appeal. By the time the court even hears it, your client'll have been locked down for a good seven, eight years. That'll hold him."

9

Veil faced the jury, his face grim and set. He walked back and forth in front of them for a few minutes, as if getting the feel of the ground. Then he spun around and looked them in the eyes, one by one.

"You think the police can protect you from the plague? From the invasion? No, I'm not talking about aliens, or UFOs, or AIDS, now—I'm talking crack. And it's here, folks. Right here. You think it can't happen in your town? You think it's only Dallas and Houston where they grow those sort of folks? Take a look around. Even in this little town, you all lock your doors at night now, don't you? And you've had shootings right at the high school, haven't you? You see the churches as full as they used to be? No, you don't. Because things are changing, people. The plague is coming, just like the Good Book says. Only it's not locusts this time, it's that crack cocaine. It's a plague, all right. And it's carried by rats, just like always. And, like we learned, there isn't but one way to turn *that* tide. Fire!

"Now, I'm not saying my client set that fire. In fact, I'm asking you to find that he did *not* set that fire. I'm asking you to turn this good citizen, this man who cared about his community, loose. So he can be with you. That's where he belongs. He stood with you . . . now it's time for you to stand with him."

Veil sat down, exhausted like he'd just gone ten rounds with a rough opponent. But, the way they do trials, it's always the prosecutor who gets to throw the last punch.

And that chubby little bastard of a DA gave it his best shot, going on and on about how two wrongs don't make a right. But you could see him slip a few times. He'd make this snide reference to Leonard being black, or being gay, or just being . . . Leonard, I guess, and of course, that part is kind of understandable. But, exactly like Veil predicted, every time he did it, there was at least one member of the jury who didn't like it. Sure, it's easy to play on people's prejudices—and we got no shortage of those down this way, I know—but if there wasn't more good folks than bad, well, the Klan would've been running the state a long time ago.

The judge told the jury what the law was, and told them to go out there and come back when they were done. Everybody got up to go to lunch, but Veil didn't move. He motioned me over.

"This is going to be over with real quick, Hap," he said. "One way or the other."

"What if it's the other?"

"Plan B," he said, his face flat as a piece of slate.

10

The jury was out about an hour. The foreman stood up and said "Not Guilty" about two dozen times—once for every crime they had charged Leonard with.

I was hugging Leonard when Veil tapped me on the shoulder. "Leonard," he said, "you need to go over there and thank those jury people. One at a time. Sincere, you understand?"

"What for?" Leonard asked.

"Because this is going to happen again," Veil said. "And maybe next time, one of the rats'll get burned."

Knowing Leonard, I couldn't argue with that. He walked over to the jury and I turned around to say something to Veil. But he was gone.

DEAD RELIABLE

I was walking through the woods behind our property when I came across a huge toadstool. It was a color I'd never seen, some kind of shimmering rose-orange, standing on a stalk so thick it looked like a miniature palm tree holding up a solid canopy.

Remington stopped when I did. The chocolate lab is getting on in years, and he always grabs any excuse for a rest. I don't think he even likes walking in the woods anymore, but Florence—my wife—says he has to do it. For the same reason I have to do it: to keep fit. Diet and exercise are very important to her. Keeping fit.

Florence bought Remington because she said he was the right kind of dog for our new life. But he's always been my dog. If I didn't go walking, he wouldn't either.

The toadstool-tree stood in a thick bed of dark green moss. It looked like it had been there for centuries. Unseen, untouched. Unspoiled.

I watched it for a long time, absently patting my pockets for the cigarettes I knew wouldn't be there anymore. I used to smoke in the woods—I would never have considered smoking in the house—but I don't do that anymore, not since I quit.

That's what I did—quit. Not stop, quit. It wasn't worth the talk. All the talk. All the statistics. All the proof. All the rightness of Florence.

She said she was sick of smelling it on me, every time I came back from a walk.

I was sick, too.

I had never seen anything like that toadstool. It was so beautiful. Timeless and perfect. God knows what it must have survived, how many years it had been on earth, to grow to that size and splendor.

I never liked living way out here, even though I kept trying to. It *was* peaceful and quiet, not like the city at all. And cheaper, a lot cheaper. Instead of an apartment, we have a house, now. And land, too. The woods I walked in, they were on our own property.

Florence said the city wasn't a good value. Because there was no room to expand, every single unit was artificially priced. Someday, when they ran out of room in the city, the land we owned now would be worth a fortune to developers.

Really, we hadn't had to give up all that much. We have cable TV, and the Internet—Florence loves the Internet; she's always researching things. And there's a nice little town only a few miles away, where they have a library and a movie theater and . . . well, all kinds of things, if you're interested.

I'm not interested. I haven't been interested in a long time.

I looked down at my feet, at the special hiking boots Florence had bought for me last Christmas. Very expensive, but worth every penny, she said. Not only do they have steel toes, in case something heavy falls on me, but the insoles are removable, and I can replace them with my orthotic supports.

I'm fragile now. Precautions must be taken.

I sat down and tried to remember when I wasn't fragile. When I was a person people listened to. Respected, even.

The memory always hurt more than the reality, but, this time, I couldn't even bring it back.

I was numb. Everything was so painless. I stood up and kicked the toadstool. The entire head flew off the stalk. I walked over and held it in my hands. Then I sat down again, and started tearing it into tiny pieces.

It took a long time. When I was done, there was nothing left but little colored scraps, scattered all over the dark moss.

When I realized there was nothing more to do, I stood up and started walking again.

I walked and walked, farther than I'd ever gone before. I walked slowly, so Remington could keep up.

We came to a tree that had been cut down by lightning. Its roots were still alive, but the tree itself was lying flat on the ground.

I sat down on it.

Remington came over and sat next to me.

All of a sudden, I started sobbing.

It just kept on and on. I didn't so much stop as run out of tears. That's been happening for a long time. I know what it feels like, to run out of things, bit by bit. And I know how it feels when you're finally empty.

I used to be somebody. Not somebody important, but not a nothing, either. I was more than just a living thing. I had work. People depended on me. People always said, "Owen is a man you can count on."

Florence would say that, too. Only, when she said it, her lips would twist so that the words came out of her mouth like they had been poisoned.

At first, I tried to do some volunteer work, but that's not for me. It's just not the same as real work. People thank you, but they don't depend on you. Not for anything that matters, I mean.

What volunteers really like to do is talk. Like at the food pantry. I went there because I'm good at organizing things, and I thought they would see that. But they didn't care about doing things better. What they really came there for was the gossip: who donated what, who didn't . . . things like that. Mostly, what they wanted to talk about was what wonderful people they were. They were always saying things like "giving back," as if it were a holy act and they were the performing saints.

After a few months, I couldn't see why they even had the food pantry at all. It doesn't change anything. The same people keep coming back. It's not a bridge you use to cross over to something better; it's a hole you fall into.

I was once a solid, reliable man.

I'm not solid anymore. Between the osteoporosis and the heart attack, I'm not solid.

I don't get opportunities to be reliable, so there's no way to know. No way to prove it, is what I'm saying. My . . . reputation, I guess you'd call it . . . I wasn't even in contact with the people I once had that with.

There're some things you can't get back. Some things you can't get back *to.*

I never even got close to being as big and great and beautiful as that toadstool. If I'd been the man I used to be, a solid, reliable man, I would have just stood there and admired it. I would have paid it the respect it earned, all those years it had stayed alive. Alive and true.

When I got back to the house, Florence wanted to know what I had been doing out there so long.

I went into the room where she keeps all the hobby stuff she buys for me. Model-building kits, a shotgun, fishing rods, things like that.

I loaded the shotgun. Then I came back out into the kitchen. I shot Florence in the back of her head.

Her face blew apart like the toadstool, but I shot the other barrel into her anyway—I wanted to make sure she didn't suffer.

Remington didn't move. He just sat there and watched. Remington had never been Florence's dog. He never forgot what a reliable man I used to be.

But he's a very old dog, with a lot of health problems, and I knew what would happen when the police took him to the animal shelter. It's a "no-kill" shelter, but, still, nobody would want him. The other dogs wouldn't respect him. He would never be what he once was. He'd die. Not from what anyone did to him, but from what he'd lost.

I sat at the kitchen table. I thought about writing a note, but I had nothing to say.

Just one more thing to do.

I wasn't even sad when I promised Remington he could go with me. I could see in his eyes that he knew I was still a reliable man. He could count on me. He never lost faith. He never would.

I made sure of that, first.

for Joel

CHOICE OF WEAPONS

1

"Liberals are always blathering about how much they love nature," Roger Kenworth lectured his rapt audience. "But the truth is, they're actually *opposed* to the natural order of things."

His pronouncement was delivered with the self-assurance of a man accustomed to respect, and Roger Kenworth looked the part. He was powerfully built and deeply tanned, with light blond hair, symmetrical features, and perfect teeth too white for a man in his fifties.

Tonight, he posed with one foot on his favorite soapbox: the extended hearth of a massive stone fireplace. He was wearing a short-sleeved shirt the color of tarnished brass over a pair of tailored beige cargo pants and natural-alligator desert boots. His bright blue eyes swept the cathedral-ceilinged living room like a prison searchlight, scanning for dissent.

Satisfied he had total control of his terrain, Roger used an orator's pause to take a generous sip from his square-cut tumbler of Johnnie Walker Blue before returning to his favorite topic. "You want a perfect example, just look at the idiots who run the School Board. The paper said they held one of their little coffee klatches and decided they're going to ban what they call 'bullying' at the high school. If they'd ever spent some time in the real world, they'd understand that what they're all hyperventilating about is nothing but Darwinism in action. The strong are *always* going to assert themselves—that's what keeps a species viable. Look at a wolf pack. If one of them's too weak to pull his weight, it's better the rest find out while he's still a cub."

"Darwinism is all about evolution," I said, mildly. I say *everything* mildly—at least that's what my wife, Tammi, is always telling me. "And part of human evolution was getting past the rule of fang and claw, wasn't it?"

"Superficially, I suppose that's true," Mark Chilton said, holding his pipe like a college professor, the way he does when he pontificates. "But, in the final analysis, it still comes down to power, doesn't it? Power and dominance, isn't that the goal of each nation?"

"Self-defense isn't the same thing as dominance," I protested. Mildly.

"Maybe not," Roger said, his resonant voice reflecting off the walls of the big room. "But, bottom line, if you can't stand up to a bully, you're *going* to be dominated. I don't care if you're some kid with his lunch money or an entire country. The point is, individually or collectively, we're all going to be tested, and we can't make that natural process disappear just by passing some stupid liberal 'rule' against it. Trying to legislate human nature never works. You might as well tell teenagers not to have sex."

Tammi giggled when he said that. You don't have to be all that clever to make her giggle, as long as you're a man. Unless you're a mild one.

She's not much of a conversationalist, my wife, but she doesn't have to say a lot to get people to look at her. Especially the way she dresses. It's a little . . . embarrassing. To me, anyway. Tammi's thirty-seven, not nineteen. She shouldn't be wearing outfits like she does, even in this climate. But every time I bring it up, all she ever says is: "I've still got the body for it, don't I?"

There's no arguing with the attention she draws. And Tammi loves attention; she always did.

Roger's wife never says much. She's Asian—from Thailand, I think, but I don't know for sure. She looks a lot younger than him, but Tammi says that's just because she's so small and skinny.

I always think of Saturdays as kind of belonging to Roger. They start in the early evening, with him at the helm of a huge stainless-steel outdoor grill. He has it positioned at the far corner of the veranda-sized flagstone patio he had custom-built. After we eat, the gatherings go on until all hours of the night. There's always music playing through his full-house sound system, but not many in our crowd are dancers. Mostly, we spend the time talking and drinking.

Listening, actually.

After the first time at Roger's, Tammi couldn't stop complaining the second we got back home. "You'd think, with all the money he's supposed to have, there would have been some live entertainment. Or at least a sit-down dinner. It was just so . . . boring." She was still carrying on when I fell asleep.

The next time Roger invited us, I thought we'd just make up some excuse. But when I told Tammi, she suddenly decided she was all for it. And she really got into the spirit of things, too. Instead of the little black cocktail dress she had worn the first time, she put on a pair of jeans—the kind the kids wear, cut way too low—and a little T-shirt that showed her navel. And, once we got there, she had a few things to say, too. Nothing I'd call profound, but she *was* participating.

Since then, it's become kind of a regular thing. By now, so many people come that we tend to break up into groups. Some of the men play cards—nothing radical, not for big stakes—nobody ever gets upset if they lose. Roger has a beautiful billiard room, too, and that always gets some action. Some even use the swimming pool; although not too often, unless it's the middle of summer.

But even with a dozen things going on at once, Roger never leaves his spot in front of the fireplace. It takes up a whole wall of what he calls the "great room." Anyone who wants to talk to Roger has to come in there to do it.

2

Usually, Tammi just leaves me alone after supper. So when she came into my study one evening, I knew there was going to be some kind of argument.

"Do you have to spend so much time building those stupid models of yours?" was the first thing out of her mouth.

"They're not models," I told her, patiently. "They're miniatures."

"What's the difference?" she said. I recognized the signs: her jaw was set and her voice was already edgy.

"Models are prefabricated. All you have to do is put them together, whereas—"

"Paul! I *meant*, what's the difference *what* you putter around with? I was talking about all the time you spend at it."

"Well, you're always on the computer and I just—"

"You're pathetic," she said. She turned and walked out of my study, wiggling her bottom extra hard to make sure I knew it was meant to be taunting, not tempting.

3

Tammi doesn't work, but that's not her fault. The way we planned it, she would be staying at home with our kids. But kids never came. Every time I mentioned maybe seeing a fertility specialist, Tammi gave me one of her looks—the kind I didn't even know she had until we had been married for over a year.

So I went on my own, without saying anything to her. "I can't tell you more without examining your wife and running additional tests," the doctor told me, "but we can definitely rule out any . . . impediment at your end. Both motility and viability are more than adequate for. . . ."

I'm not one of those men who doesn't want his wife to work. But Tammi never found anything she really likes to do. She's not stupid; in fact, she taught herself a wide variety of computer skills.

And she's certainly not lazy; her exercise regimen would exhaust a professional athlete. She once told me that keeping a small waist is the key to a woman's shape. "If you've got it down, it makes everything else kind of stick out, see, Paul?" she said, turning so her body was in profile.

I suggested she might want to go back to school. That's where I met her, in college: she was a freshman and I was a grad student. But Tammi wasn't interested in formal education, except when she got excited about some new thing. Then she would take all kinds of classes—yoga, tai chi, photography, things like that. She's always wildly enthusiastic at first, but then it just goes flat for her, somehow.

Like we had.

4

"Do you think Roger was really a mercenary in the Congo?" Tammi said to me one night, as we were getting ready for bed.

"Where did you hear that?"

"Oh, Carla's husband, Larry—he was in the army, himself—told her. And she told me."

"In the Congo? When would that have been?"

"What difference does that make?" she said, sharply. "That's just like you, Paul. Always nitpicking, checking every little detail. I mean, he *seems* like the kind of man who could have been a soldier of fortune, don't you think?"

"A 'soldier of fortune'?" I said, with maybe just a trace of sarcasm.

"What, I didn't use the proper term?" Tammi said, hands on her hips. "Are you going to correct me, Paul?"

"I wasn't trying to do that," I said.

"No," she said, the sneer thick in her voice. "I can't imagine you would."

5

I know Tammi cheats on me. Not in the flesh—well, maybe that's not the right way to put it, considering what I found out. Once I installed the spyware on our computer, it was easy enough for me to reconstruct how she spends her days when I'm at work, especially since we're on the same wireless network.

Maybe sending nude photographs of herself over the Internet doesn't meet the legal definition of adultery, but some of her e-mails were . . . well, they were considerably more than cyber-flirting. Still, no matter how diligently I checked—even after I installed the recorder on our phone lines, and the fiber-optic cameras in the house—I never uncovered any evidence that she actually met any of those men in real life.

I call her from work sporadically, so she can never know when to expect it. But she always answers when I call. She never even sounds out of breath. I guess she doesn't know forwarding our home number to her cell phone shows up on the bill every time she pulls that trick. Or maybe she doesn't care.

I use my sick days to maintain surveillance, too. I tell her I'm going to work, but I spend the day watching the house. Or following her, when she goes out. I guess I could have paid a private detective to do all this, but it's not the kind of thing I want to discuss with other people. Or even admit.

Besides, I'm not sure I could trust someone I hired. I'm the kind of man who likes to do things himself—that's the only way I can make certain it comes out properly.

6

"Sure, they're good enough to catch some moron holding up a liquor store, or a wife who poisons her husband," Roger said, one Saturday night. "But the police haven't got a chance against a highly evolved killer."

Bobby Williams started to say, "There's been plenty of murderers who thought they were geniuses until—"

"No, no," Roger interrupted. "I didn't say 'smart'; I said, 'highly evolved.' There's a big difference."

"What?" Marcy Chilton asked. She's the opposite of her husband, very parsimonious with her words.

"The highly evolved killer is one who makes a statement," Roger said. "Not some animal who guns down a shopkeeper in a holdup."

"You mean, like Ted Bundy, someone like him?" Tammi asked, breathlessly.

"Exactly!" Roger replied.

Tammi arched her back like a cat who had just been stroked.

"Ted Bundy was a sex fiend," Theresa Wright said, sharply. She's married to Sam Wright, a church deacon. The two of them generally agree with Roger on everything, especially when he starts ranting about liberals, but the idea of seeing a rapist as highly evolved apparently was too much for her to swallow.

"I'm not so sure that's true," Roger said, judiciously. "Certainly, there was a sexual . . . aura to his killings—there often is, I believe—but he was successful for a very long time before he was caught. And we *still* have no idea how many women he actually raped and killed."

"*That's* your idea of highly evolved? A killer who gets away with more murders than the authorities find out about?" Mark said.

"Well, isn't it yours?" Roger challenged him. "Isn't that the way we evaluate *any* activity: by whether you're successful at it? Look at the most famous murderer in history, Jack the Ripper. Do you think, if he had ever been caught, he'd still be in the public eye centuries later? Do you think people would still be writing books about him? Making movies? Speculating about his identity?"

"People are still speculating about who shot JFK, too," Sam Wright retorted.

I don't like the Wrights very much—I can smell their disapproval of Tammi like heavy perfume in an elevator. But I do admire the way they're always on the same side, backing each other up.

"Conspiracy buffs," Roger said, dismissively.

"But you just said—"

"The highly evolved killer is the one who kills at *random*," Roger said emphatically, veins swelling in the muscle of his voice like those in his flexed biceps. "It doesn't matter who he kills, it's just his way of making a statement. Look at the Zodiac, *another* killer they never caught. Do you think the newspapers would have published his letters if he hadn't proven himself?"

"Proven himself?" I said.

Tammi gave me one of those looks she specializes in.

"Proven his expertise," Roger said, not missing a beat. "Like providing your credentials. He killed *when* he wanted, *where* he wanted, *who* he wanted . . . and there was nothing the cops could ever do about it."

"The papers published the Unabomber's manifesto, too," Mark Chilton said, toady that he is.

"And he got caught," I rejoined, catching another look from Tammi.

"He would *never* have been caught," Roger said, in a tone that brooked no argument. "Not by all the law enforcement in America. It was his own family that turned him in."

"So he wasn't as highly evolved as the Zodiac?" I said, keeping my voice neutral.

"That's right!" Roger said, pointing his finger at me. I was glad I wasn't standing closer. Once he had made a point with that same finger, jabbing it into my chest. It felt like a piece of rebar—I had the bruise for days. "The ultimate killer never leaves himself vulnerable to the weakness of others."

"Morality isn't weakness," Sam Wright said, his voice as strong as his convictions.

"It's a good thing the military doesn't share your philosophy," Roger delivered his knockout punch. "Or we'd all be having this conversation in German."

7

"You don't even try anymore," Tammi said to me, later that night. She was wearing the black teddy she likes to pose in for her webcam.

"Try what?"

"Sex," she said, almost spitting out the word.

"You're joking," I said, disgusted. With her and myself, both. "What's the point of asking for something when you know the answer's going to be 'no'?"

"That's your problem, Paul. Can you imagine *Roger's* wife saying 'no' to him?"

"Not with him holding her green card," I said, not so mildly.

"You're disgusting," Tammi said. She rolled over, her frozen back doing the rest of her talking for her.

8

That Monday, I called Roger's house from work. His wife answered the phone. Her name is Kanya, something like that.

"Hello," she said. Her voice was like a child's.

"Good morning," I said, speaking through the harmonizer that transformed my voice into an elderly man's. "Is Mr. Kenworth at home?"

"Oh, yes, sure. I get him, okay?"

I hung up.

That night, Tammi asked me if I wanted to watch a movie with her. I was a little surprised. Usually, she spends the whole evening on the computer. I asked her, what did she want me to go out and rent? But she already had a DVD loaded.

It only took a minute before I realized what kind of movie it was.

"I don't want to watch that stuff," I said, getting off the couch.

"Oh, don't be such a little wimp *all* the time," Tammi snapped at me. "I thought, if we watched it together, maybe you'd get some ideas. Besides how to build bridges or whatever it is you do at work, I mean."

"I've got plenty of ideas," I said, defensively.

On the screen, a nurse was being raped by three men wearing stocking masks.

"She really wants it," Tammi said, making a little grunting sound of judgment. "You'll see. Watch how it ends."

I couldn't.

9

That Saturday, Roger gave a lecture on the NRA. He was thinking of canceling his membership, he said. The organization was getting too soft.

"Catering to the lefties. That's just pitiful. Just caving to the media. So a kid killed his little sister with a gun he found in the house. That wasn't a *registered* weapon, not like mine are," he said. He swept his arm in the direction of his den, a wood-and-leather room just down the hall. We had all been treated to a tour of Roger's den: it was mostly glass-fronted display cases for his collection of guns.

"Some liberal would walk back in there and start wailing about what an 'arsenal' I'm keeping. But if I want to own a hundred guns, that's my right as an American, as long as I can pay for them. Besides," he said, rotating his head on his thick neck like a tank turret, covering everyone in the room, "self-defense is the natural right of every species. What sets man apart from the animals is that we get to choose our weapons."

"What do you need them all for?" Mark Chilton asked, lobbing the softball question.

"Anyone who enters my home without my permission would find out quick enough," Roger promised. "That's why I don't have a lock on my gun case. What kind of idiot does that? By the time I find the key, unlock the cabinet, and reach for one of my guns, it's too late."

"But you don't need that many guns just to protect—"

"Who says?" Roger interrupted him. "You? If you'd ever been in combat you'd know; two loaded weapons are a lot better than one that you have to *re*load."

"You keep them all *loaded*?" Tammi asked, clasping her hands under her breasts.

"An unloaded gun's about as useful as a limp . . . Well, you get the picture," Roger said, smiling with his perfect teeth.

10

I was watching the next Thursday morning when Roger's wife drove off in their ivory Land Rover. I was still watching when Tammi walked up to the side door of his house, wearing pink shorts and a black T-shirt. I saw the flash of his smile as he let her in.

It was five more Saturdays before I was ready. Impatience always endangers the end product. Like building a bridge: you have to check and recheck every single component before you start to fit them together.

Roger's den is past a pair of bathrooms off the hall. "Just like a nightclub," Tammi had said when she first discovered there were two of them. "Especially the way he keeps the hallways so dark. But don't worry, Paul, I won't ask you to go in there with me."

Tammi knows I have weak kidneys. "You're worse than a woman," she complained once, when we had to stop driving.

That was a few years ago, the last time we tried to take a vacation together.

A bridge engineer has to be able to measure with his eyes and make rough calculations. First you visualize. Then you go back and double-check with instruments.

One of the guns in Roger's den is a Colt Python. That's a revolver, with a ventilated rib over the barrel. His is chrome, with black rubberized grips. It holds six .357 magnum cartridges. A very common gun, I discovered.

The glass case kept his guns dust-free. They all looked new. But when I opened one of the cases, I couldn't smell any gun oil. It was as if he had a maid come in to polish them, instead of cleaning them himself.

11

The round-trip to Georgia took even less than the twelve hours I had expected; eleven hours and nineteen minutes, to be exact. I had plotted the route on a map by hand—I didn't want anything on my computer.

I rented a car using the credit card that had come in the mail to "Occupant" a couple of years ago. Usually, I would have shredded something like that, but it came on a day I had to go to New York on business, so I just stuffed it in my briefcase without looking at it.

It was past midnight, and I couldn't sleep. I opened my briefcase, figuring I might as well get some work done. That's when I found the credit card.

I don't know why, but I filled out the application using the address of the mailbox rental place I had noticed on my way back from the meeting. There wasn't any logical reason. I never "go with my gut," like Tammi's always saying. But it just felt right.

The next morning, I went to that mailbox place and paid six months rental in advance. The next time I came back to New York, the credit card was waiting for me there. Apparently, the credit of the man I made up from scratch was good . . . at least up to the five thousand limit the papers that came with it said.

I always test things to make certain they work properly. So I used the card to charge a few gadgets at different stores when I went on business trips. I always dropped them into different Dumpsters on my way back to the hotel.

When I returned to the box the next month, a bill was waiting. I bought a money order with cash, and paid it.

I kept up the rent on the box, but I hadn't used the card for anything since. I told myself, if it didn't work for what I wanted, I'd forget the whole thing. But, a couple of months later, the credit card company sent me a letter saying my limit had been raised to ten thousand dollars.

12

I drove my own car to Hartsfield-Jackson Airport in Atlanta, and left it in the short-stay lot. Then I rented a car, putting down the credit card as security. They took it without blinking. The driver's license I showed them was a complete fabrication, except for my photograph. Making one only takes a few minutes: all you need is a template, a computer, and a laminator.

Then I drove straight to the first gun shop I saw in the little town I had already picked out. I made sure they had the twin to Roger's Colt Python, brand-new, still in the box. Then I walked out.

The man who walked in and bought the gun was a marginal human being. His nose was a mass of broken capillaries, his eyes were rheumy, and his whole body reeked of liquor and sweat. But the gun store took his cash. The fifty I paid him would probably hasten his imminent death—and he wouldn't remember me.

When I returned the rental car, I paid cash and they gave the credit card back to me. I used a pair of tin snips to turn it into cross-cut scraps of plastic. Then I did the same with the fake driver's license. I dropped little pieces out the window as I drove back north—I was in North Carolina before they were all gone.

13

"Do you have to carry that bag around with you *everywhere* you go?" Tammi asked me the next Saturday.

"It's very useful," I told her. "Ever since I bought it, I realize how much easier it is to walk around without a whole lot of stuff in my pockets."

"It looks like a handbag," Tammi said, just short of a sneer. "Or maybe a purse."

"It's a computer case," I told her calmly, as I was putting my wallet and house keys in one of the side pockets. "It's just the shoulder strap that you don't like."

"You're ridiculous," she said, walking out of the bedroom.

I had to use the bathroom a lot that night, but that didn't attract attention—people were used to me doing that. When I finally had the corridor to myself, I slipped into Roger's den and made the switch. My computer case had plenty of room for the latex gloves I wore to do it.

14

The Saturday after that, I was so nervous I almost spilled my first drink. When I went to use the bathroom, I peeked into Roger's den. I could see the pistol—*my* pistol—was still in his gun case. It looked untouched, but there was no way to tell for sure.

The party was over at around one-thirty in the morning. Or, at least, that's when we left. Tammi walked around our house nude when we got back. She'd been doing that for the last few weeks. She said it made her feel free.

She finally curled up on the couch to watch one of her DVDs. I waited for her to call my name, then I mixed her the vodka-and-tonic she told me to get for her before I went to bed.

With what I put in her drink, she wouldn't wake up until the middle of the next day. That gave me approximately two hours to get it done. I needed darkness, and it starts to get light pretty early in this part of the country, especially in the summertime.

15

Another Saturday night. It was mid-fall, but still warm. Roger was telling us that the stupid cops don't have a clue about three murders. "Three! Right on the street. Within a ten-mile radius of where we're standing right now. And . . . *nothing!* Mark my words, whoever did those killings knew *exactly* what he was doing. And there'll be more."

Tammi was looking at him like he was a god . . . and she couldn't wait to get down on her knees and pray.

I had to use the bathroom.

16

It was Tammi who told me all about it. "I was standing right there when the cops knocked on the door. Detectives, I guess—they were wearing suits. Anyway, they told Roger they got an anonymous tip, and they had to follow up. They were kind of laughing when they said it, like it was some kind of nut who called, but their chief told them they had to go out anyway.

"Roger invited them in, and they all sat down. I even made them a drink, like I was the hostess in a gentleman's club. Everybody got a kick out of that.

"But then one of them, an older fat guy, he asked if they could take a look at Roger's gun collection. See, they knew what kind of gun had been used in all those murders, and . . .

"Roger took them right back to his den. They didn't mind me going along, too. The fat cop tapped on the glass and asked Roger if he could look at the gun he was pointing at. Roger told him to help himself—the cabinet wasn't locked.

"The cop took out this big pistol. Roger told him that it hadn't been fired for years. The cop asked if they could take the pistol with them. 'Just to rule it out,' is what he said.

"Roger winked at him, like they had a secret joke. The cops hung around for a while. After they left, Roger was his usual self. I mean, when I heard he'd been *arrested*, I swear I almost fainted!"

17

Even the top-shelf lawyer Roger hired couldn't explain how the murder weapon the serial killer had used was sitting right in Roger's own gun case. He tried to get the judge to suppress the evidence, but the cops both testified that Roger had *invited* them to look at the gun, and even to take it with them. They'd given him a receipt for it, with the serial number and all.

The lawyer called Roger's wife as an alibi witness, but she wasn't any use to him—she said Roger sends her to her room at ten every night, because she has to get up so early every morning.

When the prosecutor started asking her questions, Roger's lawyer objected to just about every one.

But none of that really mattered. Everyone remembered Roger's speeches about highly evolved killers, and how only humans could qualify . . . because we had a choice of weapons.

18

I never asked Tammi what she had been doing in Roger's house when the cops had come over that day.

I never asked her why being terrified all the time had made her so excited, either.

for Big Wayne

THEY'RE ALL ALIKE

1

The sleek, dark coupe slipped confidently through the tight grid of narrow streets, weaving an intricate tapestry with the after-image of its taillights. Even past midnight, harsh heat still hovered over the asphalt. The humidity was so thick that a faint mist settled over the coupe's tinted windows. Through that soft filter, the man watched the brightly dressed women posture and pose as he glided past. They made him think of the lush flowers he had once seen in a jungle, long ago. All that sweet fruit, ripe on the vine.

But looks couldn't deceive him. He knew the fruit was poison. He knew what it would do to any man who tasted it.

As he turned a corner, one of the girls quickly pulled up her yellow spandex micro-skirt and gave herself a spank, her face a mockery of ecstasy. The man kept driving.

The greedy whores didn't know what he wanted. The selection wasn't up to them. *He* made the choices.

A chubby blonde in a red halter top shrieked "Faggot!" as he passed her by. In his rearview mirror, he saw a black girl in iridescent blue hot pants give the blonde a high five.

The man felt the familiar acid-bath of rage in his chest, but his expression never changed. The name-calling meant nothing to him—they didn't *know* him.

If they did, they'd never mock him.

As if by tacit agreement, the cops pretty much stayed out of the warehouse district after dark, and the night-girls didn't stray into the better parts of the little town. The good citizens liked it that way, and that's who the cops "served and protected." The man smirked at the idea that the stupid sluts felt safer without cops around. Safer from a simple prostitution bust, sure. But not from a much harsher judge than they would ever encounter in court.

He made another slow circuit, the movement of the powerful car calming him as it always did. *Careful, careful,* he cautioned himself. He'd hunted the same area for a while now. He knew night-girls vanish all the time. They get tired of The Life. Run off with a new pimp. Move on to someplace where they hear the money is better. AIDS, overdoses, jail . . . plenty of reasons for any of them to disappear from the streets.

But he also knew that if you picked too much of the fruit, sooner or later, the cops would start looking for the harvester.

Maybe it was time for him to nomad again. The prospect didn't concern him. He was rootless. And he knew that wherever he went, he would find what he needed.

Some of the girls were stunningly bold. It almost felt like an assault the way they charged his car every time he slowed down to a prowler's crawl. *If they only knew,* he thought, *they'd run like rabbits who saw the shadow of a hawk.*

A hawk. Yes. The man liked that image. A solitary, hunting hawk. A righteous hawk, circling . . . then descending suddenly out of the night sky.

Some of the girls looked fresh and new. He knew that look wouldn't last long. The Life would claim their bodies like it had their souls.

Maybe he was doing them a favor, the ones he chose.

He knew appearances didn't matter. The night-girls may come in all sizes, shapes, and colors, but they're all alike. Every one of them. Wicked, evil women. Sweet and ripe-looking on the outside, venomous at their core.

It was their fault.

They gave him no choice.

It was a lot easier now than when he'd started. He never fought the feelings anymore. He knew there was only one thing that would soothe him.

For a while, anyway.

Agony. The word was a prism in his brain, refracting all the light in his vision. *Agony.* He knew the truth now. The only way it could ever be. *Agony.* Inflict it, or suffer it.

There was nothing else.

2

I can always tell, she thought. *Sometimes, just from the way they use their cars to stalk. And when I see their faces, when I hear them talk, I know they think I can't see the truth.*

When she saw the dark coupe for the third time that night, she deliberately walked a half-block down from the corner, distancing herself from the safety of the other girls. She positioned herself against a bent aluminum lamppost with a burnt-out bulb, and clasped her hands behind her.

No fishnet stockings or five-inch spike heels for her. She had better luck in a simple little white dress, standing primly, as if waiting for a bus. Her heart fluttered in her chest. She fancied he could hear it, even from so far away.

And that it would draw him closer.

The dark coupe slid to a gentle stop next to her. As she walked toward the passenger-side window, it zipped down as if in sync with her movements. *It's like I have X-ray eyes by now,* she thought. *I can see right into his mind. Ropes. Handcuffs. Maybe a gun. Always a knife. Or a razor. And, in the trunk of his car, a Polaroid camera. Or a videocam.*

3

"Are you dating?" the man asked. *No way this one's an undercover,* he thought. *They always try to blend in, dress up outrageous, look like all the rest.*

"Maybe," the girl said, softly. "But I don't date just anyone."

"How much for a—"

"Don't talk nasty," the girl interrupted him. "That's what I mean. I only date nice men. Are you a nice man?"

"I can be *very* nice," the man assured her. "Very generous, too." Now he was certain she couldn't be a cop. They always wanted you to offer a specific amount of money for a specific sex act, so that it would stand up in court. This one, she acted like it was her first time out. If she only knew . . .

"All right," the girl said, "but not . . . not here, okay? It's not . . . private."

The man knew "here" meant the pool of darkness behind the abandoned factory building where the night-girls always directed their quick-tricks to park. Privacy didn't mean anything to hookers, but safety did. Usually, he had to talk them out of going there. This one would be easier than usual. "We could go to my house," he said.

"No," she said firmly, leaning into the car through the open window. "I'd be too scared. Maybe after we have a few dates, I would. But I know a place. It's not far from here. You know that spot off 109 where they have the picnic tables?"

"Sure," the man said.

4

Don't wait! she screamed inside herself, as the dark coupe pulled into the deserted highway rest stop. *Don't let him start.*

As the man was unzipping his fly, she brought up the tiny .25

caliber automatic and shot him in the face. He made a grunting sound, hands pressing against his temples as if he had a horrible migraine. She shot him four more times, not aware of the moaning sound coming from her mouth . . . a banshee wail louder than the muted *pops!* of the little pistol.

There wasn't much blood. There never was. And she never got any on her little white dress.

She backed out of the car carefully. Opened the trunk with the key she had pulled from the ignition switch. *Yes!*

It was about a mile through the woods to the access road where she always left her own car. From experience, she knew it would take her about a half hour, carrying her shoes in one hand.

5

Maybe they're right, he thought to himself. *Maybe I really am a natural-born wuss.* He circled the fringes of night-girl territory in his beige compact sedan for what seemed like the tenth time that night, certain they were laughing behind their hands as he passed by.

They're just plain . . . scary, he thought. *I mean, they could have diseases and everything.* And he'd heard they all had pimps. Big black guys who'd cut your throat for whatever was in your wallet.

He had promised himself it would be tonight. No more backing out at the last minute. If only he could find one that wasn't so . . . dangerous-looking.

The moment he saw her, he knew she was the one. That pretty little white dress. The sweet expression on her face. Somehow, he just knew *she* wouldn't laugh at him if he had trouble with . . .

6

She backed out of the sedan carefully. With the smaller cars, there was a greater chance of getting some of the blood on you.

She opened the trunk. Empty. That didn't matter, she told herself. It just meant he had been too cautious to bring his torture equipment with him. Probably had it back at his place. She knew it had to be *somewhere* close at hand. One thing she knew. One thing she was sure of.

They're all alike.

for Ruby

HALF-BREED

This ceremony was given to The People by the gods, when we first came to this earth.

The ceremony first brought forth Monster Slayer, and it does, still, to this day.

When The People lived below, there was no need of the ceremony. Before the Emergence, there was no Evil. Before Evil, there was no need to guard the children. But this earth is a dangerous place, so the means to call Monster Slayer were given to The People.

The ceremony carries our children on their journey, safely past Evil, until they are children no more. As each shaman who holds the ceremony must prepare whoever shall follow in his place, so must Monster Slayer walk again, for so long as The People are on this earth.

Ceremony for Greeting the Newborn Child

—

"Just tell me how it happened," the nondescript man said. His voice was low-pitched and toneless, but the man he was speaking to heard every syllable clearly.

"It was the blood transfusion," the doctor said, glancing at his wafer-thin platinum watch to underscore the value of his time. Seated in a butterscotch leather chair, he reclined slightly behind a slate-gray slab of marble that served him as a desk. He wore his white doctor's coat like a suit of armor.

The nondescript man's face was expressionless, heavy cheek-bones framing obsidian eyes.

If he were any more neutral, he would be inert, the doctor thought to himself, wondering why so detached an individual was making him feel so . . . terrified. He let his eyes wander across the immaculate eggshell-white walls of his office, as if the expensively framed diplomas held some talisman of protection.

"Why did she need a blood transfusion?" the nondescript man asked.

"She was a hemophiliac."

"Was?"

"I mean is, of course," the doctor said, hastily. "A hemophiliac at the time of the . . . event."

"So, she was cut?"

"Cut?"

"Stabbed, sliced, punctured . . ."

"Oh. I see. You mean, as a result of some deliberate act?"

"Yes."

"No! Certainly not. It was . . . entirely unintentional. You see, she—"

The doctor stopped talking, shuddering involuntarily, as though the temperature in the room had suddenly dropped. The other man had not moved. *He's way past "patient,"* the doctor thought, *he's a damn stone.*

"She had elective surgery," the doctor resumed, his voice precise and clipped. "To repair the harelip. And, while she was still—"

"Who 'elected' the surgery?"

The doctor struggled with himself, unable to identify the source of his terror. His status, his profession, the trappings of his office . . . all his treasured boundaries seemed to have gone porous. He had the overpowering feeling that wrong answers could cost him his life. *Get a grip!* he counseled himself. *You're overreacting. The man is grief-stricken at what he's just learned, that's all. Differ-*

*ent people handle traumatic news in different ways. You know that.
Relax!*

"Your sister was a ward of the court," he explained, abandoning
his habitual air of superiority for a facsimile of empathy. "She has
been, ever since the death of your parents, when she was only four.
You couldn't be reached, and—"

"That was more than twelve years ago," the unexpected visitor
said. "She's old enough to make her own decisions now, isn't she?"

"Well, not legally, of course. I mean, she's still a minor. But,
believe me, sir, your sister very much wanted this surgery. It was
her choice. The consent of her legal guardian was required, but
your sister . . ."

"Dawn."

"Dawn. Yes, I'm. . . . Yes, Dawn herself made the request.
She was at an age where . . . social considerations can become
paramount, especially in matters of self-image. You know how
adolescents can be . . ." The doctor let his voice trail off, inviting
agreement.

"She had the surgery," the nondescript man said. "She got a
transfusion. So the disease, it was in the blood she got?"

"Apparently so. We have carefully ruled out all other possibili-
ties. She certainly did not have . . ."

"AIDS."

"Yes," the doctor said. His hands balled into fists beneath the
desk, to keep their trembling from becoming apparent. "Prior to
any surgery, of course, we do a complete blood panel. I'm sure you
understand, with this type of surgery, a transfusion would not have
been anticipated. If we had thought there was even the possibility of such a need, a series of injections, essentially hemoglobin-
enhancers, could have been administered. Or, for that matter, the
patient's own blood could have been drawn and stored."

"But you didn't do any of that?" the man asked, his voice devoid
of inflection.

"The cost of such . . . precautions . . . is quite prohibitive, sir. Your sister's insurance would not cover . . ."

"Did you tell her that?"

"Tell her that? I don't understand?"

"When you were getting this 'informed consent' from Dawn, did you tell her that there were things you could do, things that would make the surgery safer . . . only you weren't going to do them, because her insurance wouldn't pay for them?"

Did I use that term, 'informed consent,' myself? Or did I just . . . ? The doctor's mind raced, approaching the redline of panic. He consciously breathed through his nose, in a futile effort to center himself. "Well," he said, carefully, "as I explained, the child is a minor. Even if such matters had been discussed with her, how would that have—?"

The other man hadn't moved, but, somehow, his body was closer to the doctor's desk. Much closer.

"She might have refused the surgery," the man said, his voice just above a whisper. "Or she might have asked a relative to put up the extra money."

"You are the only relative on record for her," the doctor said quickly. "And, as I explained, we were unable to reach you."

"Dawn can always reach me," the nondescript man said, his voice very soft. "But you didn't tell her, so she didn't try."

"I . . ."

"And now she's dying."

"We do not take that position," the doctor said, desperately trying for an authoritative tone, and failing miserably. "I mean . . . there are new drugs. And more promising ones being developed all the time. Being HIV-positive is no longer the guaranteed death sentence it once was thought to be."

The nondescript man locked the doctor's eyes. "But for her, with the hemophilia, it is, yes?" he said. "These drugs you're talking about . . . she can't take them; isn't that true?"

"Well, that is true as of this moment. But, as I said, there are new—"

The doctor blinked rapidly, interrupting himself. Because, suddenly, the visitor was standing right next to him. And the doctor had not seen him move.

"Where is she?" the nondescript man said.

—

"Is it really you?" the teenage girl asked. She was lying in a hospital bed, its upper half elevated to prop her into a sitting position.

"Yes."

"I haven't seen you since—"

"I've been away."

"I never told—"

"I know."

"Have you been to see the doctors?" the girl asked.

"Yes."

"I'm not afraid," she said, her eyes full of tears. "Not anymore. I know why you came back. You wouldn't let them keep hurting me before, and you won't let these other ones, either."

"You are not going to die," the man said.

"I know. Not now. Not with you here. Maybe I'm not all grown up yet, but I figured it out a long time ago. The private schools, the clothing money, even my horse, Thunder. It all had to come from you. Mom and Dad didn't leave that much—"

"Everything they ever had was used up a long time ago. That's right."

"You always protect me," the girl said, fervently. "Even when you're not around. I tell everyone about my big brother. My best friend, Kelly, I think she's in love with you, just from hearing me talk about you. The only picture I have is when you were in the—"

"Sure."

"You look the same."

"You don't."

"I know," she giggled. "But I was only a baby. You were almost . . . twenty, right? You didn't even live at home. I didn't even know about you. You just . . . showed up when they started—"

"It doesn't matter now."

"Where have you been?"

"Working. I travel a lot."

"But where do you live?"

"Just in hotels. I don't have a regular house."

"You never wrote. Not one time."

"I'm not good at that."

"I understand. That's what I told Kelly. When I got Thunder for my birthday, I was so surprised I almost fainted. But I knew he was from you. Kelly said, maybe you weren't my brother at all. You were like my guardian angel or something."

"I am your brother," the man said.

"Say my name," the girl commanded, her eyes pleading.

"Dawn. New Dawn."

"I haven't heard you say that since—"

"It only needs to be said when you need me. You know that."

"Wait! Aren't you going to—?"

"I have to see some people. About special medicine for you. There's a new drug. A brand-new one the doctors here don't even know about. It's in Switzerland, a long way from here. I have to go and see if it's any good."

"But you'll be back?"

"Yes."

"Promise?"

"What I speak to you, it is always a promise."

The young girl reached out to hug her brother, closing her eyes. But her arms grasped empty air; the nondescript man was gone.

—

"A million dollars?" the young Asian man said, looking up from a giant flat-screen computer monitor over to the nondescript man.

"In cash."

"How do I know—?"

The man raised the pair of black aluminum suitcases he was holding, one in each hand. "One million dollars in hundred-dollar bills. Weighs approximately three hundred and fifty pounds. I added some metal for ballast and split it into two parcels, to make it easier for you to carry."

"You expect me to believe you just walked through this neighborhood after dark with—?"

"You're a scientist," the man said, putting the suitcases down. "I don't expect you to take anything on faith. But you can verify what I just said. Open them."

The young Asian walked over to the twin suitcases. He tried to lift one, but he was unable to move it from the floor. The man flicked his right heel. One of the suitcases fell onto its side. "Open it now," he said. "They're not locked."

The young Asian man popped the latches. The suitcase was filled with neatly banded hundred-dollar bills.

"They're all odd lots," the man said. "No sequential serial numbers. Untraceable. Grab as many as you need to run your tests. Go and get them checked out. Any way you want."

The Asian man looked up from where he was kneeling over the money. "I'm a biochemist, true enough. But what you're asking, it's outside my field. AIDS research is a specialty, and—?"

"They said you were the best."

"Who said?"

The man didn't respond.

"Even if I . . . could find something. Something that might work . . . it would have to be tested. The process would take several years, even with that so-called FDA speedup."

"I don't need it to be approved."

"Look, no offense. But, for that kind of money, you could hire a whole team of experts."

"I have," the man said.

"Ah. You realize that whoever finds an actual cure for AIDS is . . . beyond rich. So what you're doing, you're gambling, right? Betting a million against more money than a computer could count."

"You find the cure, you can keep it," the nondescript man said. "Just give it to me, the formula; then go publish your papers or whatever it is people like you do."

"I never heard of—"

The Asian man suddenly realized he was alone in the room. With a million dollars in cash.

—

"How did you get in here? Past the . . . ?" the woman in the black silk business suit demanded.

The nondescript man was silent for several seconds. Then he said, "What you do here, is it for real, or is it a scam?"

"Are you serious?" the woman said, indignantly, tossing her immaculately coiffed hair. "Our clinic is the most—"

"Do you cure AIDS? Yes or no?"

"I don't know how you got past security," the woman said, a faint Germanic trace within her perfect English, "but that hardly entitles you to such confidential information."

"I don't want confidential information," the man said. "I don't care if you're running a scam. I just want to know if your stuff works."

"I don't see—"

"If it works, I'll pay you whatever you want for it," the man said. "If it doesn't work, I'll just leave, and you'll never see me again."

"I—"

"But if you say it works, and you're lying, I'll come back. Nothing you have here, nothing you can buy, nothing on this earth will protect you. If you run, I'll find you. Wherever you go, wherever you hide, I'll find you. And I'll kill you."

The woman sat still, considering. She had devoted her life to the manipulation of emotion, and prided herself on standing above such petty human weaknesses. *I must calculate the probabilities*, she thought to herself. *Logic is the ultimate weapon.*

The woman knew top-quality professional guards were posted tightly around the Swiss clinic's mountain location. She knew ultramodern intrusion-detection devices were seamlessly interwoven throughout the building. And yet . . .

Motionless, the silent man watched her.

There was a panic button under the Persian rug only a few inches from the toe of the woman's cobra-skin shoe. And a custom-made little semiautomatic pistol in her top desk drawer.

The nondescript man waited.

"It doesn't work," she said.

—

"How much of it is true?" the nondescript man asked the ancient crone. If standing in six inches of filthy water with the subway's third rail only a few steps behind bothered him in any way, it was not apparent.

"How much?" the crone cackled. "It is *all* true."

"The only thing they can live on is human blood?"

"Yes."

"They die if exposed to daylight?"

"Yes."

"Only a wooden stake through the heart can take them out?"

"Yes."

"And anybody they bite becomes one of them?"

"No! Were that so, they would already have overrun this earth. Only some."

"How can—?"

"It cannot be predicted. Some of those taken become the undead. And some just . . . die. A human's death."

"They don't have any—?"

"What? Super powers? Like in a horror tale? No. They cannot fly, they cannot change into bats. They appear as they did before they became the undead. But they do not age."

"So you could keep one . . . caged?"

"Yes. But it would die if it were not fed."

"I understand."

"Do you, human? You are the first to pass through the portals, but that signifies only that you can walk in death. I know what you paid to ask me your questions. So you are a man with great skills and no—what do mortals call it?—conscience. You paid what was asked, so human life means nothing to you."

The crone touched one eye with a long, gnarled fingernail. "There are many such humans," she said. "They often take lives for their own amusement. But only a small few kill for payment, and even fewer do so with continuing success. That much I understand. What you understand is not known to me."

"I need to find some," the man said.

"Vampires? You need to find vampires?" The crone shook her head, weighing the absurdity of the problem she had been asked to solve. "Ah!" she said suddenly. "You want revenge, is that it? One of them took one of yours, yes?"

"No."

"No? Why else would you want—?"

"I want to feed them."

The crone's eyes narrowed as she regarded him. "You cannot be one of those insane children who worship foolish myths to play at sex. Your face is not painted; you do not dress in their fashion; you are too old. And your eyes—"

"I want to feed them," the man repeated, with no change of inflection.

"Why?"

"I know what it costs to speak to you. I will pay you with more of that. I know you don't want money."

"More lives? You will take more lives for me, just to feed some of . . . them?"

"Yes."

The crone said nothing for several minutes. The nondescript man remained motionless.

"You have three sundowns to make your offering. Then come back here," the crone said, finally. "And bring your food."

—

"It could be done, I guess," the black man in the blue lab coat said. His plastic name badge read: Roger Rolange, Phlebotomist. "But a full swap? That could take, hell, a damn week, maybe. You can't just pull one supply out and pump the other in, understand? You need to have it done a little bit at a time. Maintain the pressure at both ends, monitor the signs, keep a—"

"Why couldn't you do it all at once?" the nondescript man asked.

"Theoretically, I suppose you could," the black man said, closing his eyes in concentration. "But both patients would have to be anesthetized; you'd have to monitor real close and get ready to abort if it wasn't working. So you'd need a separate supply for each and a full team, plus a . . ."

Something about the surrounding silence alerted him. When he opened his eyes, the nondescript man had vanished.

—

"Titanium? You know what that would cost?" the squat, muscular man asked. His shaven head displayed a tattoo of a lightning bolt, lancing through the number 88.

"It wouldn't weigh much, though?" the nondescript man asked him.

"Weight, that's a relative term. Of course it wouldn't weigh much, compared to steel. For the size of what you want, it would still take superhuman strength for a single person to even move it an inch, much less transport it. And the mechanism you want, well, it's simple enough, that's right. No more complicated than the way we used to catch pigeons when I was a kid. Just a box held up with a stick, a string attached to the stick. The pigeon goes to get the food and . . ."

—

"Is he—?"

"No," the nondescript man told the crone. He rolled the skinny man's body off his shoulder and placed him on the ground, face up. "He's alive. Just weak, that's all. I need to leave him here while I—"

"They are not here yet. You have come before the time we agreed, and—"

"I know. I have five more to bring. And one at a time is the best I can do."

The man turned away, and started back down the subway tunnel.

—

In less than an hour, six men were laid out on the floor of the tunnel.

"Come to me!" the crone whispered.

The nondescript man watched as the creatures materialized out of the darkness. He focused on their faces, memorizing the features of the one female and three males, moving his eyes from one to another.

"There they are," he said, gesturing toward the six bodies lying on the tunnel floor. All were in various stages of consciousness, but none was capable of movement.

Fangs bared, one of the vampires launched himself at the nondescript man, hands extended to claw. The man's hand flashed and the vampire staggered backward, a wooden stake embedded in his chest. The other vampires watched without emotion as he briefly struggled before he crumpled into a small pile of ash.

"Not me," the nondescript man said, pointing. "Them."

One of the men on the floor managed to scream weakly before he was taken.

—

The nondescript man watched, motionless. When it was over, he said, "I will bring you more in three days. On the same terms, all right?"

"Yes," the crone replied. "If you wish."

"But it has to be these same ones," the man said, pointing at the sated vampires. "Especially her."

The female vampire smiled. She was young and curvy. "My name is Darnetra," she said, twitching her hips. "Do you like me?"

"Yes," the nondescript man said.

—

"Don't say another goddamn word to me about your 'monsters,'" the powerfully built, jowly man in a rumpled plaid sports coat glared at the much younger man in a blue uniform.

"But, Sarge, I'm telling you—"

"Listen, kid. I don't have time for your stupid little wannabe informants, what do you call them, again? Goths?"

"That's right. And the word is—"

"Son," the older man shook his head sadly. "Even if there *were* vampires suddenly popping up in Manhattan, it wouldn't be close to our biggest problem."

"What do you mean?"

"I got my informants, too. Real ones, not crazed kids with white paint on their faces. And you know what mine tell me?"

"What?"

"That the most dangerous guy on the face of this earth is back in town."

"Who is—?"

"You know what they say about this guy? When he shows up, nobody knows why, but somebody's gonna die. A whole lot of some-bodies. That's his business: making bodies. He hasn't been ID'd in New York for a long time now, but we still got wants and warrants out on him for the one job we can connect him to, for sure."

"Which is?"

"His parents," the older man said.

—

"You have come seven times now," the crone said. "Each time, you pay the price. Will you tell me why?"

"I want Darnetra."

"What does that mean . . . 'want'? You want her as a man wants a woman?"

"Yes."

"You understand humans cannot mate with—"

"I want her. Only her. Tell her, the next time I come, I will bring her exactly what she wants."

"You know this? What she wants?"

"Yes. Darnetra wants women. Plump women, but not fat ones. I will bring her some. No fewer than four. And then I will have her."

"You are not a man," the crone said.

—

"I'm a little scared," Dawn said.

"Fear is not a god," the nondescript man said. "It is an enemy."

"Have you ever . . . ? Oh! I know. When they were—"

"You are no longer a little child," the man told her. "Your time will come soon. Then we will fight, together."

"Truly?"

"I promise."

—

"I couldn't bring them all the way here," the nondescript man told Darnetra. "They weighed too much. You said plump, right?"

"Yesss. . . ." the vampire said, licking her lips.

"They're a thousand yards or so back the way I came. Will you come with me?"

"I saw what you did to Tortrine," she said. "How do I know you won't—"

"If I wanted to kill you, I could do it anytime I wanted to," the man said, looking toward the crone. The old woman nodded her agreement.

"What do you want?" Darnetra asked.

"I want you," the man said. "I want you as I have never wanted any woman."

Darnetra locked eyes with the man before her. Finally, she reached out her hand. The man took it, exchanging a final, bargain-sealing look with the crone.

They walked down the subway tunnel together, around a series of turns. "There they are," the man said.

"Ummm!" Darnetra replied, dropping the man's hand and running toward them.

She was deep into the first one's jugular when the titanium cage dropped over her.

—

Twenty-four hours passed before the nondescript man returned. "It's a trade," he said, speaking through the bars of the cage.

"Trade?" Darnetra snarled. "You tricked me."

"Yes. And, by now, you know you can't get out. The others of your pack, they can't move the cage. Or they won't, I don't know which. They haven't even tried to come for you. So I know you're not a tribe. Each one is only for itself."

"Why did you—?"

"You have to feed to live," the man went on, as if she had not spoken. "But I don't know how long you can go between kills. So that's not the threat."

The man came closer to the front of the cage. "This isn't either," he said, pulling a sharpened wooden stake from inside his coat. Darnetra shrank back against the far wall of bars.

"This is the trade," the man said. "The people whose blood you've been feeding on, the ones I brought you, they all had AIDS. Full-blown AIDS. I got them right out of the hospital's terminal ward. A couple of them were only hours from death when you took them.

"But their blood didn't kill you. Any of you. I don't have the time to find out if it eventually would. I'm betting it would not.

There's something about the way you process blood that makes you immune. Or kills the virus. Either way is just as good.

"I don't know much about it, and I don't have the time to learn. So what we're going to do is this: you are going to swap your blood with a human. A human who is HIV-positive. I don't know what will happen. Maybe your blood will cure her. Maybe it will turn her into . . . what you are. Maybe it will kill her. But it's her only chance, so there is no choice. Any fight is better than surrendering. And when you are surrounded, anyone you attack is an enemy."

"But what about me?" Darnetra said. "I would be getting human blood. I can't—"

"You probably can," the man said. "I've been asking a lot of questions, and I think I know, now. You feed off the blood of humans; you should be able to *live* off it, too."

"I don't want—"

"You vampires can't be born, right? If you mate, you can't make a vampire baby. So you were something else, once. Before you got taken. Maybe the human blood will turn you back into that."

"Into what? A human dying of AIDS? I won't—"

"It's not your choice," the man said. "I can't bring a whole hospital down here. Even if I could, it wouldn't be . . . clean enough. So you have to come with me. Or die right here."

"Die?" she sneered, disdainfully. "Even without food, I can last for—"

"Only a few more hours," the man interrupted. "Then I pull another lever, and the sunlight comes right in. You're just under a subway grate. Only that plate above you blocks the light.

"So what you're going to do is this: You're going to turn around, and back toward me. You're going to put your wrists through that slot in the bars," he said. "For these"—holding up a pair of handcuffs. "Then I'm going to open the cage, and you're going to come out. If you try to bite, I'll put this stake in your heart before you can take a breath."

Darnetra watched, silent except for her eyes.

"Then you're going to climb into this," the man said, showing her a black Kevlar body bag. "You can't bite through it. I'll carry you, while it's still dark. When you wake up, you'll be indoors. No sunlight."

"What if I don't cooperate?" she spat at this . . . whatever he was. "What good are your threats, then? You can kill me, but I'm no good to you dead."

"The next one will be," the man said. "Or the one after that. See, like I said, there's one thing I found out about you vampires. You're not a tribe. You don't care about anyone except your own selves. So I'll just get the old lady to bring me some more, until I find one who will take the chance."

"I . . ."

"You have nothing to bargain with, except your blood. If you want to test me, just wait a few more hours. By then, the sun will be up."

—

"I can't believe we're doing this," one nurse whispered to another.

Darnetra and Dawn lay on separate tables, connected by a complicated network of tubing, all monitored by vital-signs gauges.

"Why not, girl?" the other nurse said. "These damn interns, they've been doing secret plastic surgery down here for years. Making an off-the-books fortune at it, too. What's wrong with us getting a taste?"

"But look at her. She's not even . . . human."

"Way I heard it, neither was the guy who brought her in here. But he's paying for the party. I don't know what he thinks he's buying for all the money he spent, but he just bought *me* a new car, honey."

The overhead lights flickered briefly. The fluids started to move in the tubes.

Invisible in the shadows, the nondescript man waited.

for Champion Joe Lansdale

PIG

Pig was my friend, so I didn't have any choice. I don't mean I ran with him, or even that he could claim my crew. But I was in his house a lot, and there's no keeping something like that a secret around here.

His mother treated me better than I thought mothers ever did. Any mothers. I ate the food she made. Food she cooked, I'm saying. I even slept over more than a few times. Times when I couldn't stay where I lived.

I don't know why I'm making this sound better than it was. The truth is, once I got too big for my mother to have around when she brought a man home, that was the end. She said I made them uncomfortable, even though I stayed out of sight and never said a word. The first time one actually got up and left without . . . Ah, it doesn't matter. My mother told me how it was going to be from then on out. She made it real clear. In case I was deaf and blind, I guess. Or maybe she just figured me for stupid—she'd said *that* enough.

But nobody ever called me out of my name behind being seen with Pig. My name, it wasn't one I put on myself. I don't know exactly when people started calling me Viper, but it stuck. That's a joke—if you don't get it, you live somewhere else.

I earned that name. Move on me, and your next meal was going to be the steel-in-the stomach special.

One more year and they'd stop giving me ninety days in juvie. Or probation and all that counseling crap. I'd be old enough for the state pen. That's where they all said I was going anyway.

My destiny, like.

I didn't care about that. But I was glad I was so good with a blade. Plenty of bad guys who made their name behind being shooters didn't last long behind bars. You don't get to carry a Tec-9 in there, but you can always get your hands on a spike. Specially if you had a crew waiting on you.

If it wasn't too bad out, I had plenty of other places to spend the night. Our clubhouse was one. I don't mean some cute little shack guys built out in the woods, with a "No Girls Allowed" sign. Our clubhouse was a filthy basement . . . and it stayed filthy. Not because we wanted it that way—although some of the guys probably wouldn't have cared—but it didn't have lights or running water, so what could we do?

Girls were definitely allowed. Any girl who came down those steps knew what was waiting on her. And what came after that. It didn't stop them. Some of them, anyway.

The building was going to get torn down one day. Most of it was already gone. But around here, we didn't think about things like that.

Tomorrow things.

A number on a building, that might matter if you were looking for some house. But we all knew where we were going, so who gave a rat's ass?

And once they put a number on your back, everyone would have the same address. In the winter, even trying to sleep under a pile of old rugs, the place was just too . . . ah, it was impossible. Bone-eating cold and junkies, too. They only came around when it was way below freezing. They weren't afraid of anything we might do to them; they were past that. What scared them was the thought of anyone grabbing their stuff before they could fire up their pipes. Hardcore crackheads, they're not scared of nothing. Nothing except losing the rock they just scored.

I could see how Pig got the way he was. If my mother fed me like that, I'd probably weigh three hundred pounds, too.

Pig's mother, she'd make you eat. No matter how much you chowed down, she'd ask you fifty times if you had enough.

Pig didn't have a father around. Most of us don't. Some of us knew a name our mothers told us. Some actually knew a man who they could point to—even had his name on their birth certificate. But nobody had one like on TV. You know, one that lived with them and all.

A father like that, a guy who had a job, took care of his family, that was just crazy. Nobody who had all that would ever stay where we did. Everything was rotting wood and broken concrete. A place where you could have your application in for the projects your whole life, but they'd never call your name.

I don't know how they'd do that, anyway. Nobody had telephones. Not in their houses, I mean. Everybody had a cell. You didn't have a cell, how could you do business?

Pig lived on the far edge of our turf, just a couple of blocks away from a real nice neighborhood. One with little houses with lawns and all.

All those houses had burglar bars. And nasty dogs inside those bars, in case someone from where we lived wanted to visit.

We didn't need that stuff—kids from those neighborhoods never wanted to visit us. Or maybe they did. I couldn't read their minds. But if I was them, I knew I wouldn't. I guess that was as close as I could ever get to thinking like they did.

—

I remember the first time I came to Pig's house, how he kept telling me it would be okay. Every step we walked, it seemed he had to keep telling me that.

It was so cold that even the corner boys were inside someplace. Night, it would be different. No matter how cold, sellers would have to be there for the buyers. Didn't matter if was dope or pussy.

You sign up for that gig, you better show up. I got plenty of offers, but I never took those jobs. I had plans for myself. Big plans. After I did my first bit, I mean. For what I wanted, you have to prove in, first. Show you can do time the right way. Come in alone, and stand up once you get there, put in some work. I've seen whores out in weather that kept the cop cars inside their garages. I knew why that was. I saw the way my mother acted, anytime she could get a man to come home with her.

That first time, Pig's mother must have seen us coming—she had the door open before we even got to it.

"Mom, this is Viper. He's my friend."

Any other mother, you bring home a guy named Viper, she's gonna ask a lot of questions. Pig's mother didn't ask a single one. Just put another plate out like I was going to be there for dinner. Or supper, or whatever they called it—I remember it was around four in the afternoon.

That night, she said I'd have to share a room with Pig. That's when I found out his real name was Alexander. I put up a little fuss, but she said there was a spare bed, and plenty of blankets.

I never expected she'd do any more than let me sleep in the basement. That would have been fine with me—you don't cop an attitude when someone does you a solid.

In the morning, she gave me fresh clothes. I don't mean she washed mine; I'd slept in what I'd been wearing.

"These were my late husband's," she said. "Alexander's father. He was about your size. Maybe a little bigger, but I'm sure they'll fit."

There was a winter coat that fit pretty good, too.

—

Then it stopped being winter. Why in hell Pig had to pick such a beautiful spring day to go sit in the luncheonette I'll never know.

I guess maybe he thought he was waiting for me. All our crew went there after school—the ones on probation, I mean. If you cut school, they'd put you back in juvie.

But he had to know I wouldn't be going home with him that day, not with the weather being so nice.

It doesn't matter now.

Our club had never claimed the luncheonette. It was too big of a place, and right on the border, too. No one club could ever hold it.

And if the owner blamed us for losing business, we'd be out. He could do it, too. Always had three or four guys behind the counter. From the look of them, they sold a lot more than those slimy sandwiches nobody ever tried to eat twice.

Pig saw me come in and called out my name. Waved me over to the back booth like we had a meeting set up or something.

When he did that, I didn't have any choice. If I acted like I didn't know him, punked him out like that, it would have been serious disrespect. Pig showed a lot of heart, taking that risk. I couldn't put him down in front of everybody; that would have been just wrong.

So I walked all the way over toward him, passing between the round seats at the counter to my right and the booths on my left. I was going all the way to that back booth. That's all I wanted to do. Go there, sit down, and tell Pig how things were.

Only I never got that far. I was only about halfway there when someone on my right said, "You gonna pork that piggy tonight, faggot?"

Later I learned the guy's name had been Tico. Tico something, it doesn't matter. I keep telling myself I'd been headed straight for that back booth. Over and over, I say that in my mind. That's the only way I can make what happened come out right.

I was still walking, not looking back, wiping the blood off my blade on a paper napkin, when I heard the first shots. I snapped my knife closed, wiped it down again, and threw it over the counter.

Tico's boys were there way before the cops. What else? I mean, they were *already* there.

Mine, too.

When the cops finally rolled Pig off of me, he was dead weight. Over twenty slugs in him, the way it's told now.

Any crew would be proud to claim a man like that. So when I poured his "X" onto the sidewalk a few nights later, I wasn't alone.

Neither was Pig.

for Greg and Marilyn

A PIECE OF THE CITY

1

Just because you live someplace, that doesn't mean you understand how it works. The city where I came up is a perfect example. Everybody who lives there talks like they know all about it, but they never will. If you want to figure out how the city really works, you have to get far away from it. When you're down too deep in it, all you can see is your own little piece.

I know what I'm saying. I've been away, for a long time now. There isn't much to do here, once you figure out how to stay alive. So I've been studying the city long distance, getting ready for when I come back.

What I finally figured out was that there isn't just the one city, like people think. I mean, everybody knows there's different parts, like Queens and Brooklyn. And there's parts inside the parts, like Harlem and Greenwich Village. But the city is really cut up a lot smaller than even that.

2

When I was a kid, the city was split up into little tiny pieces, all the way right down to the blocks. Our territory was three streets, plus a vacant lot, where they had torn down some buildings. Any time you left your territory, no matter where you went, you were an outsider.

Mostly, we got around by subway. You might think, nobody owns the subway, but you would be wrong. The subway, it's just like the city itself. It's a great big huge thing; but, the minute you put people into it, it starts getting cut up into pieces.

Like, if you got on a subway car, and it was full of boys from another club, it was their car. And if you had enough boys get on with you, you could maybe make it your car.

Other people riding the subway, they would watch this happen right in front of them, and not pay it any mind. When I was a kid, I thought that was because they didn't understand what they were seeing. Now I know different. They knew. But to them, the subway was like a bad neighborhood they had to go through every day to get to work. They would never want to live in a neighborhood like that, so they never wanted a piece of it for themselves, that's all.

But the block, that wasn't like the subway. The block was permanent. You were there every day. When outsiders came into your block, you had to make them pay tolls. Because if people could go through your territory without paying, it was like it wasn't yours at all.

The City—that's the government, not the territory—it owns the subway, so everyone who rides has to pay. But, if you were riding with some of your boys, and a kid got on alone, you could collect, too. Charge a toll, because that was your piece he was standing on, then.

It was the same on our block. We didn't own the buildings— nobody around there did. Even the men who came to collect the rents, they lived somewhere else. The City owned the streets, just like it owned the subway. But the City wasn't around all the time, and we were.

3

It was that rule, about paying the tolls, that got me sent away. The vacant lot was between two territories, ours and the Renegades'. We both used it, for different stuff, but neither of us claimed it. If a coolie—a kid who wasn't with a club, or what they would call an off-brand today—went through the lot, any club that was there could take the tolls from him.

We had little clashes with the Renegades about the lot, but it was mostly just selling wolf tickets, loudmouthing around. Both clubs knew; that vacant lot, it didn't move, but it was just like the subway. The only time you had a piece of it was when you were right there to hold it.

The leader of the Renegades was a skinny little guy called Junta. All of the Renegades had those PR names, but PRs, they don't always look like each other. Some of them were so black, if they didn't speak that Spanish, you would think they were colored. And some of them were as white as us, with everything in between. The only way you could tell for sure was from listening to them talk— even the ones that talked English, they didn't talk white.

I didn't know how Junta got to be leader. He wasn't a great fist fighter, he didn't have any kind of rep with a knife, and no one ever saw him with a pistol. I didn't see where he was any great brains, either.

The reason I knew about Junta is that I had to meet with him a few times, one-on-one. I was president of the Royal Vikings, and, sometimes, we would have a sit-down, to settle a dispute. If the presidents couldn't settle things, then the warlords would get together, to set the rules for a clash. But it never came to that, between the Renegades and us.

Junta and me, we made a treaty, to have our clubs share the vacant lot. The way Junta explained it, the lot was kind of like the gateway to our two territories. If we fought each other over it, we'd always be having that same fight, over and over. We needed to protect the gateway from outsiders; that was most important. Better to share a little piece than not to have any at all, he said, and he was right. So our treaty was, whoever was on the set, for right then, it was their piece.

4

It started when one of the Mystic Dragons got himself a girlfriend in our territory. He would walk right through our block, flying his colors, and nobody was crazy enough to make him pay tolls. The Mystic Dragons, they were a major club. People said they could put a thousand men into a meet, and a couple of hundred of them would have guns. Real guns, not zips.

The way guys in gangs talk, a lot of that was probably just blowing smoke, but there was enough truth in it to keep us all chilled. Our club, the Royal Vikings, we could put, maybe, twenty guys out for a meet . . . and some of them would make it only because they'd be scared not to. If a club like ours ever vamped on a Mystic Dragon, we'd be finished.

What kicked it off was the day Bunchie came charging down the steps to the basement we use for a clubhouse.

"Mystic Dragons!" he yelled.

"What?!" Tony Boy said.

"Mystic Dragons! All over the block. They got a car at both ends. And one parked right across from here!"

Everybody was getting all excited, talking at once. "Cool it," I told them. "If this was a raid, they would have been down here already."

"The president is right," Little Augie backed me up. But I could see he was nervous.

I looked around the basement. Just five men, plus me. I thought about sending Sammy out to see what the Mystic Dragons wanted—it wouldn't look good for the president to go himself. But if they saw the guy we sent was our warlord, they could get the wrong idea.

I could send Little Augie, but he's not a good talker. And bringing the Mystic Dragons down to that ratty basement would be showing them too much.

I had to think. Everyone went quiet, waiting on me. All we had in the clubhouse was Sammy's zip, and some bats and chains. I knew at least a couple of the boys always had knives, but Bunchie had said there were three carloads of Mystic Dragons.

"I'll handle it," I told the others. "I'll go see what they want. No reason to let them see what we're holding down here."

"You want we should go with?" Little Augie asked me.

"Yeah," I said. "But stay back. Right against the building, understand? Don't crowd nobody."

I was proud of my boys. They looked sharp and hard, in their white silk jackets with *Royal Vikings* across the back. Our jackets are all custom-made, by this very classy place down in Little Italy. They cost a lot, but they say a lot about us, too, so they're worth it. Two of the boys stepped out first, then moved off to the side to let me through, while the others filled in behind.

The Mystic Dragons' car was a big black Buick. A four-door. Facing the wrong direction on our one-way street, so the driver was against the curb. As I walked over, the back door opened, and three men got out. They didn't say anything. The driver looked at me out of his window.

"You Hawk?" he asked.

"Right," I said. That's the name I go by. It was written in purple script on the left side of my jacket. On my right sleeve, there were four little hearts; meaning, I'm the president. Sammy, our warlord, had three on his. We didn't spell out the offices, the way some clubs do.

"The man wants to talk to you," the driver said.

"Here I am," I told him, cool.

"Boss," he said, as he climbed out of the car, holding the door open.

I couldn't tell if he meant, "boss!" it was good I was willing to talk, or that I would be talking to his boss, but I got in. It was classy, the way they set it up. I didn't have an excuse to refuse, because I would be the one behind the wheel, so they couldn't take off with me as a prisoner. Besides, all their men were already standing on the sidewalk. Except for the ones in the cars at the end of the block.

The guy in the passenger seat was colored. I expected that, him being a Mystic Dragon and all. But I was surprised at how old he was.

"I'm Baron James," he said. "You know my name?"

"I heard it," I said. Which was the truth. Everybody in the city who ran with a club had heard of Baron James. He killed two men in a clash a long time ago, when he was real little. Baron James was famous. His name was in the *Daily News*, with headlines and everything. The paper said it was wrong that they couldn't send him to the state pen, just because he was only fourteen at the time. People wrote letters to the paper, saying, for what Baron James did, they should give him the electric chair, no matter how old he was.

"You're leader of . . . what's the name of your club?"

"The Royal Vikings," I told him, like I didn't know he was saying that just to say we were nothing.

"Yeah. Well, then you're the man I have to talk to. About what happened to Chango."

"Who's Chango?"

"All you need to know about Chango is two things, man. One, Chango is a Mystic Dragon. And, two, some of your boys jumped him two nights ago, in the vacant lot over by Twenty-ninth."

"Not my boys."

"Yeah, your boys. Chango's got himself a little twist around here. She's a PR, but she lives over in your turf."

"I don't know any names," I said. "But we know a guy who flies Mystic Dragon colors has a girl around here. He comes and goes. Whenever he wants. Nobody ever bothers him."

"That's the way it's supposed to be," Baron James said. "Only, it wasn't. Chango, he's going to make it. But he got hurt pretty bad."

"Shot?"

"Stomped," Baron James said. "Wasn't no fair one, either. No challenge, nothing. He said he was just cutting through the lot when he got piled on."

"It wasn't any of my—"

"You Vikings, you going to pull something like that, you should've left those jackets at home," he said. He reached over and rubbed the back of his fingers against where my name was. "Nice," he said.

"Look," I said, being reasonable, "you know a club like ours, we'd never start anything with—"

"Oh, I don't think it was your club," he said. "We thought it was your club, there wouldn't be no Royal Vikings now. No, what we figure is, it was a couple of members of your club. See the difference?"

"No," I said. I took out my pack of smokes, held it out toward Baron James—I wanted him to see my hand wasn't shaking. I was a little surprised when he took one. I lit us both up from my lighter.

Baron James took a deep drag. Then he said, "Difference is, a club makes a move, it has to be approved, am I right? The president has to give his okay."

"Unless it's—"

"This wasn't no self-defense," he said. "Don't even try to run that."

"I wasn't saying—"

"And, if it's not approved, that means the boys went freelance. Now, if that was one of the Mystic Dragons, anybody who would try a breakaway move like that, he'd be disciplined, understand?"

"Yeah."

"And that's all we're asking for," he said. "A little discipline."

"But none of our—"

"Only thing is," he said, talking right over me, "we'd kind of like to do the discipline ourselves. I mean, you do whatever you think needs to be done. But, when that's over, we get our turn. Fair enough?"

"If one of the Vikings did anything like that, I would—"

"Not one," Baron James said. "At least two. Probably three, but we'll settle for two."

"Who are you saying jumped your man?"

"I just told you," he said.

"You said Vikings," I said. I knew, if I backed off, even a little, we were all done. "I asked you, which ones?"

"How would Chango know your boys?"

"Well, you said—"

"I said Vikings. I didn't say which ones. That's for you to find out. And deal with."

"There's no way any of—"

"This here is Wednesday," Baron James said. His voice was soft, but it was ice cold. "We give you until Sunday night. Now, your boys, they seen us talking for a while now. Seen us talking like men. No screaming and yelling. Calm and cool, am I right? So, when you go on back, what you tell them is, the Mystic Dragons thinking about making you Vikings an affiliate club. You know what that is?"

"Yeah. But I thought you guys only took—"

"Times are changing," Baron James said. "This color thing, it put a lot of good men in the ground. And a lot more in the penitentiary. There ain't no money in it. The Mystic Dragons, we got plans. There's all kinds of rackets going on in the city, and we're going to take our place, soon enough. This is a big city, and we entitled to our piece of it.

"Now, the only way we make the right people listen is behind numbers. Big numbers. What we got to do is consolidate," he said, like he loved the word. "We can't be fighting each other all the time; what we get out of that? So, that's what you tell your boys."

"But you're not really . . ."

"What I just tell you, that's the stone truth," Baron James said. "Everybody be doing this, you see soon enough. Even the Chinaboys, way downtown, they stepping past color when it come to business. Us, too. We reaching out to the little clubs . . . no offense . . . to bring them in. You don't get to be Mystic Dragons, but you get to be with us; you understand?"

"I think I do."

"But you know the rules," he said. "And the toll you got to pay. You got to give us the boys who stomped Chango."

I didn't say anything. I knew more was coming.

"Sunday night," Baron James said, "we pull up to the curb, just like now. We get out, just like now. You walk over to us, just like now. Only, Sunday night, you have two men with you. The ones we want." Baron James looked at me. His eyes were green—I never saw that on a colored, before. "Everybody gets in the car," he said. "The car takes off. Later, when you come back, you president of an official Mystic Dragons affiliate."

Baron James leaned in, close to me. "Only, when you come back, you come back alone."

5

We started that same night. First, I put out the word—all the Royal Vikings had to come in, emergency. Then I questioned every single one of the boys.

Little Augie and Bunchie helped me. Sammy, too. I knew it couldn't have been any of those three, because they had all been with me the night Chango got stomped.

Everybody denied doing it. I expected that. What I didn't

expect was that I couldn't tell which ones were lying, the way I usually can.

Even in our own little piece of the city, you didn't see Royal Vikings out by themselves too often. We had our clubhouse, the candy store, the corner; that was about it. The school had dances at night, sometimes, but that was too far out of our territory for anyone to go alone. And, if you did go alone, it would take a lot of heart to fly colors. Sammy might do it, or Little Augie, but not the rest, I didn't think.

And Baron James had said it was at least two men.

The clubhouse had a backroom. We used it for initiations, and for when we got the debs to come down. That night, we used it for the interrogations.

We all suspected these particular two boys might be guilty. They were real tight with each other, partners, and we figured they might be plotting to move up in the organization. But even after Sammy hurt one of them pretty bad, they wouldn't admit anything.

By Friday night, I knew I wouldn't have anyone I could give to Baron James.

6

I got my men together, and I told them how it had to be. I talked for a long time before I was finished.

"What happens to us?" Little Augie asked. He was talking to me, but I knew he was speaking for the whole club.

"The Mystic Dragons don't know any of our real names," I said. "Not even mine. Just Hawk. The first thing, the jackets have to go. I mean, burn them. The Royal Vikings are done. Once this is over, the only one the Mystic Dragons are going to be looking for is me."

"You sure you want to . . ." Sammy said.

"What choice is there?" I told them. "I'm not going to play

Judas on guys who didn't do anything. If we want to keep our little piece, here, we'd have to go to war against the Mystic Dragons. That's crazy; we'd all be wiped out in a day. I'm the president; I know what I have to do. I got people in Chicago. Soon as it's done, that's where I'll go."

"The hell with that," Little Augie said. "Just go. Tonight."

Little Augie was a good man. I was sorry to lie to him, about having people in Chicago. But the whole club was there when I was talking, and I wasn't sure of them all. I knew the Mystic Dragons would be around right after I took off, asking questions, and I couldn't take a chance that one of them wouldn't turn rat, if they got scared enough.

"No," I said. "The way I have to do it is the only way. They're going to get me, anyway. I might as well have a name."

"Where are you going to get a real pistol?" Bunchie said. "Nobody around here has one to sell."

"The same place we get our jackets," I said. "The guy who makes them up for us, I heard, if you bring the right money, he can get you anything. Now, everybody, put up your coin. Tomorrow, I'm going shopping."

7

I didn't blink when the old man in the shop told me it would be three hundred dollars for the pistol and the bullets. I told him I'd leave the money with him, come back in a couple of hours. He looked at me for a minute, then he said, "That's not how it's done. You want the piece, you wait right here for it. Understand?"

I said I did. Right then is when I started to understand a lot of things. Like why people call a pistol a "piece."

The old man picked up the phone and said something in Italian. I didn't speak it, but I figured what it was about.

When he hung up, he looked at me. "You're getting bigger," he said. "All the time."

"I'm almost eighteen," I told him.

"I mean your . . . ambitions," the old man said.

"Oh. Like what I just—?"

"Sure, that. A business expense. And I see you've been recruiting, too. Outside the tribe. Very smart. All over the city, you can see, that's the trend among . . . businessmen."

I think I knew it right then, but I gave myself a minute to make sure I was under control. Then I asked the old man, "What do you mean, outside the tribe?"

"The last bunch who came in here for your jackets, that was a surprise," he said. "I never saw Spanish boys in your . . . organization before."

8

Right after that, I straightened things out with Baron James. We agreed on the tolls. I paid them, and the Mystic Dragons never moved on the Royal Vikings.

The pistol the old man sold me worked perfect. The only way I could use it was by calling for a one-on-one, so the cops found out pretty quick it was me who aced Junta.

I thought, maybe, the Renegades wouldn't testify against me . . . you're not supposed to. But they did. By the time the court was through with me, I was doing The Book. That's what they call a life sentence . . . from throwing the book at you, I guess.

When I got to prison, I came in with a name. Not just from what I did—there were plenty of guys who had a body up there. But I was the first white guy inside who had friends in the Mystic Dragons, just like Baron James promised. It made me kind of a leader in there, even that young.

I see the Board again in another year. Maybe they'll cut me loose this time. I've got a perfect institutional record—I know how to do time.

I'm only forty-two years old now. It's not too late for me to get my little piece of the city.

for Matt Kinney

SEEDING THE GROUND

A malevolent fog reduced the morning sun to a hazy, rancid-butter splotch. It descended as it always did: inexorably, until it merged with the prison walls to form a sea of the dullest gray.

The inner gates opened, and the yard slowly came to life. Convicts moved in intricate patterns; some to their own territory, others to the no-man's-land where the unaffiliated were allowed to congregate. The boundary lines were invisible to outsiders. To the prisoners, they were as clear as the concertina wire that topped the surrounding wall, occasionally glittering in sunlight like a necklace of razors.

Domino players set up their tables, weight lifters assembled their iron, joggers started on their first circuit. A few men began limbering up on the handball court, their gloveless hands marking them as veterans of the sport.

Only the shadowy shark of sudden, explosive violence moved freely across the boundaries, swimming silently through the tight clusters of convicts. A lethal shape-shifter, never motionless, it would stop only to strike.

The yard was a border town on the edge of a frontier that few of its residents would ever cross. And now it was open for business. Bets were placed, debts collected, sex threatened, plots hatched. . . .

—

One of the last cons to enter the yard was an elderly man, so old he had become an ancient, unnoticed relic. He moved glacially, his back bent from the weight of his Life-Without term. His destination was a tiny patch of stone-hard dirt, in a corner that never saw the sun.

The old man was mostly bald, with only a fringe of bleached-out white hair remaining. The eyes behind his taped-together, steel-rimmed glasses were the color of denim after a thousand turns in the laundry.

As the old man settled into position in front of his patch, a guard strolled by, a muscular young man with a military haircut and a bodybuilder's biceps.

"What're you up to, Pop?"

"Ah, you know me, Rico. I'm planting my seeds, like I always do."

"Yeah, I know. What I meant was, how are you feeling?"

"Pretty good, son. All things considered. What about you?"

The guard stepped closer to the old man. He rotated his head on his thick neck as if to get out a kink, scanning the yard in the same motion. Satisfied, he began telling the old man about how his dumb-fuck brother-in-law had gotten himself in trouble. Again. And how that made his wife so upset she wasn't fit to live with. Again.

"But if I say one word about that useless slug, she gets mad at *me*. So what am I supposed to do?" the guard finished, five minutes later.

The old man nodded sympathetically, knowing no answer was expected.

The guard watched the yard with hands behind his back and his chest expanded. Playing his role. "So, you still won't let your granddaughter come for a visit?" he said.

"You know how it is when girls come here, Rico. She's been through enough."

"But, Pop, I know she wants to—"

"It's better this way," the old man said, closing the subject. For today.

—

After the guard moved off, two men passed by where the old man was working. They were both in their late twenties, cold-eyed and prison-complected. One nodded curtly to the old man, as if deigning to acknowledge his existence. The old man nodded back—just a meaningless movement of his head.

The two men kept moving, walking the track around the outer yard in a leisurely circuit as they did every day. They walked in perfect synchronization, shoulders almost, but never quite, touching.

The shorter of the two was stocky, round-faced, with curly brown hair. His forearms were so thick with crude, prison-artist tattoos that they looked as if they'd been dipped in ink.

"You really think he knows the whole layout, like he said?" he asked his partner.

The taller man was hawk-faced, with jet-black hair worn short on the sides and long in back. "Why shouldn't he?" he demanded. "I mean, he worked there, right? He was the gardener, had the run of the place."

"But that was, like, what? Five, six years ago? And, anyway, he's an old man, could be soft in the head."

"Being old don't make him stupid."

"Stupid wouldn't bother me. *Crazy,* that's what bothers me."

"Crazy people can still know things, Eugene," the taller man said, confidently. "Anyway, you think he's crazy just because he keeps trying to make something grow on the yard?"

"Maybe not when he first started, okay," Eugene agreed. "But he's sure crazy by *now.* That ground's like concrete. Even if you could break it deep enough to plant a lousy seed, nothing would ever grow there—not without sunlight."

"It's his money. What else has he got to spend it on in here?"

"You city guys don't know nothing about growing things," the stocky man said. "You ever look at the packets those seeds come in? The commissary's had them for a thousand years. They're way too old to work. Got no life left in them. That old man's stone lunar, Pete. Trying the same thing, over and over, like a robot."

"Maybe he's just stubborn."

"Even a damn mule quits after a while, bro. But the old man don't even have *that* much sense. You ever put a worm in a glass bottle, watch what happens? The worm crawls a little bit up the side, then he falls back down. Then he goes back, does the same thing. Over and over."

"What *else* has the worm got to do?" the taller man said.

"Huh?"

"What I'm saying is, so *what*, Eugene? It's not like he's going to be going along with us."

"Yeah, but what if he *is* crazy? I mean, that place he used to work at is a damn long ways from here. We don't know nothing about that part of the state." The stocky man eye-swept the yard, dropped his voice even lower. "I don't know about you, bro, but I can't stand another jolt. I had two rides already. You know the deal; the next one's The Book. That means you end up like that old man."

"Right. That's why there's not going to be any witnesses."

"You think I don't know that? But . . . four people. That's going to draw heavy heat. There would have to be a serious pile of cash to make it—"

"The old man says more than half a *million*," the hawk-faced one said urgently. "All in those—what did he call them, Krugerrands? Gold coins. *Solid* gold. Untraceable. They're good anywhere. And in Mexico, they're *better* than money. Remember that article he showed us in the newspaper? About that Mexican money? Nobody down there wants it; they all want American dollars. But gold, that's even better. We'd be kings, Eugene."

"Kings? We'd be *gods,* bro. I wonder how much the lawyer would cost."

"The lawyer the old man wants?"

"Yeah. For his 'appeal.' Like any lawyer's going to do *him* any good. How old is he, anyway? Seventy-five?"

"Hell, he's older than that. It was the old man's *granddaughter* those guys raped. And she wasn't no kid herself."

"That's right. Man, you'd think a jury would have cut him some slack, behind what they did to her. Specially with him being in World War Two and all."

"Probably would have," the hawk-faced man said, thought-fully, "if he'd just gone berserk and blown them away. But that old man, he was one cold-blooded bastard. Hunted all three of them down, one by one. And I heard he'd done some time, too, back in the day. You know they hold that against you forever. Only reason he's not in the Death House is, the jury figured, guy his age, he's going to die soon enough, anyway."

"For a guy who's supposed to be such a stone killer, he's sure going out quiet, bro. Won't even let his own granddaughter, the one he *did* it for, come to visit him. All he does is plant those seeds of his. Talks to himself, too. A real wet-brain."

"But he *remembers* real good. Don't forget, he worked for Rexum himself. Right on that big estate. Hell, that's where it hap-pened. With his granddaughter, I mean."

"Yeah. I heard, the guys who did it, they worked for—"

"Point is," the hawk-faced man interrupted, "he *knows,* okay? Those maps he drew us . . ."

"Yeah, well, I guess it couldn't hurt to go down there and take a look; see if it's like he remembered it."

"We're doing it, Eugene," the hawk-faced man said, flatly, taking control. "I get out in two weeks. I'll get everything set. You raise a month after that; that's when we move. *I'm* the one show-ing the discipline, right? No partying, no booze, no speed, no . . . nothing that could attract any attention. You understand? Soon as you make the door, we *go* for it."

"No witnesses, bro," the stocky man said, extending a clenched fist at waist level.

"No witnesses," the hawk-faced man agreed, tapping his fist against his partner's. "Now, let's go see if we can pump any more out of the geezer, while he's still got a memory."

—

Two months later, the old man walked slowly out to his patch of ground. He dropped a handful of seeds, bowed his head.

The guard walked up. "What's going on?" he greeted the old man.

"I want to see my granddaughter, Rico. One more time, before I die."

"You mean you're finally going to let her come for a visit? Hey, Pop, that's great! I knew you'd finally—"

"No. She's never coming in this place. I want to *go* and see her."

"What are you talking about?"

"A little furlough. But, first, I have to go and see the warden."

"You? About what, Pop?"

"About that special visit."

"Sure," the guard chuckled. "Just go off all by yourself, and promise to come back, right? Yeah; you and every con on the yard."

"I got something to trade."

"Come on, Pop. What could *you* have to trade?"

The old man looked up from the ground, his pale eyes holding the guard's. "The Rexum family murders," he said, softly. "Those four people killed downstate a couple of weeks ago. It was in all the papers."

"Come on, Pop. What could you possibly know about that?"

"I know who did it. I know for sure. And, you know what else? I know what all that knowledge is worth," the old man said, tossing his last handful of dry seeds on the dead ground.

for Kamau Marcharia

AS THE CROW FLIES

Alfred Hitchcock is dead. He's lying there dead, and I don't know what to do about it.

I wasn't surprised when I found him dead on the ground. The woods behind our house are wild—a country where Darwin makes the rules. I'm no philosopher to be saying that; it's just that I've been in places like that myself, so I know how they work.

Alfred Hitchcock was one of those crow-raven hybrids you see around this piece of the coast all the time—too big for a crow, but without that classic thick raven's beak. You couldn't miss him, even at a distance. He had a white streak along one side of his head, like the fire-scar a bullet leaves when it just kisses you on the cheek as it goes by.

He hadn't shown up for a few days, but that didn't worry Dolly. She loves all her animals, but she doesn't regard them as pets. "They have their own ways" is what she always says.

It was Dolly who named him Alfred Hitchcock. "Look how he walks," she said to me one day, pointing out behind the house. "See how *dignified* he is? Not raucous like the others. You never hear a peep out of him. He just paces back and forth, like he's deep in thought."

I realized he *did* kind of look like that famous profile of Alfred Hitchcock, especially the way his head wobbled when he walked. Dolly had names for all the creatures who came to visit, and you could tell she thought about each and every one before she finally decided what to call them.

Take Winston. He's a chipmunk, but not one of those little

things they have back east; this one's damn near the size of a squirrel. Dolly named him because he had a stance like a bulldog. And he was fearless, too. When he saw Dolly on the back deck, he'd rush right up and take a peanut out of her hand. Then he'd just sit on his haunches and strip away the shell casing, the way you'd sit and share a beer with a pal.

Winston had a mate—Dolly called her Mrs. Churchill—and a whole family of little ones. They all lived under one of the sheds in the backyard. The entrance to their den was marked by two jagged pieces of granite I put there, leaving just enough room between them to form a portal. It looked like they'd hired an architect to build it that way.

Dolly also had herself a whole flock of jays. They were a lot bigger than what I'd grown up with in West Virginia. Out here, they're called Steller's jays—big-bodied thugs with black heads and high crests. If Dolly doesn't get out there quick enough in the morning, they hammer on the door with their beaks like a mob of crazed woodpeckers. Dolly goes out with a little bucket of peanuts and just flings the whole thing into the yard. "Slopping the jays" is what she calls it, and that's pretty much on the money; they *do* act like a gang of hogs. No manners at all, wings flailing, shrieking loud enough to empty a cemetery.

Dolly doesn't care how much noise they make, but she won't let them fight. I know it doesn't make sense, but the birds actually seem to mind her. Once, I saw a couple of the jays really get into it over a big fat peanut, leaping into the air and ripping at each other like spurred gamecocks. Dolly yelled, "You two just stop that!" and they did. Even looked a little ashamed of themselves, too.

Sometimes, one of the bolder chipmunks will charge right into the middle of a mob of jays and try and swipe a peanut for himself. But mostly they hang around by their portal, standing straight up like prairie dogs, until I wind up and throw long distance over the jays' heads. The peanuts bounce off the shed, and the jays don't even pay attention.

The roof of the shed is where Alfred Hitchcock always waited. He had his own spot all to himself, and he seemed content to just watch all the ranting and raving without getting involved.

And something was *always* going on back there. Like a couple of hummingbirds duking it out over one particular spot. Those little guys are as territorial as wolverines, and they buzz-bomb each other almost too fast for the eye to follow.

Or maybe a neighbor's cat from down the way would come visiting. Big mistake. The misbegotten mutt Dolly had rescued from the shelter lived out there too, in this little house I built for him. And any cat that walked into the yard would launch Rascal out of his doghouse door like a mortar round.

I think that's why we have so many birds around all the time—Rascal is hell-bent on turning the whole place into a cat-free zone. A dog is like a person—he needs a job and a family to be what he's meant to be. Rascal always came inside for supper, and he'd stay inside until daybreak. He slept on this sheepskin mat I cut for him. First I put it by the door, but Rascal dragged it over until it was just outside our bedroom, and we left it there.

When things got quiet enough to suit him, Alfred Hitchcock would kind of float on down to the yard. He'd go right into his back-and-forth pacing until Dolly would call his name. Then it would be my job to lob a peanut close enough for him to pick it up without acting all undignified, but not so close that he thought I was trying to hit him. I got real good at it.

One day, I was out on the deck by myself, testing some new optics I was putting together, when Alfred showed up. He watched me from his perch on the shed for a long time before he finally dropped into the yard and started his walk.

"Alfred!" I called to him, but he just ignored me.

When Dolly came out later, I told her what happened. "I guess he only likes you," I said.

"It's not that, honey. It's what you said to him."

"I said the same thing you do. Called his name."

"His name is Alfred Hitchcock," Dolly said. "Not Alfred. He's a very dignified bird."

When he came back a few days later, we were both outside. "You try it," Dolly insisted.

"Alfred Hitchcock!" I called.

And damned if the bird didn't stop his walk and cock his head, like he was waiting. I tossed him a peanut. He slowly strolled over, picked it up, very dignified, and lofted himself back to the shed. Dolly and I watched him eat the peanut.

It was a fine moment.

2

Now Alfred Hitchcock is dead, deep back in the woods. If it had been a bobcat that had nailed him, I would have been okay with it. Maybe a little sad, but not all that worked up about it. Dolly doesn't feed the night-hunters, and they have to look out for themselves.

But I know a human kill when I see one. No animal could have wrapped one of Alfred Hitchcock's legs with a strand of wire. No animal uses gasoline. Or matches.

And no animal kills for fun.

3

If it had been a natural predator that killed Alfred Hitchcock, I wouldn't have said a word to Dolly. I would have just given him a proper burial, and let her think he'd moved on. Maybe found himself a girl bird that wanted a dignified mate.

But I knew better than to bury him. I couldn't let whoever had tortured Alfred Hitchcock to death know anybody had seen their work. So I just slipped back the way I'd come.

I didn't leave tracks. I learned that the same place I learned that you don't always get to bury your dead.

4

When I finally got back to the house that day, it was full of kids, like it always is in the afternoons during the week. Teenagers. Dolly's just a magnet for them. Mostly girls, but any time you've got that many girls, there's going to be some boys, too.

She knows how to have fun, my Dolly. Dolly used to be a Rockette, and she can *tell* some stories, believe me. But what she's best at is listening. I know that for a fact. I've told Dolly things I never told anyone else. I had to do that before I asked her to marry me—she had a right to know what she was getting if she said yes.

But there's a lot of stuff I never told Dolly, not out loud. Not because I wanted to keep them a secret. Dolly's got this . . . I don't know the word for it, exactly, but she feels things inside her that *other* people are feeling. I wouldn't ever want Dolly to have some of the feelings I have.

Maybe that's why those kids are always talking to her. Not like some guidance counselor, but like she's the kind of aunt you trust, the kind who'd never rat you out to your folks, no matter what you told her.

She's always teaching those kids something, like how to stitch up those crazy costumes they're wearing out in public today. And they're always teaching *her* stuff, too. Like how to work her cell phone with her thumbs to send messages. She showed me one of those messages one time—it was like it was in a different language. When she tried to explain it to me, I told her I didn't care about stuff like that.

I don't . . . well, I don't *dis*like kids, exactly, but I don't have anything to say to them. And I'm not interested in anything they've got to say, either. What could they know at their age?

The kids are used to me staying in my workshop in the basement, and they never bother me when I'm down there. Dolly doesn't have a lot of rules in her house, but the ones she has, you better follow, or you're eighty-sixed. Like bringing drugs or booze into her house. First time, it's two weeks. If there's a next time, it's your last.

I've actually got *two* places of my own. The basement, and what Dolly calls my den. She fixed it up real fine. It's got a big dark red leather easy chair, and a flat-screen TV with earphones, so I can watch the news without the racket from all those kids bothering me. One wall is nothing but bookshelves. The others have my terrain maps, from different places I've been. And a big porthole window, so I can see right out into the yard.

Some days, I'd be sitting there and Alfred Hitchcock would pace right past that window.

6

Every once in a while, a couple of the boys will wander back to the den. If my door's open, they know they can just walk right in. Sometimes, girls come in there, too.

The boys always want to talk about Vietnam. That was my mistake, I guess, but we never could have bought the house Dolly wanted if it wasn't for me saying I was a vet, and showing them the papers to prove it. A town this size, especially nestled away in a cove of its own, word gets around.

"Did you ever kill anyone?" That's their favorite question.

I always tell them the truth and lie at the same time. "Yes," I would always tell them, "but that's what war is. I never killed anyone who wasn't trying to kill me at the same time."

They think I was infantry. That's what it says on my papers. No Special Forces, no Airborne Ranger, just your basic grunt.

That's all a lie, too. I was in Vietnam, all right, but way after the war. And a lot of other places, too. But I never wore a uniform, and I never carried dog tags.

"Does it make you mad, when people say they're against the war?" they'd want to know. They meant that mess in Afghanistan— the one that spilled back over from Iraq. Some of their relatives had told them stories, about how it hurt them to be fighting for their country and be hated for doing it.

"It doesn't make me angry," I always tell them. And that part's the truth.

"My father says Jane Fonda was a traitor," one of them said, once. I could see he was trying to get me going.

"I can see where he'd think that," I answered.

"But do *you* think that?" one of the girls asked. At that age, they're a lot sharper than boys.

"It's not people like me who matter," I told them. "It's people like you."

"How come?"

"Because the only way anyone listens to someone like Jane Fonda is when people treat them like they're important. You get famous enough, you start to think you're special. If someone's a big enough movie star, journalists ask them questions about stuff they don't know anything about, because their *fans* want to know what a celebrity thinks.

"Jane Fonda was never a soldier. She wasn't a political scientist, or a historian. And she sure was no expert on Southeast Asia. But if she calls a press conference, everybody shows up. That's all that happened."

"That's true!" one of the other girls said, backing me up. A tough-looking little freckle-face with big owl glasses, she looked like she was used to standing her ground. "Once I saw Britney Spears on TV. They were asking her about global warming. I'll bet her idea of global warming is when the air-conditioning breaks."

I caught a glimpse of Dolly smiling at me over the girl's shoulder. I treasure how that makes me feel.

7

The morning after the day I found Alfred Hitchcock, I told Dolly I was driving up to the city. There's always some little things I need for my projects, and she knows I'd never buy anything over the Internet. I asked her if she wanted me to bring back anything for her and she said what she always does: "A surprise!"

I stopped at the nursery first, picked up a whole mess of stuff for Dolly. A couple of gay guys own the place. They're nuts about Dolly. I'm not sure how they feel about me, but that doesn't matter. Not to them; not to me.

I never ask for anything in particular; they just load up whatever they think Dolly might like. We've got Asian lilies growing in big tubs I made out of cut-down barrels. I put some PVC to work as a liner, drilled a few drainage holes, and Dolly did the rest. We've got purple-and-white lilacs, what Dolly calls a butterfly bush. Fuchsia for the hummingbirds. Even some black bamboo— thin, strange-looking stalks with green blades for leaves, not the sharp-edged kind I'd felt before.

This time, I got Dolly some new orchids, for inside the house. Those were my own idea. I know I should have left the nursery stop for last, to keep everything fresh. But I had to get Dolly's surprise done first—I wasn't sure how late I'd be out looking for what I needed. So I misted everything down real good, and covered it all with a dark mesh tarp.

As it turned out, I had to drive quite a distance until I found the place I wanted. They've got a lot of those places in a city about ninety miles away, and they all kind of look alike. Either the glass in the windows is all blacked out or there's no windows at all.

The guy at the desk didn't look up when I came in the door. That's part of his job, same reason they don't have security cameras in those places.

I found what I was looking for easy enough—there was a big selection.

I paid for what I bought the same way I paid for Dolly's plants. I don't have any credit cards, and I don't have a checking account.

Dolly didn't say a word about how long I'd been gone. And she loved everything I brought back. I took the other stuff I'd bought down to my workshop.

8

I knew who he was. Just like I knew Alfred Hitchcock hadn't been his first one.

I didn't need his name, because I had his path. His kind, they always move in straight lines. You may not know where they're going, but you always know where they've been.

The local paper keeps the crime reports on a separate page. Not big crimes, like an armed robbery or a murder. Around here, something like that's so rare it would make headlines. The Crime Beat page is just a printout of the entire police blotter. Drunk driving takes up most of it, with some domestic violence sprinkled in. Lately, a lot of meth busts, too. But you also see things like shoplifting, disorderly conduct, urinating in public . . . any petty little thing you could get arrested for.

The library has a complete archive, going all the way back for years and years. I read three years' worth. Found seven little notices that qualified: five "animal cruelties"—no details; it wasn't that kind of newspaper—and two fires they called "arson, unsolved."

After I marked the locations on my close-terrain map, I could see they were all within a two-and-a-half-mile area. You wouldn't need a car to cover that much ground, no matter where you started from.

I started leaving the door of my den open all the time, even when I wasn't around.

Under the bookshelves, there's a cabinet. It has a lock built into it, but I sometimes forget to use it. You can tell that by looking— the key would still be in the lock, sticking out.

There're magazines in there now. All kinds, from *Soldier of Fortune* to *Playboy* to the stuff I bought on that last visit to the city.

It took a couple of weeks for one of those new ones to go missing. Whoever took it would never notice that I had removed the staples and replaced them with a pair of wire-thin transmitters.

Those transmitters were real short-range, but I was sure I wouldn't need much. I knew he was close.

9

Dolly was asleep when I slipped out that night. Rascal was awake, but he kept his mouth shut. He gave me a look, so I'd know he wasn't sleeping on the job.

When I picked up the signal, I didn't try to track it to the exact house—I wasn't dressed for that kind of risk. All I really needed was the general area, anyway. The library had a city directory, and every school yearbook, too.

The high school was closed for the summer. There was no security guard. The alarm system was probably older than me.

The guidance counselor's office wasn't even locked.

I could tell it was a woman's office without even turning on my fiber-optic pin light. Whoever she was, she kept her file cabinets locked. Cost me an extra fifteen seconds.

Jerrald had a thick file. He'd been evaluated a number of times.

I kept seeing stuff like "attachment disorder." I skipped over the flabby labels and went right to the stone foundation they built those on—the boy had been torturing animals since he was in the second grade.

The counselors wrote that Jerrald was "acting out." Or "crying for help." Some mentioned "conduct disorder." Some talked about medications.

To read what they wrote, you'd think they knew what they were talking about. Every one of his "behaviors" always had some explanation.

But I knew what Jerrald was doing.

Practicing.

10

The counselors had done all kinds of things for Jerrald. Individual therapy. Group therapy. Medication.

The most recent report said he had been making real progress. Jerrald was keeping a blog. I knew what that was from those kids Dolly always had around—a kind of diary they keep on their computers, so other people can see it.

I read some of Jerrald's stuff the counselor had printed out. Torture-rape-murder. The counselor said that the blog was a good outlet for Jerrald; a "safe place for him to vent."

Jerrald's English teacher said his writing showed real promise.

I knew what promises he was going to keep.

I left the school the same way I'd left Alfred Hitchcock's body in the woods.

11

You never work angry—that could get you killed. The best way to keep anger out of your blood is to always do it by the numbers. First, secure the perimeter. By August, I knew Jerrald's parents were going on vacation. To Hawaii. They were taking his little sister with them, but not Jerrald. He was eighteen, more than old enough to leave on his own for a couple of weeks.

I don't know whose idea that was. Or, I guess, whose idea they *thought* it was.

12

The newspapers said Jerrald must have been building some kind of bomb in his room. A pretty serious one, too—it blew out the whole back of his house, where his bedroom was.

They brought in the FBI. Anytime a high school kid gets caught with heavy explosives, they figure it for a terrorist plot. If that doesn't pan out, they look for a Columbine connection.

It was the FBI that told the local TV people the bomb was probably a crude, homemade device. "Very simplistic," their expert said. "You can get instructions how to build one on the Internet."

They printed parts of Jerrald's blog in the papers, and the Columbine connection was all over it. He was obviously a very disturbed young man, most probably the target of school bullying.

13

The town had a big funeral for him. A lot of kids were crying. Dolly went too; some of the kids really wanted her there.

I didn't go. I was out in the deep woods giving Alfred Hitchcock a proper burial. The way he would have wanted it.

for Zak

BLOOD TEST

"Don't put that on!" the gray man driving the generic-looking gray sedan hissed at the much younger man in the passenger seat.

"The boss said—"

"What the boss said was, I'm in charge."

"Yeah, but—"

"The cops see a guy driving around this hour of the night, wearing a ski mask in the middle of June, they make up some excuse—busted taillight, smeared license plate, doesn't matter—and they pull us over."

"They got to have probable cause—"

"Where'd you hear that, from one of the big-time gangsters last time you were in the county tank? The cops tell the judge how they found us both wearing latex gloves, with a couple of unregistered pieces under the seat, and the judge, he's going to, what? Toss out the case?"

"That's why the boss has lawyers, man. He said no matter what happened, he could always—"

"You know what we're supposed to do tonight, right?"

"Yeah. We're going take out that—"

"That's the *job,* understand? That's what we have to get done. That's what a job is, something you have to get done. You think we could go ahead and get it done *after* we got stopped by the law? Gun-felony bust, this town, even if some bought-and-paid-for judge eventually kicked us loose, they'd hold us for twenty-four hours, minimum, just waiting on arraignment. You think the boss is gonna like paying out a bunch of bribes instead of paying *us*?"

"I—"

"You *never* get impatient. That's a rule you can't break. We put the masks on *just* before we go in, understand? That way, anybody spots us back of the joint, they make us for a couple of drunks, or maybe we're trying to wait on one of the girls when they come out."

"I don't see why we got to do it right where he—"

"You want to learn, the first thing you learn is, pay attention. This is a *job,* all right? It's *work.* And part of every job is doing it the way the client wants it done. *Where* he wants it done, *when* he wants it done, and *how* he wants it done, understand?"

"The boss—"

"The boss *is* the client."

"Yeah, yeah. I got it. But why does he want it done like this?"

"You ask a lot of questions."

"Hey, I'm just trying to learn, okay? You're supposed to be the big pro, right? The boss said I got to do this one with you, so I'm doing it, ain't I? I mean, I could do it myself, but—"

"Only you never have."

"Everybody's a virgin once. Even you. When was your first one, about a hundred years ago?"

"More questions?"

"I didn't mean nothing by it."

"Yeah."

"Look, after tonight, you ain't going to have to put up with me, okay? The boss said, I do this one with you, I pass the test, I'm blooded in. After that, I can work on my own. Just like you."

"That's between you and the boss."

The gray car rolled past a free-standing one-story building set in the middle of an unlit parking lot. The building had no windows; its slab-sided monotony was broken only by the glowing red outline of an impossibly proportioned woman and various other promises, wrapped around three sides of the building in streams of neon:

XXX TOTALLY NUDE XXX GIRL-GIRL SHOWS
XXX PRIVATE ROOMS XXX

The gray man checked his watch, said, "Four-fifteen is the time we move. We've got a seven, eight minute margin. We'll pull into the back, sit there for a minute, make sure it's clear."

"What's the big deal, a few minutes either way?"

The gray man made a sound of disgust, but didn't speak. He slowly wheeled the gray sedan around the back of the strip joint, positioning it carefully at an angle so he could watch both the back door of the building and the streets that ran along either side of the parking lot.

"Yeah, well, I guess you ain't perfect, pal," the younger man said. "I heard you did a real long stretch a while back."

"Is that right? What else did you 'hear' about that?"

"I heard you did almost twenty years. For a contract hit."

"It was seventeen and change. And it was for a homicide—nobody ever proved it was paid for. In fact, I'm still on parole; I pulled a Life for that one. But it looks like you didn't 'hear' anything you could use."

"What're you talking about, man? I'm not planning on doing no seventeen years."

"Nobody *plans* on doing time. It's *how* you do it, that's the test."

"What's that supposed to mean?"

"I went down by myself. Just me, nobody else. You following me?"

"Sure. You didn't rat nobody out."

"Which is why I'm still working for the same people, see? Like I said, that was a test. And I passed it."

"You did all that time, and you're still doing . . . this?"

"If I was a plumber, and I did seventeen years inside, what would I do when I got out, be an architect?"

"The boss should've taken care of you. I mean, seventeen *years . . .*"

"*I* was the one who got caught, not the boss. So I was the one who had to do the time. That's the way it works."

"But he *did* take care of you while you were—?"

"Everyone makes their own arrangement. I made mine, and I stuck to it."

"Big deal. I—"

"Put that away! No smoking on the job."

"Why not? We ain't playing with gasoline, here."

"We're not *playing* at all. They can get DNA from saliva."

"Fine! Jesus, look, how come it's gotta be exactly four-fifteen."

"Because that's when he'll be in the back office."

"The bouncers—"

"They'll all be out front. He likes to bring a couple of the girls back there with him when the last shift's almost over, and he doesn't like to be interrupted."

"The back door might be—"

"It'll be open."

"How can you be so sure?"

"Sometimes a man's on more than one payroll."

"You mean one of the bouncers—?"

"It's time," the gray man said.

He opened the door. The sedan's interior light did not come on. The gray man stepped out into the night, slipped the ski mask over his head, and motioned for the younger man to do the same.

The gray man reached under the front seat and extracted a blued steel semi-auto. By the time the younger man joined him, holding a similar weapon, the gray man was screwing a long tube onto the front of his pistol. Again, the younger man copied each move.

They walked casually to the back door of the club. No lights shone on the back side of the building. The gray man held his weapon straight down, dangling by his side, and used his free hand to turn the doorknob. Slowly. It yielded.

He stepped inside, the younger man close behind.

To their left, a sign said DRESSING ROOMS. The gray man turned right, walked a short length of hall, then turned right again, heading for the farthest corner of the building. He motioned for the younger man to stay back a few steps. The only sound was the music coming from the front of the strip club.

The gray man stepped through the door of the dimly lit office. A pudgy man with a red face was sprawled in an office chair. He was fully dressed, but the pants of his suit were puddled around his ankles. A skinny brunette with improbable breasts knelt in front of him; a heftier blonde with a more believable chest stood slightly to one side, as if waiting her turn.

"Anybody screams, everybody dies," the gray man said.

All three pairs of eyes magneted to the silenced pistol he was holding.

"You," he said, pointing to the kneeling brunette with the pistol, "get up. Go over and stand with the other one."

The brunette got up without a word. The gray man nodded. The younger man walked over to the two women, stuck his pistol awkwardly in his waistband, and handcuffed the women together, using two cuffs on each wrist and crossing the chains.

"Turn around and face the wall," the gray man told them.

They did it, moving in sync as if accustomed to being yoked together.

"Where's the rest of it?" the gray man asked the man in the office chair, indicating a half dozen lines of cocaine on a hand mirror resting on top of the desk.

"In the safe," the man in the office chair said, his voice tired and resigned, just on the edge of boredom.

"Get it."

"Sure," the red-faced man said, scrambling to pull up his pants as he rose. "Whatever you—"

"Open the safe," the gray man said.

As soon as the red-faced man started to turn the safe's dial, the gray man stepped close to him and fired a single shot into the back of his head. The red-faced man dropped. The gray man knelt next to him and put a bullet into each eye. Then another into his right ear. Each shot made a *splaat!* sound, inaudible outside the office.

The gray man stood up, unscrewed the silencer, and pocketed each half of the disassembled weapon in a separate pocket of his coat. Empty-handed, he motioned for the younger man to move away from the women.

"Hey, wait a minute," the younger man said. "You know what the boss said."

"Shut up."

"The boss said 'no witnesses,' man!" the younger man whispered harshly, nodding his head urgently in the direction of the handcuffed women, who were still facing the wall. "We got plenty of time. No reason I can't have a little taste of that stuff, first."

"No."

"No? The test is whether I can follow orders, right? Well, the order was 'no witnesses.' You were right there when the boss said it. He didn't say nothing about not—"

"When the boss said 'no witnesses,' he wasn't talking to you; he was talking to me."

"So? What difference does that—?"

"All right," the gray man said. "But hurry it up. And give me that piece—you're gonna need both hands free."

The younger man handed his pistol to the gray man, and turned toward the women. The gray man briefly examined the weapon in his hand, shook his head, flicked off the safety, said "Hey!" very softly. The younger man turned. The gray man shot him between the eyebrows. The gray man knelt next to the body and added three more bullets, exactly as he had done to the man in the office chair.

The gray man took the pistol he had used to kill the club owner from his pocket and reattached the silencer. He put the weapon on the desk, his movements sure and unhurried. Then he stripped off the surgeon's gloves he had been wearing, being careful to turn them inside out, revealing still another pair of gloves underneath. He removed the single-layer gloves from the body of the younger man, pocketed them, then regloved the body with the outer gloves he had removed from his own hands.

Satisfied, he wrapped the younger man's hand around the pistol used to kill the club owner. He broke down the younger man's weapon and stowed the separate pieces.

The gray man got to his feet. "You know the story you have to tell," he said to the handcuffed women. "And what happens if you don't."

They didn't answer him. He hadn't expected them to.

The gray man walked out of the office, down the hall, and out into the night, pulling the ski mask off his head as he moved. The gray sedan was gone. A black sedan was parked in its place, engine idling quietly.

The gray man got into the backseat. The black sedan pulled away.

for Mike MacNamara

PROFILE
A Cross Story

1

"This one is mine," the girl said, as her fingers danced over an ergonomic keyboard with an attached wrist cushion. Her posture was boarding-school perfect: back straight, wrists resting on the keyboard's cushion, forearms parallel to the floor.

The girl was almost thirteen. To her wealthy father, an ongoing source of bafflement. To the three men in the room with her, a job.

The man standing close to the girl's right side was utterly unremarkable, a human generic. "He looks like every guy you ever saw walking down the street," a cop named McNamara had once described him. "Probably could get a job being the extra at line-ups." The man was wearing a dark business suit over a white Kevlar shirt and a plain black tie.

Several feet to that man's left was a creature so mammoth as to cause gasps at first sight, his huge, formless body encased in a putty-gray jumpsuit. He stood motionless, right hand gripping his left wrist. The tip to the forefinger of that hand was missing—the remaining digit as smoothly polished as an aluminum cigar tube. And roughly the same size.

Directly behind the girl, peering over her shoulder excitedly, was a man who would have been described as "huge" if not for the contrast of the monster in the same room. This glowing specimen was dressed in a chartreuse tank top over a pair of sunburst-yellow parachute pants, his impossibly overdeveloped arms and chest bulging even at rest. Every visible inch of his body was ripped with corded muscle, as chiseled as a quarry-stone statue. His head was shaved, and polished to cue-ball smoothness. But the overdone body and outrageous costume were seemingly mocked by a mud-thick application of makeup. His eyes were surrounded with enough mascara to print a page. A heavy blush of rouge adorned his cheeks. And his Eau de Walmart cologne was slathered on heavily enough to displace smog.

The computer's screen popped into life.

> Name: AriaBlue11888
>
> Location: Chicago
>
> Sex: You wish!
>
> Marital Status: Shut up!
>
> Birthdate: I'm almost legal.
>
> Computer: Pul-leeze!
>
> Hobbies: HangN wiD mah girlz, Buffy TVS, gettin' in trouble.
>
> Personal Quote: "The Internet's no different from any other piece of technology. It's neutral, like a scalpel. In the hands of a surgeon, it cuts out cancer. In the hands of a freak, it cuts out hearts."
>
> —Andrew Vachss

"That's a profile," the girl explained. "So anyone who wants to check you out can see what's up with you, understand?"

"You make it up yourself?" the unremarkable man asked quietly.

"Sure. I never put photos on my page, though. That would make it . . . well, make it too real."

"But you *could* put anything. . . ."

"Of *course.* I mean, that's part of the fun too, see? It's all just . . . fun. Don't you get tired of just using e-mail?"

"I don't use it."

"You *what*? I mean, how do you, like, send messages and stuff?"

"Face-to-face."

"But what if the other person's far away?"

"Nobody's ever far away enough that you can't reach out and touch them."

"You're . . . so, like, strange. Here," she challenged, pointing a blue-lacquered fingernail at the screen. "Do you even know what that means?"

"I know! I know!" the hypermuscled man said excitedly. "Buffy TVS. That's *Buffy the Vampire Slayer,* right?"

"No-oh," the girl said, mock-annoyed. "That's 'Buffy, TV Show.' See, there was a *movie,* too. Very OldSchool, but it *was* the first one. Most people, fans, I mean, they like the TV show. But there's always the ones just have to start where *it* started. That's so—"

"There was a *movie?*" the bodybuilder demanded, turning slowly toward the jump-suited monster, an accusatory tone in his voice.

"Well, of *course,*" the girl said. "I mean . . . it's old now, but it's still around. You can still catch it on cable, on one of those movie channels. And there's all kinds of Web sites for Buffy fans, so if you really wanted, you could—"

"Rhino . . . ?" the bodybuilder asked, plaintively.

"Yes," the monster replied. The single word came out a high-pitched squeak. "We'll check the Internet. We'll find out when the movie will be on TV. And we'll watch it. And if we're not around, we'll record it, and then watch it later. All right, Princess?"

"Awwwriiight!" the bodybuilder shouted, firing a high five that the behemoth met deftly. The sound was slightly softer than a sledgehammer on steel. The girl turned toward the unremarkable man. He made a "don't mind them" face, then asked, "So how do you know, then? The people you talk to online, how do you know who they are in real life?"

"You *don't,*" the girl said tartly. "You sound just like my father." She sighed, larding the words with that world-weary emphasis only teenage girls have ever mastered. "*I* know this is all a game. Like I actually believe I have a thousand 'friends' just because they're on my Facebook page. As if!

"This is . . . it's just playing. But *he* thinks there are monsters hiding under my bed. Is that what you're here to do, check under my bed, make sure the closets are clear? You're not going to find anything."

"We get paid to look," the unremarkable man said mildly.

2

"You know what?" the girl said an hour later. "If I *did* tell anyone about this, they'd never believe me."

"Is that right?" the unremarkable man said, indifferently.

"Oh, I don't mean *you*," she said haughtily. "I mean Princess. He's like . . . I mean, you're *all* like—I didn't mean to talk about you like you aren't even here, that's what *they* do all the time with me—but you really *are* like something out of a movie."

"What movie?" Princess eagerly asked the girl.

"One of those kung fu ones, maybe," she answered thoughtfully. "Only, with your . . . with all that . . . I mean, maybe a rock video . . . ?"

"I don't like those so much," the human rock sculpture said, petulantly. "They're no fun. People are mean in them. The karate ones are good, though, right, Rhino? Especially when they fly around and stuff."

"They're swell," the mammoth said, busy with an oversized keyboard he had connected to the girl's computer. A maze of anaconda wires ran from the back of the girl's computer into two separate boxy devices he had removed from a duffel bag big enough to house RPGs.

"What *is* all that stuff?" the girl asked, bouncing slightly on her bed, to which she had retreated in a huff, arms crossed over her chest.

"Test equipment," the unremarkable man told her.

"What *kind* of equipment? I'm not dumb. If you explain it to me, I'll understand."

"We're trying to find out if anyone has put anything into your computer."

"You mean, like a virus?"

"Sure."

"I don't believe you," she said, sternly. "There's no way my father paid all you . . . guys to come in here and see if I got some stupid virus—you're not exactly geeks, if you know what I mean. I think he'd be *glad* if I did, anyway. Then I couldn't go online for a while."

"There's different kinds of bugs," the unremarkable man replied.

"Well, *what* kinds?" she demanded.

"Yeah, what kinds, Cross?" Princess joined in.

The unremarkable man squeezed his eyes tightly shut, as if fighting off a severe headache. Then he breathed deeply through his nose, exhaled slowly, and said, "When we came in, your computer was already on, right? You were using it for . . . whatever you do."

"Uh . . . *yes,*" the girl said, managing to blend annoyance and sarcasm into a single word.

"For how long?"

"For how . . . ? Oh, I see what you mean. I was online for, I don't know, maybe an hour or so."

"Then there's no way we could have seen your password, right?"

"Well . . . no. Especially with the one I—"

"And nobody but you *has* your password?"

"Not a chance," she sneered. "I mean, who's that stupid? You give even your BFF your password, you have a little fight, and, the next thing you know, your page is all vandalized. Anyway, it's *my* computer, and I—"

"Sure," he interrupted. "You're right. Okay, Rhino, let her back at the keyboard for a minute."

"What do you want me to do?" she said, as she reclaimed her chair.

"Just turn it off."

"The IM I was talking on, the Facebook I get off Mozilla, or the whole thing?"

"You have a password just to turn the computer itself on, or only for the online stuff?"

"I'm always online. I mean, it's a DSL connection, so I don't have to log on to—"

"Never mind. Just shut it *all* down, okay?"

"Well, I don't see why. . . .." the girl muttered to herself, but she haughtily tapped on the keyboard, clicked her mouse, and the computer went quiet. "There! Happy now? Or do you want me to disengage the monitor, too."

The unremarkable man ignored her. "Rhino . . ."

As the girl went back to sitting on her bed, the mammoth immediately keyed in a series of commands. The screen blinked, flashed twice, and then "Recovery in Progress" appeared.

"What's he doing?" the girl asked.

"Running a password-recovery program."

"What's that?"

"It's for people who forget their passwords. It works just as good for people who want to get inside your system."

"You mean he can just—" she asked, suddenly cutting herself off as her screen name popped into life.

"You're back online," the unremarkable man said. "You've even got mail. And DMs waiting, too. Now how about you go play with Princess or something and let us finish what we're doing?"

"Play? I'm not a—"

"Yeah. Sure. Right. Fine. Okay. Why don't you and Princess go have a few drinks or smoke some dope? How's that?"

3

"Do you have an appointment?" the brunette behind the blue-veined white marble reception cube asked the unremarkable man.

"Three-fifteen."

"Yes, I understand," the brunette said, speaking slowly, so she wouldn't confuse the obviously dull individual standing before her. "You told me that. All I need is your name, if you don't mind."

"Winslow, he's the boss, right?"

"Mr. Anthony Winslow is the CEO of Rampartel Enterprises, if that's what you mean."

"That's who I have the appointment with. At three-fifteen."

"Yes," she said patiently. "I understand, sir. But I *still* don't have your—"

"Call his secretary," the man said. "Ask *her* my name."

"That's not the way we—"

"Yeah, it is."

The brunette hadn't been hired just for decoration. "Please wait over there," she said, gesturing toward a white leather couch.

The man didn't seem to move. But when the brunette looked up from her console, he was standing in front of the couch, still facing her.

"Jani," she whispered into her headset. "There's a man here who says he—"

The brunette listened for a minute, intently. Then she looked up saying, "Sir? You can go right . . ." But she was talking to empty space—the man was gone.

4

"You're certain you can . . . solve this problem?"

Cross scanned the speaker. He clocked the facts: a man in his late forties, trim and tanned, with a haircut that cost more than some men pay for a suit. The man's own suit was bespoke dark green alpaca, with just a hint of ecru raw silk peeking out from the arms, hinting at high-status cufflinks.

Probably has a different wristwatch for each outfit, Cross thought to himself. But all he said aloud was, "Yes."

"Just . . . 'yes'?"

"I don't get paid by the word."

"What *do* you get paid by, then?" the man behind the desk asked, the faintest trace of annoyance wafting over his words.

"Degree of difficulty."

"And how . . . uh, *difficult* do you anticipate this particular solution to be?"

"The most difficult solutions are the permanent ones."

The man behind the desk turned pale under his eye-color-matched tan. "I won't have my daughter . . . bothered. I suppose that isn't the right word. I don't know what the right word for all this would *be*. You're certain she's being . . . what was that word you used . . . lured? Enticed?"

"The person or persons making contact through her computer are trying to get her to meet them, yes."

"How do you know this? Are you just guessing, or do you have some form of wiretap on her computer?"

"No," Cross told him. "We hijacked it."

"I'm not following you."

"We took over your daughter's address," Cross said. "We let all the traffic through except for when whoever's trying to get her to meet them sends a message. That's diverted, so it goes to us. And the answer they get, it *comes* from us. We've been dialoguing with whoever it is for a couple of weeks, now."

"But when Ariel writes to him . . . ?"

"It's mostly messages, not really e-mails, but that doesn't matter. When she talks to him, she's talking to us, real-time or e-mail. And we answer her. We use *their* answers, so it always sounds right. To both sides, okay?"

"I . . . see," the man said, making a steeple of his fingertips, thinking.

Cross sat in silence, his face as expressionless as the bare top of the man's desk.

"Let me just understand. This . . . person or persons, as you put it . . . is only in contact with *you,* now. So if all Ariel's attempts to communicate with whoever they are go through you, she's not in any danger, is she?"

"She talked too much," Cross said, flatly.

"You mean, before you . . . ?"

"Yeah. If she'd stayed virtual, it wouldn't matter—your DSL IP floats. But whoever she was talking to wormed her real name out of her. They know where she lives. Where she goes to school. All kinds of intel, right down to what her bedroom looks like. The only thing she's held back—so far—is a picture of herself. And they've probably already got one. School yearbook, places like that."

"Ariel told you she—?"

"Ariel didn't tell us anything. She thinks it's all a game. But once we plugged in, we could see it all for ourselves."

"I see. What do you propose, then?"

"We set up a meet. Whoever's on the other end thinks they're meeting your daughter. Instead, they meet us."

"And then . . . ?"

"Degree of difficulty."

The man behind the desk said nothing.

Cross looked through the man's skull to the wall behind it.

Finally, the man broke the silence. "One of the reasons I'm successful is that I know how to listen," he said. "You're the professional. So I leave it up to you. If you conclude this 'person or persons' represents an actual danger to my daughter . . .'"

"You *don't* know how to listen," Cross said, very quietly. "That 'actual' qualifier you added, it's like a string. You cut it, somebody comes along and reties it. You set it on fire in the middle, it burns down each side until there's nothing left to tie."

The man behind the desk didn't hesitate. His nod wasn't an indication of understanding, it was one of agreement.

"I already told you how to send the money," Cross said. "Just a few keystrokes. Transfer the money. When we get half, we go to work."

"Half of . . ."

"Half of the max."

"But what if you don't have to . . . ?"

"Then the half *is* the max."

5

"Take out the shunt, Rhino," the unremarkable man said.

"But keep it on real-time monitoring?"

"Yeah. If he's going to go for it, we have to give him the chance. It's the only way we'll ever know, and we need to wrap this up, one way or the other."

"Go for what?" Princess demanded. "He's not going to hurt Ariel, is he?"

"No," Cross reassured the walking menace. "No, he's not."

6

Three weeks later, the girl strolled out the elaborately carved front doors of the private school she had attended since kindergarten. She was wearing her school uniform, but there was a complete change of clothes in the backpack she carried.

The note from her father asking that she be excused from afternoon classes because of a family trip had not drawn a second glance. Despite the perfect forgery of her father's signature—Ariel had a great deal of practice—the school had still called to verify.

Ariel didn't know who would be answering the number printed next to her father's name on the stationery Cross had handed to her, but her special friend had promised her he could get someone who sounded "old" to take the call.

Ariel thought about that special friend as she walked around the corner. She felt a shiver at the base of her spine when she spied the black limousine. Waiting for her, just as he had promised. Just right for the star she was going to be.

A man in a chauffeur's uniform opened the back door, and Ariel climbed into the backseat. The partition was closed, but she wasn't concerned. Her special friend had told her about that in advance. It certainly wasn't any of some *driver's* business who she was.

The limo smoothly negotiated the streets of Chicago. Ariel recognized the route to O'Hare—her father was always flying in and out of town, and, sometimes, she got to go to the airport to meet him.

The limo pulled up to a motel court. The seediness of the place was no surprise—her special friend had explained that another car would meet them both later, and they'd go to someplace more appropriate.

The limo moved slowly, like a majestic ship through a dirty-water canal. It stopped at the door of Cabin 6. Ariel hopped out, her backpack in one hand, and knocked on the door.

"Come in," she heard.

She turned the doorknob and walked inside.

"Sit over there," Cross told her, pointing to a bed covered in plastic garbage bags. "And be quiet."

7

"He was lying all the time?" Ariel said, an hour later, looking up from her laptop computer screen.

"Not about what he wanted to do with you," Cross told her.

"I wasn't going to do *that*! I was just . . ."

"Playing, yeah," Cross said. "You were. He wasn't."

"He's *really* a . . . ?"

"Convicted child molester, yes. That's him; that's what he does. He even belongs to an organization that 'loves' little girls. Rhino, pull up their site for her."

8

"I'm scared," Ariel said. "I told him . . . stuff. Stuff about me. Maybe he told some of those other . . ."

"Don't be afraid," Princess told her. Ariel unconsciously moved closer to the hypermuscled man, her mind not registering that he was dressed in a gray sweatshirt and matching drawstring pants, with a black watch cap covering his shaven skull. Or that his face was scrubbed clean of makeup.

"You understand, there's no more of this, right?" Cross told her. "You change your e-mail address, you stay out of chat rooms, you do all the stuff Rhino showed you how to do if you want to make friends online. . . ."

"And you won't tell my father?"

"That's our deal," Cross said, reaching out his hand for the girl to shake. She finally noticed something unusual about the man—a bull's-eye tattoo on the back on his right hand.

9

An hour later, Ariel turned to Cross. They were both sitting in the backseat of the heavy sedan that was taking her home. The man at the wheel was wearing the same dark watch cap as Princess had, but he was half the muscleman's size. He piloted the big car expertly, sliding through the streets like a shark that had recently fed. It wasn't hungry, but it still wouldn't be a good idea to attract its attention.

"He's going to . . . ? He's going to do this with other girls, isn't he?"

"No."

"How can you be so *sure?*"

"The FBI is on to him," Cross said, his voice unchanged even when it moved from certain truth to outrageous lie. "He got the word, and took off for Cambodia. That's why he wanted to meet you so near the airport. He's running scared, now. He can't come back here, not ever."

"But on the computer—"

"No one's ever going to hear from him again," Cross told her. "The kind of technology he'd need for that hasn't been invented yet."

10

Ariel's father pushed a button on what looked like a miniature version of a spaceship's console. He noted that neither the caller ID nor the GPS locator seemed to be working properly. They were blinking and changing colors, but not providing any information. Before he could speak, a voice came through the console's speaker.

"You know where to send the other half."

"Yes, I know *where* to send it. What I don't know is if it was earned."

"What would prove it to you?"

"If Ariel isn't—"

"She won't be."

"How do I know that? How do I know you even . . . identified the right person?"

"You want to be sure, we can send you his profile," Cross said. "It'll come FedEx, packed in dry ice. Billed to recipient—I'll need your account number for that. Tell your secretary not to open any package from Mr. Green, just bring it in to you. And make sure you're alone when you open it. Once you see what's inside, you send the money. *Disposing* of what's inside, that's your problem."

Five seconds of silence followed. Dead silence.

The girl's father, finally realizing his only options were to speak or hang up, said, "That's all right," hastily. "I'll take your word for it. Just wait a . . . *There!* The money's in your account, all right? There's no further need to—"

"Not anymore, there isn't," Cross said, just before he severed the connection.

for Buddha

LAST RIGHTS

1

The priest had not been a young man for many years. Yet his face was serenely unlined, his chestnut hair still thick and full, and the set of his trim body radiated self-assurance. He strode toward the confessional with the measured gait of an experienced boxer making his way to the ring.

Still doing this, a rueful bitterness misted his thoughts. *With all the time I have devoted to service, I should be . . . a monsignor, perhaps? The head of a diocese? Director of a prestigious parochial school? Instead, that endless series of transfers, each one a step down the ladder I should have been climbing. And now this dying parish in a neighborhood from which most of the true believers have fled. Yet there is no anger in me, for I accept that I am but an instrument of God's will. I serve him, as I was chosen to serve.*

The priest could make out the vague outline of the person on the other side of the screen. His scanning skills, honed by decades of practice, instantly computed that the penitent was a white male with a prominent jaw, his head covered with one of those stupid watch caps, even though it was a sweltering August morning.

Not one of the old congregation stopping by, the priest thought. *Not one of today's regulars, either; too young. But this was no teenager—he was a grown man. And a stranger.*

The priest tuned out the ritualistic preconfessional words spoken by the man on the other side of the screen. He had a library of standard responses, cataloged by whatever sins were acknowledged. Forgiveness was his to dispense, and he was always generous with it. No matter what sin was confessed, forgiveness would never be withheld. *Whatever this one has to say, it won't be the first time I've heard it.*

"Father, I have violated the Sixth Commandment."

"How did this come about, my son?"

"I entered a man's home while he was asleep. I paralyzed him by jamming a nerve-juncture, then I blocked his air passages and locked him down until he was gone."

"What would cause you to commit such an act?" the priest asked, more curious than shocked.

"Because that's what I do."

"I don't understand. Are you saying that . . . that you have done this before?"

"Killed? Yes. Many times."

"Is this something you feel compelled to do, my son?" the priest asked, genuine empathy embracing the timbre of his resonant voice. "Are there times when you—"

"I killed that man for money, Father. That's what I do. That is my work."

"You are . . . you are an assassin, then?"

"Yes. For a long time."

"Then why seek forgiveness now?" the priest asked, wondering if he was listening to a demented man's fantasy, or, Lord forbid, some foul little degenerate's idea of a "prank."

"It was time."

"I understand," the priest said, soothingly. "But something must have occurred for you to have decided this was the time to seek forgiveness."

"It was time because it *took* time."

The priest peered at the screen. Was it his imagination, or had the other man's shape shifted? He seemed . . . not smaller, exactly, but more difficult to focus on.

"Perhaps if you told me . . ."

"Told you? Is God listening now, Father?"

"God is always listening, my son."

"And always watching."

"Of course."

"So, when I tell you, it's the same as if I was telling—?"

"Yes," the priest interrupted, feeling the power inside himself grow as the man on the other side of the screen's appearance faded. It had been many years since that feeling had raced through his blood, but he always knew it would come to him again. He had faith in the knowledge that the power he had been given could never die—it was a banked fire, awaiting its time to blaze anew. "Perhaps if you told me when this began?" he said, encouraging with both his will and his words.

The man on the other side was silent for thirty seconds. Again, his shape seemed to shift, but the priest realized this was just a light-and-shadow play—the truth never changes, no matter what the senses perceive.

"When I was a boy, a man made me do things. And he did things to me. He didn't force me. I wasn't beaten, or tied up, or even threatened. I was . . . what was that word you used before? 'Compelled'? I think that's right. I was compelled. The man was . . . very special. I believed in him. I knew he had powers.

"Then one day, the man was gone. There was another man in his place. I felt . . . I felt relieved and betrayed at the same time, if that makes any sense. So I told him, the new man, what I had done, and he granted me forgiveness. And that, that was when I knew."

"Knew what, my son?"

"Knew that I must have wanted those things to happen. They didn't happen to everyone, so I must have wanted them to happen to me. But I hated those things, those things I did, so I was con-fused. When I told this to the new man, he explained it all. I had a moral weakness in me, but, if I worked hard, I could fight the weakness and defeat it. With the Lord's help.

"I believed. So the first thing I did was to make myself strong. I spent all my time in a place for weight lifters. I wanted to be big. Huge. So people would look at me and say, 'He couldn't possibly be a . . .'"

The priest waited. Patience had been difficult for him to master when he first began, but, over time, he had learned how valuable an asset it could be.

"But those places were full of them," the man continued. "I couldn't ever be sure. I didn't even want to take a shower there. So I went to another kind of gym. A boxing gym.

"I wasn't good at it, but I never, ever showed fear. No matter how hard I got hit, I didn't even feel it. But, even there, those showers . . ."

The priest debated within himself, then decided that too much prompting would interrupt the flow. Another skill he had learned over the years.

"In high school, before I dropped out, I had girlfriends," the man said. "Never for long, because I was always grabbing at them, like I was trying to make them put out. Force them. I wanted to show them. Show them all. Show them right then. In school, people said things about me, but I didn't care. Because they never said the one word that would kill me.

"Besides, I never wanted one of the nice girls, anyway. I wanted one of my own kind.

"Like I said, I quit school. I went in the army. I was so lucky there was a war. I got to be brave, out where everyone could see it for themselves. Even the ones who whispered about me being crazy, that was the same as high school—there's worse things to be called, and I never was.

"The only scary part came when my platoon caught this girl. Everyone took a turn with her. I had to do it."

"You had to rape a defenseless woman?"

"Yes," the man said, as if the answer was self-evident.

"Did you ever do anything like that again?"

"No. I had already proved myself. When I got out, I had the proof. Medals and everything. But I never felt . . . safe."

"Safe from what, my son?"

"Safe from the truth. The truth in me. The truth that special man had told me about myself. He told me, if I hadn't wanted it, it never would have happened."

"You were afraid you were a—?"

"No. I already knew that was what I was. What I was afraid of was anyone finding out. So I had to be the opposite. The opposite of the truth."

"So you got married and—?"

"No. No, I didn't get married. What would that prove? Plenty of *them* are married. I went someplace far away. Where they have holy men. Not the same kind of holy man I told you about, but sort of like that. Only I didn't ever talk to them. I went to the place where they are so I could learn what I needed to be safe."

"Did you learn those things?"

"Yes. But not from them. I went to their . . . place because I thought only holy men knew these things. But they didn't want me. I told them I was willing to do anything to prove myself worthy, but it didn't matter. They didn't want me.

"At first, I thought it was because they knew. So I kept looking. And I found other men who would sell the secrets I needed. That's when I knew there was nothing holy about what I was looking for, because a holy man would not sell secrets."

"I don't understand. What secrets do you mean?"

"The secrets of their training. There was nothing . . . spiritual about it, not the way they taught. But it wasn't for everyone. You had to find them, first. If you could find them, you knew you would have to pay."

"Yes. You already said—"

"No. Money was only part of the price. You also pay with pain.

It took a long time. They did all kinds of things to me. Sometimes, it was so bad that my whole world was a throbbing red blaze. But they never actually hurt me; nobody can do that."

"And you endured all of that because of . . . ?"

"Yes. And it was years before I truly felt safe. I was still alone, but that's what I wanted. It's the only way to be safe, to be alone.

"I don't know if the people who hired me ever judged me, but it never felt as if they did. Maybe because they didn't care, maybe because they were afraid of me. But as long as I didn't feel anything, it didn't matter."

"How many—"

"What difference?" the man said. "I don't keep score. I'm not in a contest. It's not something they give awards for. Nobody will ever know who's the best at it, because anyone who is truly the best will never be known."

"Your sin is—"

"The worst one of all," the man interrupted. "I committed the sin of forgiveness."

"There is no such sin!" the priest said, sharply. "God teaches us that—"

"It was all a lie," the man said, as calmly as if he were giving directions to a stranger. "I never secretly wanted any of those things. It was never inside me. I didn't have some moral weakness. I was not a degenerate.

"It took me a whole lifetime to understand that. What that special man saw in me wasn't that I wanted to . . . do those things. No, what he saw was weakness, the same way a predator always sees the easiest prey. A special man always sees a special weakness. And I had that. That weakness that makes me . . . *made* me . . . think I had been chosen because the special man could see me for what I really was.

"I was supposed to be the sinner. And when the special man

left, the one who took his place, he proved that. He granted me forgiveness for what I had done. For my sins.

"See? That forgiveness meant that those things I did, they had to have been in me all along. The special man could see it. But I knew nobody else ever would if I did all the right things. And that's what I did. All the right things."

"You ask for forgiveness, yet you blaspheme with your very request," the priest said, voice thickening with condemnation.

"You still don't understand, do you?" the man said. "The only sin I committed was accepting the forgiveness. All those things I did, those right things, to prove I wasn't what the special man said I was, I never would have done any of that if I hadn't been forgiven, first."

"You are very confused, my son. But it is not too—"

"This is my confession. You listen to me. When I took the blame, when I accepted forgiveness for what had been done to me, it was the same as forgiving the man who was the true sinner. That was my sin."

"Forgiveness is never a—"

"Is that what they told you, every time you got discovered? Is that what they told you when they transferred you to another parish, where you could just pick a new target, and do it again? Is that what you really, truly believe? Is that your faith? That you can rape little boys, over and over and over again, and you will always be forgiven?"

"Who are—?"

"You know," the man's voice said.

How could his voice be coming from behind me? was the priest's last thought. And that thought lasted throughout his final test of faith.

for Grier

POSTWAR BOOM

"What's your name, anyway?"

"What difference?"

"Come on, pal. We're gonna be working together next couple of weeks or so. Just two vets, riding around, seeing the country. That's the story they gave us. So I gotta have *something* to call you by, just in case."

"Case of what?"

"It's one hell of a drive, all the way to L.A. Cops stop us, I should know what name's on your ID, right?"

"I was hitching a ride."

"In that suit? Not gonna fly. No reason to make things complicated, I gotta call you quick. Down the road, I mean."

The short, compactly built man in the passenger seat of the big sedan said nothing for a few seconds. Finally, as if conceding the reasonableness of the driver's request, said, "Mendil," without turning his head.

"Mendil?" the thickset man behind the wheel said. "What kind of name is that?"

"Just a name."

"There ain't no such thing as 'just a name,' pal. Take me, for instance. I tell you my name is Seamus O'Reilly, you know I'm Irish, am I right?"

"No."

"No What other kind of name *could* it be?"

"Fake."

"Huh! Well, right you are at that one. But my mug's a map of

Galway, as my mother used to say. Every chance she got, matter of fact."

The passenger pulled the front of his felt fedora down over his eyes, as if to shield them from the sun.

The driver took the hint . . . for about ten minutes. "Seems funny, don't it? The war's been over for a couple of years, and here we are, driving all the way across the country right back to where it started."

"The war didn't start in L.A."

"Christ, you must think I'm as thick as a paving stone! I just meant the West Coast. That's where the Japs made their move. Fucking ambush, it was. After that, even a pansy like Roosevelt, he didn't have no choice."

The passenger snatched a pack of Lucky Strikes from the top of the dashboard.

Damn! I didn't even see his hand move, the driver thought to himself.

The passenger flicked his wrist. A single cigarette shot into his mouth. His thumb cracked, and a wooden match flared into life. He took a measured drag, carefully replaced the pack, and used the tap of a single finger to send it sliding across the dashboard.

"Nice to see these in a full pack again," the driver said, pushing in the dashboard lighter.

Silence reigned for another twenty minutes. The miles slipped past as the big car gobbled long patches of concrete.

"They say, you go without smoking for a few weeks, you lose your taste for them. What a crock. Me, I didn't have one for months. Fucking Japs. I still don't know how I made it through that march. Walk or die, that's what they kept saying. Walk or die. Far as I'm concerned, we should have bombed that whole island into the ocean."

"Too valuable."

"Yeah, I guess it was. The island, I mean. But those little yellow monkeys . . . I wish I'd killed a few more of them. Actually, a *lot* more. It feels better when you handle that kind of work yourself."

"True enough."

"You were there?"

"Europe."

"So you didn't see how they—"

"I saw how they fought."

"How the hell could you see Japs fight in Europe?"

"Nisei brigades."

"Oh, yeah. I heard about them. Crazy bastards, they were."

"They had something to prove."

"I guess so. Maybe. I don't know."

"I do."

"Yeah? How could that be?"

"I had something to prove, too."

"You? The boss told me you did stuff, but he didn't say what."

The passenger leaned back in his seat, rolled down his window, snapped out the still-burning stub of his last cigarette, and closed the window again.

"I got a Dishonorable," he said, after another minute of silence.

"For what?"

"Killing Nazis."

"Huh? That was the whole point, am I right? I mean, that's why they sent us over. Guys like me and you, we were *supposed* to kill the other guys."

"They said I killed some Nazis after they surrendered."

"How were you gonna do that? Once it was over . . ."

"It wasn't over. What they said was, I gunned down a bunch of them while they had their hands in the air."

"What the fuck? Who cares?"

"Eisenhower, I guess. Whoever was in charge."

"Why'd you—"

"Camp guards," the passenger said, as if that explained everything.

"How'd they even find out? There weren't any generals on the frontlines, pal—that much I know for sure."

"Somebody talked."

"Ratted you out?"

"You could say that."

"I'll bet the louse got a medal for it, too."

"Maybe posthumously."

"What?"

"After his death."

"He got killed over there, you mean?"

"After he testified."

"You mean, like, right in the barracks?"

"Barracks? No. He was back home. In this clubhouse they had. Yorkville, you know where that is?"

"Way over on the East Side?"

"Yeah. He was supposed to make a speech or something; I'm not sure."

"He got drilled right there?"

"Not just him. Whole place blew up."

"Hey, I *heard* about that. It was on the front page and everything. That was some blast."

"There's been bigger."

"Wait a minute! That guy, he wouldn't happen to be . . . ? Ah, what the hell was his name? He was going to run for city council, am I right?"

"Hendricks."

"That's the one! Supposed to be this big war hero. I heard he was a shoo-in. What the hell was he doing over in Yorkville?"

"That's the district he was running in."

"But that's Germantown."

"They get to vote there, too."

"I guess that's right. At least he was a white man. When we had to pass through Chicago to change cars? One thing the boss was *clear* about—we stay outta the South Side. The niggers're bunching up over there. Making their own plays. That's what we get for letting them fight."

"Yeah, that was a real privilege."

"Come on, buddy, you know what I'm saying. I mean, teaching them all about . . . you know, guns and stuff."

"You think they didn't know before?"

"Down south, sure. But back home—the City, I'm saying—they never turned those guns in the wrong direction. Not until after the war, anyway."

"Rifles for food, pistols for each other."

"Yep! That's it, exactly. But we send them over, we're *telling* 'em to shoot at white men. Probably never thought of it before."

"You really believe that?"

"Huh?"

"The IRA never thought of shooting a Protestant?"

"Hey! You don't know what you're talking about, okay? The IRA, all they ever killed was—"

"Enemies."

"That's right, enemies!"

"Enemies come in all colors, yeah? That's what camouflage is for."

"I . . . Okay, I see what you're saying."

"Hitler and Hirohito, they kept everything down to one color. What do you think happens if they'd've won?"

"I guess they'd . . . Wait! They'd start in on each other, that's what you're saying?"

"You see any coloreds fighting alongside the Japs?"

"And you didn't see any in your unit, either. Yeah, I get it."

"Up to you?"

"What's that's supposed to mean?"

"You get it, you don't get it, that's your choice. It's not a puzzle you figure out. There's no right answer to guess at—it's just the way you look at things."

The driver turned his head and stared at the man in the passenger seat for a long minute. Then he said, "You see that sign back there? Says we're in Idaho."

"Odometer show another four hundred?"

"Three sixty-eight."

"Try and find a gas station. Better if we make the switch without stopping on the side of the road."

"I know. Damn, this is one endless journey, you know? Why the boss has to send us all the way across country just to do this one job, I'll never know."

"What difference?"

"What difference? You're joking, pal. We got to change drivers every few hundred miles, change cars every day or two, spend every night in some crumby motel, eat diner food, no stopping for even a little bit of fun. . . . And all for what?"

"You know."

"Yeah, I know. But this job, it ain't no big deal. Must be a hundred local boys who could handle it."

"A hundred suspects."

"*That's* what you think this is all about?"

The passenger shrugged. As if acting in sync with his shoulders, dusk started its fade to black.

—

"This is more like it," O'Reilly said. "Brand-new Buick. Rides like a cloud. Too bad we can't take it the rest of the way."

"Only a couple of more switches to go," the passenger said. "Maybe we'll get lucky again."

"All the guineas want Cadillacs. Course, they can't have one even if they save up the scratch—bosses wouldn't like that. Freelancers like you and me, we don't got that problem. You know what I'm getting? Present for myself when this job is done?"

"No."

"A Lincoln Continental. Now *that's* the cream of the crop. Don't see many of them. Something special. You drive a car like that, everybody pays attention."

"That's what you want?"

"Not while we're working, for Christ's sake. Hey! Maybe that's the idea."

The driver lit another of his endless smokes. "What's the idea?"

"We cancel this guy in L.A., and we come back home. Doesn't matter who the cops are looking for—it won't be us. Yeah, now I get it. Airplanes, you got to buy a ticket. Even trains, buses, there's people to deal with. But we go back just like we got out there, there's nothing. We pay cash for gas, and we change cars all along the way. By the time we roll out of Cleveland, we're driving a car with New York plates. Going home."

—

The cream-colored Oldsmobile fastback coupe turned off the highway and slowly made its way through the city, the passenger calling out directions as they rolled.

A huge billboard high above the boulevard announced Lana Turner would soon be blazing across the screen in *Green Dolphin Street.*

"Now *that's* a babe," the driver said.

"Turn left two blocks down."

"You see the all those palm trees? I thought it never rained in this part of the country."

"It rains everywhere."

"Bullshit. What about deserts?"

"Rains less, that's all. Four more lights, turn left again. The garage on Barton Avenue, that's what we want."

—

As the car pulled inside the no-name garage, the doors closed behind it.

The two men climbed out slowly.

"Over here," a voice called.

A morbidly obese man sat behind a desk covered with food platters of varying age. The free-range cockroaches who roamed the desktop without pushing each other seemed to understand that there was plenty enough for all of them.

"I guess I don't have to ask which one of you is O'Reilly," the fat man said, tilting his watermelon head to one side. "The car's over there. Got it all fixed up so it looks like one of those zoot-suit boys hit it big. Being a Mex, naturally, all the dough goes into his car. They ain't hotrodders. In fact, they drop those things so low you can't drive 'em fast at all. They're all show, no go.

"Now here's the beauty part. You'd think, with all that crap that happened a few years ago, the beaners would get themselves together. At least, *stick* together. But, no, not those chumps.

"They don't got time to find jobs, but they got all the time in the world to shoot each other. Got gangs all over the East Side. And *territories,* can you feature that? It ain't like they *do* nothing with these 'territories' of theirs. But if you ain't a member of this club or that club, they will seriously fucking shoot you in the head for just walking down 'their' street."

"How's that help us?" O'Reilly asked. "That car may be what your spics drive out here; I wouldn't know. But him and me, we don't exactly look the part."

The piggish man laughed. "The part. Yeah, that's it. This town's fulla broads who'll drop right down and suck your cock, you even say those words: 'the part.' Movies. That's the magic word in this town. You wouldn't believe how much stag film we got stored up."

"Why store it? That don't make you any money."

"We store it 'cause the boss *said* to store it. But I know why he said it, and it makes sense, you give it some thought. Some of those broads, they're gonna be famous. Actual movie stars. *That's* when we cash in, see? The boss, he's even got things on schedule, like. We shoot the footage, then the girl's got five years to make it. She does, we cash *big*—those studios, they'll pay anything to keep stuff like that quiet . . . specially if the star's supposed to be lily-white. You own a nice piece of property, you put up a strong fence around it, see what I'm saying?

"And if the broad never makes it, we just put the movies on the market. Pretty slick, huh?"

"Yeah. Yeah, it is. But you still haven't told us how any of that's gonna make this job so easy."

"Those stag films, we shoot them right here," the fat man said. "In the back. It's like a real studio and all. Now it wouldn't be a studio without a prop department, am I right? We got all kinds of stuff back there. Even some of those zoot suits.

"Now this guy, the one who's gotta go, he operates out of a dump on Melrose. Actually, it's on the street just *behind* Melrose. From the front, looks like a liquor store. But for his real business, he just walks out the back door and right through to the other joint.

"Now you don't never wanna park on Melrose. Too many cars, you can't be sure of a spot. So this guy, he parks around back, then he walks down the street, makes a sharp right, and goes in the front door. Every night.

"Still with me? Okay, at eleven, he's walking down the street to his joint. On Melrose. And that car over there? It's waiting just around the corner. One of you walks up Melrose, the other stays behind the wheel. When the target gets close, whoever's walking plugs him. It's that easy. The shooter—I don't even want to know who that's gonna be—he gets in that Mex car and the driver moves out. You come straight back here . . . it's not even ten minutes away, that time of night.

"You drive in here, and you drive right out in that nice little Ford we got for you. California plates. You change clothes first, head north. The Mex car disappears, and so do you. Sound good?"

"Good enough," the smaller man said.

"Not for me, it ain't," O'Reilly said. "What if the cops decide to stop that car? Me, I don't speak Spanish."

"The cops?" the man behind the desk laughed. "Who do you think runs this town, the fucking mayor? The studios, that's who's in charge. The cops already got the license plate. If there's one car anywhere near this part of town that *ain't* gonna be stopped tomorrow night, it's that one over there."

The man with O'Reilly lit a cigarette.

"You'd think they'd learn, wouldn't you?" the fat man chuckled. "I mean, it was only a couple of months ago that they had to take out that yid? You know, the one that Virginia Hill ended up with? Now *this* fuck, he thinks he's out on this coast, they can't reach out and touch him, too?"

—

"I've spent the night in better places," O'Reilly said, surveying the space above the garage.

It was bare bones, lacking even a radio, but it had two separate cots, a bathroom, and a refrigerator.

"And worse."

"That, too," O'Reilly agreed, watching his companion nail a large blow-up map of their target area to the wall. "You really think it'll be as easy as fat boy says?"

"We come south on Formosa," the other man said, drawing a line with a thick red wax pencil. "Then left on Melrose. We wait for the target to walk toward us. Soon as he passes by the car, I wait a few seconds. Then I get out, step behind him, catch up quick, and put a couple in his head.

"I get back in the car. You take off. Make a left on Mansfield—see, right here? Then a quick left again on Waring, takes us right back to Formosa. Go up a couple of blocks, make a right, and follow it all the way back here . . . Barton Avenue, that's where we are now. After that, there's nothing for us to do but change clothes, climb in that Ford, and drive back home."

"How come I drive?"

"You're a better driver than me."

—

"What kind of piece is that?"

"Luger."

"Never heard of it," O'Reilly said. "Me, there's nothing like the Army-issue .45. It ain't no target pistol, but whatever you hit with it, down they go. They *stay* down, too."

"This one's Army-issue, too."

"Huh?"

"German army. Just for officers—like yours was—and very precise."

"It don't look like much."

"Smaller rounds. Nine millimeter. A little less than a .38, but very fast. Has to be—the way they designed these things, you need a lot of recoil to chamber the next cartridge."

"Nine millimeter. Even *sounds* weird."

"Nine millimeter Parabellum, they called it. The Krauts, I mean. It's from Latin. Means: if you want to be left in peace, be prepared for war."

"Yeah? Well, makes sense to me, then. You want the shower first?"

"I'm good."

—

The next night, at 10:57 p.m., a man wearing a black coat with red silk lining turned on Melrose and began to walk down the block. He glanced neither right nor left, but drew covert glances from a wide variety of night crawlers.

As he passed by a curb-parked blood-orange 1945 Chevrolet that had been dropped over the wheels almost to street level, a man got out of the passenger seat. The man fell into step behind him, pulled a pistol from his suit jacket, and shot him in the back of the head.

He fell to the sidewalk, face up, the red lining of his overcoat mocking the neon wash from a nearby window.

The shooter stepped close and shot him three more times, carefully placing each round into the dead man's face.

Instantly, the shooter spun, eyes sweeping a suddenly empty street. He walked back toward the low-rider. As he passed the driver's rolled-down window, he emptied the magazine of his Luger into the wheelman's face, head, and neck without breaking stride.

The shooter pocketed his pistol and kept walking to the end of the block. There, he climbed into the backseat of a fog-gray Cadillac that had been idling at the corner.

The Cadillac slid into traffic. Neither of the two men in the front seat turned around.

The man in the backseat snapped a new magazine into his pistol.

for Lou Bank, Ten Angry Pitbulls

CORAZÓN

Blanca was a flame in the night, beckoning. But whenever a man reached for her, his arms would grasp only smoke. And, if he reached deeper, pain would be his only reward.

One could always tell, later, which men had reached for the flame. By the scars on their hands.

But, always in the season when blood rises, some men would try.

—

Jorge was a quiet, solid, honest man who lived alone in the village. He did not dance, or sing in the cantina, as did the other young men. He could not be persuaded to gamble or cajoled to drink. Like a block of stone, the villagers said of him; an ancient man, in his ways.

Jorge could fix anything. It was not so much the gift in his hands—it was his patience. He would worry at a stubborn piece of machinery for days at a time, until it yielded and worked once again. Some said Jorge could fix even the old rusty guns discarded by the government soldiers in the jungle. But only the rebels would want such weapons, and to aid them was an act of suicide.

Besides, Jorge had no politics, and the rebels had no money.

When Blanca's spell fell upon Jorge, some of the villagers predicted her power would not prevail. No fire can consume stone. But, in their hearts, they knew this was not true, and they feared for the man they so respected.

But, although Blanca's fire blazed as none had ever seen, still Jorge held her.

And when the two of them announced in church one Sunday

that they soon would wed, the villagers were forced to believe in the truth of their intertwined lives. Because fiery Blanca had never before promised herself to a man, and honest Jorge never lied.

Jorge bought a patch of ground and began work on the house he and Blanca would live in after their marriage.

Because Jorge spent his days fixing machinery, he could work on the house only in the evenings. But that was of no concern. The jungle days are long, and, many times, other villagers would come by to help.

Jorge was too proud a man to ask for their labor. But the villagers remembered well that none of them had ever had to ask Jorge when they were in need. It would be against honor to allow their friend to work alone on such a task.

The villagers not only helped Jorge build his little house, they also prayed for him to be blessed with many healthy children. Children as beautiful as Blanca, if that was possible. Children as strong and patient and honest as Jorge, if the gods willed it.

Months passed, and the season of rising blood came again. An old woman came to Jorge's shop and told him that Blanca had been out late the night before, dancing with a lobo named Hector.

Jorge was not a man to listen to gossip. So he went to Blanca and asked her if what he had been told was true.

"Yes," she told him, tartly, hands on her perfect hips. "I cannot stay home every night and do nothing—there will be time enough for that when I am old."

Although all agreed that it was his right, Jorge did not beat her. He did not become angry, and he did not argue. Jorge said that life is a choice. He had made his choice, and Blanca must be allowed to make her own. "A man cannot own a woman," he said. "He can possess her only if she wills it."

A week passed. The village waited expectantly, but Jorge did not seek revenge against Hector. Finally, a group of the elders came to Jorge's shop, to ask him why. "Blanca is not my property," he told them. "She is a woman, not a goat. And, Hector, he is only a fool, not a thief. A heart cannot be stolen."

When the elders argued, Jorge patiently explained that Hector had not imposed himself on Blanca by force. And he did not deserve to die just because her flame had drawn him, too.

The next Sunday, Jorge went to church alone. He told the villagers that his wedding was not to be.

When Blanca heard what Jorge had done, she just laughed and shook her hips, running both hands through her thick midnight hair. "He will be back," she told the disapproving villagers. "He knows he cannot find all this anyplace else."

But months passed, and Jorge did not return to her. He still fixed machinery for the villagers. He still saved his money. He still worked on the little house—but all alone now. The villagers did not understand. But they did not question Jorge, and only watched in respect and in wonder.

All were watching the day that Blanca walked slowly through the village, all the way out to the little house. Some of the watchers whispered that Jorge had been right all along to have kept working on the house . . . because they all heard Blanca beg Jorge to forgive her. When Blanca told Jorge she had never lain with Hector, that her body was still pure, the whole village knew she spoke the truth. Blanca was a fickle, dancing butterfly, teasing all those who looked . . . but she was not a whore.

And Jorge did forgive her. But he would not accept her return to him. Blanca stalked off . . . but she returned the next evening. And the next. Still, no amount of pleading would make Jorge relent. He would not marry Blanca.

He would love her forever, Jorge said, but he could not marry the woman who had not been true to him.

He told Blanca she had not betrayed him with her body, but with her heart.

After that night, several of the girls in the village brought small machines to Jorge's shop for him to fix. At church, they fluttered around him like glorious tropical birds.

But no matter what was said to him, Jorge always replied the same. He said a man must bring his heart to a marriage, and his was gone forever, given to another. He would never marry.

Another season passed. One morning, when Jorge came to his shop, he found a note anchored to his door by a sharp knife. "By the time you read this, I will be dead," the note said. He did not need the signature to know it was from Blanca.

Jorge worked all that day. That same evening, he walked over to the still-unfinished little house. He stepped through the doorway. The villagers heard the sound of a shot. They came running, and found Jorge inside. Dead, his broken heart shattered by a bullet, holding Blanca's farewell note as gently as he once held her hand.

When Blanca came back two weeks later from visiting a cousin in another village, she learned that Jorge was dead.

The villagers expected Blanca to laugh at the result of her cruel joke. But never did she laugh again.

"I must apologize for my betrayal," she told her mother.

"You cannot apologize to Jorge," her mother said. "Jorge is gone. Go to church and pray for forgiveness."

Blanca put on the dress she was to have worn to her wedding. She walked alone to the graveyard at the edge of the village.

That night she went to Jorge. To prove that he was her one true love, and to be with him forever.

For X

SAVIOR

Some say that this is when it began.

It was not long afterward that the forest began to be taken from the villagers.

After that, the famine came.

And, finally, the soldiers.

—

Between the Government soldiers and the guerillas, our people had no safe place. My father protested that the Government soldiers took too much for their taxes. So they said he was a communist, and beat him until he could no longer work. Then the guerillas came. And they said my father must have collaborated with the fascist oppressors; otherwise, they would have killed him. So the guerillas executed my father, as an example to the village of what happens when people do not support their liberators.

My mother watched as they shot my father. She nodded her head, to show she understood that this was justice.

For that, she lived long enough to give me my father's folding knife and all our coins, and to tell me to run for the city.

I did not want to leave my mother, though she beat me and ordered me to go. Only when she told me if I loved her, I would go, did I run for the city.

When they put me in prison, I was not what they called me. I was no revolutionary—I was a thief. And I was a child, with a child's faith and a child's innocence.

Every night in my cell, I would pray. No one ever answered. Sometimes, the priest would come and I would ask him, "Why?"

It was a test, the priest would say.

"Padre, when do I find out if I passed that test?" I asked.

"When you die," he told me.

In prison, I came very close to the answer. Many times. Does that mean I passed? Was I closer to God?

I do not know.

After seven years, all that was gone. If I were still a thief, I would try to steal back what they took from me.

But I am a thief no longer.

They whisper about me now, but the whispers are lies. What I do, it is for myself, for my own heart. I have no politics.

Now I am a savior of both the Government soldiers and the guerillas. As they pass through the jungle where I was born, I bring them closer to God, as the priest did me.

But I am not as cruel as the priest. I never make them wait for the answer.

For Geof

BLOOD ORCHID

Nothing is written. There are only whispers. The villagers know there was a time before the helicopters, though none could remember it. Some of the elders say that children have always been offered, even before the coming of the god who descends from the air like a bird.

In the time before the convoys, each year, the snake god took some of the children. The justice for this was simple and pure: a snake may be poison, but that kills only the man who ventures too close. But the rats, they bring the plague.

Snakes may take a life; rats can take a village. What people eat, rats eat. If the rats grow too plentiful and strong, they devour all, until the people starve. And then the rats eat their flesh.

The gods know all, so they knew about the rats. The gods sent the snakes to kill the rats. But the snakes required tribute, to ensure their return. The priests did the harvesting, then.

—

The word is passed quickly. It starts at the border where the convoy assembles. By the time the first Land Rovers veer off the paved roads and chug their way into the jungle, the villagers of La Corazón have known of their coming for many days.

Awaiting the convoy's arrival, the villagers celebrate. The celebrations are quiet, held in private.

When the convoy arrives, the children must all be present. If a child's mother cannot bring the child—perhaps she has gone with the rebels in the mountains, perhaps she is in prison, perhaps dead—the villagers will act for her. At the edge of the jungle, the culture is that of the pack. All the children belong to the village, and all the village to them.

The hands of the convoy doctors are sure, inspiring confidence. The nurses are gentle-voiced. Each child is weighed and measured so that growth and development can be charted. Blood samples are drawn and examined under microscopes. Portable devices check for defects in bones and teeth and organs.

If any of the children are broken, the medical team fixes them. Some of the repairs are wizardry—a sickly child gains weight and thrives, a harelip vanishes, a painful limp becomes a joyous lope.

The convoy never takes any of the children they repair. That would be against justice. And never is more than one child taken from one mother.

The convoy harvests only nine of the children each time, three for each of the seasons.

Three is a holy number. Even the priests say that is so.

Each mother whose child is taken receives a large sum of money. It is customary for the mother to divide the money in half—one half is hers to keep, the other belongs to the village fund.

The villagers use the fund to buy supplies for the year. The land close to the border is not fertile, but there is nowhere else to farm. The rebels control the lower mountain steppes and the untilled forest.

Deep in the forest, children of the rebels are healed by shamans. But the Government has proclaimed that all those who aid the rebels are themselves enemies of the State, and no shaman will come to the border villages.

The Government soldiers come and take—they call it tax-collecting. The rebels come and take too—they call it contributing to the struggle for liberation. Without the money from the harvest, there would be nothing left.

It is whispered that, if the convoy comes and harvests nothing, it will never return. Nobody in the village knows if this is true, but all are frightened by the possibility.

Without the convoy, the village would die. So the priests have blessed the harvests. For some of the villagers, this is a source of great confusion. And some sadness.

But none of that matters. Truth is truth, no matter how it is dressed. People are on this earth not to question the gods, but only to serve them.

The doctors do not call in the helicopter until just before the end of their stay. The removals must all be done before crossing the border—in other countries, harvesting children is against the law. But it is not against the law to fly the harvested parts to the waiting hospitals, and the village of La Corazón is always proud to be true to its name.

—

Only the shamans know if what is said is true, but the People of No Colors believe it, every one.

The shamans call the orchid *Renacimiento*. It grows only in the place where the jungle is always dark. Its petals are flames of orange, and its center is pure white; so white it stuns the eyes, as if staring directly into the sun.

And like the sun, the orchid renews.

The orchid will return whatever you have lost. It cannot create, but it can restore.

So, if you were born to blindness, the orchid could not make you see. But if you once had sight, and later lost it, the orchid could make your eyes work again.

The orchid has power only if eaten on its stalk. It cannot be preserved, and it will die if transplanted.

Many seek the *Renacimiento*. Some are deaf, or blind, or crippled. They come in groups, with hired guides; but they never find the orchid. Perhaps this is because, as the shamans say, he who seeks *Renacimiento* must come to it alone.

Of those who make the journey alone, most seek sex. Predators who can no longer prey, venturing deep into the jungle to have their power restored. Such men always go in alone. The villagers say none has ever returned.

More dangerous men come. They listen to the warnings. But they do not hesitate to follow those who have gone before. Liars trust no one.

Not all call the orchid by the name the shamans have given it. The orchid takes whatever name it is called by its seekers. Some think it is a fountain. Others believe it is in the powder made from the horn of a beast, or that it lies just past the barrier of a virgin girl-child.

Those are all lies, told by merchants.

There is a rumor. Or a myth. Or a legend. That, in the deepest depths of the jungle, there is a tribe no outsider has ever seen. The villagers call its people *Los Renacimientos.*

But all that is truly known is this: the jungle where *Renacimiento* grows is ever nourished by the blood of those who seek it.

—

In the season of the gods, a woman called Sosima was told her child had been selected for harvest. Sosima offered herself instead, but the doctors explained that only children were acceptable. And the priests said this was as the gods demanded.

The villagers caught Sosima trying to escape into the jungle with her son. She fought so viciously that three strong men died, but, finally, she was overcome. The villagers left her body in a clearing.

They took her son back to the convoy. As his heart was harvested, the village elders decreed Sosima's half of the prize would be forfeited to the families of the men she had killed.

After the convoy was gone, the villagers returned to the clearing to bury Sosima. But her body was not where they had left it. Perhaps a jaguar had hauled the corpse away, one villager said.

The others shuddered. A jaguar big enough to drag a woman away, a jaguar with a taste for human flesh . . .

—

There is another border, a border not of governments. It lies between the known jungle and a forest so dense that its only light is said to come from the orchid sought by the dangerous men. In that forest there is a beast of terrifying power. No man can describe the beast, for to see it is to die.

Some say the beast is the jaguar who took the body of Sosima. They say that the beast eats the *Renacimiento*, so that even if it could be wounded, it can never be killed.

Villagers sometimes find men at the edge of the forest. The men cannot speak. They do not eat or take water. And they soon die.

The shamans say their hearts have been harvested.

Sometimes, the rebels go into the forest of the *Renacimiento*, to hide from the soldiers. Sometimes, the soldiers are ordered to follow. But what they find cannot be known, because neither the rebels nor the soldiers ever return.

—

Now there is a new legend. A legend of a tribe of children. Children born of Sosima and the jaguar. Children who now harvest to keep their own hearts.

None knows if this is true.

But the convoys no longer come to the villages. Children are no longer taken. And yet, the villages live.

for Rose Dawn

UNDERGROUND

A Screenplay

EXT: The remains of an industrial park. Most of the buildings have collapsed, some have a wall or two standing, some have no roof; most have no windows.

   CLOSER TO:

   EXT: A primitively fortified building. It has been shored up solidly: concrete walls repaired, with large solar panels covering the roof. It vaguely resembles an educational institution . . . with barbed wire replacing the ivy. Armed guards—male and female—are patrolling the area. Beyond them, a dog pack sleeps in the bright sunlight. Farther out on the perimeter are what look like mini-Edmontonia (armor-plated dinosaurs) only with unusually large eyes, rhino-type horns, and fearsome teeth. These beasts appear to be invulnerable to anything but high explosives. Each one is also "patrolling," moving within what seem to be strictly defined territories, although no fencing is visible.

   A distinctive high-pitched humming noise spills out of the building. The sound fades as the camera approaches. . . .

   BUILDING INT: A vaguely churchlike setting, but absent any religious references . . . even the stained-glass windows are clearly intended as works of art. The ceiling is the roof, so about as high as a three-story structure. Inside, rows of straight benches, irregularly constructed from scrap wood, but well maintained. At the front of the large room is a height-adjustable podium, built of tubular metal, behind which is an acoustic cone large enough to encompass several people. The auditorium is full. The crowd ranges from infants to the elderly. All races are represented, but scattered randomly, as if there is no significance to any individual's color.

   A woman steps to the podium. She is neither young nor old, with long hair worn in two thick braids, clad in a simple denim garment.

WOMAN

Who will share a Pass-Down with us today?

A very serious-looking boy, vaguely Asian in appearance, suggesting mixed blood, stands. He is young, but tall for his age.

WOMAN
(beckoning him forward)
Lincoln Su, come teach us.

She steps aside as the boy takes the stage. He adjusts the podium height, places an open book on it. Then he stands very still and closes his eyes. (Beat) He opens his eyes and faces the audience.

LINCOLN SU
(no microphone, the acoustic cone carries his voice)
An uncountable number of spans ago, there was a place called Underground. The history of our people begins with those who escaped to our world. Each one brought . . . stories. Some were true; some were lies; some were a blend. Only those that proved true-true became the Truths of our people. I have studied with the Tribe of Truth-Tellers since I was small. I am a man now. And the Tribe of Truth-Tellers is my tribe. So it is both my right and my duty to speak of what I have learned. This Truth is from the Book of Crews.

As Lincoln Su begins to speak we . . .
FADE OUT (on visual of his lips moving)
OPEN ON: UNDERGROUND
EXT/INT:

NOTES: In Underground, all "exterior" shots are still "interiors," as within an encapsulated area. The degree of illumination varies from blazing white to total blackness, but the change is controlled . . . either by individuals or by location, not by passage of time. This is not a sci-fi or "futuristic" setting. The tools, the technology, the furnishings, etc., are all salvaged, recycled, or simply holdovers from an earlier time. Clearly, it took many, many years to construct Underground, using sophisticated machinery and manual labor to dig the many tunnels . . . but equally clear that Underground itself has been around a long time. The terminology may have changed—e.g., the "blasters" referred to in the opening sequence are a motley collection of conventional pistols—and some new things have been invented—e.g., fabrics—but this is not a Matrix-type set: no robots, no computers running people through a "program," no SFX, no teleporting. . . .

IMPORTANT! DIRECTOR'S OPTION

AT ANY PLACE WITHIN THE SCRIPT WHEN A CHARACTER IS UTILIZING V/O OR INTERIOR MONOLOGUE, THE ACTION DESCRIBED MAY BE SHOWN . . . EITHER AS A "SILENT MOVIE" WHILE THE CHARACTER IS "SPEAKING," OR AS A SEPARATE STAND-ALONE SCENE.

ESTABLISHING:

Vaguely resembles a subway station, but the "ceiling" is as tall as a twenty-story building, hidden somewhere behind a complex gridwork composed of tubing thicker than redwoods interlaced with those of smaller diameters, the narrowest of which emit a barely discernible pale green glow. The platform is antiseptically clean, very wide, with numerous "stands" of varying sizes running its full length, placed a uniform distance from one another. A Times Square–size flat screen hovers over the station, visible from both sides. It is constantly scrolling, text only. This is the Info-Board.

PAN LEFT TO:

Seven young men, all dressed alike in orange jackets with white sleeves. The collars of their jackets are turned up, showing that the underside is white. *The jackets are clearly expensive, custom-made. These are the Game Boys.*

An old man staggers toward them. He is wearing a ragged coat; his hair is long: greasy and matted. He is holding what obviously is a bottle in a soiled paper bag. In today's terms, he would look "homeless."

Seeing him coming, the gang spreads out in a purposeful fan, with its leader at the apex. This forces the "bum" to the very edge of the platform, where he turns sideways to avoid the oncoming gang. The bum's hands are shaking. Suddenly, a spurt of red wine spills out of the bag and splatters the leader's jacket.

CLOSE UP: The leader's left jacket sleeve, white with four orange slashes on it, now blotched with the red wine.

PULL OUT TO: The leader's jaw drops at this impossible affront. The gang stands in stunned silence—the unthinkable has just happened before their very eyes.

A dynamo sound fills the station. In Underground, there are no "tracks"—a conveyor belt moves the trains.

One of the Game Boys pulls a small pistol from his jacket pocket. He looks at it dubiously for a second (this is an old .25 caliber Saturday Night Special; he isn't ambivalent about using it; just not sure it will work), then shoots the bum, who immediately falls. The pistol makes a soft popping sound as the boy continues to fire. The leader kicks the fallen bum until he disappears over the edge of the platform.

The Game Boys all turn and walk away. Slowly. The essence of cool.

FADE OUT

FADE IN TO:

The Game Boys walking past the same spot. On the Info-Board, it says:

SANITATION SQUAD TO STATION 29

DISPOSAL: LDC1788-GR4

They board the train, ride several stops to a station marked APEX.

When they leave the train, they face a series of neon signs, each designating a separate route:

MEDICAL
PERSONNEL
HOUSING
SAGES
SEX
ARCADE

and many more.

They walk to the ARCADE, a tunnel that opens into what seems to be hundreds of different gaming parlors. They enter one. The other players immediately look up as they enter. Some are more overtly deferential than others, but all show respect. The gang walks through the gaming parlor to a back door with a coded keypad. The leader taps several keys, and they all walk through.

Now they are in an unlighted, narrow tunnel. Each pulls a light-producing tube from his jacket, but it is clear they know where they are going.

INT: A cave dug into the side of a tunnel. The Game Boys are all present, wearing their jackets. There are roughly fifteen of them, all facing in one direction where an older man, perhaps late twenties, sits facing them. This is Merlin, the gang's leader.

MERLIN

The bum was on the Info-Board. That's a certified kill. Dante was the one who shot him, so Dante should get a mark for it.

He points at his own white sleeve, which is covered cuff-to-shoulder with orange slashes.

RAJAH

That's bogus! We're Game Boys, aren't we? The only way to get a mark is to score a perfect game. That's why I'm a fan leader (his hand indicating the crew we saw in the opening)—I've got the most marks.

MERLIN
(not so much reasoning as ruling*)*

Game Boys play. And the only game we play is Anarchy. That's the hardest of the kill games, and we are the best at it. Dante was playing a kill game with the bum, so he deserves to get a mark.

RAJAH

That's changing the rules! And we can't change the rules if there's a True Dispute, right?

General chorus of assent.

RAJAH
(angry, edging toward challenge)

And this *is* a True Dispute. So what does *that* rule say?

MERLIN
(not rising to the bait . . . and not blinking)

Game Boys don't fight each other. No real crew can let that happen; a crew has to be united, like we're all one person.

We can't even fight *as* a crew. The Rulers don't let crews fight each other, not anymore. People say that used to happen all the time—one crew fighting another for territory—but no one actually *saw* it, so maybe it is only a Myth.

But none of that matters. Only The Rules matter. If The Rulers catch two crews fighting, everyone they grab gets put on the HydroFarm for ten to twenty. All that time, and you don't even get a single credit for it.

And if you *kill* someone in another crew, they put you Outside.

Chorus of agreement

MERLIN

But any crew can make its own rules, so long as they don't go against The Rulers. Every crew plays something, because you are what you do. The Scooter Boys all ride. The Magic Girls do potions. I don't know what the Cricket Boys do, but those bats they carry are serious weapons.

You said it yourself, Rajah: Game Boys play video games. So that's how we settle this dispute.

UNIDENTIFIED GAME BOY
A duel!

FADE TO:

Rajah and Dante are standing side by side, each positioned before a complex set of hand controls on a small podium, facing identical screens.

The screens display numbers, counting down from 10-9-8-7-6 . . .

ANARCHY

lights up both screens, which immediately fill with what looks like a post-apocalyptic city, overrun with all kinds of creatures, human and otherwise. As Rajah and Dante fire various-colored laser beams at the screen, the upper corner of each shows their kill-count like an odometer.

Rajah is up 1122 to 1009 when Dante launches a triangulated tricolor beam at a suddenly revealed BREEDING CENTER. His screen goes dark. Then it flashes . . .

TOTAL ANNIHILATION!!!

The Game Boys all congratulate Dante.

FADE OUT

FADE IN

In the Arcade, the Game Boys are gathered, but not playing. A close-up of Dante's sleeve shows his mark, an orange slash. Another Game Boy walks in, very excited.

TURBO

I got one, too!

UNIDENTIFIED GAME BOY

One what?

TURBO

A bum! Just like Dante did. I shot him right in the back of the head, just outside the Feeding Station. You could tell he was a bum; he was, like, talking to himself, and talking back, you know?

FADE OUT

FADE IN

INT: Game Boys' crew-cave

MERLIN
(to Turbo)

Yeah, I *know* it was on the Info-Board. But the Dead Score never says *how* they die—they just put the number up. So we don't know, not for sure. Everyone *saw* Dante get his bum. But you were all alone when you got yours.

TURBO

That's not fair! I couldn't help being alone. I just saw the chance, and I went for it.

MERLIN

Nobody says you're lying, Turbo. But the only Dispute was whether Dante should get a mark for his kill, not whether he actually *made* one. Remember what it means to be a Game Boy: It has to be about what we *do*, not what we *say*. So we can't settle this the same way we did before. From now on (RULING) anyone who claims a mark has to have witnesses.

Chorus of: "That's right." "Yeah!"
   FADE OUT
   FADE IN
   The Game Boys are walking in a pack, exactly as they were when first shown. But there is a predatory air about them, subtle but obvious.

UNIDENTIFIED GAME BOY
There's one!

Turbo shoves his way clear, charges over to the sleeping bum, and shoots him in the face.

FADE OUT

FADE IN

Quick cuts of:

Rajah shooting a bum who is trying to hide behind a pillar.

Four different Game Boys all shooting the same bum as he tries to flee down a dark tunnel.

FADE OUT

FADE IN

The Game Boys step off a Conveyor Car just as a crew of Music Boys are getting on, each carrying a boom box on his shoulder. Their leader, Mohawk, has three yellow X's on his sleeve.

                              RAJAH
                    (pointing at the yellow X's)
          What're those supposed to mean?

                             MOHAWK
                    (pointing at Rajah's sleeve)
          Same as yours.

FADE OUT

FADE IN

The Game Boys are approaching the Sex Tunnel. Lounging around the entrance, they encounter the Dancing Girls. Their leader, Charm, is wearing skin-tight black pants made from a very shiny material . . . with five red slashes on the thigh. The Game Boys pass by without a word, but the looks they exchange clearly indicate that they realize every crew is playing the same game now.

They each hand a plastic card to the woman at the entrance. She scans each card, then listens to each Game Boy whisper to her, individually.

Different Game Boys follow different arrows.

Rajah enters a door with a blinking chartreuse light.

A girl stands up and starts to struggle with the same skin-tight black pants Charm was wearing. As she does, we see hers have a single red slash on the thigh.

FADE OUT

FADE IN

Rajah is on a pallet with the girl. Both are nude. Above them, two digital clocks: one is the "time" in Underground; the other is counting down (the time left in his session).

DANCING GIRL

How did I get mine? You know all Dancing Girls carry razors. So we don't have to do it in front of a whole lot of people like you guys do; we just bring back a piece of the bum, and that's proof enough for a mark. It's a good thing, too—the bums are on the watch, now. Most of them stay way back in the deep tunnels.

FADE OUT

FADE IN

CLOSE-UP OF WHAT APPEARS TO BE GRAFFITI, SPRAYED ON ONE OF THE TUNNEL WALLS IN BLUE PAINT.

BEING IN STYLE WENT ON TRIAL
THE SENTENCE WAS DEATH
MAKE YOUR MARK, AND WE'LL FIND YOU
EVEN IN THE DARK

Shots of individual crew members, still wearing their uniforms, but working alone, interspersed with shots of individual bums, running as soon as they spot a crew uniform.

FADE OUT
FADE IN
A man is moving stealthily through a pitch-black tunnel. He is wearing a long coat and a slouch hat.

RAJAH
(V/O)

I'm the king now. Because I play the game better than anyone else. Not just Game Boys, either; I'm ahead of everyone who hunts bums: The Deaf Boys, the Muscle Boys, even the Love Boys . . . the ones who sell in the Sex Tunnels . . . they're all doing it.

But I still always have the most marks.

Every time we hunted as a crew, it turned into a mess. "There's one of them," the scout would whisper, and we'd all close in and do it. But then we'd argue over who'd take the ears. That's when I decided to work alone. Like the bums I hunt.

The bums started to run the minute they'd see a crew jacket. That made some of the Game Boys feel good, but it doesn't get you any marks.

The bums can't go into the Safety Tunnels where most of the old ones stay. You have to have credits for that. Bums don't have credits, and they don't have any way to get them. They can't even sell their blood—it's all dirty from the stuff they take.

The bums used to beg for credits. If they tried that now, they'd be begging to be killed.

At first, I just went into the side tunnels. The Medical Tunnel was the best—all the bums have to go there, sooner or later. I remembered what that Dancing Girl said, so I brought back some fingers. But Merlin x'd that—he said you could take more than one finger from a bum, so you needed all of them for *one* mark. Even ears were only good if you brought back both.

Whoever had the most marks had whatever else he wanted. You didn't even need credits, it was just . . . yours. I *had* to have those marks.

Rajah continues to move, very skillfully, just a shadow inside darkness.

RAJAH
(V/O)

But the thing about bums is that they don't have crews—that's what makes them bums. So I never wear my jacket when I hunt.

I can tell when a bum is close by—they all smell, even down here.

Sometimes I go in so deep that I don't come out for a week. But I always come out with ears. The Book Boys keep score. It's on the walls; every twenty-four, something new. Everybody knows: If it's written in blue; it must be true. So everybody knows I'm still the leader.

When I go deep, I look just like a bum myself. I always carry a paper bag with a bottle of wine in it. I have my blaster—a much better one, now. I have this big knife, too. It's perfect for taking proof, sure . . . but the best thing about it is how you can make a kill without making a sound. That way, you can keep on hunting, instead of going right back.

Suddenly Rajah turns. He hears the sound of boots. Several men, running. He sneaks a look, sees it's the Cricket Boys, running toward him, bats held high.

Rajah turns and runs. The Cricket Boys are closing ground, screaming, "Bum! Bum!"

WHISPERED VOICE

In here!

Rajah ducks into a side tunnel. A bum is hiding there. He pulls Rajah down next to him, under a pile of garbage.

The Cricket Boys run on by.

THE BUM

They're everywhere now, the crews. It's like they're trying to kill us all.

RAJAH

Damn! You really saved my ass, man.

He offers his bottle of wine.

THE BUM
(taking a drink, handing the bottle back)
Thanks, bro. We have to stick together now.

RAJAH

Oh, yeah!

Rajah stabs the bum in the chest. Waits a few seconds to make sure it's safe to leave. Then he starts hacking off the bum's ears.

FADE OUT

FADE IN

Shots of Rajah being treated like a god: Shopkeepers waving away his proffered card (for credit-extraction), girls draped all over him, boys offering him all kinds of free gear, hanging on his every word.

FADE OUT

FADE IN

Rajah is working the tunnels, dressed in his hunting gear.

RAJAH
(V/O)

Everybody hunts down here now. I get spotted a lot by different crews, but they can never catch me. I know these deep tunnels better than anyone.

I used to pop Zoners when I first went out, but now I don't need them anymore.

All I need is the marks.

Rajah stops, satisfies himself that he's safe, sits with his back against the wall, and lights a cigarette, carefully cupping the tip.

LOUD VOICE

There's one of them!

Rajah acts almost bored. He moves with the air of a man who has done the same acts many times: gets up slowly, stubs out his smoke, and pockets the butt. He walks a few feet, steps into a crevice, and peers out, using a periscope-like device with a light-illuminator.

The onrushing group is closer than he first thought. Rajah takes a deep breath, gets ready to run for the deep tunnels. He looks over his shoulder and sees . . .

A crew of bums, screaming for his blood.

FADE OUT ON RAJAH BEING TORN APART LIKE HUMAN
TISSUE PAPER
 FADE BACK TO:

LINCOLN SU
(still at the podium)
 The Book of Crews teaches that the desire to kill
becomes death itself. From this came our First
Law.

 FADE OUT
 FADE IN ON:
 Shot of another section of wall . . . same color, style—as if only one tag-
ger is at work*
 *Every message from the Book Boys is in the exact *same color, and, while*
sprayed as graffiti would be, it is always in the exact *same handwriting, too.*

THE SAGES SEE THROUGH THE AGES
THE TERROR WAS NO ERROR
FIRST CAME THE AGENCIES

 FADE OUT
 FADE IN ON:
 INT: Same "gathering hall" as in the opening. we see a rotund black
man stepping away from the podium as an androgynous individual takes
his place and faces the audience. The Androgynous Individual has short
brown hair, long white-painted nails, and is wearing a lilac-colored, loose-
fitting garment.

ANDROGYNOUS INDIVIDUAL
(self-assured voice, gives no clue to gender)

This is the Tale of the Charter. It is from the Book of Records. Through study of this Book, we learn the value of maintaining truth.

FADE OUT as the Androgynous Individual begins to speak
FADE IN
INT: A man in his early thirties is sitting on the floor of a small cave laboriously hand-carved into the wall of one of the Tunnels. He is whispering to himself, occasionally pausing to write feverishly, using a long black stick to make entries in an old leather book. This is the Charter.

CHARTER
(speaking to himself)

I know this is all so complicated, but I have to make a record. My blood demands: Leave a record. Not on the wall, like the Book Boys. Write it all down, but bury it away. Then, maybe, someday . . .

CHARTER
(aloud, as he writes)

Before the Terror, the Rulers kept changing. Different ones, in different places. But the *real* rulers were always the same—they were called Agencies. The Health Agency ruled Health; the War Agency ruled Wars. There was an Agency for everything people did.

We don't have wars anymore. We have Warlocks, but the name doesn't mean what it sounds

like: In Underground, the Warlocks are potion-
ers. The best ones can make stuff that lets you see
Outside. Not with your eyes, in your head.

FADE AWAY TO:

*The Charter is entering the Trade Tunnel. His head is down, and he
moves slowly. He walks past stall after stall until he comes to one marked
POTIONS.*

A crone looks up as the Charter enters. Her eyes are empty sockets.

CRONE
(extending her fingertips like sensory organs)
You want something to stop you from being sad?

CHARTER
For what? Those never last.

CRONE
(indifferently)
They last forever, as long as you keeping taking
them.

CHARTER
Zoners do that, too. But after a while, there's
nothing left of you.

CRONE
What *do* you want, then?

CHARTER

I want to see Outside.

CRONE

A vision potion.

CHARTER
(determined)

Yes.

CRONE

Outside is too big to see in a vision. You have to say what *part* of it you want to see.

CHARTER

I want to see one of the Agencies. The Agencies that ruled there. I want to see the Agency that protected the children.

The Crone nods; she doesn't need to hear any more.

CRONE

One hundred credits. *Open* credits, not Tunnel credits.

The Charter hands over his plastic card. The Crone places it into the slot of a Transaction Box. Then she beckons him forward. The Charter places his palm over the slot, intones solemnly.

CHARTER

One hundred open credits.

The box hums for a second, then makes a pinging sound, indicating the Charter's card was good for that amount, and that it has been deducted.

CRONE
(decanting droplets from various colored bottles into a small vial)
You must be in a very safe place before you take this. While you are having the vision, only your body will still be here. You will not be able to defend yourself. Do you understand?

FADE OUT
FADE IN
INT: Charter's mini-cave
The Charter blocks the opening, sits with his back to the far wall, and takes out a vial of swirl-colored liquid. He tilts back his head, and pours the contents into his mouth. His face goes slack, his eyes slip closed.
The Camera sees:
A huge blob, throbbing with energy. Every spasm emits another blob, much smaller. The smaller blobs subsume whatever they encounter, and grow with each success. Those that do not find something to subsume grow smaller . . . until they vanish.
FADE OUT
FADE IN
Sense of time having passed.
The Charter is walking along the Conveyor Platform, his affect clearly indicating he is searching. He spots a teenager wearing a pale yellow jumpsuit, standing immobile. The Charter steps close to him.

CHARTER
I had a Vision. I need to know what it means.

TEENAGER
Only a Sage can tell you that.

CHARTER
(pointing at the yellow jumpsuit)
You're a Messenger, aren't you? So you could tell me how to—

MESSENGER
(warningly)
No one Sage knows everything. You have to find the right one.

CHARTER
(intensely)
But if I tell you the Vision, you can find the Sage who can answer my question?

MESSENGER
(smugly)
Sure. Only a Messenger can do that. The Book Boys don't answer questions; they just say things. True things, sure. But unless what they say is the answer *you're* looking for, it won't help you.

CHARTER
I know.

FADE OUT
FADE IN
The Charter and the Messenger are sitting across from one another, a board game of some kind between them, like one of the outdoor chess tables in Washington Square Park. They move pieces, but it is clear they are merely using this as a prop to speak. We have to come in close to hear the conversation.

MESSENGER

None of the Sages on Border knew the whole answer. But one of them told me where I could find what you wanted. In the Uncharted Zone.

CHARTER
(wary)

Yeah?

MESSENGER

I heard you can buy and sell anything— *anything*—in the Uncharted Zone. They call it the Black Market, because there's no overhead lights like they have here . . . just little ones.

CHARTER
(not impressed, striking at the Messenger's vanity)

Everybody hears things. Even the crazies.

MESSENGER

What *I* heard was that, before the Terror, Agencies were very, very big. And they gave birth. There would be like a super Agency, and it would have many, many littler Agencies coming from it.

CHARTER
(staring at the Messenger)

You hear anything else?

MESSENGER

(vanity restored, smug)

Oh, *now* you're interested? Okay. I heard it was a *huge* Agency that gave birth to the Agency that protected the children. That one was a lot smaller.

CHARTER

Did it . . . ?

MESSENGER

(moving a piece on the board, not looking up)

I told you everything. I took the Message, and I brought back what I got from the Sage, didn't I?

CHARTER

(nodding, but not satisfied)

Yeah. And I paid you, too, didn't I? But I still don't have the answer.

MESSENGER

(just short of condescending)

You asked if there ever was an Agency that protected the children. That's a Truth Question; three hundred credits. You paid me; I did my job. I told you what the Sage said. But the Sage also said that asking if the Agency *worked* isn't a Truth Question; it's a Judgment Question. One thousand credits. And every Judgment Question has to be asked three times—you need a different Sage each time you ask. And the only ones who can do Judgment Questions are in the Uncharted Zone. And Messengers never go there.

FADE OUT
FADE IN
INT: Charter's mini-cave

CHARTER
(eyes closed, smoking, V/O)

I know this is taking a long time. Making a record is hard. I have to explain everything. I found a way to get things Outside. Not people, but things. That's why I need to make this record. For Outside.

If there *is* anyone there. Nobody knows. Not for sure.

I want my record to go Outside, but I don't want to go there myself. That's why nobody can ever find my record until I'm ready to send it.

I thought I could find the answers I need, but I'll never have three thousand credits in my life.

All I have is my record.

That's how I found a way to get things Outside. Doing what I was trained to do. Making records.

FADE OUT
FADE IN
The same Charter, only much younger. He is moving through narrow, twisting tunnels with calm assurance. Every once in a while, he stops and makes a note on a pad strapped to his thigh.

CHARTER
(V/O)

When I was a kid, they trained me to be a Charter. I could move through the tunnels without a map or markers or a sonar-pack. I had this . . . gift for finding my way; that's why the Rulers picked me. They tested me when I was still a baby. Then they took me away.

The tunnels outside the Charted Zone never have any light. The Rulers said we have to chart *all* the tunnels. Once a tunnel has been charted, the Rulers give it a name, so it can have a purpose. Once the tunnel has a name, it's in the Charted Zone. Some of them have always been here, like the Medical Tunnels. Some are pretty new, like the Sanitation Tunnels. That's where the Conveyor takes people who have died.

A Charter makes a record. He gives the record to the Rulers, so they can add new tunnels to the Charted Zone.

The Rulers said I was special, because I could always find my way, and make a path. But I never found my own path until one time when I heard a sound echoing through the deep tunnels. It called to me. I'd heard children cry before. Plenty of times. But this was different: it was the thin, bitter sadness of a child seeing his own future.

I first thought the sound was some kind of prayer. But who could they be praying to in Underground?

The child never knew I was listening.

Image of the Charter sliding through darkness toward the sound of a child sobbing. A man is standing, a knotted cord of some kind in his hand, lashing down.

THE MAN WITH THE WHIP
You like *that*, you little—?

The Charter looms out of the shadows, a black-bladed knife in his hand.

FADE OUT
FADE IN

CHARTER
(V/O)
That first time, I thought I could stop the crying
by taking the heart that was closed. If I took the
heart, the crying would stop.

Image of the Conveyor pulling to a stop. SANITATION is marked on its front. It stops, robotic arms lift the body of the man the Charter had stabbed. It moves silently away.

CHARTER
(V/O)
But I could never be sure. Not certain-sure.

IMAGE:
    A group of people all wearing white jumpsuits enter the area where the Charter killed the man with the whip. They grab the crying child and carry him to a conveyor. A train marked HydroFarm *stops. The creatures in the white jumpsuits toss the child inside.*
    IMAGE:

The Charter, standing invisibly in a tunnel, using an infrared scope to scan the HydroFarm.

CHARTER
(V/O)

At first, I couldn't see the baby. The HydroFarm is too big, and he'd be too young to work, anyway. Then I spotted him. One of the Enforcers was holding him. But he was still crying.

I don't know if he ever stopped.

CUT TO:

The Charter standing outside a room, listening to a child cry. Inside, a woman is screaming a torrent of verbal abuse. The Charter settles in to wait.

BACK IN TO:

Same exact spot. The Charter ghosts his way into the room. When he comes back out, he is carrying a female child.

CUT TO:

Interior of the Charter's cave. He is cuddling the child. They are both asleep.

CUT TO:

Shot of the Charter talking to the child. She is animated; no longer crying.

CUT TO:

The Charter is back outside the room where he took the child. This time; his knife is unsheathed.

FADE OUT

FADE IN

Distinct sense that time has passed

A tunnel full of children. The older ones are caring for the younger ones. Some are grave, some are cheerful. None are frightened.

A different Charter approaches (this tells us that the tunnel itself is in the Uncharted Zone). The new Charter is still some distance away when a squeaking sound fills the tunnel. Mutated rats, the size of dogs.

CHARTER
(V/O)

Charters are supposed to stay out until they find a new tunnel. Sometimes, they're gone for fifty cycles, even more. But I always take them early, just past the perimeter. If they don't come back, the Rulers are never surprised: Zone Rats are dangerous, but not nearly as dangerous as the Traxyls who feed on them.

Charters are supposed to always leave a trail behind them. That way, if they don't come back, the next Charter can find the body . . . and pick up where the last one left off. That's why I always make sure to change their markings after I kill them.

CUT TO:

Children feeding a mixed pack of vicious-looking dogs. They treat the dogs like puppies, and the dogs frolic like puppies, too.

A rat-squeak is heard. The ears on several of the dogs shoot up. The entire pack charges out of the tunnel, as purposeful as a guided missile.

CHARTER
(V/O)

The Rulers don't have this tunnel on any of their charts. One of the little girls I took called it the Tunnel of Love. Now we all call it that.

When the first children get old enough, I will teach them to do what I do. Some will be Charters, but Charters for *us*, not the Rulers. Some will be Enforcers, but Enforcers for *us*, not the Rulers.

There will always be children who belong with us.

They will all have jobs. Not jobs the Rulers make children do, jobs they want to do. Having a job makes you feel good. Even the dogs know this.

If we live, someday there will be many of us. But if the Rulers find us before we are ready, they will make everything we build disappear.

That's why I have to make this record.

ANDROGYNOUS INDIVIDUAL
(speaking from the podium)

By this we learn that the only true records are *tested* accounts. Truth may be written. Truth may be spoken. Just as lies may be written or spoken. The only test for truth is not what is written, or what is said. The test is what has been *done*.

FADE TO BLACK
FADE IN:
INT: The Gathering Hall
A couple stands at the podium; both Native American in appearance. The man is wearing black-lensed goggles; the woman is facially scarred, but with clear eyes. Blue eyes.

COUPLE AT PODIUM
(woman speaking, man nodding as she does)

Shall it be Axel, then?

They step aside as an extremely muscular man strides purposefully to the
podium. His head is shaven, nose crooked, face a roadmap of battle scars.
When we close in on his hands gripping the podium, we see the first two
knuckles of each hand are raised and are a bluish color.

AXEL
(facing the audience as if ready for battle)
The Book of Obligations takes many, many
spans to learn. Not all those who enter the school
remain. Those who do are tested. I stand here
now with the pride of one who has been granted
the honor of carrying the burden of truth.

FADE OUT as Axel begins to speak
FADE IN ON VOICE (speaker not visible: voice of an older teen,
speaking in that half-knowledgeable, half-superior air of an adolescent
speaking to a younger boy, just on the cusp of puberty)

NARRATOR
You have to know how things work if you want
to survive here. There's the Rules; and there's the
Truth. You need to know both. And how to tell
them apart.

Everybody writes on the walls, but only the
Book Boys have this special blue paint. Whatever
they write doesn't always stay up on the walls, but
their messages can't really be removed, because
everybody in Underground knows: If it's written
in Blue, it must be True.

The Guardians protect the Book Boys. Anyone can write on the walls, but there's two things
you can't ever do: you can't mess up what the

Book Boys write, and you can't sign their tag to anything you write yourself.

COME UP ON:

A group of young people, all dressed for combat, but not in the matching uniforms favored by crews. They are making their way through a tunnel.

> **NARRATOR**
> *(V/O, depicting what he speaks)*
> The Guardians are a mixed crew. Most crews have only boys or girls. Some of them allow only one skin/shade band—the Turf crews are the strictest about that. The Guardians don't care about stuff like that, but, remember, they're still a crew, so they can't punish you the way the Rulers can. The Guardians can't send you to the HydroFarm. They can't send you Outside, either.
>
> But if you mess up what the Book Boys write, they *will* hurt you.

CUT TO:

A pair of Dancing Girls, standing on either side of a Book Boys message:

TAKING EARS WON'T KILL YOUR FEARS

The girls each pull out a can of black spray paint and begin to black out the blue writing.

The Guardians descend on them, mercilessly. When they walk away, the two Dancing Girls are lying on the ground, bloody and beaten.

> **NARRATOR**
> And if you claim a Book Boys tag . . .

CUT TO:

A youth is spraying MUSIC BOYS RULE! *in blue. His work is skillful: not perfect, but a close imitation of the distinct Book Boys script.*

One of the Guardians steps away from the pack. She aims a small crossbow. The arrow hits the Music Boy in the back of his neck. Another Guardian runs close and swings a heavy machete, neatly decapitating the Music Boy.

They leave the Music Boy's dead body beneath what he wrote—a message of their own.

NARRATOR

What the Guardians do is against the Rules. They get caught at it, too. Every once in a while, you see it on the Info-Board. That's where they announce the Crimes and Punishments.

Everybody knows the Crimes.

Everybody knows the Punishments.

But nobody knows who the Guardians are.

CUT TO:

A Guardian being subjected to electric shock torture. She is strapped to a gurney, convulsing. A hooded man comes into view.

HOODED MAN

All you have to do is tell us. You're going to tell us anyway—why go through all this pain?

GUARDIAN GIRL

You don't know what pain is, you little maggot. But you will soon. When the Book Boys write *your* name on the walls, you'll see—

*The Hooded Man recoils just as another jolt hits the Guardian Girl . . .
killing her.*

    FADE TO BLACK

    OPEN TO A LARGE MESSAGE FROM THE BOOK BOYS

LM24-GG77-6Δ29

TUNNEL 29

BLOCK 7

CAVE 4

    *PAN DOWN TO: The supine body of a man, pinned to the ground by
a heavy steel spike driven through his body, obviously by the sledge hammer
propped against the wall. A black hood lies just past his fingertips.*

NARRATOR

Nobody knows why they're called the Book
Boys—everybody knows some of them are girls.
But not *which* girls, of course. The Book Boys are
invisible. They write the truth, so they have to be
everywhere the truth is.

    Whispers say the Rulers sent so many of them
Outside that there's a whole colony of Book Boys
there.

    That could be true. The Book Boys write
about Outside sometimes; maybe that's where
they get it from.

    There's no way to know.

CUT TO:

    *Various shots of different crews spraying on the walls. The usual gang-
turf graffiti.*

NARRATOR

Lots of turf crews write on the walls, but nobody pays attention. Like when they claim a Tunnel . . . as if anyone could own a Tunnel except the Rulers! Well, maybe in the Uncharted Zone, but who would ever know *that*?

Turf crew names are just stupid. They don't tell you anything about them, the way other crew names do. Like the Golden Dragons. What does that tell you? It doesn't mean they're all skin/ shade band 70, like gold. And everyone knows giant lizards can only live Outside anyway, where there is light coming down on you even without the generators. At least that's the way it was before the Terror. That's what the Book Boys say.

The Turf crews fight each other, too. That's *all* they do. You can watch it happening. Not the fighting, the score: you read it on the walls. One Turf crew will write that they own something. Another crew will cross out what they wrote. That goes on for a while, one crew slashing over what another crew writes. On and on. Until, finally, one crew writes something and it stays there. That means they won.

But nothing like that ever stays too long.

People say the Turf crews did the same thing before the Terror.

CUT TO:

Two turf crews moving toward each other, in classic rumble style.

NARRATOR

But that's too stupid to believe. I mean, why would they kill each other over something they could never really own? That's as stupid as them saying they own a Tunnel.

You learn the Big Rules first. Because if you break one of the Big Rules, you go to the Hydro-Farm . . . if you're lucky.

There are other Rules too. So many Rules, you could never learn them all. You're supposed to ask if you don't know. You can't ask the Rulers—nobody has ever seen one of them. But in every Tunnel there are little pockets all along the walls. Just little indentations, not deep enough to be caves.

SHOW:

Inside one of those indentations. It has no door, and contains nothing but a murkily viewed person seated behind a desk, which stands between the person and whoever enters. A flat screen sits on the desk, facing the person behind it.

A teenager with a shaved head steps into the indentation, his muscular upper body covered only by a lilac-colored vest. A small tattoo of some kind is visible on the back of his neck.

TEENAGER

Is there a Rule about lifting weights?

PERSON BEHIND DESK

(taps some keys, looks at the screen)

No. *(He hands the teenager a piece of paper.)* Sign at the bottom. Your index number, not your name. This signifies that you asked a Rules Question, and the answer was given to you.

The Teenager signs.

PERSON BEHIND DESK
Give me your card. You get two credits for asking a Rules Question. Not Open Credits—you have to say what you want them for before they're loaded into your card.

TEENAGER
The Sex Tunnel.

NARRATOR
The people who explain the Rules to you are called Bureaucrats. There are lots of them. They come in every skin/shade, but they all look alike. I mean, they don't all have the same faces, but all their faces have the same look.

I once asked a Bureaucrat about the reason for a certain Rule. He told me that was against the Rules, asking for reasons. But he gave me the two credits after I signed the paper, because even though I didn't ask a Rules question, I got a Rules answer.

CUT TO:

BUREAUCRAT
Every Rule is for your own good. That's because every Rule is for *everyone's* good.

NARRATOR

Where the break really started—the one between the Rulers and the Book Boys, I mean—was probably about the Bad Babies. A Bad Baby is one born against the Rules. You can't have sex until Year 14 if you are a boy. And not until Year 17 if you are a girl. The Bad Babies all came from girls under Year 17 since those girls must have had sex before it was allowed.

If a girl had a Bad Baby, she would have to go into one of the Medical Tunnels and get fixed. After that, she couldn't have babies anymore.

CUT TO A MESSAGE FROM THE BOOK BOYS:

MAKE THE RULES

TIE THE TUBES

BUT THAT HEX WON'T STOP THE SEX

NARRATOR

But the Bad Babies kept happening.

If the Rulers want to know something, they send you to a Synapse Squad. They put this metal band around your head and ask you the questions. Then they just look at the screen and they know the truth. But everybody knows this doesn't work on girls.

So when a girl would get pregnant before she was allowed, the Rulers would make every boy she knew go to a Synapse Squad.

But sometimes, no matter how far they looked, they couldn't find the boy who was guilty.

CUT TO:

A man in a lab coat, looking at DNA profiles on a large screen, shaking his head.

NARRATOR

Remember, the Rulers *never* give up. They started checking the Bad Baby's own spray. That's when they found out that the father of those girls was also the father of their babies. The father *was* the father, that's what the Book Boys wrote. In blue.

The fathers were old enough to have sex, but their daughters weren't. Anyway, children belong to their parents; they own them. Everybody knows that.

So the Rulers made an Exception. An Exception is when the Rules don't apply. Whenever a girl had a Bad Baby, they would put her on the HydroFarm. While a girl was pregnant, she wasn't much good to her owners, anyway. They eat more; and they work less, even if you beat them. Nobody wanted them in the Sex Tunnels either. That wasn't fair to the owners, so the Rulers took the babies, and paid the fathers compensation-credits.

After the girl did her punishment time, the Rulers would send her back to her own spray, if they still wanted her. If not, they just let her go.

CUT TO:

Adolescent girl standing on a platform, waiting for a Conveyor. The HydroFarm is in the background: It looks like row after row of different kinds of plants, all being hand-harvested by various individuals wearing the same ecru-colored uniforms with red stripes, working under a sky of Gro-Lights. The girl is holding a plastic carry-all marked DISCHARGE in one hand. She looks more frightened than relieved.

CUT TO:

On the Wall, in Blue:

WHEN YOU CAN'T CHANGE PEOPLE
JUST CHANGE THE RULES
FOOLS

NARRATOR

Now, if you're the owner of a girl, you have to
bring her to the Medical Tunnel when she reaches
Year 11. They give her an implant there, a little
fan-shaped thing, five lines with a star at the base.
They put it on the outside of the right thigh,
where anyone could see it.

The implants work for six years, so there won't
be any more Bad Babies.

A young male steps out of the shadows, a heavy duffel of some thick material slung over one shoulder, with a clearly visible locking device on its top. He is staring at the latest posting of the Book Boys:

YOU CAN'T TAKE THE CREDIT
IF YOU DON'T MAKE THE CREDITS

When he speaks, we realize it is the same VOICE we have been
hearing; this is the voice of HEXON, as he explains:

HEXON
(V/O)

My name is Hexon. Even though a Warlock named me, I am a Merchant Boy. People buy and sell stuff all the time. There's even a Barter Tunnel, where you can trade without worrying about getting your stuff stolen . . . but you need credits to get in there. Only Merchant Boys work in the Black Market, outside the Charted Zone. We deal in anything. And everything we score goes into our vault. Merchant Boys share. We get *our* marks from bringing in stuff, not from keeping it.

CUT TO:

Hexon offloading his duffel. An older man checks off every item; others carry the stacked-up goods away.

HEXON

I was the one who heard the whisper first: someone wanted to buy the Bad Babies. That was crazy. With the implants, how could there be any more of the Bad Babies.

But I remembered a message I saw once . . .

CUT TO:

WHAT CAME FIRST : GREED OR NEED?

HEXON
(V/O)

That's what Merchant Boys do—we scout for new opportunities. New frontiers, we call them. You have to start in the Charted Zone, but you have to be *very* careful in the Open Tunnels. There's a No-Name crew in some of them. They went in there to hide. The Book Boys wrote that it was the Game Boys who started it. Then the Dancing Girls got in on it, too. Killing. Not for stuff, for marks. Marks on their crew clothes. It was like a contest. They only killed No-Names—"bums" they called them.

None of the crews play that game anymore, but you still have to be careful in the Edge-Tunnels. Some of the No-Names never came out, even after the killing stopped. And if they think you're hunting them, you won't be coming out either.

CUT TO:

Mob of bums, tearing apart a pair of bodies.

HEXON
(V/O)

There's an endless market for baby parts. Hearts are worth the most, but even spares—like kidneys and lungs—are worth a lot of credits. I heard you used to be able to just buy the parts, right in the Medical Tunnel. That's what the Rulers used the Bad Babies for.

CUT TO VISUAL OF A BOOK BOYS MESSAGE:

THE TRANSPLANTS ARE A FAKE
THE ORGANS NEVER TAKE
THERE ARE NO BAD BABIES
IF YOU BUY THAT LIE, YOUR BABY DIES

HEXON

(V/O)

Now it's against the Rules to sell a baby for parts. Of course, some people do it anyway, because some mothers and fathers will pay anything to keep their own babies alive.

Underground is a weird place: some mothers and fathers will kill their babies for the credits. And some mothers and fathers, if you even *asked* them about doing that, they'd kill *you*.

The Rules don't protect babies, because some people will always risk breaking a Rule if there's enough credits in it for them. Maybe that's why there's such a monster Bounty on any Book Boy: they keep telling everyone that, over and over.

CUT TO:

Δ RULE IS Δ TOOL

WΔLK THE PΔTH, BECOME THE PΔTH

HEXON

(V/O)

I spent thirteen days in the Open Tunnels, but I couldn't pick up a clue. Not a whisper, not a trail, not even a scent.

SHOW:

Hexon talking with various people, sometimes furtively, sometimes at a table in what looks like a bar, sometimes using sign language.

HEXON
(V/O)

Some of the Traders had heard the same whisper I had, but they all thought it was too crazy to be true. Even down here.

I don't know why, but I wanted to know. The longer I stayed out, the more I needed to find the answer. If the Book Boys said there are no Bad Babies, it must be true. So how could there be a price on them?

SHOW:

Hexon penetrating into the Uncharted Zone. Sometimes, he is recognized, sometimes he hides. Once, he encounters a crew of Bums. He squats, opens his duffel, and hands out various small items.

HEXON
(V/O)

I went out past the Open Tunnels, past the Black Market, looking for the crew that wanted the Bad Babies.

But I never found anything except those freakish Zone Rats. The noise they make is something you never forget once you hear it.

SHOW:

The mutated rats, their tiny heads almost completely dominated by eyes. They are much *bigger than conventional rats, and come in every color (and combination of colors) imaginable.*

HEXON
(V/O)

It's really dark outside the Charted Zone, except for the little pools of light where traffickers set up shop. That's why it's called the Black Market, I guess—it's mostly black, with just little spots of light.

I kept moving, using my crystal-flash only once in a while, to preserve the charge. Once I thought I saw a dog . . . just a flash of fur, I guess. But it was way too big to be a rat . . . even a Zone Rat.

I was on my way back when I stopped into a provisions stand near the Rim. They only sell maintenance food, like water or freeze-dry. Zoners too—some of the prospectors won't go outside the Charted Zone without them.

CUT TO:

Hexon standing at the Provisions Stand, neither casual nor nervous. A girl steps up into view, holding out a plastic card. She is much shorter than Hexon, fairly slim, but with bare, muscled arms. Caucasian, lighter-skinned than Hexon, but not subway-pale.

GIRL
(business-like)

Four freeze-dries; two green; two white.

Hexon opens his mouth to say something, then slams it shut. Realizing she is about to leave, he approaches.

HEXON
(proffering his pack)
Would you like a smoke?

GIRL
(polite, but very clear)
No, thank you.

The Girl walks away. Hexon's eyes are drawn to her hips—a natural reaction, given her more-than-necessary wiggle—when he realizes she is wearing the skin-tight black pants of a Dancing Girl [Note: we should SEE this image within-an-image]. She turns her head slightly, looks back over her shoulder. Hexon immediately forgets any thoughts of razors.

They find a place to sit—a makeshift bench just a little past the halo of light from the Provisions Stand.

GIRL
(facing Hexon; straightforward)
My name is Fyyah. Not like the kind that burns.
F like Favor, Y like Yellow, Y like Yellow, A like
Apple, H like Happy.

HEXON
That's a beautiful name. Mine is Hexon. But it
doesn't mean anything. I don't put hexes on people; I'm a Merchant Boy.

FYYAH
Then you already know what I am.

HEXON
A Dancing Girl, you mean? That's not what you
are—that's just the crew you're in.

FYYAH

If it doesn't mean anything, why did you tell me
you're a Merchant Boy?

HEXON
(looking down)

'Cause I didn't know what else to say. I didn't
want you to go. I wanted to say something, I
don't know . . . cool? But I'm no good at talking
to girls.

FYYAH
(giving him an appraising look)

You're doing pretty good so far.

PULL OUT TO:

Hexon and Fyyah talking. Sometimes earnestly, sometimes very serious,
occasionally smiling. They are sitting close, but not touching. Clear impres-
sion that a great deal of time has passed, as different people keep walking
back and forth in front of them. Everyone who passes draws a look from
both of them—threat assessment—but nobody looks in their direction . . .
they're all there on business of one kind or another.

FYYAH

I . . . I wish I could keep . . . I wish I could just
stay here. But I have to find a place to sleep. The
cold is coming, and we're out too deep to make it
back across to the lights.

HEXON

I could—

FYYAH
(sharply, with a hint of disappointment)
I don't trade, Hexon. I know some of the Dancing Girls work the Sex Tunnels, but we don't *have* to, and I never would. I'm not trading sex for a night in one of the Stay-Overs.

HEXON
(angry and hurt)
I wasn't going to say anything like that. I already knew you wouldn't—

FYYAH
(turning to face him; seriously interested)
How? How could you know something like that?

HEXON
Like what?

FYYAH
That I wouldn't . . .

HEXON
I just knew. I always know . . . things like that, I mean. I'm a Merchant Boy, but a Warlock named me. Maybe that's why. Because I always *do* know, for real. That's why I'm the top Merchant Boy—I never get cheated.

FYYAH
What's that got to do with sex? I thought you weren't even any good at *talking* to girls.

HEXON

Not sex things, *trade* things. I can always tell
when somebody wants something, and what
they'll give for it.

FYYAH
(not sure what to make of this statement)
Oh.

HEXON

You could use my sleep-tube. It's right in my
pack; a 33-Z, the very best, one hundred percent
Raytell. It's even got a heat exchanger and a bub-
ble visor. Sometimes I'm out here for a few cycles
at a time, so I need to carry one.

FYYAH
(firmly)
I couldn't do that. It wouldn't be fair.

HEXON

It's fair if I *want* you to.

*They exchange a look. Then, as if by mutual agreement, they get up and start
walking. When they come to a flat spot slightly off the ground, Hexon pops
open his sleep-tube.*

FYYAH

Are you sure you can . . .

HEXON

Sure. It's easy. Give me your jacket.

As Fyyah is removing her waist-length jacket, Hexon takes off his much longer coat, which he doubles up and lays flat on the ground. Then he gently places her jacket on top of his and sits down.

FYYAH
(insistently)

Are you *sure*?

HEXON

I've been making trading trips out here a long time. It took forever to save enough for the 33-Z. So I slept on less than this plenty of times. The trick is to keep something between yourself and the ground. The more the better.

Fyyah gives him an unreadable look, then fastens the sleep-tube around her, and shifts her body so it's right against Hexon's.

HEXON

The heat-exchanger is—

FYYAH

I know how they work. If I turn it on, then the outside of the tube will get all cold, right? If I leave it off, it'll be like I'm another blanket. And if I don't pull the visor down, we can still talk. I'm not sleepy yet, anyway. Are you?

Hexon deliberately turns away from her, shifting his body to a guard-alert position.

HEXON

There's . . . things out here. It takes a long time
to learn how to sleep so any sound wakes you up.
We'll take turns staying awake. Pull up the visor
and I'll wake you when it's your turn.

*He lights a cigarette by inserting it into a flameless box, cups the tip, and
takes a drag.*

FYYAH

(ignoring him; not touching the visor)
Have you been out here *that* long?

HEXON

(not turning around)
Long enough.

FYYAH

Not out here, *out*. Away from your spray, I mean.

HEXON

(soberly, turning slightly to face her)
Almost twelve years.

FYYAH

You don't look that old.

HEXON

I'll have my Year 19 soon. You?

FYYAH

A little over two years.

HEXON

Did you run from . . . ?

FYYAH

My spray, yeah. In my Year 13, they sold me on a three-year contract to the HydroFarm. I worked out the contract, but I never went back, even though my spray still owned me. But they never caught me, and I'm too old, now. Even if they found me, they couldn't bring me back.

HEXON

Couldn't they still snatch—?

FYYAH
(closing her eyes)
I'm a Dancing Girl. You come for one of us, you come for us all. When we used to take kill-marks, a Drover counted for ten regular ones.

Hexon lights another cigarette and looks into the darkness, as if he's watching for intruders.

HEXON
(V/O)
It was like I was talking to her and thinking inside my mind at the same time. They used to have a different name for sprays once. Families, they were called. The Book Boys wrote that, in blue. Families were supposed to really want kids. To keep, not to sell. They were supposed to love children. And protect them. But after a while,

they all stopped doing that. Or most of them, anyway. That was part of the Terror. I don't really understand it all. The Book Boys wrote it in blue.

SHOW:

YOU KILLED THOSE WHO TRIED TO WARN
THE FABRIC WAS TORN
FAMILY WAS DEAD——SPRAY WAS BORN

HEXON
(V/O)

Spray means DNA connection. When people have sex, sometimes a baby comes. The Rulers can always tell your spray. From your blood, that's how they tell.

He sneaks a glance at Fyyah, almost as if to reassure himself she's still there. She seems to be sleeping peacefully.

HEXON
(V/O)

It felt good to look at her. Rats can't get into the sleep-tube, not with the visor down. But she had the visor up. I had to keep watch, so nothing would hurt her.

It felt funny, doing that. No, wait. That isn't what felt so strange. She was probably real good with her razor and all, but, going to sleep like she did, she was . . . trusting me. Why should she do that?

I talked to her. Real soft, so it wouldn't wake her up. I told her about the stuff I had to do when I ran off from the work site. The first two times, they caught me. They know how to hurt you without crippling you . . . because they need you to go back to work when they're done hurting you. The last time, I finally made it.

I had to do a lot of things after that. Bad things. But it got easier to do them, after a while. And once I found a crew that would have me, once I became a Merchant Boy, I knew they would never get me back into a work site again. It was like she said for her crew—if anyone came after one of us, it was the same as coming after us all.

FYYAH
(in a voice that indicates she was never asleep)
You didn't have any choice, Hexon.

HEXON
(startled)
When did you wake up?

FYYAH
I never really went to sleep. I was just lying here with my eyes closed. Feeling safe. I loved that feeling. I didn't go to sleep because I didn't want it to end.

But I know we have to sleep. We'll do it like you said, okay? You watch me for a while, then wake me up and I'll watch for you.

HEXON

I'm not sleepy.

FYYAH

Me neither. What were you looking for out here?

HEXON

I'm . . . looking for someone who wants to buy Bad Babies.

FYYAH

(on the verge of a terrible sadness)

The Merchant Boys are going to—?

HEXON

(disgusted)

We *never* did that. And this isn't for the Merchant Boys, anyway; it's for me. I heard on the whisper-stream that somebody wanted the Bad Babies. I had to see if it was true.

FYYAH

(opening the sleep-tube, sitting up, intense)

It *is* true! That's why I came . . . to find them.

HEXON

How can you know it's really true? Why would anyone want to—

FYYAH

It's a crew that takes the babies. It has to be. You heard about them, too, didn't you?

HEXON

Them? You mean the ones who used to—

FYYAH

Not them. They only bought the Bad Babies to sell. You're only allowed to sell babies from your own spray, but there's no market for the . . . parts from the Bad Babies anymore. And the Rulers know how to test the . . . organs. So whoever's taking the babies, they're not taking them to sell; they're taking them to keep.

HEXON

The Book Boys never wrote—

FYYAH
(with absolute assurance)

Not yet. But they will.

HEXON

Do you know where—?

FYYAH

Nobody does. But it has to be somewhere here in the Uncharted Zone. That's the only place the Rulers don't have sensors.

HEXON
(warningly)

The deeper you go, the worse it gets. All kinds of things that you never—

FYYAH
(*thoughtfully*)

You're not just talking, the way some boys do when they're trying to make themselves big. You've been out there yourself, haven't you, Hexon? Out real deep?

HEXON

A few times, but . . .

FYYAH
(*calmly urgent*)

I have to find them, Hexon. I think they have my little sister.

HEXON

Your sister-for-real? From your own spray?

FYYAH
(*excitedly*)

Yes! After I worked off my contract, I never went back to my spray. I knew they'd just sell me again, so I went on my own. Once the Dancing Girls chose me, I learned a lot of tricks. When I got good at stalking, I snuck back to see what was happening in my spray. My baby sister, Fiona, she was still with them; the only one left. I knew, as soon as she got old enough, my mother would—

HEXON
(*Hexon is all business, now; calculating trade value. Cutting her off—*)

How old is she?

FYYAH

Almost Year 6. Next cycle, she turns.

HEXON
(matter-of-factly)
That's too young to sell to a work site.

FYYAH

But not for the Sex Tunnels. You know where they list kids gone missing on the Info-Board? They don't do that if the kid is sold. The Rulers know where the kid is, so that doesn't count as missing.

HEXON

Why not try your . . . mother, first. If she was going to sell her, couldn't we negotiate with—?

FYYAH
(flatly, just the facts)
She's dead. My father, too. That's happening all the time now. First, someone steals a kid from the kid's spray. Then, after a while, the kid's owners end up getting killed themselves. How could a little kid kill grown people? And not just one kid; this is like a regular thing, so it has to be a crew at work. Some call them the Spray-Slayers, but that's just talk—the Book Boys never wrote anything on the walls. Anyway, it doesn't matter what they're called; Fiona's with them, whoever they are. I know that, even if I can't explain it. She's with them. And I'm going to find her.

HEXON
(V/O, hearing his thoughts)

Dancing Girls are all tough. They have to be—when they say "dance," they mean fight. All Dancing Girls carry razors. Some of them work in the Sex Tunnels, but most of them don't work. They steal, mostly. But going outside the Charted Zone takes more than being tough. I know. A few of the Merchant Boys have gone out but not come back. Me, I've come back every time. So far.

HEXON
(aloud)

We both need to find that crew, if that's what it is. If they have your sister, we'll get her back.

Fyyah reaches out, takes Hexon's hand, places it on her breast, over her heart, and closes her eyes.

HEXON
(V/O)

A Merchant Boy isn't allowed to do anything unless he gets something back. Dancing Girls aren't supposed to have anything to do with their own spray. In Underground, every crew has its own rules.

But none of that counts in the Uncharted Zone.

FADE OUT
FADE IN
Hexon and Fyyah, working their way through the tunnels. Hexon trades for the provisions they need. During one of the trades, two men suddenly

jump out of the shadows. Fyyah slashes expertly with her razor. Both men
are bleeding out as they stagger away. The man Hexon was trading with is
staring open-mouthed.

HEXON
(to the man he had been trading with)
That's two mistakes.

MAN
Hey! I didn't—

HEXON
(not listening)
That's what happens to people who live out here.
You lose touch. You thought Merchant Boys would
be easy, because all we do is talk. And you never
even heard of Dancing Girls, did you?

MAN
I don't know what you're—

HEXON
The deal is off. Give me back my barter.

The Man hands it over, says . . .

MAN
What about mine?

HEXON
(taking a small blaster out of his coat)
Here's what's yours.

FADE OUT
FADE IN
INT: Side-tunnel

Rats squeaking madly. Hexon and Fyyah stand side by side. Fyyah has a razor in each hand, Hexon is holding his blaster.

A pack of dogs—ranging in size, shape, color, of no known breed—suddenly burst into view, plowing through the rats like elephants through grass.

Hexon tries to step in front of Fyyah, but she hip-slams him to one side, flicks her razors closed, and pockets them. In almost the same motion, she squats down and holds out her hands, palms facing down.

The lead dog sniffs Fyyah's hands, then looks up at Hexon. A near-mechanical sound resonates deep within his chest, as if "threat" could be a physical thing.

FYYAH

Put your blaster away and get down here with me, Hexon! Do what I'm doing. Quick!

Hexon hesitates for a split second, then follows her command.
Everyone stays frozen for a long second.
Then a male child steps out of the shadows.

FYYAH
(to the child)

I want Fiona. I want my sister.

The child runs away. Seconds pass before he is replaced by a tall, broad-shouldered man, with a prizefighter's face. He speaks some unrecognizable word. The dogs part like a gate opening.

He then turns and walks away wordlessly.

Fyyah follows without hesitation. Hexon is a step behind her. Unlike Fyyah, he keeps looking back over his shoulder, and sees:

The dogs close in behind them, like cage doors slamming shut.

The man keeps walking until they come to a honeycomb of caves. There is plenty of light, but its source is not obvious. The caves are full of children, one of which is the boy who had first approached them. They range in age; the youngest are tiny infants.

The man steps aside. Fyyah carefully approaches the children, examining them one by one. Suddenly, she kneels and scoops up a chubby little girl, hugging the child to her chest.

FYYAH

Fiona!

Fyyah backs away toward Hexon. She holds the child with one arm, uses the other to pull one of her razors free. Hexon immediately draws his blaster.

FYYAH
(to the tall man)
We're going. Don't try to stop us.

FIONA
(struggling in Fyyah's arm, screaming like a baby)
No! No go!

FYYAH

It's okay, baby. We're going to take you out of here.

FIONA
(frantically, waving her arms)
No! No! No!

Hexon turns and finds himself facing a solid blockade of dogs. They are completely calm. And clearly ready to kill.

TALL MAN
(to Fiona)

Be still, child.

Fiona immediately stops crying and struggling

TALL MAN
(to Fyyah)

You can take her. But you have to pay.

HEXON
(stepping forward confidently—bargaining is his turf)

Credits, barter, or task?

TALL MAN
(his voice is completely neutral)

Tasks.

HEXON
(nodding)

Time tasks, or results tasks?

TALL MAN

Time tasks. One full cycle.

FYYAH
(standing on her toes, whispering to Hexon)

He means a woman's cycle. About twenty-four days.

HEXON
(walking toward the Tall Man, hands open)

Done.

FYYAH

Hexon! You can't—

HEXON

(to Fyyah, just short of commanding)

Take your sister and go. We made a bargain; sealed. They have to let me go when my time is over. Figure it'll take me ten, maybe twelve 24's to get back out. Take my pack. It's got the sleep-tube and plenty of freeze-dry. My card's in there, too. It's my Trader's Card, so it has about six hundred credits on it. Bring the kid to the West-Orange Medical Tunnel, get her a checkup.

FYYAH

But . . .

HEXON

(as if she had not spoken; one eye on the Tall Man)

You know you can't bring a child to the Dancing Girls—you have to protect her yourself. My blaster's in there, too.

I can't know exactly how long it will take, so you keep watch for me by the Merchant Boys. When I come back, we can both keep your sister safe.

As Fyyah starts to say something, Hexon turns his back on her, ending any "discussion." He strides away from her toward the Tall Man, dropping his duffel on the ground behind him, as if distancing himself from it. The Tall Man has not moved. Hexon steps close to him, holding out his wrists as if he expects to be cuffed.

TALL MAN
(holding up his palm like a traffic cop)
Both of you. One cycle.

HEXON
(to Fyyah, without turning his head)
Pull out my blaster, quick! Cover me!

HEXON
(to the Tall Man)
We made a bargain. Now let them go.

TALL MAN
You *offered* a bargain. You are a Merchant Boy. It
is one of your tricks to seal a bargain before you
have heard the other man's terms. I just told you
mine.

HEXON
(nodding ruefully, acknowledging he's been caught)
Okay. But I'm all you're getting. Look, I'll just
double my time. Two cycles. Deal?

TALL MAN
No. *(deliberately staring at Hexon's blaster, which
Fyyah now has trained on his chest)* I am not ready
to die yet, but that isn't important. *This* is: if you
kill me, you will never leave. *(He points a long
finger at the furry mass behind them)* You cannot
frighten animals with weapons. And you cannot
bargain with them, either.

FYYAH
(louder than a whisper, but very quietly)
Hexon, he's right!

TALL MAN
Both of you. No bargaining, no dealing, no nego-
tiating. Both of you, one full cycle. Yes or No?

FADE TO BLACK
Gradually open on the honeycomb of tunnels.

HEXON
(V/O)
That was about a year ago. We learned the truth
in those caves, and not from the Book Boys—we
learned it by living it. This is a family, not a spray.
The tall man never did tell us his name. He never
talked much at all, except for one time. But some
of the little ones called him Father, and we kind
of got into the habit too.

Father knows the Outlaw Tunnels better than
anyone. He showed me, a little at a time. Some of
them run so close to the Charted Zone that you
can just step across and step back, before anyone
even knows.

I do that now. To get things we need. Sometimes I trade, sometimes I steal. It doesn't matter.
I'm not a Merchant Boy anymore—their rules
don't matter. Only my family does.

After a while, Father showed us how he gets
the babies. It's easy. Real easy.

FLASHBACK TO:

INT: Separate cave

Sparsely furnished, clearly, Father's private headquarters. No children are present. Father is a man in perhaps his early fifties. He moves with the intuitive grace of a martial artist, but has no trace of "guru" in his mannerisms or affects.

FATHER

(speaking to Hexon and Fyyah together)

I began by simply buying the Bad Babies. They weren't worth much once the Word got out that all the transplants were failing. Then the Rulers ordered the implants, and fathers couldn't make babies with their own daughters anymore.

The Book Boys wrote there *are* no Bad Babies. And that was true: the babies weren't the bad ones; the bad one were the fathers who made them. And I knew, if there are bad fathers, there must be bad mothers, too.

Those are Closed Hearts. I began to take their children from them. Sometimes, I took their hearts, too. For that task, I had to learn many skills.

The Voice connects—it is now clear that Father was the Charter in previous scenes.

FYYAH

(respectfully)

You were one of those . . . cage-fighters? I thought that whole thing was just one of the Myths.

FATHER

It was no myth, child. Even before the Rulers started calling children born of a girl and her own father the Bad Babies, there were others who carried that brand. Others like me. We were bad at birth. That's what the Trainers said when they beat us. They started when we were very young. The first test was to stop crying. If you learned not to cry, they increased the pain—then you had to learn not to scream. After that, they used sticks. Clubs. Rocks. Anything that could tear flesh or break bone.

FYYAH

That's—

FATHER

Yes. Whatever you were going to say would be true, but words don't tell. Behavior is the only truth. The fathers who made the Bad Babies, didn't they say they "loved" their daughters?

The Trainers always told us they were teaching us special skills. But, first, we had to learn pain tolerance. Only the ones who learned it *all* were allowed to remain. The others were disposed of. The Trainers called that "culling." Only those who survived to the end of the teachings were permitted to fight in the cages.

HEXON

People *bet* on those fights?

FATHER

(mildly, but firmly)

Just as they bet on Traxyl fights now. Only Traxyls don't have to be trained to attack each other. They don't have to be . . . motivated. We were taught fighting skills, yes. But we always understood that the winner lives and the loser dies.

FYYAH

If they were . . . evil enough to do that. To do that to *babies*, what ever made them stop?

FATHER

They swallowed their own poison. Cage-fighters often escaped. Usually, it would be because they went mad. They would just run amok until the Police Squad executed them. But some ran in the other direction. They ran for the deep tunnels. And no one ever followed.

I don't know what happened to any of the others who ran. I was somewhere in the Uncharted Zone when people from the Temple found me.

FYYAH

The Temple?

FATHER

The Temple is where the Book Boys are. They had older people there. Old, but with great skills. They taught me. I spent a long time there. Then it was my task to teach others. Every Book Boy knows capture looms each time they write. So none may leave the Temple to write until they know how to do . . . certain things.

HEXON

But you didn't stop the cage-fighting . . . not all by yourself, did you? I mean, how could . . . ?

FATHER

I stopped nothing. The Rulers did. Every time they captured a Book Boy, they learned a truth of their own. It wasn't only what the Book Boys wrote on the walls that made them dangerous; every Book Boy is dangerous, too. The Analysts did their calculations. They reasoned it out. They understood they could never find the Temple; it cannot *be* found, because it is not a place . . . it is wherever we are. But they did learn that the Book Boys were being trained in the death arts. And who best to train them but the escaped cage-fighters?

The Rulers could never stop the cage-fighters from escaping. Most, but not all. They tried having them fight inside their prisons, but nobody would bet on the matches unless they could see the fights up close. It cost too much to train a cage-fighter, and it wasn't returning the invest-ment. So the Rulers killed them all. Every one.

The Rulers know: if you don't pull out the root, more will grow. So they killed everyone in the chain: breeders, inflicters, cullers . . . and the Trainers—they were the first to go.

The Rulers know: no matter how high the risk,

some people will take it if the possible reward is
high enough. If the reward sought is a pure one,
death is no deterrent. But if the reward is credits,
death works perfectly. After the Rulers finished
the killing, no one ever tried to start the cage-
fighting business up again.

FYYAH
Why didn't they just make a Rule?

FATHER
There is no need for a Rule against suicide. How
do you punish the person who breaks it?

FADE OUT
    *COME IN ON Hexon, carrying a huge duffel over one shoulder, pres-
ent tense:*

HEXON
(V/O)
When I come back from the Charted Zone, I
bring the things we need. And I know ways to
get credits that I never dreamed of when I was a
Merchant Boy.

Soon we are going to buy children. The ones
in Year 8 that their parents want to sell to the
work sites. All we have to do to get those Bad
Babies is offer them more credits.

Fyyah cut the implant out of her own thigh.
She said it was supposed to stop working after her
Year 17, but she didn't trust that. I told her that
was crazy, but she wouldn't listen:

CUT TO:

Fyyah, dressed only in a T-shirt and underpants, one leg braced on a low table, a gleaming razor in her hand.

FYYAH

I don't want them in my body, Hexon. Not any *part* of them. It's time for what I *do* want. Just hold my hand; it'll be quick.

FADE OUT

FADE IN

INT: Fyyah and Hexon walking together. Fyyah is obviously pregnant. The children around them are visibly older.

HEXON
(V/O)

When I step across, I bring messages, too. Fyyah already knows three Dancing Girls who want to come and be with us. I know only one Merchant Boy so far, but there have to be others.

We'll find them. They'll find others.

By the time the Book Boys get to write about us on the walls, we'll be too strong.

There will be too many of us.

The Rulers won't come back here. And Father says he knows a way Outside.

FADE TO BLACK

BACK TO:

AXEL

This was once a Traveler's Tale called "The Journey of Hexon and Fyyah." It is now the Book of Obligations. Mine (touching his heart) and yours (pointing at the audience, somewhere between a message and a threat).

FADE TO BLACK
(Characteristic) Humming Sound in the blackness, then:
OPEN ON INT: Gathering Hall
This time the podium is empty. A very tall, very slender, pale-skinned woman makes her way to the front. Her most striking feature is spiky jet-black hair streaked in red slashes. She turns to face the audience.

WOMAN

(bowing slightly)

My name is Tech. I come before you to speak from the Book of Connection.

FADE OUT as she beings to speak . . .
OPEN SLOWLY TO . . .
EXT: Wide shot of what had once been a city close in on windowless brick building. Remnants of signage indicate it was once a factory of some kind.
INT: Open space on the top floor of the factory.
A young woman with long, straight blonde hair is speaking into what looks like a jury-rigged microphone. . . .

YOUNG WOMAN

I hope you get this, Lynny. The cyber-link up here is real old, three or even four spans. We don't have generators like you do. But we have panels that store energy. Big ones, too. Most of them were broken, but there's quite a few good ones left. Besides, there aren't many people up here, so we usually have power, but it doesn't last.

I know that sounds crazy, but I'll try and explain. Anyway, if you're listening to this, you know I made it.

Nobody thinks much about Outside. I mean, not really. It was too many spans ago. I heard that some of the Ancients were even born Outside, but I never believed it—people just don't live that long.

CUT TO:

Shots of the destruction of newspaper office, government hunter-killer teams executing individual journalists, bloggers being cyber-tracked by government agents (of all races)—uniformed soldiers ripping them from their computer terminals. World leaders banning news broadcasting, demonstrators mowed down by soldiers who act as emotionlessly as if harvesting wheat. Finally, even graffiti taggers being "sprayed" with machine-gun fire.

Finally, scenes of total planetary destruction, progressing in a loop from jungle combat to urban guerilla warfare to ICBMs. Show a radically shrinking Arctic ice cap to rainforests disappearing. Humans end up fighting with the crudest of weapons.

YOUNG WOMAN

The Rulers say it was the Terror that brought us all Underground. They said that people couldn't live Outside anymore. If that's true, they must have known it was coming, because it took a long time for Underground to be built. I guess most of the Originals died while they were still digging the tunnels.

I don't know if you ever think of me, Lynny. I left when you were only Year 4. I know you cried. You yelled that you hated me. But I *had* to go.

I don't know if you even think about Outside, but I *always* did. I got up to Learn-Rite/Seven before I had to go to work, so I had plenty of programs. But none of them ever said what the Terror was. They just said that Outside had something in the air. Like chemicals, or even radioactive stuff. All the programs say that; I was only in Learn-Rite/Two when I first heard it.

If it wasn't for the Book Boys, I never would have heard anything else.

CUT TO:

ON A TUNNEL WALL:

THEY TEACH US LIES ABOUT OUTSIDE
IF THEY TOLD THE TRUTH, THEY'D ALL DIE

YOUNG WOMAN
(into the microphone)
That was the truth, sister-of-my-spray. There's nothing wrong with the air up here—at least not where I am. The only thing is, I don't know where I am, not exactly. See, there *is* no Outside.

I mean, it's not a . . . destination. It's not a *place* you can go to, like going to the Medical Tunnel. It's . . . too big to see. Or maybe even imagine.

The Travelers come through here all the time. They come to trade. Some of them trade stories.

SHOW:

Various individuals passing through clusters of destroyed buildings. Some carry sacks, some a musical instrument, some weapons . . . not invaders, mercenaries looking for work.

Transactions taking place.

A Traveler standing before a few dozen seated people, clearly narrating a story, complete with hand gestures.

YOUNG WOMAN

They tell us, in some places, it's warm all the time. And in others, believe it or not, it's cold all the time. And where I am, it's both. Not at the same time, but at different times. It's about three slice-turns for each change. When I got here, it was very warm. Hot, sometimes. Then it got cooler. Then real cold. Then warmer a bit. Then it was back to where it was when I got here.

The slice is way above us. You can see it when it gets dark. It gets dark, and then it gets light. Every day. Not like home . . . I mean, not like Underground.

Anyway, sometimes the slice is round, like a ball. And sometimes it's so skinny you can barely see it.

Things . . . *change* up here, Lynny. One Traveler even told us there aren't any Rulers anymore. Nothing happened to him when he said that, so maybe . . . maybe it's even true. But I'll have to wait until I see that one again. If I do, then I'll know for sure he was telling the truth.

I sure hope so. Otherwise, there's no way to really know anything—there's no Book Boys here.

She pauses, checks a soft red light on a makeshift console. It throbs weakly, like the pulse of a man struggling to live. She looks out the broken window to a sundial on the ground. She nods grimly, as if she understands she will not have much more time.

YOUNG WOMAN

You should be in your Year 12 pretty soon, Lynny. I don't think things have changed *that* much. People still wonder about Outside, don't they?

Wondering, that isn't the same as thinking. If you *think* about it, there's only two things that could be true. Either everyone the Rulers put Outside died because the air was so bad . . . or they didn't die at all.

Remember what I said about the air here? I always thought *that* was a lie. I mean, if the Rulers wanted to kill someone, why wouldn't they just do it right there, instead of sending them away? Then I thought, maybe the Rulers were scaring us for our own good. Maybe the Terror was still here, and they wanted to protect us.

Now that I know the air up here is safe, either the Rulers are lying, or they just don't know the truth.

Unaware that her actions are underscoring her words, she takes a deep breath. Holds it for a long time, then exhales very slowly before she picks up the microphone again:

YOUNG WOMAN

Cain was my boy, Lynny. When the Drover came to our sector, he said I had to go to the Sex Tunnels. I was just in my Year 14. Cain told the Drover they can't make you go until your Year 16, that was the Rule.

The Drover told Cain the Rule had been changed. Cain stabbed him and the Drover died.

The camera shows the above as the young woman continues to narrate over it, as if it were a silent movie. The drover is wearing a cattleman's duster, with a thick leather strap over one shoulder, to which rings are attached. Cain is wearing a crew uniform, a snow-white jacket with a red lightning bolt across the back. His hands are empty as they argue: the knife appears in Cain's hand so quickly that it is obvious he has used it many times before.

YOUNG WOMAN

Cain had to go in front of the Video-Counsel. It turned out the Rule really hadn't changed at all—the Drover was lying. But they said Cain should have put in a Dispute Ticket. Cain told them, by the time the ticket was processed, I would be gone. They said that didn't matter—killing is against the Rules. So they put Cain Outside.

SHOW:

A teenage boy and girl standing before a video screen. On the screen:

UYUT77-KJ09
OUTSIDE
RB11L-M331
SEX TUNNEL AT YEAR 16

YOUNG WOMAN

That's when I decided to go, Lynny. If I just stayed around and waited until my Year 16 to go into the Sex Tunnels, then what Cain did, it was all for nothing. I figured if they can *put* you Outside, there had to be a way to *get* to Outside, too.

I couldn't go out the way they took Cain. That way is guarded. And there's always a crowd of people standing around, waiting to see if anyone comes back. They all want the first person to come back to be theirs. Nobody has ever come back yet, so the crowd is big, really, really big; I saw it for myself. I went there when they took Cain. Some actually *live* there now. Just waiting.

So I just kept walking, until I was out of the Charted Zone.

I can't tell you where I went after that. Or who I stayed with. I can't take a chance that the Rulers might be listening. They haven't found the channel to Outside yet, or they would have closed it off.

Listen to me, Lynny: The Rulers lie. Cain

didn't die from the bad air. He didn't die from the Terror, either. I know this for sure. Because I found him.

You know what we have, Lynny? A baby. Our own baby.

Other people have babies here, too. They protect the babies. The Travelers said people learned that from the animals. The Terror only killed the humans, not the animals. I mean, sure, a lot of animals died. But not their ways.

We don't have Rules here. But there are things you can't do. Like a contract everyone signs. If we didn't have one, we would all die. Like, you can't take somebody's tools. If you get caught doing that, you have to pay it back double. But the most important thing is about children; they call it the Unspoken Law. You can't hurt children here, Lynny. It's not like Underground, even though the Rule there sounds the same. In Underground, you can't hurt children either, unless you own them. But here, you can't hurt *any* children, even your own. You can't have sex with them either, no matter how many credits you have. Not that we have credits up here, but you understand what I'm telling you.

We call ourselves the People. If we catch anyone hurting a child, they have to go away. And they have to leave the child they hurt behind. With us.

In the beginning, the ones who had to go, the Loners, they kept moving. But no matter where they went, nobody wanted them. So they tried to form a group of their own, like a crew, but then they started fighting with each other. So now they stay away from everyone.

You can feel them sometimes. At night, by the fire, you can feel them looking down at us.

Every group has its own code. That's what it's called up here, Lynny . . . a code. A Moral Code. That means, you live a certain way because it's right. Even if there are no Rules to make you.

Some of the groups are called Families. Not spray, like in Underground; it doesn't have anything to do with your blood. Our Family is called the Warriors. We guard the other Families. That's our work, like the Weavers and the Builders have their work. We don't trade, not like the Exchanges in Underground. But we all have what we need because we all have each other's work.

And I have a name now, Lynny. A real name. My own birth-name plus my Family name. So I'm not Rachel/RB11L-M331 anymore. I am Rachel Guardian now.

One of the old Travelers told us that Outside is just another word for Starting Over. We are Beginning Again, he said.

It's not like Underground, my sister. Sometimes it's cold and sometimes it's hot. There are animals. Big ones, so big they are scary. And some of the humans hunt, too. It's not quiet and clean and safe, like it is Underground.

But if our Codes win, Outside will be a better place than Underground ever was.

And if we lose, we just die, that's all. That's the code of our family: Die Trying.

The ones who get put Outside are the ones who broke the Rules. That means the Rulers are sending us the *best*. I know, some of them aren't the best. But plenty of them are.

I wanted to go back down into the tunnels and show people the way out, but Cain said if too many people came out at once, there would be an overload. And that would stop our Code from growing. Besides, he was afraid for me.

But Cain's a man, sister. He's my man, but he's still a man. My heart doesn't have a brain, but it knows what's right. It's so easy now, to know what's right.

This damn tape is almost done. Listen, my sister . . . sister-of-my-spray, sister-for-real, sister-of-my-Family, sister-of-my-Code. *Listen* now: When we were very small we had a game; a game of counting. Please remember. You could do any calculations in your head. Please remember, Lynny. Remember the time I counted the most cargo crates on the Conveyor? The most anyone had ever counted? Take that number, the number I counted, all right? Now take thirty-one and a quarter percent of that number, and round it off to the nearest hundredth. When you're ready, go back to the tunnel where you last saw me. Then walk that number of steps times twelve. No more, no less. When you get there, stop! You'll be in the Uncharted Zone, but nobody will bother you if you *stay* there. Just wait.

Bring food and water. It may take a while, a long while even. But someone will come. They

will ask your name. When you tell them, they'll
lead you to the channel to Outside. Those people
are a Family too. My Family. My first Family.
But they're not coming Outside for a while; their
work is to Guide.

Come Outside, sister. We're starting over.
Come be with us. Walk into the darkness, and
you can come into the light.

FADE TO BLACK
FADE IN ON:

TECH

By this we learn that Connection requires
Courage.

She bows again as we . . .
FADE TO BLACK
OPEN TO INT: Gathering Hall

*A Latino-appearing man is at the podium. He is impeccably groomed,
very "Latin-lover" in appearance. He speaks with only a trace of a Spanish
accent.*

LATINO AT PODIUM
(as if passing judgment)
Welcome, Solon and Sensa. Your wish to present
as a unit will be honored.

*He rather elaborately steps aside, making an ushering movement with his
hands. A man and a woman take the podium. The man is short and slim;
the female is both taller and heavier-built. The only physical characteristic they share is a blue lightning bolt branded into the right side of their
faces.*

SENSA
(unaggressive but inexorable)
The Book of the Mission is the parent of all. We
are here to do its work.

FADE OUT on her speaking
COME IN ON:
INT: Interrogation chamber
A hooded woman—THE QUESTIONER—waits serenely. A door
opens and a Young Man is marched inside by two people wearing full-body
coverings: impossible to determine their age, sex, or any other characteristic,
except that they are both much larger than their charge. The Young Man has
been branded: BOOK BOY has been laser-engraved across his forehead . . .
in blue, as if to mock his life's work.
The Book Boy is pushed into a seat across from the Questioner.
Utter silence.
Time passes.
The same two figures enter, and remove the Book Boy.
The same scene is repeated several times, with one subtle difference: At
first, we see the Book Boy inching closer and closer to the Questioner. But
then he begins inching backward. Then forward once again. He displays no
nervousness. It becomes clear that his pattern is to create no pattern. A Tao-
ist would recognize this as "The Way of No Way."

QUESTIONER
(harshly)
Patience is not one of your privileges here, Book
Boy. You know where you are: if you will not talk
to me, you will talk to others.

The Book Boy does not respond.
FADE OUT
BACK TO SAME EXACT SCENE

                    QUESTIONER
                     (sweetly)
Won't you at least tell me your name?

The Book Boy inches his chair closer to her.

                    BOOK BOY

YT555-4JD303

                    QUESTIONER
              (throaty, sexy . . . promising)
Not your ID, your *real* name. That way, we can
talk . . . privately. My name is Syreen.

                    BOOK BOY
                  (inching closer)
I'm Tracer.

                    QUESTIONER
                 (arching her back)
See? Isn't this nicer?

                    BOOK BOY
    (as if soothed, but actually soothing Questioner)
It . . . feels better, anyway.

                    QUESTIONER
Is there anything we could do that would make
things better for you here, Tracer? They *did* give
you permission to write on the walls of your compartment, didn't they? If they didn't, I can fix that.

BOOK BOY

I can't write if I don't have paint.

QUESTIONER

Now that's only fair. How about a trade? If you'll tell me where I can find some of your paint, I'll bring it to you.

BOOK BOY

I don't know where the paint is.

QUESTIONER

But you . . . all of you, I mean . . . you must have paint to work, yes?

BOOK BOY

Yes. But they give us the paint each time we go out.

QUESTIONER
(leaning forward)
Who gives you the paint, Tracer?

BOOK BOY
(breathing shallowly through his nose)
(literally radiating calmness)
Our teachers.

QUESTIONER

Teachers? You mean, from your temple?

BOOK BOY
(moving slightly closer)

Yes.

QUESTIONER
(smiling at Tracer)

I *love* it when a man tells me the truth. It feels as if
he's . . . stroking me. We know about the Temple,
Tracer. So I know you are being truthful with me.
That gets me very excited, the truth. Can you tell
me what they teach there?

BOOK BOY
(microscopically closer; lowering his voice slightly)

They teach us that truth is sacred. It was even
a religion once, before the Terror. It was called
"Journalism."

QUESTIONER
(surprised)

They teach myths?

BOOK BOY
(shrugs)

If truth is a myth, what is a lie?

QUESTIONER
(switching gears)

All right, Tracer. Tell me the *truth*, then . . . does
the Temple have a link to Outside?

BOOK BOY

You already know the answer.

QUESTIONER

How would we know such a thing?

BOOK BOY

Because the Rulers have always tried to match our blue paint. Then they could write what *they* want, and people would trust it. If it's written in blue, it must be true . . . everyone knows that. But the Rulers can't copy the paint, no matter what they do. They scrape it off the walls; they even confiscate our spray cans when one of us is captured. But they can't copy our Blue. Every time they try, the same tag goes up:

CUT TO:

   EXT: Wall

     IF YOU CAN'T MAKE IT, MAKE IT UP

COME BACK ON:

BOOK BOY

That's how you know our Temple has a link to Outside. The Rulers own everything Underground, don't they? So if they can't make something here, it must come from Outside.

QUESTIONER

(licking her lips)

I love it when a man teaches me things. Maybe tomorrow, you'll teach me something else, Tracer.

FADE OUT
FADE IN ON:
INT: Tracer's "compartment." Clearly a confinement area, but spacious and clean. Tracer is in a yoga position on the floor, breathing correctly, eyes closed.

TRACER
(interior monologue, as if reciting a lesson he has learned)
When a Book Boy is captured, the wave becomes the way. *Radiate.* Flow your fear to the men; flow your gentleness to the women. This will make the men brave, and the women unafraid. They will become calm. Move through the calm. You must be close to finish your work.

Tracer rotates his neck. The crack of adhesions breaking is audible. He stands up, walks to his pallet, lies back, and closes his eyes.

TRACER
(interior monologue)
The Questioner makes promises she can't keep. The whisper-stream says the Rulers don't have sex—they clone. But we don't write that on the walls, because we never write rumors. Our way is our path. When truth turns to lies, everything dies.

FADE OUT
COME IN ON . . .
INT: Interrogation chamber
Tracer's chair is closer to the Questioner than ever before.

QUESTIONER
(almost purring)
Come on, Tracer. You promised. *(Said petulantly, with a pout. The Questioner has removed her hooded cape, revealing a truly beautiful, extravagantly endowed young woman with long red hair.)*

TRACER
(almost as if mesmerized)
All Book Boys have the same handwriting. The exact same. The Rulers can't tell which of us wrote any particular message.

QUESTIONER
(opening a snap to deepen the V of her top)
Oh, that's *good*, Tracer.

Tracer leans forward, tentatively reaches out to touch her hair.

QUESTIONER
(teasingly)
I thought you were a Book Boy, not a *bad* boy.

Tracer pulls back his hand, looks somewhat shamefaced.

QUESTIONER
(taking his hand and putting it back where it was)
This isn't the only Interrogation Room, you know. There're lots of different kinds. One of them's in the back. It's dark in there. With a nice soft couch. But we're only allowed to bring any-

one back there if we can be sure it would . . . help.
Do you understand what I'm telling you, Tracer?

TRACER
(softly)
Sometimes it's easier to talk after. . . .

QUESTIONER
(wicked smile)
You go back to your place and think about that,
Tracer. Tomorrow, if you're ready to *really* talk to
me, maybe we can go to that other room.

FADE OUT
COME UP ON:
*INT: Tracer's "compartment." He is flat on his back on the floor, feet
and hands suspended in the air. His eyes are closed and his breathing is
almost undetectable.*

TRACER
(interior monologue)
I send out gentle waves to her. In and out like
the tide. Or sex. She thinks being inside her will
weaken me, not knowing I am already there. *Send*
the tide, *become* the tide.

Our tides have an undertow. What they pull
beneath will never surface again.

Tracer visibly relaxes, breathing shallowly.

TRACER

(interior monologue; thoughtful, not reciting doctrine)

The Rulers know the truth about some things. They know some of the Book Boys are girls. But in the whisper-stream, we will always be the Book Boys. That was one of the first lessons: whatever the name, the truth stays the same.

Like the Guardians. They don't come from the Temple, but they protect us. They're a war crew, mixed. All different skin/shades. We write their truth on the walls:

CUT TO IMAGE OF:

YOU CAN'T SEE US
SO YOU'LL NEVER SEE US COMING

BACK TO:

TRACER

(interior monologue)

Just *being* a Guardian is enough to get you sent Outside; same as being a Book Boy. We never meet; we never talk. But it is the same for us both: Once you truly learn a lesson, once it gets in deep enough, you *become* the lesson. The Rulers think all our work is writing on the walls. They think, if they capture one of us, that one's work is done.

CUT TO:

Tracer, fleeing into a tunnel. He has a spray can in one hand, empty-ing it as he runs, a Police Squad on his heels. Most of the pursuers are *picked off by arrows, laser blasts, and throwing stars. But Tracer runs right into another Squad, coming from the opposite direction. One Police Squad member zaps him with a purple-tinged beam, and he drops, paralyzed.*

TRACER
(interior monologue)

It is time for my other work now. Focus! Even knowing how to convert the enemy's strength into your own power, is not enough for this. It is all timing. Had I moved too quickly, the cello-curtain would have come down between us. Floor to ceiling, like the see-throughs they have in the Sex Tunnels.

The Rulers always ask different questions when they have one of us, but the only thing they really care about is finding our Temple.

They have serum. Electrodes. Girls who offer you sex. Or boys, if that's what you want. Promises. Threats. None of that ever works . . . because it *can't*. The Temple isn't a place, it's a truth. And all truth travels. Whenever one of us needs to return, we just step into the Uncharted Zone. Then we walk our path until the truth finds us. If we sense anyone following us, we just stop. If the Tracker stops, waiting for us to move, the truth will find him, too.

But when you tell the Rulers you don't know where the Temple is, they're sure you're lying. As we have been taught: the best way to lie to the Rulers is to tell them the truth.

The Rulers have a lot of information, but no knowledge . . . and no way to get any. Even if they

could read our minds, the path to the Temple
isn't in there.

It's in us.

*Tracer flows into a sitting position, so fluidly it appears he transformed. He
opens his eyes: they are dry ice. He closes them again, quickly.*

TRACER
(interior monologue)
Tomorrow might be the day. I'll be close to the
Questioner, with no curtain between us.

She says the truth makes her excited.

*Image of the Book Boy and the Questioner on a large cushion. She is on her
knees, facing away from him, in what is meant to seem like a submissive
position, but she has her head turned sufficiently to keep whispering insistently. The Book Boy murmurs some sound as he slips one arm around her
neck. One quick twist and the Questioner falls away, lifeless. Instantly, the
door bursts open and a squad in full-body gear bursts in, long weapons at
the ready, the tips crackling with electricity. The Book Boy is on his feet in a
classic martial arts horse stance: one hand is fisted, the other ridged to chop.*

TRACER
I will be last the Book Boy she ever tells that
lie to.

FADE TO BLUE
  HUMMING NOISE FILLS THE VOID
  OPEN ON INT: Gathering hall

SOLON

The Book of the Mission *is* our mission. And the
Book of Obligations requires that we defend it.

FADE TO BLACK
OPEN ON INT: Gathering hall
Four women are standing at the podium, dressed in identical black
robes with purple sleeve-stripes. They speak in a continual stream, one pick-
ing up exactly where the other leaves off . . .

FIRST WOMAN

This is from the Book of Revelations . . .

SECOND WOMAN

. . . and Transformations.

THIRD WOMAN

The order is no accident.

FOURTH WOMAN

First came the Revelation. . . . .

FADE OUT on a shot of them all speaking
FADE IN:
Open on a crew of music boys stalking toward THE SEX TUNNEL.
Boom boxes are on their shoulders, each holds a different sort of short club in
the other hand. One of the youngest in the crew points to a group of differ-
ent individuals, all garbed in one-time-use-only plastic suits, hard at work
doing various cleaning tasks.

YOUNG MUSIC BOY
(tugging at the vest of an older boy)
What crew is that, Lyric?

LYRIC
That's no crew, kid. That's a horde. You have to be
chosen to get in a crew. If no crew wants you, you
end up in a horde.

YOUNG MUSIC BOY
And the hordes do all the cleaning?

LYRIC
(cold-laughing)
Hordes do *all* the dirty jobs in Underground.
That's why you have to be in a crew. If you're in a
horde, you're nothing.

*The Music Boys pass through the entrance to the Sex Tunnels. The camera
watches them go, then pulls back out to one of the horde workers. He is
scrubbing the exterior wall, but his attention is focused on a young woman
who is also entering the same tunnel. She's round-faced and kind of chubby,
with her hair tied in a long ponytail, wearing nondescript jeans and a plain
white sweatshirt. Another horde boy approaches as he works, and speaks to
the scrubber out of the side of his mouth.*

HORDE BOY #1 (scrubber)
What're you staring at, Esau? You act like you
never seen a whore before.

HORDE BOY #2
She's not a whore, Zimmy.

ZIMMY

Yeah? What do you think she does in there every
day?

ESAU

I don't know, but she isn't a sex worker. They
always live in the Tunnel. You never see them
coming and going. Only the customers do that.
The workers can't leave until they finish their
contract. And most of them just sign up again,
anyway. Once you work a full contract in there,
what else *could* you do?

ZIMMY

I never thought about it.

ESAU

There's a lot of jobs in there that don't have anything to do with sex. Look at our horde: we don't
have anything to do with sex either, but we help
the tunnel keep running, don't we?

ZIMMY

No we don't; we just clean things. Come on,
Esau. What's the worst job in Underground?
Cleaning the walls, right? We have to keep them
so pure and bright it hurts your eyes to look at
them. What's that got to do with sex? Nothing!
It's what the Rulers tell us to do, so we do it.

ESAU

Most of the stuff people write on the walls is just
silly. Sex stuff. Drawings of people doing . . .
whatever.

ZIMMY

That crap isn't what I'm talking about—one shot
of Chloroscrape from a hydroblaster and it's
gone. It's those damn Book Boys that make us
use the AC7—that's the only thing that removes
that blue paint of theirs. It eats the cover right
off the wall. Then we have to put on the plastic
spray-sheets, and layer it back until it looks new
again. I wish they'd just stay away from here—
there's enough walls in Underground for them to
work on.

ESAU

They only write on *these* walls when it's something about sex.

ZIMMY

Who cares? I just wish I could catch one of them
doing it. The bounty is five hundred thousand
credits! That's enough to buy anything you want,
even your own crew. But the Rulers only pay off if
you catch one of them actually writing. And you
have to get the special blue paint too—that's the
only real proof it's one of them.

ESAU

I never heard of one of them getting caught.

ZIMMY
(confidently)

Oh, they get caught, all right. It's just that we
don't see it happen. Book Boys don't wear crew
gear. They could be anywhere, anytime. Hell, for
all I know, you could be one yourself.

ESAU
(shocked, but kind of flattered, too)

Me?

ZIMMY
(letting the wind out of his sails)

Relax, man. I know you don't have the balls
for anything like that. Everybody knows what
happens to a Book Boy when the Rulers get
them.

FADE TO BLACK
FADE IN:
INT: Outside the sex tunnel
Note, the artificial lighting outside the sex tunnels roughly approximates
a daylight cycle, starting off faint (dawn), growing steadily brighter (noon),
then darkening as time passes (dusk, then night).

The horde arrives, and sees the Book Boys have been at work:

SEX WITH KIDS
THE RULERS AREN'T THE ONLY ONES
WE ALL KNOW WHAT YOU DID

ZIMMY

Damn! It's going to take hours to get *that* off.

ESAU

Don't touch it, Zimmy.

ZIMMY

Are you insane, man? If we don't take it off, the
Rulers will . . .

ESAU

Check out the right bank. Don't turn your head!
Use your mirror ring.

*The camera comes in close on the reflection in Zimmy's ring: a pack of
Guardians, standing together, weapons at the ready.*

ESAU
(whispering)

Guardians! We have to wait until they're gone
before we touch anything the Book Boys put
up. The Police Squad will be here in another *(he
glances up at one of the digital clocks that are omni-
present in Underground)* sixty clicks or so. *Then* we
can start cleaning that part of the wall.

ZIMMY

There's a bounty on Guardians, too.

ESAU
(sarcastically)

So go grab one.

ZIMMY

Maybe if there was only one of them. . . .

ESAU

(rolls his eyes; says nothing)

ZIMMY

Look! *(pointing)* There's *another* one!

CAMERA PANS TO:

THEY NEVER WANTED TO DO IT
AND YOU ALWAYS KNEW IT

ESAU

(tilting his head in the direction of the Guardians)
Calm down! There's plenty of other work to do
until the Police Squad comes. And once we get
both of those signs off, the Book Boys probably
won't be back for weeks.

FADE OUT

Passage of time indicated by showing the horde at work over several days.

COME IN ON: *Zimmy and Esau, staring open-mouthed at:*

YOU THINK PAIN IS A GAME?
YOU THINK WE DON'T KNOW YOUR NAMES?

ZIMMY
(incensed)

That's *it*!

He opens an alarm box on the wall, and presses a red button. The Police Squad rumbles into position.

ESAU

Good move, genius. The tunnel won't be getting a lot of customers today.

ZIMMY

So what? I'm not getting any of those credits, anyway.

The entire horde is still working when the girl Esau had first noticed departs the Sex Tunnel. She flashes a smile at him . . . very quick and very private.
FADE OUT
NEXT "MORNING"
On the wall. Same script, same color paint, but in a much larger font:

THE RULERS KNOW YOU RAPE THEY HAVE IT ALL ON TAPE SO DO WE

FADE OUT on the horde starting to work.
They are still working when the Girl exits. She makes the slightest gesture with her head. Esau slides away from the horde and stands close to her.

THE GIRL
I know you can't stay here long. My name is Rose.

                    ESAU

I'm Esau. Are you with a crew?

                    Rose

No. I don't have a horde, either. So I have to pay
tolls to get to my job every time.

They are still walking as . . .
    FADE OUT
    *Camera shows the passage of days. Esau is working when Rose arrives;
and he is still working when she leaves. Each day, they manage to talk a
little longer, but we don't hear whatever they are saying.*
    FADE OUT
    COME IN ON:
    Esau, walking through a tunnel, occasionally using a pencil flash.
    *INT: Esau and Rose, inside Rose's cell. It's about half the size of a studio
apartment. They are sitting at a table built from salvage, talking.*

                    ROSE

Was it bad today?

                    ESAU

You mean, did the Book Boys tag? No. But, really,
I don't care.

                    ROSE

Because you have to work the same number of
hours, no matter how you spend them?

ESAU
(thoughtfully)

It's not just that. I guess I was trying to say . . . I
don't know, what they write, it's the truth. If it's
written in Blue, it must be True. But sometimes
you have to figure out what they're saying.

ROSE
(tilting her head)

You like doing that, Esau?

ESAU

I . . . I guess I do. I never thought about it before.
Until you asked me, I mean. I mean, it's not the
kind of thing you tell people. You know . . .

FADE OUT

COME IN ON

INT: Rose's cell. Esau is there, too. But now they are in bed together. He
is lying on his back; she is cuddled against his chest.

ROSE

Esau?

ESAU

Hmmm?

ROSE

How come you never talk about your work? You
always ask me about mine, but you never say a
word about yours.

ESAU

(shifting position, now on one elbow)

I'm . . . embarrassed, I guess. I mean, you're a cashier. People tell you what they want, and you point them to the right arrow. The color of the arrow tells them how many credits it's going to cost. Most of them, they already know, so you don't have to . . . deal with them, really. You have a *good* job. Me, I only scrub dirt off walls. I'm nothing.

ROSE

How can you say that?

ESAU

Why not? It's true. I'm in a horde because none of the crews wanted me. But you . . . you're by yourself because that's what *you* wanted.

ROSE

(gazing at Esau very carefully, as if searching)

A crew doesn't make you anything. Neither does a job. What I do in there, yes, it's a good job . . . if you mean the pay. But some of it's dirty. A lot dirtier than anything you have to do. Dirty and ugly. Evil.

ESAU

What's "evil"?

ROSE

When the customers have sex with children. The children don't want to do it, but the Rulers make them.

ESAU

But the Rulers make *everybody* do things they don't want to do. That's what the Rules are. If people *wanted* to do things, you wouldn't have to make them do them, isn't that right?

ROSE

No. That's wrong. I don't mean you're not telling the truth; I mean, what the Rulers do, *that's* wrong.

ESAU

But if the Rulers make the Rules, how can any rule they make be wrong?

ROSE
(wistfully)

I thought you *read* what the Books Boys write, Esau. And thought about it, too.

ESAU

I *do* read it. But I don't always understand it.

FADE OUT
FADE IN
Clear that time has passed.
INT: Rose's cell.

ESAU
(takes a deep breath)

Rose, would you . . . would you be with me? My cell isn't even as big as yours, but if we each sold ours, we could get a pretty nice one. Big enough for us both. Then we could—

ROSE
(sadly)

I do love you, Esau. But you're not ready to be with me. You have to—

ESAU
(almost frantically)

I can get more credits! All I have to do is—

Rose slaps Esau. Hard. Then she puts her face in her hands and starts sobbing.

ESAU
(knows he did something wrong; not sure what)

Don't cry, Rose. I'm sorry. Just tell me . . .

FADE OUT on Esau as he walks out of the cell. Rose is still crying.
FADE IN
EXT: Sex Tunnel
Esau is at work with his horde. Rose walks past him without a word or even a glance.
FADE OUT
FADE IN ON
INT: Esau's tiny cell. He is writing something on a tablet. We see the word "Rose." He looks at what he's just written, then rips the note to shreds, fighting back his own tears.

FADE OUT

FADE IN ON

Esau's cell. He clearly has not slept. Looks up at the digital clock. 13:54. He puts on his work clothes and walks out the door.

EXT: Sex Tunnels. Very dark. Esau trudges along, knowing he is way early for work, but with no other place to go.

EXT: Sex Tunnels.

Esau sees what is clearly a Book Boy at work, spraying the wall in their special blue.

He glances up at the BOUNTY sign, flashing.

He moves closer.

It's Rose.

FADE OUT on Esau, retreating.

FADE IN

Rose is in her cell. She hears a tap. Opens the door. Esau steps inside.

ROSE

Esau! I told you—

ESAU

(rock-determined)

I know what you told me. You told me you loved me. And you told me I wasn't ready to be with you. But you told me something else . . . I was just too hurt to listen.

ROSE

You don't—

ESAU

You've *been* telling me all along, haven't you? But I couldn't figure it out. I tried and tried, but I never understood.

                              ROSE

Esau, if you don't—

                              ESAU

I spent all that time trying to understand what
the Book Boys were saying. And you even told
me yourself that people who have sex with kids,
that's wrong. Even if there's a Rule that allows
it, it's wrong. But I never put it together. I never
understood it. Because . . .

                              ROSE
            (seeing his distress, stepping in close to him)
Because what, Esau?

                              ESAU

Because I was one of those kids, Rose. They only
let me leave the Sex Tunnel when I got too old.

                              ROSE
            (first stunned, then she reaches for Esau)
                   (as if appealing to God)
Oh Blue be True!

                              ESAU

I tried to find a kill-crew to join. I figured there
had to be one that hunted the . . . people who
used the Sex Tunnel for kids. The whisper-stream
is always talking about the Children of the Secret,
like they're a crew. But I never found them.

CUT TO:
    INT: Deep tunnel

A young man is moving carefully but with confidence. His face is scarred to the point of disfigurement, barely visible under a black bodysuit. He is armed to the teeth, clearly looking for a victim. . . .

HUNTER
(interior voice, as he moves)

The safest place in all Underground is the Sex Tunnels. A long time ago, the Sex Tunnels were the most dangerous. They scared people, just being there. Nothing is forbidden in the Sex Tunnels. But that doesn't mean there are no Rules. The Book Boys wrote it on the wall.

IF YOU DON'T HAVE THE CREDITS
YOU DON'T GET IT

What they were talking about was First Rule: you *always* have to pay. You can buy anything in the Sex Tunnels. Any skin/shade, any age. Do anything you want to do . . . so long as you have the credits.

The Rulers keep count. It goes on your encoder, so they always know. As soon as you go inside, the scanner tells the truth about you, and the arrows point you to the subtunnel where they have what you want. After you see the cashier.

You can buy anything. That's what the Sex Tunnels are for. You just have to remember that nothing is for free. That's why kill-sex costs the most credits, because they can only use the product once.

Nobody is supposed to be afraid to go into the

Sex Tunnels anymore, because the Rulers made it safe for everyone.

But the Book Boys still scare some people off. The Rulers say they are terrorists—there's a reward for naming any of them. The whisper-stream always flows when one of them is caught, but that never changes anything.

CUT TO:

THE RULERS LIE
THE TRUTH CAN'T DIE

HUNTER
(still on the prowl)

People have sex outside the Sex Tunnels, but that has to be sanctioned . . . and only approved sex is sanctioned. So, if people want to have unsanctioned sex and don't want to pay for it, they have to go into the Uncharted Zone.

Some of those who wanted to have sex with children, that's where they went. They took the children with them. They said this was different from the Sex Tunnels—what they were doing was love. They said you shouldn't have to pay for love, just for sex. So they went where they could do what they wanted without paying.

But none of them ever came out.

CUT TO BOOK BOYS MESSAGE:

YOU PAY IN CREDITS
AND WE COLLECT YOUR DEBITS

HUNTER

That one was tricky. A debit is a death. Everyone knows that. But . . . who died? And why?

Whatever it meant, it didn't stop anything. The people who say they love children still go into the Uncharted Zone. You can even buy maps of how to get to the places where the children are kept. But nobody knows if the maps work, because the people who sell them keep disappearing.

Maybe they never go into the Uncharted Zone at all. Maybe they go Outside. Maybe that's what the Book Boys are telling us.

CUT TO:

WE ARE NOT THE TERRORISTS
THE TERROR WAS OUTSIDE
THEN, NOT NOW

HUNTER
(sits down, unwraps a bar, chews slowly)
(interior monologue)

Sometimes, I wonder if there are any Rulers at all. The whisper-stream says there was a computer program. It was built Outside, because Underground had to be built before the Terror took over. It had to be ready for people a long, long time before anyone came down here. At least the life-support systems had to be in place. Some say the tunnels were all dug by prisoners, like the people sent to the HydroFarm work to make the power that drives everything here. And some say it was mostly children, the used-up children.

Everybody says. Nobody knows.

Some say the Rulers don't ever put you Outside at all—they just kill you. That part could be true. My friend, Horto, he wanted to go Outside. You can't buy something like that—it's supposed to be a punishment. So Horto broke a Major Rule, and they came and took him.

Horto promised to contact me. Everybody says there are transmissions from Outside; they come into the Uncharted Zone. If you're in there, you can pick them up. Merchant Boys bring them back, and sell them to the people they're meant for. And you can even hire a Messenger to look for you, if you expect one. But nobody knows if the messages are real, or just made up. Made up in Underground, I mean. I think, if Horto ever contacted me, I'd know. We were true friends. But he never did.

The Hunter finishes his meal, carefully pockets the wrapper, and goes back to work. His movements are more calculated now. Stealthy. His face is a mask as he opens his eyes WIDE, then closes them, repeating the exercise to accustom himself to a deeper darkness ahead.

HUNTER
(interior monologue, as he moves)

I know secrets even the Book Boys don't. The man who took me into the Uncharted Zone when I was a child told me it was the only place where we could share our love.

After a while, he shared me.

When I got too old, they walked me far away and left me there. I found my way out, just stumbling along. I didn't have anything to trade so I had to do other things.

Later, I joined a kill-crew. The initiation was easy. The only rule they had was that you couldn't kill anyone for a reason, like getting even or something. You had to kill for the killing. We covered all the tunnels.

That's how I found out that other kids like me had made it out, too. They never said anything, but I could see it on them like a sign. Some of them had grown into the ones who took me into the Uncharted Zone—now they say they love children, too.

After I killed the first four of those, my crew realized I was doing it for a personal reason, so they kicked me out.

That's when I discovered not all the other kids who got kicked out turned into the ones who took me. They hated them, too. Just like I did.

A party of three men passes by where the Hunter lies in wait. One has a pale-beamed flash, another carries what is clearly some form of tranquilizer gun, the third all different kinds of restraints.

The Hunter slides along until he is standing in the direction they are headed. As they close in, he raises a small spotlight in one hand and triggers it. The blast of light is so extreme that the three men fall to the ground, temporarily blinded. The Hunter drops the spotlight, unsheathes a two-handed sword, and steps forward.

HUNTER
(interior monologue, as he walks off . . . deeper)

I shouldn't say, "Just like me." I can always tell who they are, but that's the only thing we share. Some of us turn into the men who love boys; some of us turn into men who hate those men. But most of us, we just . . . blend in, I guess. We'll never be a crew. Never be together. All we share is the Secret.

But that doesn't matter. I learned one thing from those men who loved me: I don't need love. I don't need a crew. I don't need any friends. I don't need anything. I don't even need to keep doing this.

The Hunter shifts to a listening posture. He nods, as if confirming a deep truth, then flattens himself against the tunnel wall until he becomes invisible.

HUNTER
(unseen; we are hearing his thoughts as V/O)

No, I don't need it; I just like it. I like it a lot. Maybe this is my love.

FADE TO BLACK
COME IN ON INT: Rose's cave

ESAU
(still talking)

Or maybe I did, and I never knew. So I ended
up . . . where you found me. Scrubbing the truth
off the walls.

ROSE
(reacting to Esau's self-loathing tone)

Maybe you were just—

ESAU

I was just . . . nothing. Look, Rose, I never realized that Book Boys could be girls. I know I'm not
good enough to be a Book Boy myself. I couldn't
be a Guardian, either—they wouldn't have someone like me. But I could be *your* guardian, Rose.
If you'll have me, you can have my life, too.

Rose watches Esau's face, searchingly, but her expression is unyielding.

ESAU

I'd never let you down, Rose. Never, I swear.
I don't just love you; I love that you stand for
something. I'd be proud to die for you, Rose. At
least then I wouldn't be a nothing anymore.

ROSE
(sets her jaw)

You were never a nothing, Esau.

*She reaches her arms out to him. FADE OUT on Rose holding Esau, so
tightly they seem to merge into a single being.*
    FADE TO BLUE (SAME EXACT COLOR AS BOOK BOYS' PAINT)

FADE IN
INT: Gathering hall

ALL FOUR WOMEN
(in unison)
The Book of Revelations and Transformation is
proof of the power of true knowledge. And the
danger of false knowledge.

FADE TO BLACK
Humming noise fills the black
FADE IN
INT: Gathering hall
*At the podium is a man in his late thirties. This is Zak. His face is smooth
to the point of elasticity—his eyes, especially: they switch back and forth
constantly between the empathy of a nurse and the iciness of an executioner.*

ZAK
We are many colors, but we are *all* the People.
How we appear has no meaning; how we act is
where the truth is always found. The Book of the
Mind explains the teachings of the Book of Transformations, and clarifies the Book of Obligations.
Inside, we are *not* all alike. My name is Zak; I
am an Insighter. Our work is to see the inside of
people, and to decide. Some we can help; some
we can heal. And some we must expel.

FADE OUT on the man speaking . . .
OPEN ON:
*A young man dressed in Game Boy gear. He is alone, moving with
the resolute stride of a man-on-a-mission. Because he displays a variety of
twitches and tics (tardive dyskinesia) others quickly clear a path for him.*

A Game Boy is dangerous enough, but a crazy one is walking dynamite, and this one is talking to himself in classic schizophrenic fashion.

RADIOMAN
(as if addressing another person)

I know she's on the HydroFarm—it was on the Info-Board. Not her name; they never do that. But I know her ID! And when she is finally with me, I'll know *everything* about her. All I have to do is take her away. She wants me to do that. I don't care what you say; *I* know she does.

FADE TO:

Long shot of the hydrofarm, the camera making it clear that the scope of the entire enterprise is too vast for a single shot—"overheads" are limited in underground—but enough to show work fields, gro-lights, and "quarters" for the workers.

Close in on a girl who is hand-harvesting under the watchful eye of an overseer. As we come in closer, we see this is the infamous Charm, leader of the Dancing Girls.

CHARM
(interior monologue, as she works)

The trick in here is to keep your place without killing. If you kill anyone on the Farm, you never get to leave.

I've been here before. That was only a 4-cycle punishment, but I didn't have my name then, so it was hard.

But now I have my name. Charm, Leader of the Dancing Girls. Dancing Girls don't stand on platforms and take off our clothes for credits. "Dance" means fight. And I'm not charming.

None of the other crews want to dance with us. Even those crazy Game Boys, the ones with their little blasters, they step off. Their blasters aren't that good; you have to be real close for them to work. And if you get close enough to us, you're going to die. Razors never jam the way their blasters do. And they never miss, either.

Razors are better for scaring people, too. A lot of people don't even know what blasters are, but everyone knows a razor. Everyone gets afraid when they see that thin blue edge. Everyone knows how easy it goes through flesh.

A giant misting machine releases a blanket of fine spray over the work field. The workers all stand still, waiting for it to pass.

CHARM
(still interior monologue, almost musing)

That water; I don't know how they make it. One time, an old man told us that, before the Terror, water just dropped down by itself. Nobody made the water; it just happened. Those real old men are insane—this one wouldn't stop jabbering about this "rain" nonsense, not even when I told him we were going to take his tongue.

All boys are crazy. And the Game Boys are even crazier. But none of them are as mad as that Radioman. He tells everyone that I love him because he hears it in his head. That's the most psycho thing I ever heard in my life. I don't love anyone. I don't even know what it means when people use that word. I know it doesn't mean sex.

Some of the Dancing Girls work the Sex Tunnels, for credits. They all say the same thing: you never hear the word "love" in there.

Radioman is a Game Boy. They're the ones who started the whole thing about the marks. You got a mark for every life you took. I had a lot of them. I'm a Dancing Girl, so I wore them on my thigh, since it was so fashionable.

(Charm gazes down at the drab uniform she now wears, as if she knows a secret, but her expression never changes, and she continues to work at the steady, measured pace of an experienced bracero.)

CHARM
(still interior, but tone almost regretful)
But then it all went bad. Word got around that if you killed someone who already had marks, then their marks belonged to you. So people stopped going after the easy kills and went after the ones who already had marks. It was harder, but you could get marks so much faster. A lot of people in crews got put Outside, because it's against the Rules for crews to fight each other. The Rulers were all confused, but then the Book Boys straightened them out:

CUT TO:
    A Wall-warning:

EVEN IN THE DARK
YOU CAN'T SHARE THE MARKS
WHEN YOU KILL JUST FOR YOU,
YOU KILL YOUR OWN CREW

CHARM

(interior voice, as she rotates her neck to loosen up)

By the time the Rulers figured out this wasn't gang war, the bums had their *own* crew. That was a surprise. And I guess it made the Rulers very upset. You could tell because they changed the Rules, and they do that only when they get angry.

By then, most of the crews had already stopped wearing their costumes. And when they did, it was on the fringes, near the Uncharted Zone. That wasn't much fun. People don't recognize you're moving all together in a fan unless you're all dressed the same. Without the gear, it was lousy. What's the good of being the boss of a crew if nobody even knows it *is* a crew?

And not everybody was into the marks thing, anyway. Radioman was a Game Boy, but he never got a signal inside his head to take a mark, so he never did. That made him the lowest in his crew, but he didn't care.

Radioman doesn't care about anything. One time, he just walked up and said he loved me. Right in front of everyone. It was so insane I couldn't even get mad; I just laughed at him. One of the other Game Boys laughed at him, too. *That* one had a lot of marks, so I ripped him. The other

Game Boys were scared to shoot, because we all had our razors out. That was before it stopped being fashionable. Taking marks, I mean.

CUT TO:

Radioman is still walking, moving deeper into the tunnels. Still talking to himself.

RADIOMAN
(not thinking; talking inside his head)

There has to be a way to get people to the Hydro-Farm. The Rulers must use a Conveyor. It's too far to walk. The ones who come back always say it took a long time to make the trip. They couldn't see anything, but they knew they were moving. And new ones come back every twenty-four.

Shots of Radioman pathetically trying to "interview" recently discharged inmates—all still wearing HyroFarm uniforms—as they depart the Conveyor.

RADIOMAN

I am always polite, so I guess they don't tell me because they don't know. But it has to be some-where inside the Charted Zone. All the power for Underground has to come from the HydroFarm. The Rulers could never risk losing it. Besides, the Conveyor runs only inside the Charted Zone.

RADIOMAN

(making it clear he is addressing the Voice)

I'm sorry. I apologize. I know I shouldn't ask people questions. Only you. *You* know, don't you? Just tell me, and I'll do anything you want. I always do, don't I?

Radioman resumes his walk through the tunnel until he fades from view. We come back in on . . .

CHARM

(grimly resigned, but not defeated)

It's all a circle. You work here to make electricity. They use electricity to make you work. And *that* works. Nobody wants electricity on them. Being wet all the time, it doesn't take much. All one of the Overseers has to do is tap you with the prod. . . .

It's easy enough to get away, but not many even try. They never keep you more than twenty cycles, and you can have Zoners for free. Some of the people here, they don't feel anything, they just smile. They can still work, though, so they never get jolted. Plus, if you escape, they double whatever time you had left.

And even if you could get away, where could you go? If you have a crew, it would a Betrayal to go back to them—Harboring, that's breaking a Major Rule. If you ever want to go back as Leader, you can't get the others in that kind of trouble. A leader has to protect her crew. Even if you're the best dancer, that's not enough.

Show next monologue as a v/o to a "silent movie"

The Love Boys leader was Cameo. He was huge. And a great fighter, too. But when the Police Squad came, and one of the Love Boys twisted his ankle, Cameo didn't go back for him. The Love Boys beat Cameo to death. They put his body on the Conveyor, so everyone could see it.

If I just wait until my time is done, I can go back and be Leader again. There'll be a new girl who wants to keep her place, so we'll have to dance. I can't wait. That's the worst punishment of all—you can't dance here.

Charm squats, as if having difficulty with a stubborn root. The camera shows us she just wants an excuse to look at a tiny slice of metal glued to the underside of her thumbnail.

CHARM
(twisting her lips ever so slightly)

I had to buy that tiny little slice of nuim. Not with credits, they don't have any in here. If you're caught with credits, they think you're getting ready to escape . . . and then you get jolted. Nobody can take too many of those; it makes you like you're on Zoners all the time: always smiling, but you can't even eat. They have to feed you with tubes so you can work. So I paid with sex. I didn't even have to look at the Overseer while he did it.

They all like to sex me, because I have a reputation. They all know how I get so excited and wet and make the noises they like. It's easy: I just

close my eyes and think I'm slicing on them. That
always works.

CUT TO:

Artificial darkness

*Charm is alone in her dorm. That is, others are present, but they are
resolutely looking away as . . .*

*Charm sits naked on her bunk, and uses the nuim to cut a thin, straight
line across the front of her left thigh. Her touch is practiced; the blood is so
faint that it looks as if she drew a red line with a fine-point marker.*

CHARM
(inside her own head, watching the blood dry)

I have to be careful not to go too deep. Blood
dries quick here, and the moisture keeps it clean.
By tomorrow, it'll look like a tattoo. Besides, even
the Scanners know—you can't work the fields
without getting cuts on you every so often.

FADE TO:

*Radioman talking to a Merchant Boy, gesturing frantically. Finally, he
hands over a bone-handled knife. As the Merchant Boy speaks, he listens
intently, then walks off.*

RADIOMAN
(aloud, as if speaking to someone next to him)

Now I know where it is. I'm going there. *Now.*

FADE TO:

*Charm is on her bunk, wearing a regulation sleep-suit. But she is wide-
awake, her slitted eyes sweeping the dorm.*

CHARM
(inner voice)

There's other Dancing Girls here. But even talking to a member of your own crew means you get a jolt. Everything is on video. Even in the dark, they have infra and thermal. There's no way to connect.

Marking myself is all I have. The Rulers know the Overseers are going to want sex, so they make them take pills. But they don't work—they don't erase things, they just bury them. You have to know how to dig down deep. The nuim helps me do that.

I can do it anytime I want now. And I have only three cycles left.

She closes her eyes and fades into a peaceful sleep as the camera comes in on Radioman, checking the map he bought from the Merchant Boy.

RADIOMAN
(to the voice in his head)

Why are you lying? Charm *will* come with me. What she said that time, she only did that to fool the others. The only thing that scares me is how the HydroFarm changes people. I remember when Ithar got off the Discharge Conveyor; he was like a different person. Maybe it's the jolts. That's when I first started hearing you. When I was there myself before, I mean.

CUT TO:

Charm, back to working in the fields. She drops to her knees and puts her head down, pulling at a stubborn root. She cants her head to one side,

sweeping the area. When she picks up on an Overseer watching her, she twitches her bottom subtly. Her mouth is an ugly slash in her face.
CUT TO:
Radioman, now standing on the far perimeter of the HydroFarm:

RADIOMAN
(to the voice)

I can see Charm now, but I have to make sure she sees me before I take her away. I have to be quiet until then. No moving!

CUT TO:
Charm, still in the same position, still eye-sweeping the area. She knows the show she's putting on will keep the Overseer from ordering her back to work.

CHARM
(inner voice)

That crazy Radioman has been here for three turns now, just standing outside the perimeter. He came for me because I have what he needs. I have what they all need. And I can't wait anymore.

She stands up, holds up two fingers. Looking at the Overseer. She licks her lips.
The Overseer nods, pointing at his wrist.
Charm takes off.

RADIOMAN
(to the voice)

Here she comes. She wants to be with me. I *told* you!

FADE TO BLACK
COME IN ON CHARM
She is working in the fields, really moving her way down the row, pick-
ing expertly. Energized.

CHARM
(inner voice, still excited)

Radioman even brought my razor. Now I can
keep the feeling inside me for a long time. Long
enough to finish my cycles and get back to where
I belong. Radioman was so good to me. He knew
what I really needed. Maybe that's what love is—
giving someone what they need . . . no matter
what.

FADE OUT TO RED/BLACK
FADE IN

ZAK

The Book of the Mind teaches that some can
be transformed through revelation. Helped and
healed. But it also teaches that understanding is
not transformation. Some are beyond our reach.
We must learn to know such people, because they
cannot be allowed to walk among us.

FADE OUT
Humming noise on emerging screen
FADE IN
INT: Gathering hall
At the podium stands a man in his late forties/early fifties. His long hair
is gray-streaked, his face is craggy, and his voice has a preacher's carrying
power.

MAN AT PODIUM
My name is of no consequence; I am my father's father's father's son. I will not be staying among you. It takes many, many spans to learn the Book of the Path, and I must use the time left to me to teach it.

FADE OUT on the man gesturing, accompanying a speech we don't hear . . .

FADE IN

INT: A murky dive that could be a bar or a café or a diner, depending on viewing angle. There is no uniformity to the place—the furnishings were all randomly assembled from scrap and salvage.

A man is seated in a booth in the farthest corner. The seat against the wall is an individual chair, so that whoever occupies it can use the table as a work desk. The other side of the desk is piled-up scrap, creating a wall. A small terminal to the right of the single chair shows strings of trailing data, much like an electronic stock ticker.

CLOSE UP: The man in the booth is maybe in his mid-thirties, but with a very old man's eyes, cold behind clear bifocals. He is scanning various publications, including individual sheets, occasionally glancing at the terminal. A colorless drink is just past his left elbow. He makes a few more marks on a long, narrow sheet of paper, like an adding machine tape. This is a man at work.

A woman approaches. She has long blonde hair, a very short skirt, and extravagant (implanted) breasts on display via a tight-fitting top. Her face is something like the man's mid-thirties but with much older eyes. She looks like a hooker past her sell-by date if you're flying first class.

WAITRESS
Want something to eat, Ace?

ACE

(shakes his head no)

WAITRESS

Business first, huh?

ACE

(twists his mouth in a half-smile)

WAITRESS

Well, I had to ask. I mean, I know how you are, but people change, right?

ACE

That's like saying the favorite doesn't always win, Candy. It's true enough, but what're the odds? *That's* what counts.

CANDY

That's for . . . things, not people. Nothing's ever going to change here. Underground, that's for-ever. But every single person is a separate thing. You can never be sure.

ACE

That's how I earn my living, little girl.

CANDY

You're the only one who calls me that. Some of them, they're old enough for that to be true, maybe, but you're not. And you never grab my ass, either.

ACE

(interested in her reasoning)

So you add that up, what do you get?

CANDY

(hands on hips)

You mean, like in the Sex Tunnels? Some of the buyers only want little girls; they wouldn't go near a grown woman. So, one: that's not you.

ACE

(even more interested: this could be info he could use)

How do you know?

CANDY

(her lips curl: smile-sneer-snarl)

I know because I took the course, and I paid the tuition. Maybe I don't know much, but what I know, I know for real. You don't say "little girl" like you want to dress me up and spank me. And you're not putting me down, either. I know what *that* means (she pauses, folds her arms under her breasts) even if you don't.

ACE

I know good logic when I hear it.

CANDY

Yeah? What's all that logic good *for*, Ace? You're here every day. It's like this is your office. And I'm your secretary. More than that. I take care of you, don't I? You get the best food, the cleanest drinks. Anybody wants to see you; they have to see me first.

ACE
(quietly, not softly)
And I take care of—

CANDY
'Cause you always leave a tip that's way too big? That's not taking care of me; that's paying me.

ACE
What's the—

CANDY
You know how many of the men who come in here offer me credits to . . . "take care" of them, Ace? Got any idea? What's the *odds*, Ace? *(not quite angry, but close)*

ACE
(not reacting to her mood)
Off the charts.

CANDY
(mockingly)
Very good. But, then again, you're the *best*, aren't you? Try a harder one. Do I ever do it? Do I ever "take care" of any of them? Come on, smart guy. You don't miss a thing. Tell me.

ACE
(studying her closely)
Same call.

CANDY
(leaning close, both sexy and angry)
I'm a little slow about that whole odds thing, Ace.
How about you spell it out for me.

ACE
(flat toned, full eye contact)
You get offered credits for sex every single day.
You never go for it. And there's no chance you
would, no matter how much anyone had on their
card.

CANDY
(appraisingly)
I see why everyone says you're the best. You see it
all, don't you? Except I'm not a Traxyl, Ace; I'm a
woman. I've got something for you . . . and you
know it. But you won't ante up, will you?

ACE
I don't know what you—

CANDY
You're afraid. *(Not said snidely, more like a diagno-
sis.)* This *(she pats her left breast)* is what scares you.
Emotion is the enemy, right? If you start *feeling*
things, that gets in the way. You make your living
betting on things with no feelings. They just do
what they do; they never think about it. But you

bet *against* people who have feelings. All kinds of feelings. Superstitions, hunches . . . stuff like that. That's why they don't have a chance against you. That's your edge.

> ACE
> *(gives her a long, slow look)*
> You don't miss much yourself.

> CANDY
> *(as she turns and walks away)*
> You may be the best, Ace. But you don't play to win.

FADE OUT

> *BACK IN ON SAME INT: A man approaches Ace's booth. Ace hands him a strip of paper and a plastic card. The man inserts the card into a hand-held device, then taps in the information Ace just gave him, and displays the screen for Ace's approval:*

| B/4 | UF44TT | 1,000 | 7-1 |
| B/6 | OOR2II6 | 4,000 | 9-1 |

Ace nods. The man extracts Ace's card, returns it to him, and leaves. Candy approaches. She is carrying a tray of food.

> ACE
> I didn't—

> CANDY
> *(just short of bossy)*
> Business is over. Time to eat.

ACE

Yeah, yeah, okay. But I didn't tell you what I wanted.

CANDY
(putting out the food)
Since when do *you* order food? I picked this out for you, like always. The same way I make the Runner wait until you're ready before I send him over. I know you don't care what food tastes like, all you want is the fuel. That's not good for you, so it's my job to make sure you get the best. Like always.

ACE

I never—

CANDY

What? Put me in charge? That's right; *I* put me in charge. Any time you want to change things, you just put in your own damn orders, okay?

ACE
(not just looking at her, capturing her eyes)
I *do* want to change things. But that's not something I can do here.

FADE OUT
OPEN ON
INT: *A private cave that is both luxurious and monastic. All the equipment has a top-of-the-line look, but there are no cooking facilities, just a cold-box big enough to hold several small unlabeled cans. The place is*

heavily carpeted; even the walls and ceiling are lined with sound-absorbing
pads. The single chair is a recliner, with an ottoman. A data-screen—very
similar to what was in Ace's booth, only much bigger—covers one wall.
Various charts and graphs are pinned to another.

ACE

I built it just for me. But I could put in a—

CANDY

(looking around)

With that carpet, we won't need any—

ACE

(offended)

I wasn't talking about—

CANDY

(pulling off her top as she speaks)

I know, stupid. But I waited long enough. You're
the man I can prove it with.

ACE

(befuddled)

I don't—

CANDY

You know what I . . . did. Before I went to work
at the Den. That's no secret. But there *is* a secret. I
hated what I . . . did before. It was only my secret
that kept me from killing myself before my time
was up.

CANDY

(slipping out of her skirt, a seamless, latex-like garment)
I never told anyone my secret, not any of the
other girls. You want to know my secret, Ace?

ACE

(deliberately looking away from the strip tease)
Yes.

CANDY

(walks over and stands very close)
My secret was that I knew someone loved me. I
didn't know when he would come for me, but I
knew he would. So what they . . . took from me
there, that was *nothing*, see? All that time, I was
saving. Saving it all up, like storing it on a special card. I saved a lot, but I was always afraid it
wouldn't be worth anything.

ACE

Your —?

CANDY

Love? No. Listen; this is hard to say. I knew, when
the man who loved me found me, I would love
him, too. I would do anything for him. Not . . .
what you think. I mean I would . . . die for him.
That *had* to be worth something. But the stuff I
got *paid* for, I hated that.

Ace closes his eyes, as if he doesn't want to see what Candy is seeing.

CANDY

I could never understand when the video stories
talked about people "making love." How can you
make love? So I never knew if the man who loved
me would feel . . . cheated when he finally came
for me. I waited until I was *sure*. But now I have
to *prove* it, don't I?

ACE

Candy, you don't have to—

CANDY
(unhooking her bra)
Prove it to my*self*, honey. Prove they . . . *none* of
them . . . they never really took anything from
me. I still have it. All saved up. Saved up for you.
(She reaches out her hand) Come on. Come on,
Ace. It's time to find out if my secret was the real
thing . . . or just a get-numb dream.

Candy leads Ace over to the sleep-mat as we FADE TO BLACK
OPEN ON INT: Ace's cave.
*Now significantly redecorated to accommodate two residents. All his
gambling tools are still present, but the place is softer, somehow. The sleep-
mat has been replaced with a double-wide futon, the cold-box is much
larger, and there is a series of burners over what might be an oven. It is
obvious that some significant time has passed.*
The digital clock reads: 03:03:16
*CLOSE-UP: Ace is lying on his back, smoking. Candy is next to him,
in a sitting position. The room is very dark.*

ACE

You really want to hear all this?

CANDY

(reaching over to stroke his hair)

From the beginning. Every word. I want that
inside me, too. Just like I always want you inside
me. Deep. So deep it makes us like one person.
I have to feel what you feel. And I can't do that
unless I know. But I can wait, sweetheart. I waited
a long time for my secret to come true; I can wait
some more for the rest of it.

ACE

(reaches out and holds Candy's thigh)

FADE OUT as Ace starts to speak . . .

*FADE IN . . . Ace has been speaking for a while . . . we come in on him
in the middle:*

ACE

They *always* had these fights. Before the Terror,
I mean.

CANDY

(not challenging; interested)

How could you know that?

ACE

You can check out stuff like that—I mean, stuff
that happened before Underground—if you
really want to. There's history terminals in the
Knowledge Tunnels, if you have the credits. But

those are all a sucker play—the only truth in Underground is free.

CANDY
(nodding)
The Book Boys.

ACE
Yeah. But they tell only truths; not info. And that's what I need, info. Most of the players aren't like me—they're gamblers, not professionals. It's just like you said once, Candy: they never think about the odds, they don't do the research . . . they just go with their blood, with their feelings. That's my edge. And you figured that out just from watching me.

CANDY
(knowingly)
Everybody's always looking for an edge. And some people try and make their own.

ACE
You can't fix a Traxyl fight, little girl. There's always rumors about drugs and stuff, but it would be real hard to drug a Traxyl. You could never get a needle into them, so it would have to be in their food. And Traxyls eat only Zone Rats. I guess you could maybe drug one of the rats; then, when the Traxyl ate it . . . But I can't see anyone pulling that off—everyone could tell right off if a Traxyl had been poisoned.

CANDY

So what if they could tell; who would they tell it *to*? Gambling on Traxyl fights is against the Rules, so if anyone complained to the Rulers about cheating, they'd be telling on themselves, right?

ACE

Gambling is only a Minor Violation. If they catch you, all you do is pay a fine. That's part of the cost of doing business; it doesn't bother me. But there's other rules, too. Player's Rules. If anyone got caught fixing a fight, it would be . . . very bad.

I saw that happen once. A Handler cut his Traxyl's eye with a razor ring just before he sent him out. Traxyls can't smell; I don't know if they can hear too good, either. But they need their eyes. Big, huge eyes, so they can see in the dark when they go after the Zone Rats. The other Traxyl locked on to the one with the cut eye and it was over quick. I wasn't the only one who saw what the Handler had done. The other players just threw him into the pit.

CANDY

The Traxyl who won . . .

ACE

Traxyls don't feed on other Traxyls. They kill each other, but the winner never eats the loser. They kill for territory, like hunting space. Any time one Traxyl enters another's space, they fight. That's how the pit fights started, I guess. No human

would have a chance against a Traxyl if he came
into their space. And when a Traxyl wins a fight,
the pit *is* his space, see?

CANDY

I don't feel bad for that Handler. He got what he
deserved, doing that to his own—

ACE

Nobody felt sorry for him. Traxyls aren't that big;
even the largest ones are only about thirty kilos.
But they're armor-plated, and once their jaws
lock, there's no way to open them. Every once in
a while, one breaks loose, and the Police have to
kill it. Traxyls don't feel electricity, and shooting
doesn't stop them, either. The Police are so scared
of them, they always blow them up. Whenever
they do that, everyone around the area gets killed,
too.

CANDY

Even if it's not their fault the Traxyl got loose?

ACE

It's a Rule that no Traxyls can run loose. So killing people to stop one, that would be sanctioned.
Besides, you know the Rule: if the Police do it, it's
never against the Rules.

CANDY

They don't have any choice, the Traxyls. It's not
like they . . . get paid or anything.

ACE
(glances at Candy, sees she identifies with the Traxyls)
Well, it's not going to go on much longer. When a Traxyl gets loose, it just keeps killing until they blow it up. A Traxyl doesn't care about the Rules. So the places where they hold the fights keep getting moved farther and farther away from the Central Tunnels. Now almost all the fights happen near the Border, just this side of the Uncharted Zone. Some are so far away that you need to hire one of the Guides to take you there and bring you back.

CANDY
The Guides? Are they a crew? I never heard of them.

ACE
More like a spray, I think. Every one I've ever seen is a skin/shade 40+, almost a reddish color. That's weird, right? I mean, you'd think they'd be real pale from spending so much time in the Deep Tunnels, but they're not.

CANDY
Do Guides capture the Traxyls?

ACE
No. Only Trappers do that. Traxyls live in the Uncharted Zone. A good fighting Traxyl is worth enough credits to live on for a few years. Live *nice*, not just get by. Most of the Trappers don't succeed; that's why Traxyls are so rare.

CANDY

What if they go out and never catch a Traxyl?

ACE

(flat, unsympathetic)

In a way, they're gamblers, too. Some go into the Uncharted Zone and never come back; some go in a few times and bring back a Traxyl. But if you go in too many times, the odds shift. Shift way down.

If you believe the whisper-stream, there's people in the Uncharted Zone. *Living* there, not just going in and coming out. I even heard that the Traxyls guard those people from the rats, but that sounds so crazy . . . I mean, what're the odds on *that?* But, one time, I was walking to a fight, and the Guide showed me a Book Boys sign:

CUT TO:

SURVIVE, STAY ALIVE
BREED WHAT YOU NEED

ACE

And it was the real thing, too. In their blue and everything. I didn't think the Book Boys ever went back that far—the only way you could even see what they wrote was with a flash . . . I can't figure out how the Guide saw it.

One of the girls who lived in the Sex Tunnels *(Ace stops and steals a glance at Candy, who gives him a "What?" look—meaning she never thought*

Ace had been celibate, and no-emotion sex would be exactly what she would have expected him to engage in) . . . she told me that the people who live in the Uncharted Zone bred the Traxyls themselves. Like . . . *created* them, to protect them from the rats. But girls in the Sex Tunnels say anything. *(This brings him another "Tell me something I don't know" look from Candy)* Anyway, she said she was going to go out to the Uncharted Zone herself one day. To join them, she said. I asked her what she meant, but then her buzzer went off, and she just got up and left.

CANDY

Did you ever—?

ACE

I never saw her again. The next time I was there, I even asked for her, 'cause I wanted her to tell me what she meant. But they said she was gone. That could mean anything, so I just . . . I don't know, forgot about it, I guess.

CANDY

Yeah. What's another missing whore?

ACE

What do you want to put that on me for, girl? I was just . . . Look, you *asked* me, remember?

CANDY

(contrite and *worried)*

I'm sorry, honey. I'm sorry for real. Didn't you ever have something just . . . slip up on you? So many years of . . . wearing my shell, I guess. I . . . don't know what to say. I did a wrong thing. I mean, I wronged you. I asked you to tell me your secret, and I had to be a goddamn wise-ass when you did. I'm just a—

ACE

Remember what you said before? About how food was nothing but fuel to me? What do you think changed that?

CANDY

Changed that? Nothing changed that. If it wasn't for me, you'd still be eating whatever damn—

ACE

If it wasn't for you, I'd still be having sex with whores, too, you stupid bitch. Now just shut your big mouth and listen, okay?

CANDY

(sunburst-grinning)

Yes, sir!

ACE

The only thing I ever *really* paid any attention to was the Traxyl sheet. It's fifteen credits; comes out about ten 24's before the fight card.

CANDY

I've seen those, but I never looked close. It, like, tells you which of them won and stuff?

ACE

That wouldn't be worth anything. The loser always dies, so any Traxyl on the sheet never lost. What the sheet tells you is how many fights each Traxyl had before, their weight and height, any permanent injuries—they fight Traxyls even if they're crippled, and some of them win that way for a while, too—the name of the Handler, stuff like that. Every fighting Traxyl has an alphanumeric burned into its side. It doesn't hurt them, just makes a mark on their armor. The hardest thing to guess is when a new one's going to be good. You can't train Traxyls. A Trapper brings one in, a Backer buys it, then he turns it over to a Handler . . . that's the guy who actually puts it into the pit to fight.

You can't tell anything about how good a Traxyl's going to fight just by looking at it. I had to learn that for myself. See, what I wanted was what every Gambler is always looking for. . . .

CANDY
(knowledgeably)
Sure. That one big score, right?

ACE

Yeah. But that was before I knew the difference. Gamblers . . . gamble. A *player* uses a *system*. That

means you have to be . . . disciplined, I guess.
What good is an edge if you can't cut with it?

CANDY

I don't get it. The losers who spend every day in
the place I work, they never stop talking about
their "systems." But they don't seem to win much.

ACE

Those aren't real systems, girl. They're just habits.
I studied that, too.

CANDY

Habits?

ACE

(gets out of bed, stands up, and pulls a book from a shelf)
No, honey—studying habits wouldn't be any
good. Habits are . . . personal. Different ones for
different people. Like when you see one of them
hunch-betting. Or betting based on stupid stuff,
like which Traxyl is the biggest. But the *odds*,
that's more like . . . numbers, okay? Numbers
don't have feelings. (Ace holds up the book so
Candy can see the cover: STATISTICS I.) This
is where I started.

CANDY

Wow! That's an *old* one. Like it came from
Outside.

ACE

Cost like it did, too. But it was worth it.

CANDY

But if it came from Outside, it couldn't be about Traxyls. . . .

ACE

I didn't want to learn about Traxyls; I wanted to learn about odds. Come here; I'll show you. *(Candy walks over to where Ace is holding the book open on the desk)* Say a Gambler sees a Traxyl with a limp. The odds are big against that Traxyl, but the Gambler plays a hunch. And he wins. What does that mean?

CANDY

That he got lucky.

ACE

(pleased)

That's *exactly* what happened. Luck. *Just* luck. That gambler, he had an idea that a Traxyl with a limp *meant* something . . . like an omen. He bet, and he won. He had what this book calls a hypothesis. *(Pointing to a page in the book)* His was that a Traxyl with a limp is a better fighter. When he won, the hypothesis was what they call "valid." That means it proved true . . . *once*. But if *every* Traxyl with a limp won, then his hypothesis wouldn't just be valid, it would be what they call "reliable." Otherwise what happened that one

time was just a coincidence . . . that's the word
this book uses for "luck."

CANDY

And that's what a system . . . a *real* system is?
Reliable?

ACE

Sure thing. Only, see, *nothing* is ever a sure thing;
that's the part you can rely on. You know what
Gamblers call a sure thing? A "mortal lock."
I guess that comes from what happens when a
Traxyl clamps down . . . the fight's over, then.

I tried all kinds of things until I figured it out:
But you can't tell *anything* about a Traxyl. There
was one—I still remember him, M6MSY—who
won eleven in a row. That was a record—no
Traxyl had ever done that before. When I came to
the fights that night, I saw M6MSY was matched
against a Traxyl that had fought only one time
before. The odds on the one-win Traxyl were
about 50 to 1. But I waited until just before it
went off, and I found a Taker who was offering
75 to 1. I put up two hundred credits. And my
Traxyl won. I'm probably the only one who *did*
win that night.

CANDY

How is that any different from just getting lucky?

ACE

Don't you see? I was testing *my* hypothesis: that any Traxyl can kill another, no matter what their records are. The first time, it was valid. Lucky, fair enough. But, by now, I know it's reliable. So if the odds are crazy enough, I play. See, I'm not betting on a Traxyl; I'm betting *against* everyone else. The Takers each set their own odds, but they do it from the way the betting is going. The more money on one Traxyl, the longer the odds on the other.

CANDY

But if you don't win—

ACE

I don't have to win every time, girl. I just have to win more often than the *odds*, see?

CANDY
(nodding in understanding)
So, if the odds are 50 to 1, and you win only two out of every fifty bets, you're still ahead.

ACE
(admiringly)
You are the quickest girl—the quickest *person*—I ever met in my life. Yeah, that's it. In one sentence. My system. It's not Traxyls; it's people.

All Gamblers are always looking for a system. When M6MSY got killed, a lot of them figured eleven wins was the maximum. So, the more a Traxyl won, the more they'd bet on it . . . until it got close to eleven, and then they'd back off. But when J44B8 won thirteen fights before *it* was killed, that theory got killed too.

The Takers love those Gamblers, because the Takers have a system of their own. That's why I have to bet on every single match. Otherwise the Takers would catch on that I'm working a *real* system, and I couldn't get any action. One of the hardest things about being a professional is to look like an amateur.

> **CANDY**
> *(nodding to herself)*
> That's why you never wear any flash.

> **ACE**
> Right. No ego. That's another thing I noticed. Some of the Handlers acted as if they *liked* their Traxyls. I could never be sure, because you can't touch one or anything, but it looked that way. I saw one Handler crying when his Traxyl died. I figured he was probably upset because he lost so much money. But I couldn't be sure . . . so, whenever I see a Handler like that, I never bet.

> **CANDY**
> You don't trust emotions.

> **ACE**
> I had a lot of reasons not to. Just like you.

CUT TO:
> *A Book Boys message:*

THE CLOSED HEARTS STAND APART
BUT YOUR FUN IS ALMOST DONE
THE TIME WILL COME
WHEN THE CHILDREN OF THE SECRET
REJOICE IN THEIR CHOICE
THERE WILL BE NO PLACE WHERE YOU ARE SAFE

ACE
(holding both Candy's hands)
I never would have . . . stepped across the line. It was like a . . . shield I put around me. If it hadn't been for you, I'd still be . . .

CANDY
(crying softly through her smile)
I'm no Gambler, either, Ace. I played only once. And when I did, I put everything I had on the line.

FADE OUT
FADE IN
EXT, CAFÉ
Candy steps out the door. Ace is waiting for her. They start walking together, hand in hand.

ACE
Any problems?

CANDY
With Umal? He hardly even looked up. I don't know why you thought he'd—

ACE
(lamely)

I guess I thought . . . I don't know, maybe you
were good for business or something. So maybe
he'd kick up a fuss if you wanted to—

CANDY
(deliberately bumping ACE with her hip)

Good for business? In *that* place? It's like a Zoner-
pipe den in there. The Gamblers come in, get
their fix, and just stare into space. I could walk
around nude; it wouldn't make any difference to
them.

ACE

Is that right? Then how come you always bring
home so much tip money?

CANDY

Hey! You know how it works: when a Gambler's
flush, everybody gets a tip. Umal can get someone to replace me in ten minutes. *You're* the one
who kicked up a fuss, remember? There was no
reason for me to quit. Now that I'm not going to
be working, it feels . . . I don't know. Like I'm not
pulling my weight or something.

ACE
(lightly smacking CANDY's bottom)

All this weight?

CANDY

You think I don't know my own man, you big
dope? I know how you slip around things that
scare you. I did what you wanted, now it's your
turn.

ACE

To do what? I already said I'd—

CANDY

If the next sentence that comes out of your
mouth has the word "credits" in it, you're in serious trouble, mister. I quit my job out of faith.
Not faith that you'd pay my bills, faith that I'd
be *part* of you. If you don't understand that, then
you can just—

ACE
(very serious)

Oh, now it's *your* turn, huh? You think I don't
know *you*? You didn't find me, Candy. And I
didn't find you. It was like we bumped into each
other in the dark. We went in blind. Who does
that in Underground? Suckers. Chumps. Fools.
Idiots. That's not either of us. So *you* explain it.
Go ahead!

*Candy doesn't say anything, but she slows her pace, and moves so her body
is right next to Ace's.*

ACE
(when she doesn't reply)

Yeah. I thought so. Why did I bring you back to
my place? *(pause)* And don't give me one of your
smart cracks, miss; I'm not in the mood.

CANDY

I wasn't trying to make you mad, honey.

ACE

I know. *(He touches her breast—exactly where she
touched herself the first time she told Ace he was
afraid of what's in there.)* You're just scared.

CANDY

Me?

ACE

You, little girl. You don't want to say it out loud,
because you're afraid you'll be wrong. But you're
not. I never brought *anyone* to my place. *Ever.* I
was raised on the same rules you were. Not the
ones the Rulers made; the ones that you have to
learn for yourself or . . . Always keep your back
to the wall, right? When I brought you to my
place, you knew what that meant. My place isn't
just a cave; it's me. I brought you in there. Plenty
of things in Underground can kill you. Plenty of
them will. Some for credits; some for fun; some
for . . . who knows? When I was a kid, people
hurt me. Like they hurt you.

CANDY

Plenty of—

ACE

Right. That doesn't make us special. It doesn't make us anything. But when I say they hurt me, I don't mean like with a whip, or an electrode. Hurt me *in* me. And I fixed that the same way you did.

CANDY

Built a shell.

ACE

Uh-huh. And I built a beauty, didn't I? So when I opened it up to you, that made you special.

CANDY

Because you love me for real?

ACE
(sadly)

I do love you for real, Candy. But what makes you special is that I made you the only person in Underground who can hurt me. Now you think you can shut up until we get home, or do I have to explain how you're going to pull your weight right here?

CANDY

You don't have to explain anything to me, Ace. Not now, not—

ACE

(smacks her bottom again, but, this time, hard enough for the crack! to
resound through the tunnel)
You never know when to be quiet, do you?

FADE OUT
INT: Ace's cave
Several hours have passed.
Candy is wearing one of Ace's flannel shirts; it comes down to mid-calf.
She is barefoot, and obviously nude beneath it. Ace is also barefoot, in a
pair of cargo pants and an old T-shirt. He is seated at their "kitchen" table;
Candy is pacing back and forth as they speak.

ACE

Okay, now? You get it? I didn't want you to quit
because I was jealous (catching a glimpse of Candy's
legs as she paces past). Okay, maybe I was, a little . . . but I knew that was stupid.

Candy stops, hands on her hips.

ACE

Will you stop? What I meant was, it'd be stupid
because you . . . opened yourself, too. You're not
my . . . girlfriend or something; you're my . . .
(searches for the right word) . . . you're my partner.
Not like a business partner, part of me. Like I'm
part of you.

CANDY

You don't have to calm me down, like I'm going
to explode or something.

                    ACE
               (sarcastically)
No?

                   CANDY
No! Who's always giving who a smack?

                    ACE
         (angry at the false allegation)
Yeah, that's me, the big mate-beater, huh? Did I
ever throw a dish at *you*? Or bust up the furni-
ture? Or punch you in the chest? Or even *yell* at
you? Oh, that's right . . . that's what *you* do.

Candy looks down. Then she puts her face in her hands and starts to cry.

                    ACE
       (grabs her wrist, pulls her onto his lap)
Smacking your fat ass shouldn't even count—
that's like whipping a rock with a pillow.

                   CANDY
            (trying to suppress a giggle)
You're nothing but a bully.

                    ACE
That's me, all right.

(Raises the flannel shirt and gives her a smack, very lightly.)

CANDY
(triumphantly)

At least you admit it. *(Buries her face in Ace's neck for a second, pulls back, gives him a quick kiss, stands up, and steps back.)*

ACE

Being a bully? *You're* the one who's always—

CANDY

Oh, don't be such an idiot. You said it yourself, didn't you? *Mate*-beater.

FADE OUT
INT: Ace's cave

Considerable *time has passed. Candy is sitting at a desk that wasn't there before, making notes from the terminal attached to one end. She consults various charts, marks them in different colors, using incomprehensible symbols. She is clearly concentrating.*

A series of LEDs suddenly begin to flash in what seems like a random sequence. She watches for a full ten seconds, then taps in a series of numbers on a keypad.

The door opens, and Ace enters.

CANDY

Come here, honey. Remember that pattern I told you about? My hypothesis? I think it's almost ready. Take a look.

                              ACE
          (walking over, putting his hand on the back of her neck)
          It *does* look good, girl. But it doesn't matter, not
          anymore.

          FADE OUT
          COME IN ON INT: Ace's cave
          Ace and Candy are sitting together in one chair; his recliner having been
      replaced by one built for two.

                              ACE
          It had to happen. You could see it coming a few
          cycles ago. The Info-Board said Traxyl-fighting
          had been upgraded to a Major Rule infraction.
          That means a year on the HydroFarm if you're
          caught. Nobody understood it at first, but then
          the Book Boys set us straight:

      CUT TO:

                  NOT JUST THE HANDLERS
              THEY COUNT THE GAMBLERS, TOO
                 AND THEY'RE COUNTING YOU

                              ACE
          The Rulers don't know what a Gambler is, but
          they know what a Gambler *does*. All the new Rule
          meant was that going to a Traxyl fight to bet *was*
          a bet . . . a bet that you wouldn't get caught. If
          the Rulers knew anything about Gamblers, they
          wouldn't have bothered changing the Rules.

But then the whisper-stream started really throbbing, saying the people in the Uncharted Zone were going to stop the Traxyl-fighting by themselves. That sounded crazy, like a rumor inside another rumor. Nobody even knows if there *are* people in the Uncharted Zone.

But it's been eighteen cycles, and not one single Trapper has come back. Even when the price for a Traxyl went up to fifty thousand credits, there were no takers. Like it wasn't a gamble anymore; it was a mortal lock: if a Trapper goes in, *he's* the one who gets trapped.

When they realized nobody was going to trap any more Traxyls, they tried to breed them. They never did that before, because it was so risky: if you put two of them together to have sex, they might kill each other, and you wouldn't make a single credit off *that*. But they found out that Traxyls won't mate after they're captured. I don't even know how you tell males from females, but the ones in cages never have babies. Or eggs.

I've been doing this so long, I guess I never figured on doing anything else. But the word just got passed. They're going to put every Traxyl they have left into one last fight. It's going to run for as long as it takes—maybe a whole cycle. When it's over, there'll only be one Traxyl left.

I know that's true, too.

CUT TO BOOK BOYS SIGN:

DEATH WIND WALKING

Ace leans forward, thousand-yard stare:

ACE

The last fight is going to be way out in the tunnels. It's right next to the Uncharted Zone, but there's no other place to hold a fight this size. There's over three hundred Traxyls left, and there has to be room for people to stay—a full cycle is a long time. Traders are already out there, setting it up. It'll be a huge score for them; out on the border, you can charge whatever you want.

It's hard to keep something this big quiet, and that makes me nervous, sure. But it's our last chance, little girl. We've got almost three hundred thousand credits saved, but, after this, there'll be no way for us to earn any more. What we have can't last forever, not if we want to stay here.

CANDY

We don't have to stay here. We just have to stay together.

ACE

Underground's no place to be old, honey. It costs credits to be safe. Protection, the Medical Tunnels . . . you know. We don't have enough to go the distance.

CANDY
(sensing what's coming)

Ace . . .

ACE

I'm going to the fights, girl. I'll take two-fifty with
me. If I come back, I'll have enough for us to go
all the way. If I don't, you can get seventy-five
for this place, easy. Plus the fifty, you should be
okay for a real long time, until you find another
way to—

CANDY

(immovable)

No.

ACE

We don't have any choice, baby.

Candy stands up.

ACE

I'm sorry, Candy. But *you* don't have any choice,
either. I'm going.

CANDY

I know you're going, you stupid man. But you're
not going with two hundred and fifty thousand
credits—

ACE

How much do you—?

CANDY

Have you been lying to me, Ace. All this time,
lying?

ACE

Lying? I never once—

CANDY

Then you're not taking two-fifty; you're taking the whole stash. And you're taking *me*, too.

Ace just stares at her.

CANDY

All in, mister. *All* in. That means you *and* me, right?

FADE TO BLACK
Open on a shot of moving through barely lit tunnels to . . .
INT: A small cave, obviously built for transient business, the equivalent of a cheap motel. Ace and Candy are sitting together on the floor mat.

ACE

I took a good look around. They keep the Traxyls in little clear Jexan cages before the fights, so the Gamblers can look them over. The cages have slots in the back, so all the Handlers have to do is reach in and shove them into the pit once they throw the switch.

CANDY

You have one picked?

ACE

It's too early, honey. For a move like this, you can't be wrong.

CANDY

Our move.

ACE
(patting her shoulder)
Our move. But we have to stay with the system,
little girl. People, not Traxyls. So—

CANDY

So this is where *I* come in! It can't be one bet; it's
got to be a lot of them, and you can't place them
all. Anyway, I already know what you're going
to do.

ACE
(smiling)
Yeah?

CANDY
(as if reciting a lesson)
People, not Traxyls. This is the last of the fights,
so it's the last chance for the Gamblers to make
that one big score. That means they're all going to
be looking for the long shot, because they don't
have that many credits to start with. What good
is a two-to-one win going to do them . . . keep
them alive for another couple of cycles? And if
they lose, they're going to . . . chase, you call it,
right?

ACE
(proud of her)

Oh yeah. If they lose a hundred credits on one
fight; they'll bet two hundred on the next one,
the fools. None of the Takers know you. Just be
patient, wait until the last minute . . . that's when
the odds are going to *jump*, because all the sucker
money will be on the long shots . . . which will
make them the favorites. Then *we* go long on the
Traxyls that *should* have been the favorites. They'd
expect a girl to do that, anyway.

FADE OUT

INT: A circular Traxyl pit.

*Two Traxyls are stationed across from one another, in their cages. The
audience is still betting, as Takers move from one person to another in
response to waves of betting cards.*

A high, humming noise fills the entire area.

*An army of children are coming through a back tunnel, holding hands.
The noise is coming from them. This is not a noise they are* making*; it is an
emanation of some kind. Should be clear that no one child could make this
sound—only the gestalt of their mutual presence can produce it.*

*Two of the older children separate from the rest. One boy; one girl. Each
walks over to a Traxyl cage and calmly throws it open.*

*Instead of charging each other, the Traxyls rush into the audience, which
scatters in panic.*

*All the children are now opening cages as the high, humming noise
increases.*

*The freed Traxyls are ripping apart every human in sight . . . except the
children.*

*The man we know as Father appears. He blows into some kind of flute-
like instrument. No sound comes out, but both the children and the Traxyls
stop moving.*

The children immediately start walking back the way they came. The Traxyls follow. Not chasing the children, walking alongside of them, as if they belong.

ACE

I see it now, little girl. *There's* our bet.

He stands up, holds out his hand.

ACE

All in? You and me?

CANDY
(taking his hand)

Let's go home, honey. Where we belong.

Ace and Candy begin to follow the children. A couple of the Traxyls suddenly whirl around to face them.
The humming noise sounds.
As if summoned, the Traxyls turn around. They follow the children.
Ace and Candy move quickly to catch up with them.
They pass the Traxyls and walk with the children, still holding hands. A different child reaches up and takes each of their other hands.
FADE OUT on blackness, illuminated only by a sign, glowing in luminescent blue:

WHAT LIES OUTSIDE
IS NO LIE
HONOR IS THE ONLY ARMOR
THE FINAL FIGHT
IS TO COME INTO THE LIGHT

FADE TO BLACK
COME IN ON
INT: Gathering hall

MAN AT PODIUM
(clearly preparing to depart, bows briefly)
I thank you for your patience. The Book of the
Path is talk. For talk to become truth, one must
walk. You will follow what you will. I must follow
my father.

for Lorraine

THE WEIGHT

Sugar's a pure professional, "time tested" and packing 255 pounds of muscle. Accused of a rape he couldn't have done because he was robbing a jewelry store at the time, the DA offers him two options: give up his partners in the heist and walk, or go back to prison alone. For Sugar, there isn't a choice; he takes the weight. When he gets out, his money is there, but so is another job. One of the heist crew has fallen off the radar, and the mastermind behind the jewelry job asks Sugar to find him and make sure their secrets are safe. Sugar suspects that there's more to this gig than what he is being told. But nothing he suspects can prepare him for what he finds.

Crime Fiction

HAIKU

When his most beloved student dies as a result of what he believes to be his misguidance, Ho renounces his position as a revered sensei, abandons his dojo and all his possessions, and embarks on a journey of atonement on the streets of New York City. Here a group of homeless men gather around him: Michael, a gambler who lost it all; Ranger, a psychotic Vietnam veteran; Lamont, an ex-con, poet, and alcoholic; Target, a compulsive "clanger"; and Brewster, the keeper of a secret library in an abandoned building. When news hits that the building is slated for demolition, the group must subsume each individual's demons into one shared goal: save Brewster's library, at all costs.

Fiction

THAT'S HOW I ROLL

Execution looms, but no prison can hold Esau Till's mind. Or his love. He sits on death row, writing his life story—his last chance to protect his brother, Tory, after he's gone. And, as too many have learned, when it comes to protecting his baby brother, Esau Till is a man without boundaries. When the genetic cards were dealt, Esau drew a genius IQ but a horribly crippled body. His brother Tory drew a "slow" mind but almost superhuman strength. A self-taught explosives expert, Esau became the top assassin for two rival local mobs. Now, as the State prepares to take his life, Esau plots going all-in on the last and most deadly hand he will ever play.

Fiction

TWO TRAINS RUNNING

It is 1959—a moment in history when the clandestine, powerful forces that will shape America to the present day are about to collide. Walker Dett is a hired gun, known for using the most extreme measures to accomplish his missions. Royal Beaumont is the "hillbilly boss" who turned Locke City from a dying town into a thriving vice capital. Add a rival Irish political machine, the nascent black power movement, turf-disputing juvenile gangs, a muckraking journalist who doubles as a blackmailer, the FBI—and Locke City is about as stable as a nitroglycerin truck stalled on the railroad tracks.

Crime Fiction

ALSO AVAILABLE

Another Life
Blossom
Blue Belle
A Bomb Built in Hell
Born Bad
Choice of Evil
Dead and Gone
Down Here
Down in the Zero
Everybody Pays
False Allegations
Flood
Footsteps of the Hawk
The Getaway Man
Hard Candy
Mask Market
Only Child
Pain Management
Sacrifice
Safe House
Shella
Strega
Terminal

VINTAGE CRIME / BLACK LIZARD
Available wherever books are sold.
www.weeklylizard.com

THE HAP AND LEONARD SERIES
BY JOE LANSDALE

SAVAGE SEASON

A rip-roaring, high-octane, Texas-sized thriller, featuring two friends, one vixen, a crew of washed-up radicals, loads of money, and bloody mayhem. Hap Collins and Leonard Pine are best friends, yet they couldn't be more different. Hap is an East Texas white boy with a weakness for Texas women. Leonard is a gay, black Vietnam vet. Together, they steer up more commotion than a firestorm. But that's just the way they like it. So when an ex-flame of Hap's returns promising a huge score, Hap lets Leonard in on the scam, and that's when things get interesting.

Crime Fiction

MUCHO MOJO

Hap and Leonard return in this incredible, mad-dash thriller, loaded with crack addicts, a serial killer, and a body count. Leonard is still nursing the injuries he sustained in the duo's last wild undertaking when he learns that his Uncle Chester has passed. Hap is of course going to be there for his best friend, and when the two are cleaning up Uncle Chester's dilapidated house, they uncover a dark little secret beneath the house's rotting floorboards—a small skeleton buried in a trunk. Hap wants to call the police. Leonard, being a black man in East Texas, persuades him this is not a good idea, and together they set out to clear Chester's name on their own.

Crime Fiction

ALSO AVAILABLE

The Two-Bear Mambo
Bad Chili
Rumble Tumble
Captains Outrageous
Vanilla Ride

VINTAGE CRIME/BLACK LIZARD
Available wherever books are sold.
www.weeklylizard.com